# Chadas
## Assassin Lord

The Second Story in

The Telling of the Maal

Steve Reilly

ISBN: 978-0-6457555-8-9

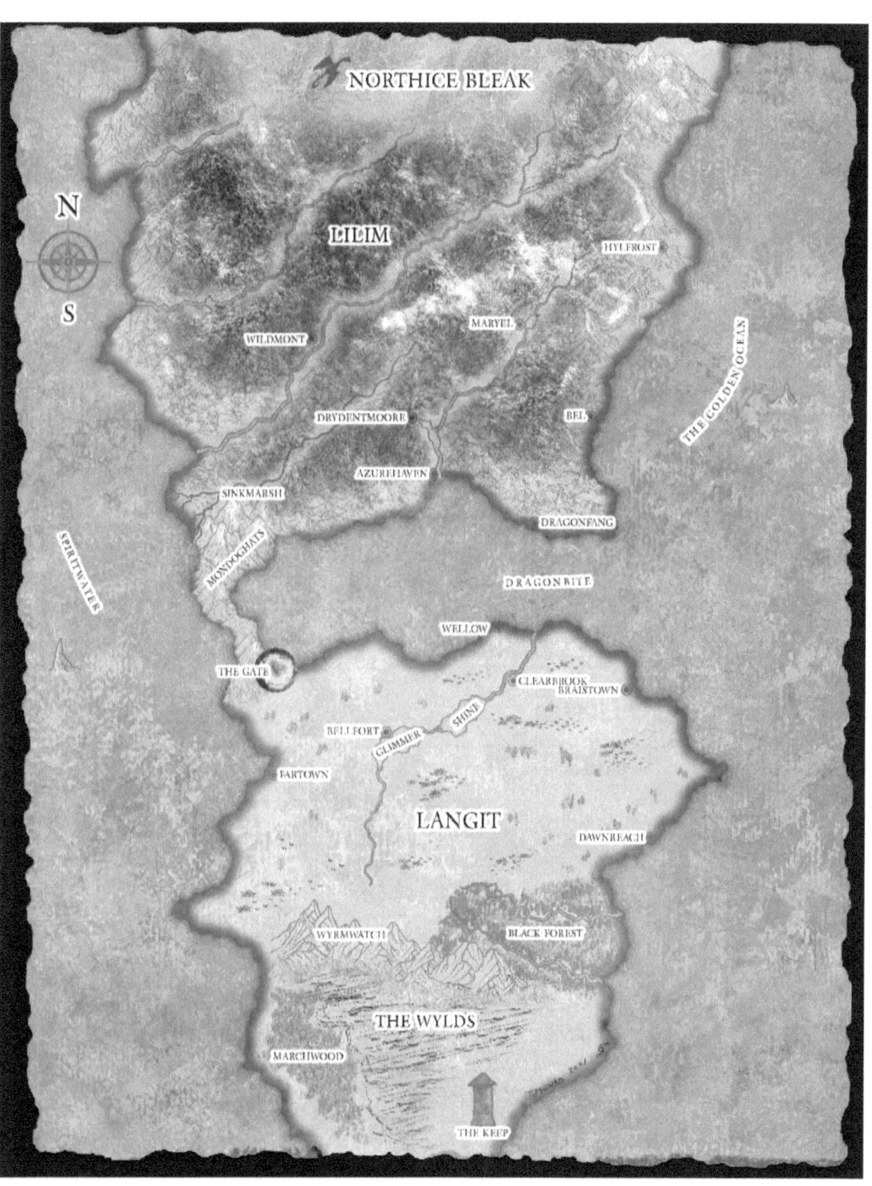
NORTHICE BLEAK
N
S
LILIM
HYLFROST
WILDMONT
MARYEL
THE GOLDEN OCEAN
DRYDENTMOORE
BEL
AZUREHAVEN
SINKMARSH
DRAGONFANG
SPIRITWATER
MONDOGHATS
DRAGONBITE
WELLOW
THE GATE
CLEARBROOK
BRAISTOWN
BELLFORT
GLIMMER
SHINE
FARTOWN
LANGIT
DAWNREACH
WYRMWATCH
BLACK FOREST
THE WYLDS
MARCHWOOD
THE KEEP

# MISE-EN-SCENE

My stories have been received well throughout the taverns and inns of Langit. I call them my stories but they are those of Kuwento, the MaalKeeper. I tell them on my travels but I also write them to keep a promise to my friend.

You see, Kuwento is the last MaalKeeper and his tales are the oral histories of our people passed down through the generations. I hear his words in my mind, the past must not be lost. He begged me to record them because Kuwento can neither read nor write. He, like those that went before him, committed these histories to their memories.

Now Kuwento is an old man and will soon have no need of this life. I must finish these stories as a record of his memory, and as a tribute to my friend.

I do not know what I believe. I once thought that death was the end of life. Kuwento is of a different opinion. Whoever is correct, I will miss him.

Kuwento wears his amulet, the symbol of his duty, with pride. The white stone with burnt red at its base and red spots above represent a campfire with stories floating into the sky. How many of these stories will I have time to relate?

Our first book told of Meeya and her siblings, left to survive in a violent world after Nodon and Rata, their parents, died in a raid, is also the story of Masima, the son who Meeya denied, and who, throughout his life, took the frustrations of his abandonment out on those around him. Together they began the history of the great city of Dragonfang.

This book is the tale of Chadas who lived when Dragonfang was reaching for greatness. I named it CHADAS : Assassin Lord. Kuwento knows it as the Chadasmaal.

I am Sumulat, the Storyteller.

# 1 CLEARBROOK

Once more I find myself returning to Clearbrook, though I am beginning to wonder if I will ever get there, or be able to deliver what lay in my saddlebags.

The rain continues, unrelenting. For eight days it added weight to my clothes, forced there by driving winds. I doubt the cold will ever leave my bones. Since yesterday morning the storm had grown more severe and the rain was now so heavy I could not see Horse's head in front of me. I must stop. As bad as the weather made me feel, I worried for my faithful steed. I had given him his name one day when, id a fit of frustration, I yelled, "Come here, horse," and he did. To this day he answers to horse. He can barely lift his massive feet from the quagmire that remains of the road. I had seen no inns or farms in which to shelter, but I could be riding past one now and not know it was there. I have never seen a storm like this. It will be something to add to my stories, once I am dry and the shivering has left my body. My stories? A storm, no matter how severe, would be of little interest compared to the stories I now had to tell, the maal of Kuwento.

A gust cleared the air long enough to glimpse a stand of trees at the side of the road. A quick tug on the reins and Horse was more than willing to stop. Dropping from his back, my boots disappeared to the ankles in squelching mud. Still gripping the reins, I trudged toward the slim promise of shelter.

I have no idea how much farther I must ride, I have lost track of distance, and even time is only a vague distraction in the foul weather. This must be a punishment sent by the spirits Kuwento so admired.

For two days we hid beneath the naked branches waiting for the storm to break. I survived on the dwindling contents of my saddlebags while Horse scavenged for grasses. I could not light a fire and so sat huddled in a ball, wrapped in my cloak. When Horse decided to move, it was only to stare at me with a desperate plea for a barn and a bag of oats. I would happily join him if one were available. Also in the saddlebags was my reason for being on this road, carefully wrapped in waxed cloth to protect it. It nestled with my flute and spare shirt.

When the storm finally passed, I was stunned. All around, the fields I remembered being filled with wildflowers now reflected the sky in a myriad of shallow lakes. I waited another day before encouraging Horse back onto the still-soft road. He seemed keen to stretch tired and cramped muscles under a sun that blinked between heavy clouds. I admit I too desired shelter in Clearbrook again, and seeing Kuwento.

#

Two days later, I sensed Clearbrook must be near. Plots of farmland bordered the road while sodden sheep paddled through grassed paddocks still soggy with remnants of the storm. Slowly, the road began to climb and soon Horse stopped at the top of the rise. Ahead, spread out as I remembered, stood Clearbrook.

Nearly a year has passed since I last looked down from this place onto the town, but nothing seemed to have changed. I should not have expected it, but I have seen towns born and die in that time. The river was muddier than I recalled, but it was busy washing away the last dregs of the rain-torn land. A large tree bobbed along as it rushed to the sea. The spring that fed the creek now gushed a small torrent to race through the town. I wondered if the weather had caused any damage. Horse accepted my gentle encouragement and began to walk towards Clearbrook.

The morning light shone from rendered walls washed clean by rain, giving the streets back their color and beauty. Against the render, the dark wood of timber framing seemed almost black. People went about the business of living, cleaning, stacking timber to dry and other daily chores. Despite the pleasant sight, there was one thing the street shared with every other one I had seen. The air hung heavy with the stench of human waste. But then, why should this street be any different? Because of the well kept houses? Or that this was where Kuwento lived? The rains may have washed the streets clean, but two days were plenty to gather their stench again.

I dismounted outside the MaalKeeper's house. It, too, was as I remembered, but as I hitched Horse to the olive tree, I saw the changes. The roof sagged a little more. The windows stared darkly as if the life was lost behind them. The cartwheel that once stood beside the door now rested in a bed of grass that grew between its spokes. Last year, the house had merely presented the image of distress. Now it was tired. Like an old man, its shoulders slumped with age. I knocked on the warped door, and after waiting and hearing nothing, knocked again. Sounds came from within, a cough followed by another, then the quiet shuffle of feet on the cobbled floor. The door squealed open to reveal Kuwento, though for a moment he did not seem to recognize me. I only knew it to be him because I expected to see him here.

I saw then the real change that had come to Clearbrook. It was not the houses or the people. The year had taken its toll on my friend. The thought surprised me, I had only met the MaalKeeper on two occasions, yet I had grown to accept him as a friend through the maal, the oral histories of past people and events. Kuwento had amazed me with his memory but the man I remembered had been thin, and alert. This Kuwento was no more than cracked skin stretched over a skeletal frame. His cheeks sagged. His mouth hung to reveal broken and dirty teeth. But the thing that surprised me most, and it hurt deeply, was that the sparkle had gone from his eyes.

"Hello Kuwento. Do you remember me? Sumulat?"

He stood for some seconds before recognition came to his face and smiled. I could not tell if it was real or if the MaalKeeper was trying to convince himself that his most prized possession, his memory, had not deserted him. I took his arm, carefully for I did not wish to break it, and led him inside. No flame burned in the hearth. There were a few pieces of wood against the wall and, after settling Kuwento into his chair, I began to construct a fire. The room felt as cold as the Northice Bleak, which only accentuated the misery of its condition. I needed to change that. Living here would be like living every day in the misery of the storm.

Soon I had a lively flame dancing on the timber, and while Kuwento warmed himself, I went to his yard in search of more to burn. There was none. I had come to read him the next book but realized he needed much more than my story, his stories. "Stay here and get warm," I said. "I will be back soon."

Going back out to the street, I looked up and down before making the obvious choice and hurried next door. This house looked twice the size of Kuwento's. The bright yellow render highlighted the little gardens of color on either side of a plain, white door. I knocked and a woman quickly answered. At first glance, I could not help but think that she suited the house. A simple dress of green trimmed with white lace at the neck and cuffs draped her middle-aged fullness. Wisps of dark hair crept from beneath a brightly patterned scarf.

"Hello," I greeted. "My name is Sumulat. I have come from next door." The woman craned her neck to take in Kuwento's house, then back at me with suspicion. "I do not live there," I told her. "My friend does, Kuwento. I have arrived and found him stiff with cold and no wood for a fire. Would you have some to spare?"

She eyed me for a moment before turning inside. When she returned, her arms were laden with cut and dried timber. "Thank you," I offered as I took the load. "What is your name?"

"Cara." Her voice was light; it tinkled on the air. It did not suit the woman's frame but it fitted her smile.

"Thank you, Cara. You must know someone who could deliver a cartload of cut timber to his house?" I reached into a pocket and withdrew a gold coin. Cara's eyes bulged at the sight of it. "Would you ask him to bring a load, and one for yourself?" I then had a thought. "If you could prepare him a meal, I would pay for it. And I am sure he would enjoy a tankard of mead if you have some. It may put some life back in his body."

"I have food on the stove," she offered, "and I will send my eldest son to see to the wood and buy you the mead." I thanked her again and returned to Kuwento.

The fire helped take the bite from the chill in the room, but it was already burning low. I added two of the logs I carried. Not long after, I heard a knock and called for Cara to enter. Her hands held a bowl of steaming stew, and while I knelt to feed my friend, she stood and looked around to take in Kuwento's tiny home. Taking a spoonful of the stew, I placed it in his mouth. He sat there until I realized he was not going to chew, maybe he did not have the energy. He needed nourishment. I retrieved the piece of meat and instead spooned some of the broth into the back of his mouth so it could trickle down his throat. It worked. I could at least put something in his belly. I fed him a second spoonful, and a third, and continued until all the broth had gone. When I looked up, Cara was cleaning and tidying the room.

Kuwento turned to me, and for the first time since my arrival, I saw genuine recognition in his smile. "Sumulat, is that you? How long have you been here?" he croaked.

"I have only just arrived," I lied. "I have come to read you another story."

He grinned, and for a moment I saw a glimmer of the old spark return to one eye. Cara stood staring, but we were interrupted when someone came to the door. He was a tall lad. His dark hair hung half across his face, hiding some of the cheeky smile that looked as if it was always present. Under one arm, he carried a firkin that I assumed would be filled with mead.

"This is Reeth, my eldest son." Cara's face lit with the pride of motherhood as she introduced him. Then, with a gesture, continued, "and this is Sumulat. I have only just come to understand who is among us. They say he is the greatest storyteller in all the land." Reeth looked unimpressed. "He is going to tell a story." She turned back to me. "May we listen?"

I assured her I would be honored, but first I wanted to fill a tankard for Kuwento. Cara rushed to do so and with drink in hand, began feeding sips to the MaalKeeper. I settled into the other chair and began unwrapping the book. I saw Kuwento smile. I saw glimmers of life return to his body with the nourishment.

This is a tale of choices, but bad decisions make good stories.

#

At this point, Kuwento grew extremely agitated. His eyes searched the room, as if lost. He wriggled. "I must show you," he repeated over and over. "It is important." He pulled himself to his feet with surprising strength.

"Sit," I encouraged. "I will read you a story."

He looked to the book, still partly wrapped, sitting on the table. I could see indecision, but finally he shook his head. "No. No. I must show you." He dragged himself to his feet with us rushing to help, then began to shuffle toward the back of the room. I had no choice but to humor him. Taking his arm, I helped him walk. Side by side we shuffled along till we came to the back wall,

"Now remember." He counted the floor boards back from the side wall with his slippered foot. "Eight." He repeated his actions counting aloud. "One, two, three…" till he reached eight. "Put your foot here," he instructed. "Against the wall." I did and was not surprised when the board seemed loose. I am sure there were many loose boards in the old home.

When I had done so, he took my hand and placed it on the wall board above my foot. "Push with your hand." The board moved only the slightest fraction. "Now push down with your foot." As I did, I heard the quiet click and a hidden door swung open. Kuwento laughed, "Yes, yes."

A stone stair leading down below the house was revealed.

"Cara, bring a candle so Sumulat can see."

In the flickering light of the single candle I descended to find a room beneath the house. There were shelves stacked with tiny items, boxes holding many more, while others were strewn on the floor. Walking among the litter of tiny treasures, I admired the skill of some while others appeared quite crude. One caught my attention, a tiny dragon carved in a strange green stone. I reached for it and the moment my fingers touched, a strange tingle filled my body. In my mind I could see the dragon flying, swooping between great mountains then soaring so high the world was so far below I could see nothing of its grandeur. It flew low again, so slow that I could count the pebbles in the river and at times, so fast the land was a blur. I released the figure and the image was gone.

I tried touching two others with different images appearing. Confused, I climbed the steps back to the room. "They are the memories," Kuwento told me, "held there by the Majick."

He shuffled back to his seat, and though I asked he seemed disinterested in saying more. He picked up the book and held it close before passing it to me. I smiled. The Kuwento I knew had returned, if only briefly. I gave my voice the tone I used in taverns to draw my audience away from their goblets, and began to read. "This story is called Chadas : Assassin Lord." I glanced around the room. Three faces hung on my words.

"Dragonfang had grown beyond its size. Too many people lived packed into the space between the outer wall and the Tower Keep."

"Dragonfang?" Reeth asked.

"It is a place far to the north, beyond the sea known as Dragonbite." Reeth stared. Like so many people, he did not know that a land existed beyond the sea. I noticed Kuwento grin as I continued.

# 2 THE GUILD OF MASIMA

In the crowded city, down a narrow lane that did its best to appear straight, among the houses that climbed over each other for space, hid a run-down little hovel. Its stone walls were cracked and breaking, the roof had long since been in need of new thatching. Its windows sagged as if ready to shed tired tears. Hidden in its dingy interior among the rickety table and beds turned hard from lack of fresh straw, lived a family, not of rats or mice. Here lived people, a family named Annear, a family who lived without hope. These people did not know that hope existed.

Chadas was the second child of this family, a shorter boy than most of his age with nothing but scavenged clothing to keep him warm. On this day, the third after his eighth birthday, Chadas sat cross-legged on the floor when he heard the roar. He knew what it meant. It was the roar of anger, the bellow of pain. Chadas searched for the nearest escape, the closest window.

Even before the thought coalesced, he was running, knowing his brothers and sisters would be doing the same. Like him, they would be diving through windows into the uncertainty that was safer than his home. They all would have heard. They would know what the bellow meant.

But even as he huddled beneath the window, he knew that what lay behind the roar was worse than pain or anger, much worse. It was a howl of sorrow, a deep, consuming despair so dark it enveloped a mind, a shadow so hot it burned a heart, a blackness so dangerous, it would feed on a person's spirit and laugh at the creature it created.

Sounds poured from the window.

The door banged.

His father was home.

He jammed his hands over his ears and hoped his brothers and sisters had escaped. He imagined the scene he had witnessed many times, his mother defiant, hands on hips, trying to face down his father.

Unwelcome tears filled his eyes. *Why does he hate us? What have I done to him?*

His father had left for the tavern before the sun had warmed the air. It gave them a day of peace. Now the shadows of night crawled through the city, but the blackness of night would never scare him. He knew the darkness that was his father. His mother always kept the way to the windows clear, offering her children the chance to escape his rage.

Hiding beneath the window, he heard his father's slurred bellow. "Food," followed almost immediately by, "And mead."

"You have been at the tavern all day," his mother growled in reply. "You have had enough." A silence followed as Chadas imagined his father trying to piece together the unexpected words. "Where are the mice? They should be scurrying about getting me mead." His mother's words must have come together in his mind. A slow growl followed. "You are my wife. It is not your place to tell me I have had enough."

"But I will tell you anyway. Lie down and stop being an old fool." *Careful mother. You do not want to anger him more.*

Moments later Chadas heard his mother's scream, cut short by the crunch of fist on flesh. Furniture tumbled as his father hunted for the children. With luck, he would not find any. He ran before his father looked out the window. He did not expect he would. Go to sleep, you old pig. He would crash about for a while before collapsing into a drunken slumber. Chadas ran down the alley and squatted behind an empty barrel, eyes squeezed shut. When he found the courage, he blinked them open. In that brief image he saw Edana, his sister, huddled into a corner. Her arm was around Keir's shoulders. Three of them had escaped. He hoped there would be two more, Alodia and Quinn. If they had got out of the house, Alodia would take care of Quinn. At almost nine, she was the eldest, and Quinn was her favorite. His youngest sister, Nari, had found her escape by not living more than two days after her birth. Sometimes, he envied her.

A stab of bravery overcame him. *I can do this.* He rose to his feet, glanced across at his sister and brother, and crept back to the house. His feet were on the edge of flight, but he came closer. No sounds came from within. He reached the window and listened. A snort. A gurgling cough followed by a loud snore. The mead had left his father too drunk to wake.

A hand on his shoulder made him jump. It was Alodia, she had come to check too. "Go and find the others," he told her. "Edana and Keir are at the end of the lane, around the corner." He was pointing to show her. "I will check on mother." Alodia nodded and was gone.

Chadas inched his way to the door and peeked in. Nothing moved. He heard his father's snore and guessed he was on the bed. He crept inside. The shadow that was his mother lay sprawled and unmoving on the floor, blood on her mouth. Moving close, he felt her unsteady breath on his face. *Rest mother. I will fix this.*

He found the cloth his mother used for cleaning. Dipping it in a pail, he wet it and began to wipe the blood from her face. Anger gnawed at his heart. His mother groaned. *Why does she take his beatings? Why does she goad him?* The answer came instantly into his head. She accepts it to protect her children. The answer made the anger grow. She suffered to protect him and the others. Someone had to protect her. A glance toward the bed. *I will protect you.* He lay the cloth across her forehead. Wisps of damp, streaked hair clung to her face. Chadas carefully picked off each one and moved it aside. Almost automatically, he rose and went to the upturned table. He knew what he wanted. His fingers searched in the shadows. *It must be here.* Feeling around on the floor, his fingers found what he knew would be there, a knife. Rising again, he moved toward the bed, slowly and deliberately. Flames of frustration engulfed him, blinding him to all but his father. The silent roar of revenge wrapped his mind in its deafening embrace.

His father lay unaware, his beard and shirt stained with spewed mead. It had fled his belly to make room for more. His breeches were wet and stank of piss. He had not paused in his drinking to relieve himself, or he was unaware that he needed to. Chadas saw these things, smelled them, but they were not part of him. Slowly, he raised the knife. Two hands gripped the handle to add strength to what he was about to do. The knife seemed to pulse with anticipation. He paused, but only to decide where he would strike.

"No!" The word hit and bounced off the shield that surrounded his mind. "No," it said again, pleading.

His mother's voice was hardly more than a croaked whisper as she tried a third time, but it carried the power of command and rang loud in his ears, "No." She spoke quietly but with urgency and desperation. He lowered his hands as slowly as they had risen. His father's death could wait, briefly. He rushed to his mother's side. There would be ample time, but the time would come. He silently promised his father that.

Chadas' head spun. Something moved at the corner of his vision, but there was nothing there. I know I saw something. He watched closely for a moment but now he saw only shadows. It must have been a rat.

His mother became more aware as Alodia and the others returned. The fires that held him burned themselves out. His mother spoke as if they were alone. "If you strike true," she explained, "the guards would soon be here. They would take you. They would likely take me too. We would face the Lord's justice, and though I would plead for mercy, it is likely we would both lose our heads. If your blade did not find its mark, your father would live and we would face him and his justice. Words could not protect us then."

The chance that his father may live stayed his hand, for now. *But I have learned one thing today. I will never fear him again.*

#

At the end of each day over the following weeks, when his father returned from the tavern, Chadas wondered if he should have plunged the knife, then Alodia turned nine. Their father spent the day at the tavern from early morning. No one expected his return until late. In the peace of the day, their mother prepared a grand feast as a treat for his sister. They began with fruit tarts followed quickly by mushroom pasties. They all gasped when their mother brought out their main meal, a pottage of mutton with horsebread. Chadas ate as if he would never need eat again. With everyone well fed, a dessert of rose pudding finished their feast.

They were all abed when their father came home. His stumbling across the floor was enough to wake them. Chadas tried to sink into the bed. His muscles trembled, his eyes darted and his breath fought to find a path through his throat. For the first time in Chadas' memory, his father staggered about, mumbled something that no one could understand, and fell on the bed, snoring.

I promised I would never fear him again, he reminded himself as he did every night, but he could not help himself. The slurred mumbling, the angry roar, crashing furniture, all these things terrified him. *I will not be afraid.* His muscles shook harder. *Stop. He does not scare me.* Tears flowed from his eyes to moisten the bed and show his thoughts to be the lie they were. Sleep finally forced out the fear.

Next morning, Chadas was woken by the sounds of his father crashing into the table as he made his way to the door. It was to be another early start at the tavern. When all seemed safe, he climbed from his bed. There were still a few fruit tarts remaining. He grabbed one and began to munch. The others were crawling from their slumber. He could not see his mother, but as the thought took him, the door opened and his mother slid quietly into the room. She carried a basket laden with fresh blackberries. "Where is Alodia?" Chadas asked. His mother did not answer. The children exchanged glances, but without Alodia, he was the eldest. He tried again. "Has Alodia gone out?" His mother remained silent.

Chadas looked to the door. "Forget about Alodia," his mother pleaded.

His eyes moved back and forth between her and the door. Had she gone to pick blackberries with their mother? If she did, why had they not returned together? Then, a terrible fear seized his heart. Had Alodia risen early? Had she disturbed their father? *What have you done, you drunken churl.*

His stomach churned at the thought he suddenly knew to be true. His father had killed Alodia.

#

Alodia never returned.

Life went on, as did their father.

Chadas' ninth birthday came too quickly. His father was at the tavern. A few insignificant clouds dotted the sky like canoes on a shining sea. Warm air tingled his skin. His mother set a pleasant feast of cabbage chowder and creamed fish, both flavored with ginger and caraway; and for dessert, a bowl of fresh figs. He enjoyed the best day he could remember. Even his father, when he arrived home, was calmer, not consumed by angry blustering. I will not forget, he had to remind himself.

As everyone slept through their father's snores, his mother woke him. Her hand was pressed to his lips to keep him quiet. *What? Are we safe? Has father woken?* She crooked a finger to show he should follow, and led him outside to a quiet place in the lane. She crouched, her face close to his. "What I tell you must never leave your lips. Your life depends on it, and mine. Promise me you will not repeat what I must tell you." He promised. " You and me, we are born of the blood of Masima." He did not understand. He had not heard of Masima. "We can both trace our parents back to the great leader. Lord Masima's vision built the city of Dragonfang, but the people turned against him. Now anyone with his blood must hide their history." Her voice barely carried to his ears, but her face and tone told him this was important.

"Why?" he whispered.

His mother spat on the ground near his feet. "Lord Masima was murdered. The ones that now rule the city killed the Great Lord, and all his family. But he had children they did not know of. Followers hid the children and his line has been kept secret since. You, Chadas, are of that line."

Chadas' head spun with the revelation. His family could have ruled Dragonfang. Is this what angered his father? But his mother had not mentioned him. "My father?" he asked. His mother shook her head.

"There are others who escaped the night of the attack, many followers and four of Lord Masima's most secret and trusted advisors. These are honored by the Children of Masima." *A Great Lord, children, advisors of Lord Masima, was he dreaming?*

"Come, I have something to show you." Without question, he followed as his mother led him into the darkened streets and alleys of Dragonfang, to a place he had never been.

They were in a part of the city where lanes turned on themselves, each one less important than the last. He was led among buildings twisted in a confusion of shapes. His mother paused. "Do not be afraid," she whispered. "We are safe here." She turned to a stone wall, the side of a building, and after a moment of thought, placed a hand on one of the stones and pressed. He heard a click and watched a change come to the shadows. Chadas gasped as a part of the wall swung inward. He had not seen the door and doubted if anyone would notice it, even in daylight. His mother took his hand and stepped through. Behind him, the door snapped shut. Everything went dark. They entered a starless, immaculate blackness.

*What is this place? Where is she taking me?* He was not afraid, only curious.

Still holding his hand in a gentle grip, his mother began to walk. He was forced to follow. If not for the touch of her fingers, he would not have known she was there. The floor sloped down, like moving down the side of a hill. They had not gone far when he felt his mother's grip tighten, and they turned right. They walked, she squeezed again, and they turned once more. Then another turn. Chadas could not see, and wondered how his mother could lead, but he suspected they were walking beneath the alley with the secret door far above. His mother led him as surely as if she were in her own kitchen.

The floor levelled. Chadas was surprised to find that he could see, not that the passage was lit, but faint hints of light seeped through small holes in the roof. His mother walked on.

Soon after, he noticed the walls. Darker patches showed where the glimmer of light did not touch. He glanced into one of these places as they passed, and then into others. Each was a niche set in the corridor, and in each a guard stood or squatted. All were alert, waiting with sword or spear, staff or bow. His mother walked on, her hand wrapping his. Another door stood waiting at the end of the corridor. Her free hand rose to her chest and the guard he had not noticed swung it open for them to pass.

Beyond was light, blinding light. "Look at the floor," his mother whispered. "Your eyes will soon feel better. I should have warned you to shut them before the door opened." She was right. After a moment, he could look up. The passage was only lit by burning torches on the walls. His mother walked on, releasing his hand. Chadas hurried to keep up. What is this place?

They were in a long tunnel, straight and level, not like the city above. The floor was a swirl of red, blue and white tiles beneath walls and a roof of polished stone. At intervals along their way, sitting on plinths of colored stone, were treasures he could not imagine. He saw dishes of the finest bone, painted with scenes that defied even the dreams of a child. Others held statues of solid gold, sculptures carved from stone or wood. One was made of a clear rock he could see through. All were beautiful. His mother walked on. Finally, they reached another door.

#

No guard waited here. His mother opened the door.

The room was unlike any he had seen. There were no walls, or walls as he knew them. A domed roof of white stone streaked with red and yellow slid down to meet a floor of gray marble. The room was circular, and apart from the door behind them, large, double doors stood opposite with four others, evenly spaced, breaking the lines of the outer edge. Twelve guards ringed the space.

As his mother moved forward, she spoke quietly. "On the floor is a dragon." Chadas could see the image inset with colored stones. The body and head in the center of the room flowed into a long tail that swept out and all around the room. Its massive head with two curved, golden horns, spat fire of red and yellow. Huge wings grew from its back while four small legs each ended with a four-pronged talon. The entire creature glowed with many shades of green and blue. Below the dragon's body, the images of three heads, a stag, a boar and a wolf were inlaid. He had time to notice that three of the doors were carved with the same heads. His mother walked to the double doors.

As they approached, the doors swung open. A woman, dressed in a long, flowing blue gown, waited. Over her shoulders hung a band of cloth that dropped to the floor, glistening in shades of blue and green. Her head carried a tall hat in similar colors. *What … ?* He could not think of what his mind was trying to tell him. His mind tried to restart itself. *What is … ?* It failed.

"Who approaches the Ama?" The woman demanded in a deep voice that echoed around the chamber.

His mother answered. "Wynne Annear returns to her true family. I bring my son, Chadas, that he, too, may come to know his family."

"Enter, Wynne Annear," the woman intoned. "Enter Chadas Annear. Your family awaits."

Inside was a smaller domed room, similar in coloring. He heard his mother whisper, "They will speak in the ancient tongue." Opposite, three people sat at three lecterns, each with one of the heads from the floor outside embossed in gold on it. The lecterns sat on a platform that was as tall as a man from the floor. But equally as high above them, and behind, a figure dressed all in black, with black cloth shrouding his face, sat a man on a huge chair of gold. In the middle of the room was a circular dais of polished, dark stone. His mother stepped up and drew him onto it.

The dark-clad man spoke. "Welcome back Wynne Annear. It is good to see you again."

"It is always pleasant to return to the Guild, Ama," his mother replied.

What brings you here tonight?"

"I bring my son to meet his family." Chadas' mind came back to life. *Who are these people? What do they want of me? Why does my mother refer to them as her family?*

His mother was speaking to him. "This man is the leader of the Guild of Masima. He is known as the Ama."

She raised herself tall. Her voice took on a tone he had never heard, a chanting melody. "Ama, I bring my son, Chadas, to meet you. I bring him to find his family. He is born of the blood of the great Lord Masima. He comes to be offered training in the ways of the Guild."

Standing there, he felt the eyes crawl over him, eyes of the three and the one who sat above them.

The man in black began to chant in low, guttural tones that filled him with warmth. *How does he do that?* "Padone tane it pane. Te so-poro Masima-to utu boor. Chadas ront-chi un tara-ten." He looked down and Chadas felt deep, blue eyes pierce him. With a wink, the Ama translated, "Rejoice brothers and sisters. A lost child of Lord Masima returns. Chadas has found his family."

Chadas turned to his mother with a grin on his face, but she was not there. She stood near the woman in blue, by the door. He turned back when the Ama began speaking again. "Your mother wishes you to learn the ways of the Guild. Is this what you wish?" Chadas nodded, not daring to speak and say the wrong words. "That would require you to apprentice to one of the Houses." His arm swept to take in the three below as he spoke. "If you choose not to apprentice yourself, you may return home with your mother. The Guild will always be open to you, but you must speak to no one of it." The Ama paused, watching his face, but Chadas had made his decision. *I will be free of my father.*

"I wish to apprentice," he stated.

"Good."

Chadas turned to see his mother's reaction, but all he saw was her back as the woman in blue closed the door on it. *Will I see her again? I hope she will be safe. I will protect you mother. When I am ready, I will kill him.* His attention returned to the Ama.

"These people represent their Houses. Each will explain briefly what they do. When you have heard of all the houses, you must choose one. Once your decision is made, you will learn the ways of the Guild and of your House. For one month in twelve, you will study in one of the other Houses so that you know and appreciate what they do. Listen carefully."

The first in line began to speak. She was a tall woman with yellow hair that hung across her shoulders. Her soft, sweet face gave her the appearance of youth, but Chadas saw the wrinkles on her neck and the backs of her hands. She sat behind the boar's head. "Tern danga mon tee Masima-to," she began. "The blood of Lord Masima flows in your veins. I am Arienh, of House Meeya, the house of the Beggars." Chadas screwed up his face.

"Do not be too quick to dismiss them," interrupted the Ama. "Meeya is revered by all. She was the best spy of Lord Masima." *A spy, that is different.*

Arienh continued with a smile. "It is said that Meeya could sit in one place all day. She could live beneath the noses of the people and yet not be seen."

She sat back and the Ama looked down on her as he added, "They are the eyes and ears of the Guild. He paused to give Chadas time to think, but Chadas had already pushed House Meeya from his mind. *I could not sit still all day. I need to do something.*

"The second is House Bela, the house of Thieves," the Ama announced.

The man sitting behind the stag leaned forward, his face both stern and ancient. He was bald with wrinkles marking more than his eyes, they wrapped his head. His dark grey shirt hung loose on his skeletal frame, and when he smiled, it was as if his mouth spread to engulf the rest of him. "I am Dyfed, of House Bela," he introduced. "Teru perlo mon tu Masima-to. The strength of Lord Masima lives in your body." He tried to smile again, with equal lack of success. "In House Bela, you will learn to purloin that which is useful to the Guild, generally from property owners or large traders, and sometimes even the Lord. Some say that Bela was such a master thief, she could steal the hearts of men and they would not notice they had gone missing. We find anything the Guild needs. We are their quick fingers and quiet feet." Chadas wondered how this man could be quick or quiet at anything, but he snickered inwardly at the story of Bela. *But he is not an old man. The face takes eyes away from the rest of him. It is a disguise.* For a moment Chadas stared. Both these people wear disguises. His eyes glanced quickly to the third leader. *It would be more fun to steal things.*

But the Ama was speaking again. "The third is House Eeva, the Assassins. It is the smallest of the Houses, but no less important. Stories say it is the assassins who will lead us back to our rightful place."

Another woman leaned forward, a short woman who had to peer to see above the wolf lectern. Dark eyes peeked from beneath the cloud of black hair.

*I think this is who she is. The little I see speaks of danger.* I am Keelia," she said, as if this needed no further explanation. "Teru zen min tu Masima-to. The spirit of Lord Masima burns in your heart." Before Chadas had time to absorb the introduction, she continued, "We kill for the Guild." She sat back.

Before the Ama could speak, Chadas rose to his full height and announced, "I wish to be an assassin."

The room waited as if there was more to be said. Finally the Ama broke the silence. "There is one more, House Alard, the guards."

"I wish to be an assassin," Chadas repeated.

The Ama stared but he met the gaze. "His decision is made. You may go, Chadas."

# 3 THE GREAT AUTHOR

Rata had long foregone the desire to walk the path to Lima, or whatever a spirit did to move to the next world. She had ignored the call of the Majick, and no longer felt its summons. She had been happy in her last life on Tatlo and discovered she could manipulate the lives and influence her old world with the control she had found in the Majick.

Watching on from the spirit world, Rata sat back and grinned, if a spirit could be said to grin, or even sit. But she was not like others of the world of Apat, the spirit world. She still chose to use the shape she had taken when she first came here, the body she last held on Tatlo. The ones she watched were her children's childrens' children. She had forgotten how many generations had passed. Around her, the clouds rolled and swam, the free shapes that most took in this world, but her heart was back in the human world. They can be anything they want. Why do they choose to be nothing? She pulled herself back. Her mind had been wandering much more recently. *Recently, ha. It had been … how long? When had her children last walked the valleys? Or their children?*

With an effort, she pushed the distraction aside. Another had come to her awareness. He would be strong. She could feel it. *I will write your name in the Book.* Again her mind wandered down a different path, this time to the Book, the Book of Majick. Someone had explained it once, all those years ago, but she could not remember who. *Whoever it was, they had moved on long ago.*

A nearby cloud began to pull together, swirling and twisting into the shape of a man. "Have you come to attack me?" Rata sneered. "Just one of you? You are not that strong. The Majick is in me, it obeys me. I am the Great Author, the writer of Majick."

"I do not come to fight."

"Do you remember when three of you tried together? Did you see how easily I cast them into the void?"

"I remember, as do many others. I have not come to fight. I know it would take more than one, or even three, and we all fear the space between worlds."

"What do you want, then?"

"To speak with you, to plead for you to stop and think."

"You waste your time, and mine. I am the Great Author. I write the story of the worlds. I am the Majick."

"Please," the man pleaded.

"Be quick. My time is needed elsewhere. I have pages to write."

The man seemed to take a slow, deep breath, pause and gulp. "What you do is not the work of the Great Author. To write the Majick, you must be the Majick. You are only a reader making notes on the side of the page." He tried a different approach. "To understand the Majick, you must know all of the worlds. Can you write what will happen in the worlds to come? You are strong in the Majick, and have learned much. No one will deny that. But your interference across the worlds angers the Majick, and weakens it. If you continue, the Majick will sicken to the point of its death. What will happen to us then? What will happen to you? And Tatlo? And the other worlds? Without the Majick, they will not exist."

When he stopped, Rata sneered, "Have you finished?"

"I beg you to think on this. Your time to move on has come many times, yet you refuse it. This is not right. The Majick must be obeyed."

"I have listened. It is you, and all those who sent you, who are wrong. I do what I must. I am the Great Author."

"You are not."

"I am!" yelled Rata, shaking the fabric of the world of white and sending echoes into neighboring worlds. She threw the Majick at him, a simple trick that bound him in invisible threads of power, unable to move and unable to escape. She sensed the fear in him. "I tire of your words. Leave now or I will cast you into the void with the others." She released him and the man disappeared.

*The void. The space between worlds. You all fear it. If I throw you there, you will be lost forever. You will never find your way back to any of the six worlds. I can do it, and I will.* Aloud, she yelled, "I am the Great Author. I am the Majick. Apat and Tatlo are mine to rule, and I will write their stories. You will not stop me, for the void is mine too."

But speaking of the six worlds dragged out memories that had been long lost, memories of her journey to this place, from her first life as a slug on the world of Isa. *That is a life I do not wish to recall. I do not want these memories.* The more she tried to push them away, the more they flooded into her mind. She lived many lives on Isa, worms and insects, snails and spiders, before the Majick called to her. Images came of the little blue beetle with black and red markings crawling along the worn dirt road, crawling for days to stand before the barrier of fallen trees so tightly packed she could see no way past. A giant bird stretched its head down, its long curved beak almost kissing her head. Two huge eyes stared out of red, green and yellow feathers. Eventually it turned away and a path opened to Dalawa.

*I do not know why I wanted to go there. It was as bad as Isa, except the creatures were larger and more dangerous.* Monstrosities crawled or walked, swam or flew. Massive creatures with long flowing necks that held twisted and hideous heads walked on four legs, or six, or eight. Bare-skinned things flew on huge, leathery wings. Armored animals with long, sinewy bodies swam in dark oceans while others scuttled on the seabed. All types of creature, scaled and armored, feathered or bald, lived and died on Dalawa, and all was black. She was trapped for twenty-two lives there. *Maybe I will hurl the next one who interferes to Dalawa instead of the void.* Thinking it, she knew how it could be done and savored the thought.

Then she lumbered up the cobbled road to the wooden gates. After being tested by the three massive snakes, each with three heads, she was allowed to pass. *And I was finally in Tatlo.*

She lived eight lives before she came to the body of Rata. *That was a good life. I was happy then, with .... what was his name? That does not matter.*

But, as it must, the Majick called to her again. She walked the silver road, surrounded by billowing white, until she reached the gates built of solid cloud, and guarded by two golden dragons.

She found herself on Apat, the spirit world. Her spirit had come but her thoughts remained on Tatlo, with her children. She learned the Majick, used it to watch and influence those still living there. When the Majick called to her, she ignored it. What she had been able to achieve had never been done before. *I can change the world. I am the Great Author. I am the Majick. No one understands. No one can stop me.* But the voice of her mind demanded attention. *You are not the Author, only a reader writing notes on the pages. The voice would fade with time.*

# 4 CONSEQUENCES

*What am I supposed to do now?* The Ama and the three were waiting. From beneath the folds of black cloth, the Ama's eyes smiled and flicked toward the door. Chadas turned. The woman in blue stood patiently holding it open. He stepped down and moved toward her. *Is mother waiting?* Hoping she would be there, he re-entered the large, white room. She was not. He was alone but one thought held his mind, I am free of my father.

The door clicked quietly shut behind him. Chadas wondered if this was the way of the Guild, doors that shut behind you, closing off your past life?

But he was not alone. Twelve guards still watched silently, and a man stood in the middle of the room. He beckoned Chadas to come closer. Chadas could not hold back his grin. The man stood in the belly of the dragon.

"Hello Chadas. I am to be your guide in House Eeva. My name is Tomlin." How could they know I would choose to be an assassin? They could not. I did not know myself. But no other Houses wait.

"Hello," he answered, looking around the room. *Was this man to be his trainer in the skills of an assassin? He looked old, but then, most people looked old. He looks almost as old as my mother, and she is five and twenty. Or will he only teach me the way of the Guild and another will come to show me the skills I will need? Tomlin, eh? He does not look like an assassin, but what does one look like?*

"Follow me." Tomlin turned and strode away as if there was no doubt he would follow. He walked quickly through dimly lit corridors and Chadas was forced to jog to keep up. They turned three times before they came to a passage with more torches. Tomlin did not slow. Two more corridors found them at a door, one of many that lined the walls, and no different from any other. "These are our rooms," Tomlin informed him. The man studied the door for a moment before pushing it open. Taking a torch from the wall, Tomlin stepped inside and moved to light three others in the room.

The room beyond was as large as the house where he had grown up. Chadas stood slack jawed. There was a bed, table and chairs, and on one wall, a cupboard filled with jars and bottles.

"How many people live here?" he asked.

"Just me." Chadas stared and Tomlin laughed loudly at his confusion. "Assassins are well respected, and I require room to practice my craft." He opened a door leading to a smaller room off to one side. "This will be your room. Apprentices do not have the same respect until they are accepted, but I will need you near if I am to teach you."

Chadas stepped through the door. Inside was a bed easily twice the size of the one he had shared with his family. Quinn would no longer kick him in his sleep. There was also a desk and an empty cupboard. Hooks on the wall waited for him to hang his clothes. He had never known such luxury.

"Time for your first lesson. I have left a package on the floor in the Dragon Hall. Run and fetch it for me." Chadas felt his stomach sink. What would Tomlin do if he could not find his way back. "I need it now, boy. Off you go." He was holding the door open. Hoping he could find the hall again, Chadas ran.

Choosing passageways he felt were right, and turning one way and another, Chadas was finally forced to admit he was lost. He was sure he could not find the hall, or find his way back. He stopped where he stood. Everything looked familiar, yet at the same time unknown. Suddenly Tomlin was at his side. He had not heard him approach, or seen him. He feared a slap, at least. But Tomlin crouched to speak with him face to face. "You have done well, boy. Not many get this close."

"Close?" he asked.

In answer, Tomlin rose, walked ten paces, and pointed. Chadas joined him. Only a short distance down a crossing passage was the Dragon Hall. The two guards still crouched either side, watching him, and they smiled.

Tomlin led him back to their rooms, and this time Chadas watched closely. If tested again, he would find the Dragon Hall without aid.

Tomlin sat him at the table and served him a glass of milk. "Your first lesson. It will be important to learn. Wherever you go, know where you are. As you walk through the passages, count your steps between each turn, and the direction. You will always be able to find your way back."

#

Sitting at the table, Tomlin asked, "Why do you choose to become an assassin?"

"It sounded most exciting," he answered.

Tomlin stared deep into his eyes, dragging forth his inner thoughts as if weighing the truth in his reply and finding the scales did not balance. Chadas cringed under the stare, he could not help it. "If you are to be my apprentice," he growled, "you will hold nothing from me."

Chadas swallowed. He knew he would be punished for withholding the truth, all of it. "I wanted…" He swallowed again before blurting out, "I wanted to learn how to kill my father."

Tomlin's face remained a mask with all emotion hidden behind it. Chadas squirmed. Finally, Tomlin smiled. "Good. Now we can begin. There are two lessons to be learned from what you say. The first, anyone can kill. The skill lies in not being caught, never being caught. And the second, you are now apprenticed to the House of Eeva, and to me. Soon enough you will become an assassin." Tomlin looked down at the table and smiled. "There is a rule you must learn, and it is important. We do not kill for personal satisfaction."

He gave Chadas time to mull over these words before explaining.

"Our skills are only employed when we have a contract, with fair payment." He laughed. "If we each killed those we thought had done us wrong, there would be no one left in the city. Do you understand?"

Chadas nodded.

"I hope so. If you fail this rule, you will shame the House, and me."

"I will obey," Chadas promised, and to himself added, for now. Tomlin watched until he was satisfied, then laughed. "As with all rules," he said, "there are exceptions. There is one reason we kill other than for coin. A person who fails to meet his obligations in a bargain would receive the same fate he ordered for his victim." When Chadas asked what this meant, he replied, "A man or woman offers payment for the death of a person. When the Guild completes the contract, and payment not made, their own lives will be forfeit, or if they intend in any other manner to betray the Guild, the punishment must be the same."

That was the moment he began thinking of his mentor as 'Old Tom'. Tomlin seemed to take no offense at his mistakes or lies. He was a friendly and knowledgeable guide, someone he could look up to. He was not his father.

"Those jars and bottles," Tomlin nodded toward the cupboard, "all hold different poisons and potions. Before your training is over, you will learn to prepare and handle each. You will know what they do, and how quickly they act. And you will make a journal with all the information you acquire."

"But…" Chadas began and his eyes dropped.

Tomlin continued as if he did not hear. "To do this, you will learn to read and write." The conversation went on, mostly about what he would learn, until he could hold his yawn no longer.

"We will continue later," Tomlin decided. "There is much to learn but enough time to learn it. Off to bed now."

Next day, his mentor led him out of the maze, below ground and above. They walked together through Dragonfang. Tomlin would sit and rest, and on these occasions, would ask, "What do you see?" At first, not knowing what his master wanted, he would reply with the obvious, the road, the houses, washing hanging from windows. "These are the things everyone sees," Tomlin explained. "What do you see? Remember, look through an assassin's eyes."

"I do not know," Chadas reluctantly admitted, expecting the back of Tomlin's hand.

"Come and sit." Tomlin was gentle. Chadas' father would have shown him his fists. "Look closely at the road. What do you see?" Chadas had not understood at the time what Tomlin wanted him to see. He shook his head. "Cobbles," Tomlin laughed, and then becoming more serious, he added, "Only a person trained to run on cobbles can do so safely and quickly. Now, off you go. Run to the blacksmith's and back. Remember, quickly and safely." He would come to run the cobbles more times than he could care to remember.

On one of their rest breaks, Tomlin asked about the houses. "They are just wood and stone. There is nothing remarkable about them." When Tomlin remained silent, he looked again. "A woman is standing at the window of the third house, and much noise comes from the tavern."

"Good. If this were where you completed your kill, that woman would raise the alarm, and her screams would empty the tavern. You could be trapped. There will be a better time and place to complete your contract."

#

After the first week, Chadas began to settle into a routine. He could see the value in the things he did and felt good because of that. He would wake when Tomlin lit the torch in his room and after he washed and dressed, there would be food for his breakfast. It still amused him that Tomlin insist he wash every day. His brothers and sisters rarely washed, and neither had he before he came here, but he pushed those memories aside. His lessons would begin when he finished eating. Tomlin would lay out the parchment on which were written letters and numbers. At first with a slate and later using a quill and fresh parchment, Chadas would try and copy them, over and over. The ornate inkwell he used was shaped from black stone with a dragon carved around it. The dragon was decorated with gold gilt. Tomlin told him it had once adorned the desk of the Lord, one that lived before his mother's parents were born. He would copy the shapes until lunch. He was both afraid and disappointed when he dripped ink on the parchment, but Tomlin only encouraged him to try again, showing him how to wipe the excess ink from the quill.

With lunch finished, Tomlin sat with him while he learned to read what he had written. Numbers confused him more than letters. How could a '1' mean one but put numbers after it and it could be ten, or a hundred or more. But Tomlin was patient, and soon the letters, words and even numbers began to make sense.

Six weeks of study passed quickly before Tomlin decided on a break in their routine. "We will walk in Dragonfang today," he announced as he cleared away breakfast.

When they were ready, Tomlin opened the door and came face to face with a woman who held her hand ready to knock, a taller woman than any he had seen, and more beautiful. Her long yellow hair framed her laughing green eyes and red pouting lips. Her pink robe was embroidered with flowers.

"Good day to you, Leena," Tomlin greeted. "Chadas and I are going walking in Dragonfang. Would you and Rill care to join us?" It was only then that Chadas noticed the girl hidden behind the woman's skirts.

Leena's smile seemed to light the corridor. Torches would not be needed with her at their side. They walked out into the alley and away from the Guild, making their way to the marketplace. Their mentors walked together, examining the wares on display while Chadas and Rill trailed behind. "What do you study?" Chadas asked. Rill looked sharply at the two ahead.

In a soft whisper she answered, "I am apprenticed to the House of Bel."

Chadas realized he may not be meant to speak of his training, and both looked to their mentors who seemed oblivious of their presence.

"What is your training like," Chadas asked. "Do you learn to read and write?"

Rill giggled. "I will have no need to write. I only learn enough of reading to know if something is important. I mainly learn to move quietly, open locks and climb walls in the dark. I like that best, the climbing."

"That sounds fun."

Rill looked toward Leena before turning her stare on Chadas. She seemed to understand that Chadas did not find her training to be fun at all.

"What about you?" she asked.

"I am apprenticed to House Eeva."

Rill's brow rose. "Is it difficult? I think I would find it so."

"It is hard work, but I have a good teacher."

"What is he like?"

"Old Tom? He is an excellent mentor, a much nicer person than my father." He looked up to see Leena and Tomlin watching them and tried to recall what he had said.

His face grew red as heat burned in his cheeks. Stepping back, he cringed. Tomlin's face was stern, but Leena broke into fits of giggles. In between she stammered, "Old Tom! Did you know, Old Tom?"

Tomlin turned, but seeing her face he, too, began laughing. "Old Tom, am I?"

Chadas tried to explain but Tomlin over-rode his words. "Old Tom?" He twisted the words around in his mouth. "I like it. You may call me that if you wish, Baby Chadas." His grin widened as he approached. Putting his hand on Chadas' shoulder he muttered, "Old Tom, eh? Well, you had better help Old Tom so he does not stumble as he shuffles between the stalls." He laughed loudly this time.

As he and Leena turned to enter the market, Rill giggled and ran after them.

Chadas followed.

# 5 OLD TOM

He had learned to read most things and could write passages his mentor dictated. He could even do numbers better than most traders.

Then one morning after Chadas had risen and breakfasted, Tomlin threw a document in front of him. Chadas stared at the parchment. The oddly shaped scrolling marks were beyond his recognition. He could make no sense of the page.

"What is this?" he asked.

"It is Belian, the letters of the city of Bel. A number of traders deal with Bel, some more than others. You will find it useful if you could read enough of their words to understand. You will never know when the knowledge you gain will be of benefit. You may learn many secrets if you seek them out."

Chadas continued to stare at the parchment as if the words would suddenly appear. A few of the shapes bore similarities with some of the letters he knew, but not enough to help him understand.

"But I thought we only concerned ourselves with a contract, and payment for it. Do we also write contracts in this?"

"We concern ourselves with many things. There is a purpose for all knowledge. A useful method of keeping a secret is to shroud it in a language that few know. Secrets are secrets for a reason. That reason may concern the Guild, and if it does, it will help to know what is planned." Chadas studied the strange script. "It says, 'Today, Chadas has been apprenticed to House Eeva for one year."

Chadas looked at the script, at Tomlin, then back at the script. He could not even recognize his own name. "A year?"

Old Tom laughed. "Yes, a year." When Chadas did not react, other than to spread confusion over his face, Tomlin asked, "You know what that means?" Chadas shook his head, not seeing the direction the conversation was leading. "Today is your tenth age-day."

A grin filled Chadas' face. His mother had provided wonderful treats on his last age-day. The memory was a good one.

"Put your studies aside. We are going to enjoy this day." There was an enthusiasm in Tomlin's voice that carried Chadas along with it. "The Lord has decided there is to be a great fair today. He wants his people to celebrate the joys of the city and the best harvest we have seen in many years. He has named it the Festival of the Tower."

Chadas scurried along trying to keep pace with Tomlin's long strides as they moved through the tunnels. At the hidden door, Tomlin took a moment to peek through the sight hole before he gave his warning and they both stepped out into the morning light. Three guards were playing knuckles in the dusty alley. One nodded a greeting before returning to the game.

The Festival was held below the tower wall where stalls backed onto the stone barrier. In front were people, a tide of flowing bodies, constantly moving but getting nowhere. Most of the stalls held produce, fresh vegetables and fruit. An equal number offered mead, ale or wine. Occasionally there were sellers of sweets, custard cakes, honey cakes and assortments of dried plums, apple and other treats. A Cryer was announcing the archery contest to be held in the afternoon. The winner would receive a gold coin. This was to be followed by a display of sword skills presented by the tower guard. There were jugglers, tumblers and musicians wherever space allowed. Chadas was absorbed with the pleasantries of the event. Everyone seemed happy.

Near one stall offering wine, a fight broke out in front of them and Tomlin turned Chadas aside to avoid the trouble. The Guards will soon put a stop to it" he said.

Tomlin stopped and tapped Chadas on the shoulder. With the slightest of nods, he indicated where Chadas should look. Lord Rodnel rode out of the tower on a tall black stallion. He was a solid man, broad shoulders and thick arms. His dark coat was trimmed in gold. At his side rode his wife, the Lady Arlette, equally as stately in her blue gown with silver embroidery and riding a brown mare. Their son, the eleven-year-old future Lord, trotted behind, on a gray pony.

It was one of the best days Chadas could remember.

When they finally returned to their rooms, he dropped into a chair, exhausted.

After a few moments of quiet, Tomlin asked, "What did you see today?"

Chadas came alert. He had experience with his mentor's questions and looked back on the day as he had been taught. "The fight, no one came to stop it."

"Good. Why?"

"It was not a serious fight, just two farmers who had drunk too much. With the Lord near, the guards did not wish to create a scene."

"Very good. What else?"

Chadas mentioned a few things but Tomlin smiled and shook his head to each. There was something he should have noticed, something more important than the things he had mentioned. He could not think of it.

"Tell me about Edur." When Chadas shook his head, he added, "The Lord's son."

*What was I meant to see? He was just another child.*

"Think," prompted Tomlin. "Tell me what he was doing."

"He was riding his pony and following his parents."

"Was he? Why was he on the pony?"

"Because he is only a child?" Chadas suggested.

"True, but he is the son of a Lord, and should be able to ride a horse."

Chadas thought. "He bounced around a lot."

Tomlin nodded. "In his position he must have received instruction on riding, but he is unable to do it, or does not listen. What else?"

Chadas cast his mind back to that moment. What was he doing? Why is Old Tom interested? Slowly at first but gaining confidence at the sight of his mentor's smile, he answered. "He was not following his father and mother, only riding behind them. His thoughts were not on them. He watched the crowds that cheered for his father, and it annoyed him. His lip sneered often. He did not want to be there. He does not like the adoration of the people for his father."

"More, he despises the people," Tomlin added. "He does not respect them the way his father does."

"Is that important?"

"It should be. One day, he will be Lord of Dragonfang. When the leader of a people holds contempt for those who serve him, trouble is brewing."

#

The day following the Festival, Chadas was ready to begin his studies of the Belian writing but Tomlin was busy reading a pile of documents and ignoring him. He had learned patience and waited for Old Tom to finish. Finally the pages were put aside and Tomlin sat with a frown creasing his forehead.

"What is wrong?"

"Nothing to worry about, just something I must attend to." He thought for a few moments before adding, "Follow me." He came quickly to his feet, his face once again relaxed, and hurried from the room with Chadas rushing to catch up. His pace did not ease as they moved through the corridors until Tomlin stopped at a door. "Wait here." Then, with a knock, Tomlin entered, shutting it behind him.

Chadas studied the door. It was no different from any other in the corridors. Then, looking closer, he saw the mark at the top corner. It appeared to be a shallow 'X', with a shorter cross at the bottom of each leg. He did not have time to look further before the door opened again. Tomlin called him in.

A woman stood beside his mentor, but unlike any woman he had seen. She had short-cropped dark hair, broad shoulders and arms thicker than Tomlin's. Although she only came to his mentor's shoulder, her presence was much bolder. She wore a tight leather jerkin over leather braccae. Why is this woman dressed like a man? Who is she?

"Welcome to the sword-room," she greeted.

"The sword-room?"

"Yes," Tomlin answered. "This is where we learn the skills of the sword." Chadas was suddenly very interested. "This is Birte. She is a swordmaster and has agreed to train you. Treat her with respect or you may come home bleeding."

Birte grinned. "Have you used a sword before? No? Then it is about time you learned about them. Today you will use a sword."

Chadas looked around. Weapons lined every wall and odd wicker figures stood in one corner. Birte pointed. "Over by the wall is a rack of swords. Find one that feels right." While Chadas obeyed, his mentor slipped from the room. "No. Those, over there," she barked. "From the children's rack." Birte pulled one of the wicker figures to the center of the room. "You have one? Good. How does it feel?"

"It seems fine."

"Well and good." She stepped back. "Attack your target."

Chadas raised his sword, exhilaration coursing through his veins. He closed and swung. The sword crashed into the wicker man sending a jolt of impact up his arm. He looked to Birte and grinned. "Do not stop," was the only command she gave. He raised his sword and struck again and again. The next stroke was in its preparation when Birte groaned "Stop! For the sake of my poor departed grandmother, please stop." Chadas froze in mid-stroke. "Do you attack a babe in arms who can not yet hold a rattle? If the person you attack is a trader, or anyone else of mild ability, you may have drawn blood, but you would be dead four times over, nine if you faced a guard."

"But I hit him with every stroke."

"Only because he cannot defend himself. Do you expect your target to wait quietly for you to kill him?" Chadas faced the wicker man. "Your target has a sword. What will he do? Anticipate his moves."

Chadas raised his sword and approached more slowly this time. His eyes were on the wicker man. He barely heard Birte when she muttered, "Better." Chadas threw his sword up, parrying an imagined blow, then to the side to stop another. As he moved the blade to deflect another blow, he ducked and brought his sword around to cut across the wicker man's belly. He moved back with care. "Much better. You only died once, and were severely wounded on another occasion."

Birte pushed the wicker man out of the way. "Now, let me see your choice of sword." Chadas moved to pass it to her. "No." Chadas stopped. "Once you have a sword in your hand, do not release it until it is time for it to be sheathed." Chadas waited. "Hold the sword out in front of you. Keep your arm straight and level. Point the sword along the line of your arm, and hold it."

Chadas did as instructed. The weapon dragged at the muscles of his arm and he could not hold it still. Slowly it sagged as if drawn by chains.

Birte shook her head. "Too heavy." She walked to the rack, looked over her shoulder at the sword Chadas carried, and searched along the line of weapons. Without drawing one, she said, "Put that away and take this one, then try again."

Chadas did as instructed, and after, stared at the blade, his eyes wide. The sword was a similar length and was fitted with the same guard, yet somehow, it felt right. Knowing he would be asked, he looked closer. The blade was a little narrower and two rounded recesses ran almost to the tip.

The wicker man came back and his exercises began in earnest. The blade flashed more quickly, its movements precise. Birte smiled. "There are a great many good weapons, but there is nothing like the feel of the right one. As you grow, your needs will change. The weapon that is right today will not be so in a year. Value a good blade but be prepared to sheath it for a final time when it becomes necessary. This advice applies to all weapons, not only swords. There will come a day when Tomlin must send you away, and you him."

Chadas knew she was right. While he learned his skills, he could think of no better teacher. But the day must come when he has learned his trade and leave. He may even begin to train another."

Training continued throughout the day and when he finally put the sword away, he could barely stand with the exhaustion that flooded his body. Birte sent him back to his room to rest. Retracing his steps, he found the room and entered. Tomlin had still not returned. Chadas fussed with lighting a couple of torches, then sat and took an apple.

He was about to take the first bite when the door crashed open. Tomlin stood there, holding himself erect with one arm on the frame. Blood dribbled down his other arm. His face was whiter than Chadas had ever seen.

Chadas was on his feet. "Tom, what happened? Quick, come and sit." After helping his mentor to a seat, Chadas tore the shirt away to examine the wound on his shoulder. It did not look too deep.

"You will need to stitch it up," Tomlin told him. "There is needle and thread in that drawer."

Chadas fetched them, and poured him a goblet of wine.

#

Jebeh sniffled as he hurried down the narrow lane, his eyes glancing toward the small house. He passed it every day, but today it was different, quiet. It struck him that this was the third day he had hear no sounds coming from within. It was never this silent. He had spoken with the woman who lived there, he thought her name was Wynne, and there was always children about. He lowered his head and strode on, but after four paces, he stopped. Something was wrong. He looked again at the run-down home. There was always a smell about it, the stink of rot, unwashed bodies, but mostly the stench of Mabon, Wynne's husband. The stink of old spew never left him and his britches emitted the smell of piss. His home had absorbed these odors. But today, in the still air, these were masked by the scent of decay.

He sniffed again, wondering, but he pushed his curiosity aside. He wanted nothing to do with Mabon, but his thoughts pushed back.

Should he do something? Should he check? He wavered. Many times he had felt the tongue of Mabon, and sometimes his fists as the man staggered home from the tavern. If there was nothing wrong … he left the thought unfinished.

Deciding it was not worth the trouble that may come his way, he moved on. But down the street he spotted the dark leather of two city guards, their short, red capes hanging from their shoulders. They should check. That is what they are here for. He waved his arms, called, and beckoned them to come.

"What?" growled one of the guards. He was tall and broad-shouldered. The second guard was a similar build though a few fingers shorter. With surprise, Jebeh realized this was a girl.

"That house," Jebeh pointed. "It is too quiet. It has been silent for three days. Mabon, the man who lives there is never this quiet. I think there is something wrong."

Both guards looked at the house and him. The man grunted and turned away, but the woman spoke. "Our job is to keep the peace in Dragonfang. We are too busy to worry about anyone who is keeping too quiet." She emphasized the 'too' before turning to leave with the other guard who was already ten paces away. Jebeh stared at the backs of the departing guards. They could at least look, he thought.

A rare moment of bravery gripped him. He took one cautious step toward the door, then another. I should go, he thought, but the moment of bravery had not yet passed. A few steps and he was standing at the door wondering what to do. The odor caused his nose to wrinkle. He took two steps to the side, to the window. The stench was stronger here. The darkness inside tried to hide the scene, without success. He spun back towards the guards.

"Wait," he yelled. "Guards, wait." The woman turned to look. She slapped the man on the shoulder as she started back. Jebeh could not help himself. His eyes returned to the scene. A woman and three children slept in their beds, a sleep from which they would never wake. Dried blood stained the beds and clothing as swarms of flies buzzed over them.

The guards were beside him, looking in, then moving to the door. He was still staring when they returned. "There is no man here. Who did you say lived here?" the man demanded.

Jebeh licked his lips. "M…Mabon," he stuttered. "Mabon Annea."

"And who are you?"

Jebeh Seff." The guards waited. He pointed. "I live down there, around the corner at the water trough."

The woman spoke again. "You said it was too quiet. Do you pass here often?"

"Every day. Three or four times every day."

"Then why did you wait so long to check?"

"Mabon, the father, is a drunk and can be very aggressive. I was afraid." She nodded.

"Run and fetch the Reeve. Quickly now," the man ordered.

As he ran, Jebeh wondered what he would say, what he should say. That the guards wanted the Reeve, of course. But should he tell of what he saw? How could he explain it and not seem hysterical? That was how it would sound.

To his surprise, the Reeve followed him back to the house without question. Jebeh looked through the door and felt his stomach twist into a knot. The woman and her young children still lay on their beds. None seemed to have tried to flee the rage that had killed them. All had gashes over their heads and bodies. The buzz of flies hovered in the room. An ax, smeared with blood, lay on the floor just inside the door.

His stomach finally won its battle with his mind and he turned aside to empty it onto the street.

When he looked up, a beggar woman was at the door. She addressed the Reeve. "If you have boxes for the bodies, I can move them, and clean the house, for a couple of coins."

The Reeve nodded. "I will send word where the bodies are to be taken." To the guards he added, "When you finish here, find the man who did this."

"He will be at the tavern. He is always at the tavern," Jebeh told them.

# 6 A LESSON IN DEATH

Not long after his tenth birthday, Chadas emerged from his room to be greeted by Tomlin's downcast expression. "Is something wrong? Does your arm still worry you?"

Tomlin pointed to the chair, and he sat. The table was prepared for their breakfast with dried fruits and cheese. This morning there was also a mug of fresh goats' milk. "I have received news," Tomlin began.

Chadas waited. From the expression on Old Tom's face, he knew the news would not be good.

Tomlin took a deep breath and swallowed. "The tower guard have been to your old house. They found your family all dead."

Chadas sat stunned, numb. He took a moment to absorb the words, then, "Mother?" Tomlin nodded.

"Edana? Keir? Quinn?" His mentor nodded to each, and with each nod his voice quietened.

After some time he decided to ask, "Father?"

With a shake of his head, Tomlin explained that his father had been arrested at the tavern. "He will face the Lord's justice for killing them."

Anger filled his question. "How?"

Tomlin would not answer.

"How?" he demanded.

"They died in their sleep."

Chadas' voice dropped low. "I will keep asking. How?"

His mentor's head dipped as he hid his face behind his hands. He clearly did not wish to answer.

"Tell me," Chadas pleaded.

Tomlin looked up. "An ax was found on the floor. It was covered with blood."

#

Tomlin suggested he take time away from his studies to mourn the loss of his family. Chadas stared at nothing until eventually he shook his head and declined. "I will continue my work." Tomlin watched with narrowed eyes. "What am I to do if I do not study. I have no home to go to, and no family." He remembered his father. "At least no family I wish to see. You are my family now, you and the Guild."

His mentor accepted his decision, but added, "If you change your mind, you need only tell me. There must be someone you would wish to see?"

"There is no one."

Silence settled between them as they ate. Chadas stared at the table, his spoon moving automatically from pate to mouth. Finally Tomlin broke the sounds of chewing with, "Then today you will begin to learn about knives." He understood that Chadas needed a distraction. With a flick of his wrist a blade appeared as if out of the air. He held it up. "This end," he indicated with his other hand, "is where you hold it. Get this wrong and you have no fingers."

Chadas' head pushed forward as he scowled. Old Tom laughed. "All right, but it is something to remember. The blade of your knife must be sharp, and it must point at your intended victim." He smiled. "Your first question. What is the difference between a knife and a dagger?"

After a moment Chadas admitted he did not know and could not guess the answer.

"It is simple, really. A knife has one sharp edge. It is meant for cutting. A dagger's two edges can cut, but the dagger is a stabbing weapon."

Tomlin opened a large box that sat against the wall. Chadas chided himself for not having noticed it. He remained quiet while his mentor placed a selection of weapons on the table. "This will give you an idea of the types of knives you could use." Chadas looked over the collection. "As you can see, some have long blades, others short. All require a skilled hand to use them. The long blades are better if your target is aware you are attacking, but in a dark alley or crowded market, the short blade will serve you better for a quick slash across the throat.

Chadas picked up one of the knives to study it.

"Many have a pommel, good for hitting, but all have a guard between grip and blade. This is to protect your hand in a fight. Some have blades that curve back, others forward, while as many are straight. We will discuss the different skills required for each later.

Admiring the knives on the table, Chadas commented, "There are so many types."

"Pick one up. Feel the weight in your hand, and the balance. Weight and balance are the reasons you should choose a knife."

Chadas reached for one, a long blade with a heavy central ridge. He moved it, felt it, and placed it back on the table. The second knife seemed to settle into his hand as if it had found a home. The blade was shorter and narrower. He smiled at the comfort it gave.

The knives began disappearing back into the box as Tomlin exchanged them for a second collection. Chadas now knew these to be daggers. All had straight, two-sided blades. To Chadas, all were weapons of great beauty.

Tomlin passed him one, a solid blade and round guard. A ruby glowed in its grip. "This belonged to a merchant from Bel. He was very disappointed when he lost it." Tomlin grinned. "It is called a rondel and gets its name from the guard."

Chadas picked up another. "And this?" he asked.

"That is a bollock dagger. Its name comes from the two oval swellings on its guard."

As Tomlin placed more on the table, Chadas' eyes lit up. Ignoring all other weapons, he reached for the most beautiful thing on the table. From its point, the diamond-shaped blade glistened in the torchlight until it met the beautiful guard. The silver mesh had been formed into the shape of a flying dragon whose head stared up the blade with small ruby eyes, while four legs and a tail wrapped the hand of the owner. The grip was bound in dark green leather finished with a pommel of a pale green gem.

It felt natural in his hand, a part of him. He moved it back and forth. The dragon protected his hand but still allowed for excellent movement. He began flicking his fingers. The blade spun so fast, it blurred in his vision.

"Careful," Tomlin warned, but Chadas knew it would offer him no harm. His fingers stopped and the blade was pointing at the roof. The spinning began again and this time, when the blade stopped, it was pointing at the table.

"The pommel is a rare form of green garnet," Tomlin offered around his smile.

Chadas looked up at Tomlin and the blade started to spin once more. His attention came back to the knife, mesmerized by the motion and the flashing of light off the blade.

"It appears to have found its owner." Chadas looked up, the blade suddenly still. "It will be your first real weapon."

"I … I cannot."

"Why?"

"It belongs to you. I cannot take a thing of such beauty away from you."

"It has chosen you. That is why it must be yours." Chadas sat shaking his head but Tomlin continued. "It is usual for a mentor to give his apprentice a gift on graduation. This will be yours, and you may hold it and learn to use it before then."

Chadas jumped from his chair and rushed to throw his arms around his mentor. "Thank you Tom, thank you," was all he was able to say.

"It is a misericord."

"What?"

"A misericord, that is the type of dagger."

"Then it shall be called Misery." Chadas smiled at the joke he made.

#

"Come," Tomlin said as he turned to the door.

"Where are we going? To the sword-room? Or is there a knife-room?"

"No. We are going for a walk. You have been studying hard and this is a trying time. You should take time to rest and think." Chadas followed but did not wish to think.

They walked together through the now-familiar tunnels and as they emerged into the alley, Chadas was not surprised to find Leena and Rill waiting. The four strolled towards the marketplace, Tomlin and Leena leading with Chadas following and Rill at his side.

"I am sorry," Rill offered. Chadas glanced at her, and she continued. "About your mother, your family."

"The guards hold my father for their killings."

"Sometimes they get it right." Chadas' look was inquisitive, and she shrugged. "Sometimes they get it wrong."

"What do you mean?"

"Just that the guards will always find the easiest answer, not necessarily the correct one. But it will save them work."

"Are you speaking generally, or about my father?"

She shrugged again. "Generally, but it could apply to your father."

"My father is a monster, a drunk. He would use his fists on my mother and us, just because we were there."

"Then the guards have probably made the right decision this time."

Rill fell silent. Chadas did not wish to continue this conversation, fearing where it could lead. They walked, no words passing between them. The narrow alleys gave way to wider streets where a horse could be ridden with ease, and further to roads made for carts. The homes still sat on top of each other, but they had no choice in the growing city. We are just like a family, Chadas thought, a rich family. Rill still trailed at his shoulder and he noticed Leena did the same with Tomlin, her hand lost in his.

When they reached the marketplace, a flowing tide of people surged around them as they searched for a bargain amongst the many traders. Everything was offered from exotic wares from other cities to weapons and fine cloth. Old Tom and Leena stopped.

"We are going to look around. You do not need to follow us." He slipped a few coins into Chadas' hand. "Wander about and see what you can find and enjoy yourselves. This is to be your day of rest. Have fun. As they left, Chadas opened his hand to count the coins. "I expect a full report when I see you this evening," Tomlin called as he and Leena disappeared among the crowd.

Chadas and Rill wandered together, examining the various goods on show. Then he grabbed her wrist and pulled her aside, his other hand covering his nose and mouth. "Are you alright?" she asked.

"It is the smell of pigfish. It always makes my stomach complain." They stood amid the surging crowd for a moment while he caught his breath.

Chadas looked to Rill and grinned. "I am going to look at knives," he said. "They are beautiful and do not smell." He walked a long path around the fish stall to one that sold blades. A number of knives were laid out for inspection, and though he looked closely, none seemed the equal of Misery, or even appeared worth considering. Rill followed at his side even though he had been ignoring her. He noticed a small knife, barely the length of his palm. The curved blade was well honed but the grip had been poorly added and the guard damaged. He offered two coins and it was accepted. Passing the knife to Rill, he said, "This is for you. Everyone needs a weapon." Her face lit up as she took the gift.

They walked on until he found an old woman selling fruit tarts. Having not seen Leena give Rill any coins, he asked, "I am going to have a plum tart. Would you like one?"

"Oh, yes please," she smiled.

Buying two, he pushed his way to a quieter spot and crouched beside a building. Rill sank down beside him and accepted the offered treat.

As they ate, she thanked him repeatedly, and her face beamed. He was pleased that such a little thing could bring such happiness. When they finished, they chatted, wondering what their mentors could be doing, watching the hectic life of the markets.

Suddenly she leaned in and kissed him firmly on the cheek. Caught by surprise, Chadas stumbled back. He saw her eyes fill with horror as her tears began to flow. "Rill," he whispered, but she jumped to her feet and rushed off into the crowds. He rose and called louder, "Rill." What had he done? She was lost in the flood of people. Why had she kissed him? "Rill," he called again.

He saw the old woman with her head lowered, shaking it slowly. Her hand flicked in a gesture he took to mean, 'Go after her'.

He searched the rest of the day without success and finally returned to his room, saddened and confused. Tomlin had not returned. Thinking about Rill, he wondered if he could sleep tonight.

# 7 LIMA

I looked up from my reading.

"Kuwento?" I asked. "I have written this next part as you told it."

"Then what is the problem?"

"The six worlds of Majick. Why are there six?"

Kuwento shook his head. "Have you not yet understood? They are the six stages we must all achieve to understand the true meaning of ourselves."

"But you say the six worlds travel side by side through time."

"Time is a meaningless abstraction."

I sat back and scratched my ear, more confused than when I first heard the stories. "How….?" My voice trailed off, not knowing what question I meant to ask.

"The Majick allows us to see our past lives if we know how to look, but the future is closed to us. We all begin our lives on Isa. There we are little more than a mindless existence that understands no more than to be. We move to Dalawa when we learn to hunt and kill. We learn to survive."

I nodded.

"To arrive here on Tatlo, we have learned much more. We find safety in herds and cities. We know what it is to love and protect others though we all fail to remember this at times."

"But if we cannot look ahead, how can we know there are six worlds?"

"Some throughout time have been visited by the spirits, so we know that Apat exists. People may deny the Majick, but few doubt the spirit world."

"Or what we must learn to get there," I added.

Kuwento smiled. "It is almost my time for the journey. I believe that to get there, I must comprehend the fact that our lives do not exist for our physical bodies. What lies beyond, I cannot say. It could be that we learn to understand each other and how they feel. Maybe it concerns common awareness, maybe not. I can only speculate using my knowledge of the maal."

I considered this. I was certain my friend knew more than he spoke but his stories fitted the tale so I must accept them. I can only speculate in my writings of Apat and Lima, and I hope you, the reader, will forgive any errors in my knowledge of these worlds. I can only promise that they fit all I have learned from Kuwento and his Majick icons.

I continued reading.

#

Lima, the world beyond the spirit world, is a strange and beautiful place. But strange and beautiful are only words, and both are inadequate and misleading. It is something far beyond these feeble words. Is it not true that whatever lies beyond our reach is always described so, whether it be in this world or the next? Or even the world beyond that? Lima is not adorned with fields of colorful flowers or the splendor of sprawling forests. You will not find the grandeur of towering mountains or the vastness of untouched oceans. Lima's beauty lies not in physical things, but in the radiance of knowledge.

A spirit who passes beyond the world of man may discover the wonders of Apat, where all can feel the Majick and bask in its glory. On Apat, they know peace. But beyond that, in the world of Lima lies wisdom.

Some tell us that on Apat the spirits remain individual entities, holding onto some memory of Tatlo. On Lima it is different. Though they remain individuals, the spirits gather in groups of twos and threes, tens or hundreds, to share their thoughts and experiences, or consider questions of immense wonder. At these times, the spirits become almost as a single entity.

They did that now.

"Did you feel it?"

"Yes, of course."

"What is happening?"

"What is causing it?"

With the passing of every moment, more minds came to join the great melding. Questions without answer ran around the massed mind of a great many thousands, a vast number never before experienced on Lima.

"Is it the Majick?"

"I have never known it to be so."

"Nothing like this has occurred before."

Another voice entered the discussion, a voice unlike all others, deep and resonating with power, sure. "*The Majick is facing its death.*"

"The Majick is going to die?

Why?"

"It cannot be. The Majick is the power of all."

"*Yet, soon the Majick will be dead.*"

"Who are you?"

"What are you?"

"Where are you?"

Then … the silence of thought. Each entity in that combined mind of Lima summoned the wisdom to understand the words of the voice. Only when they realized they had no answers did the discussion begin again.

"What is killing the Majick?"

"What will happen if the Majick dies?"

"What will become of us?"

"What will become of the worlds?"

The question once again rose. "Who are you?"

"*We are the One of Anim.*"

An awed silence followed. All knew that Anim was where they hoped to go when their time on Lima was done. Someone asked, "The One?"

"*All who enter Anim join the One. We are the One.*"

"What does that mean?"

"*We are one with each other. Just as you choose to be now, but much more. We are one with each other, with the worlds and with the Majick. Every entity who comes here joins the One.*"

"And if the Majick dies?"

"*We die. So do the worlds and all the entities on them.*"

"What can we do?"

"You are strong. You must do something.

"*The problem lies beyond Anim, just as it is beyond your world. Anim is strongly tied to the Majick. If the One interferes, the consequences to the Majick will be dire. All worlds will end. Even Lima cannot act directly. Your actions will lead us all to the same fate. Together, we must find a way to save the Majick without destroying it.*"

"Where is the danger?"

"What is the danger?"

"*The danger lies on Apat. An entity is altering the Book of Majick. It believes it is the Great Author. This being uses the Majick across worlds. That is forbidden. Rata is the name it uses.*" The voice of the One went quiet.

"What can we do?"

"The One says it is up to us."

"We must demand that it stop."

"Will it listen?"

"If it believes it is the Great Author and has control of the Majick, why would it stop?"

"It must be strong in the Majick."

"We must try."

#

After all this time, after so many generations had come and gone, Rata could sense her dream would soon be fulfilled. One had been born who would set the world of Tatlo right. He was born of Masima, of her, and he would take vengeance for the murder of her grandson. He would kill the descendants of those who had murdered Masima and take back what should be his. It will be so. She was writing it in the Book of Majick. Everywhere he went, she could sense the Majick turn to him, wrapping him in its embrace. He did not know it yet, he was still a child and while the Majick accepted him, he was not ready to accept it. He did not know or understand the power that was his to command. But there was time. Not much longer.

Rata watched through the portal she had created. Unlike those she had made earlier, she had tuned this portal to follow Chadas. He studied now. She did not understand his need to do so, but he was growing stronger. The study may be the reason. If it opened his mind to the Majick, she would be pleased. She watched as he chose Misery and felt the Majick come to him as he spun it in his fingers.

So intense was her concentration on the world of man, she did not notice the changes that came around her. The usual white world was changing slowly, glowing in a purple light. The clouds that drifted through the world were withdrawing, creeping away to put distance between them and the pending conflict. Only when the world rattled with her name was she distracted from her task.

"Rata."

Not closing the portal, but placing a shield of Majick over it, Rata turned. A shining purple star floated nearby.

"What is this? Has one of you learned more of the Majick? You will still not be strong enough. I am the Great Author."

"You must stop!"

"I have told you before, no matter how many of you try to make me cease, it will not be enough. I will cast you all into the void as I have done to those before you."

"Do not threaten that which you cannot understand."

A line of intense black opened in the shining air. It split wider until a hole appeared, a chasm into the space between worlds, the void.

"We are not who you believe."

The hole collapsed into itself. "Who are you, then?"

"We are the Gathering."

The air split again. "How many of you must I throw into the void?"

"We are not of Apat."

Once more the blackness disappeared. "Where else would you be from? Do not try to stop me. I have work to do, pages to write."

"You must not. We are the Gathering and we plead with you to stop."

"The gathering of what? Babies too afraid to use the Majick?"

"We are the Gathering of Lima."

"Lima, the world beyond?" Rata laughed. "I told you I was the Great Author. Even Lima knows what I do."

"We demand you stop. We plead with you. You must end this killing of the Majick."

A wave of Majick rushed toward the star, only to splinter and disperse into the air. A second followed, and a third. The star flared and the fourth attack was captured and held in a ball in the air. The fifth, sixth, seventh and eighth added to the collection of Majick. Now the star grew. The purple became darker until it was almost black. The ball of Majick throbbed. Energy shoved it.

"No!" The recognizable voice of the One of Anim roared, and with it the ball of Majick was gone, followed closely by the star.

#

One by one, and then in growing numbers, the Gathering opened their grip on the Majick, and with its release, the anger flowed back to where it lived.

"We would not have attacked."

"We would, but we should not."

"The Rata made us angry."

"Thank you for stopping us."

There was a humbleness in the voices of the Gathering, a knowing that they had come close to destroying everything.

"We would have killed Rata."

"And the worlds."

"And the Majick."

The Gathering contemplated what it had almost done, then the consequences of not doing it.

"The Majick will still die."

"All will die."

"We could not save it, only delay its death."

"We have a problem."

"Our anger almost tricked us into killing the Majick. We already do too much."

"What is left for us to do?"

"If we do nothing, the Majick will die."

"If we do something, we will be no better than Rata. We will be killing the Majick."

"Our use of the Majick to defeat Rata will cause more pain."

"We must not do anything, but we must do something."

"We must not use the Majick."

"It will require time to consider our actions."

"*You do not have time. The Majick will soon die. There is only one action that is safe. The One cannot act because of who we are. The spirits of Lima can do nothing. So the answer must lie away from Lima. What must be done will require great sacrifice, but only sacrifice can save the Majick.*"

"What must we do?"

"We dare not interfere further."

"You cannot mean…"

'What you ask is truly a great sacrifice."

# 8 REVENGE DENIED

"Poisons!"

"What about them?"

"It is time for you to study them. Poisons are an essential tool of an assassin." Chadas waited for his mentor to continue. He had long been waiting for his chance to learn this craft, ever since he first stepped into this room and saw the stacked shelves. "You could be eating poison now." Chadas looked at the dried figs in the bowl and it struck him that Tomlin had not taken any. "If they were poisoned, you would not know it until it was time for them to act. That is the great beauty of poison. The assassin does not need to be near when their victim dies."

Chadas sat looking between Tomlin and the figs.

"You need not worry." His mentor reached for one and ate it. "But there are many poisons and there is a good chance an assassin would not be considered."

Tomlin walked to the shelves and returned with a box of heavy oak, locked and sealed with wax. Cutting the wax, he opened it to reveal three vials. Chadas reached out a hand.

"Stop!"

He froze.

"Never touch any poison without knowing its dangers, and these three are the rarest and most dangerous." He flicked out a knife and used it to point as he explained. "These are three ancient poisons, said to be discovered by Eeva herself. The first is Torpor. It is a mixture of ground chickberries and blackbark along with rare grasses." He carefully opened the stopper, and the odor of the brown contents quickly filled the room. The stench was overwhelming and Chadas' eyes went wide. "Do not fret. The smell is no more than an irritation. It will not harm us, but when added to a dandelion or berry tea, it removes all pain before putting the drinker into a deep sleep where even their breathing seems to stop. To all who look on them, the person is dead. They still live though they will never wake. I do not know what goes through their mind when their family buries them or sends them to meet Sha."

The knife moved.

"This is Greydust. It is a powder ground from moss. It kills quickly if touched, and if eaten, causes great pain in the belly before death." Chadas looked closely at the gray powder.

And this last one is called Puff. It is the dried contents of the cheek sac of a fish of the same name." Tomlin held the vial of blue-green powder with care. "If eaten, a person will begin to feel ill in a day and grow worse over the following week. They will not want to eat and a slow and painful death awaits them. Unlike the others, there is a cure for Puff if it is discovered soon enough. Drinking powdered charcoal and honey in water every hour might save the victim."

Tomlin locked the box and replaced the wax seal. "You will learn about these later." He returned the box to the shelf and brought back another vial. "This is Sleepwort. It does not kill, but will put a man to sleep for hours. You will find it useful if you must gain entry to a place without raising suspicions. This will be your first lesson." He went on to explain how Sleepwort should be prepared, how to administer it and examples of where it could be used.

Chadas sat at the table with an assortment of implements around him. With the mortar and pestle he ground the purplish root into a fine mush and strained off the liquid which was boiled over a flame until only mud-colored crystals remained. These he ground to a fine powder. The Sleepwort was ready.

"Good. Now how much would you use on a man?" They had been over this many times, but Chadas answered again. Tomlin nodded his approval. "Now you must test it. Go into the city and find a tavern. Any tavern," he added when he saw Chadas was about to ask. "Any tavern where there is a man sitting alone with his mead." Tomlin finished his instructions.

Chadas took a small goat's scrotum pouch and carefully filled it with the powder. As he was leaving, Tomlin said, "And we will see how your lessons in stealth are progressing" A tavern was not difficult to find. He found three before he saw the man he needed. He walked on and turned to watch. The tavern did not have many customers at this time of day, but all were similarly dressed.

Chadas followed one man as he left. He went around a corner to where a group worked at two kilns making bowls or some such thing. They took turns at fanning the flames with the large bellows while one watched to control the temperature. Nearby he spotted a line with washed clothes, including two of the heavy aprons each wore. Circling well clear, he reached the line and was removing one of the aprons when he heard the shout. He froze, but it was only the head man ordering more heat, and others were rushing to help on the bellows. Chadas crept away, the apron under his arm.

No one noticed the tired-looking man enter the tavern, his face smeared with dirt and his hair disheveled. He sat at the table beside the lone man and shook his head as the serving girl approached. She turned away, seeing only a worker who needed rest before he could think of food or drink. She waited, sure that soon he would order.

Chadas' hand moved to the pouch and when he stumbled to his feet, his fingers held a pinch of Sleepwort. He staggered toward the back door, to where the latrines would be, and as he tripped over a chair, he blew and the almost-invisible cloud drifted towards the man's face.

Outside, he removed the apron and hid it behind the latrine. He wiped his face as he made his way around to the street again. The man's head slumped, hitting the table. He was sound asleep.

Chadas returned to the room where Tomlin complimented him on his success. He should have been happy, but it was only what he expected of himself. But when Tomlin mentioned the apron and his performance, he wondered how his mentor could know so soon.

#

Chadas had settled back into his studies, but he had not seen Rill for five days, and he wanted to. He needed to know why she had kissed him. Why had she acted so strangely after? He had not discussed the day with Tomlin though he was sure his mentor knew all, and even why. Girls are such odd people.

He liked Rill, but she confused him. He had once liked Alodia and his other sisters. Alodia had even kissed him once, and she did not act the way Rill did. He would never understand, so he hid in his lessons.

Tomlin entered the room and spoke quietly. "I think you need to go to the tower wall."

"But my studies…"

"Your studies can wait."

"Are you going?"

"No. You will understand when you get there."

Chadas rose and left the room. Everything is confusing, he thought, even Old Tom. Leaving the tunnels, he was making his way to the tower through the city. This was made easier than usual with everyone moving in the same direction. He overheard tiny scraps of conversation.

"… deserves it."

"… poor children…"

An interesting conversation was only beginning when he was distracted by someone calling his name. "Chadas." He stopped and searched. "Chadas." Rill was approaching, waving an arm above her head, until she drew close and asked. "Do you want to see me?"

"Of course."

Her face suddenly reddened. "I am sorry," she began.

"For what?"

"For kissing you the other day. You bought me a knife and a tart. I was so grateful. I thought you felt as I do. I was wrong."

Chadas laughed. "No. It was not wrong, just unexpected. I bought you those things because we are friends. I never suspected your feelings. I never considered them."

Rill's bottom lip began to quiver, and her eyes moistened.

"I mean, I have been concentrating on my studies. I never thought of finding a girl, any girl." Rill seemed to calm. "You did nothing wrong. It was my fault because it had never entered my mind. You startled me."

"And now?"

"Now, I do not know. The thought of having anyone other than Old Tom in my life is new to me. Can you give me time to think?"

Rill giggled. "Time for what? To decide if you have room in your life for a girl, or if I am worthy of consideration."

"Time to decide what I need to think about," he admitted, and she gave him a mock punch on the arm. They turned to walk to the tower together, her hand finding his and holding it.

After a few steps, Rill laughed loudly. "Do you know they say that if a girl decides she wants to be with a man, he has no choice in the matter." They laughed together.

"I am sorry," she repeated shortly after.

"You said that."

"No, for today. For your mother and your family."

Chadas stiffened and stopped her. "What has that to do with today?"

Again her face reddened. "I thought you knew. I thought that is why you were going to the tower."

"I only know that Old Tom said I should be there." She pulled him close and placed an arm around his waist. "Today, your father is to be executed for his crime." Chadas stiffened. Why had Tomlin not told him? "Are you all right?"

"Yes." Then after a moment, "Yes". Chadas looked toward the tower wall. "It was just that I thought I would be the one to kill him." She moved close and took his hand in hers. "We need to hurry. We would not wish to miss the Lord's grand show."

#

Chadas and Rill mingled with the crowd at the base of the wall. He looked about, then bent to speak in her ear. "Not here."

They were among the throng close the wall. "Why?" she asked.

"These people are here to see if they can catch his head and earn a coin from the Lord for their skill." His voice took on a low croaking growl she had never heard. "When they bring him out, I will see him understand at last. I want to see his face. He must pay the price for the pain he has caused. I want to watch as the ax falls, to know he suffered, if only for a moment. We are too close. We will see nothing here till after he is dead."

He began searching but Rill pointed. "There."

It was the perfect place for what he wanted. Let these people fight for his head, that was not what he needed. The stone wall off the side of a home held a family's prized goats. They pushed toward it. The wall was only shoulder high and rough built, making climbing easy. Soon, he was sitting watching the tower wall with Rill at his side. She edged closer to snuggle against his body. "Will you be satisfied when he is dead?" she whispered.

Chadas thought hard before answering. "No." Rill stiffened. "I am happy that he will pay for what he did to my mother. But I want more for the other lives he destroyed. At least my brother and sisters deserve something."

A fanfare of four horns heralded the start of proceedings, and the crowd cheered.

Lord Rodnel came along the wall, his wife at his side. He wore a dark blue cape and hat over a white doublet while the Lady Arlette was dressed in a pale blue dress that covered all but her head. Her long blond tresses cascaded over her shoulders. Following them was a child he assumed to be Edur, their son. He had not seen him for some time. His clothes were different but his demeanor remained the same. He wore bright red. Always close were the Lord's Guards.

Lord Rodnel stepped up to address his audience. "My people, citizens of Dragonfang, you all know why we are here." The crowd cheered again. "You have heard of the crimes committed in our city. I have listened to the reports of the guards who attended." He paused and turned to call, "Bring forward the prisoner."

Chadas watched his father stagger along the wall, pushed by two guards. You will not frighten anyone now, pig. His father was shirtless and red welts marked his body. His head darted this way and that, perhaps searching for mercy. Chadas hoped he found none. Behind the trio came the executioner in his black hood. They stopped near the Lord and his family.

Lord Rodnel wore a stern face, as did his wife, but Chadas could see the wide grin on the face of Edur. "People of Dragonfang," the Lord called. "This is Mabon Annear, husband of Wynne who died from a vicious ax stroke. He is the father of three young children, Edana, Keir and Quinn, who died the same way. *And I do not forget Alodia*, he thought. I have examined the testimonies and found him to be guilty." Angry shouts arose. Chadas and Rill waited for the noise to subside before the Lord continued. "He has lived a life of drunkenness and violence. I have decided the ax is too good for a man who has lived the life he did."

The executioner moved behind, bent, and placed a noose that he now held around Mabon's neck. From where they sat, Chadas thought he could see the other end tied to a peg driven into the top of the wall. "It is my decision that Mabon Annear hang for his crimes," Lord Rodnel declared and with those words he signaled the executioner who pushed.

Chadas' father fell, and stopped, dangling halfway down the wall, arms and legs flailing. Slowly they stilled as air refused to pass his oddly twisted neck. There were a few cheers, but not many.

"I know many of you hoped to catch his head and earn a coin. I would not wish to disappoint you." He raised his arm and cast a handful of coins into the crowd, causing a frantic scrambling. When calm settled enough for anyone to look up, the Lord and his family were gone. Only Mabon Annear dangled above them.

"Are you satisfied now?" Rill asked.

Chadas looked into her eyes and replied, "Almost." Then he leaned in and kissed her, clumsily and awkwardly, on the lips.

# 9 THE ART OF DEATH

Years passed quickly for Chadas. Study suited him and he found he enjoyed learning. Not only that, he needed to understand his lessons. By the age of twelve, he could write in the words of three cities. His fascination with knives had grown and his knowledge was beyond most in the Guild, or so Tomlin told him. Swords held little interest, but this did not lessen his efforts in learning all he could about them. But poisons were where his passions lay. They occupied much of the latter years of his training. He knew they would be his specialty.

Not long after his thirteenth birthday, Tomlin surprised him with news that sent a thrill through his bones. He was going with his mentor to assist with a kill. They left early on the following day and made their way through Dragonfang to a small miller's camp set up near the outer wall.

"What do you see?" asked Tomlin.

Chadas was ready with his reply. He had studied every step of their route here. "We are in a quieter part of the city. I have seen no guards and guess they do not come this way often. There are few people about at this time of day."

"And?"

There is no order to the passages and lanes between the buildings. It appears as if the houses were dropped into any piece of land they could find. We will need to study the surrounding area to know where we can run if needed."

"Good. I have familiarized myself with the area, now tell me about the camp."

Chadas' eyes came back to where the miller, wearing rough but serviceable clothing, used a scoop to pour grain from a bag into the grindstone's feed hole. "The miller is poor but hardworking. The small pony that turns the wheel is malnourished. My guess is that he only eats what spills from the stone. The grindstone is of poor quality but cared for."

"Excellent."

"But Tom, I know we only concern ourselves with the contract, but what could anyone gain by this man's death?"

Tomlin scratched his chin. "It could be anything. Maybe someone desires the land he works on, or the wife that cooks for him. He could have sold someone poor quality flour. It does not matter."

Chadas thought for a moment, then pushed the thought aside.

"Good. Now keep watch. Warn me if anyone becomes too inquisitive. Just sing a song, I will understand." Chadas gave him a twisted grin. "I know you have no singing voice, that will not matter."

Tomlin wandered toward the man at the grindstone. The miller looked up but went back to his work. He sensed no sale here and had no time for questions. He preferred the solitude of his work with only the pony walking its endless circle to keep him company. Chadas' eyes scanned the surrounding houses. *Who paid to have this man killed? He could be of no danger to anyone.* Chadas' mind kept asking its questions.

He watched his mentor take in everything around him. Tomlin seemed to start a conversation about the quality of his wares. As the man turned, a knife flicked from Tomlin's sleeve and slashed a line across the man's throat. He slumped silently to the ground.

Old Tom turned casually away and walked off between the small homes that scattered the area. As he did so, he glanced toward Chadas and gave a slight flick of his head. Minutes later, Chadas turned a corner to find Tomlin waiting. They strolled further into the city and only faintly heard the calls of alarm behind them.

Chadas went out many times with Tomlin after that, always as an observer.

#

It was not until Chadas was fifteen that he was told that he would be given his first assignment, one where he was to act on his own. Tomlin would not be with him for support.

"There is no need to rush. You have a week to complete the assignment. Enough time can be given to study your target and learn his movements. Then you may choose the weapon of your choice. I wish you good luck. Do not disappoint me."

Chadas spent the next four days learning all he could of the man who was to be his first kill. He was a weaver from the outer reaches of Dragonfang, a man who had wronged someone. Chadas forced himself to not concern himself with these facts. They did not matter. Tomlin had ordered him to kill, so someone must be paying. He began to wonder if he was chosen for this kill because his mentor knew he would relish it.

The man began work each morning but he was always in a tavern for lunch, a meal that continued the rest of the day. When he went home, it was with a temper that his wife and children suffered. She may have issued the contract, but there were many who complained about the quality and tardiness of his work. None of this seemed to worry him. Anger grew as an image of his mother laying bleeding on the floor assailed his thoughts. He decided he would use a knife the way he should have done when his mother stopped him. Now she was dead. He would not be stopped this time.

This is not your father, his mind argued. He ignored it. The time had come to avenge his mother. *Was he given this assignment because of his family?* He struggled but pushed the thought aside. This was an assignment, to be completed according to the rules of Masima.

On the day he had chosen, he arrived at the tavern just as the man was entering. Moving past, he waited until food and drink were delivered before stepping through the door into the shadowed interior. His target was placing his mead back on the table and, with spoon in hand, beginning to shovel rabbit stew into his mouth. The only things he was aware of were his food and drink.

Chadas wandered around the room, checking each of the few patrons. None paid him any attention. As he walked behind his target, Misery flicked from his sleeve and entered the man's back as his free hand grabbed the man's throat and pulled back. An image of a knife raised above his father's chest held by tiny hands filled his thoughts. By the time his blade was again hidden, it appeared the man was resting. He had made no sound. Chadas continued to circle the room and was out the door and moving away before the alarm was raised. He could not help himself; he turned and joined the gathering crowd at the tavern door. A job well done. I promised I would learn, father. He only gave himself time for a quick look before disappearing among the streets.

#

Over the following two months, Chadas saw more of Rill. He knew their friendship had grown into something far more. Whenever he thought of her, he felt the breath tighten in his chest as he wondered what she was doing. Often, he would imagine her at her studies or out in Dragonfang with her mentor. He knew it was his mind playing tricks with him, but at those times, he would see Rill raise her head and smile as if sensing his presence. His studies did not suffer. He made sure of that. No matter what happened, he would not disappoint Old Tom.

He discovered that whenever his mentor left him to his studies, Leena would also go missing, and Rill was left alone. Rill began visiting him in his room on those occasions, or sometimes he would visit her. Chadas could sense when she was coming or when he should go to her. The stolen kisses became premeditated, more energetic, and more practiced.

Old Tom sat and listened as Chadas recited his list of swords and knives, their similarities and differences, their advantages and disadvantages. He finished and was about to start again when his mentor rose.

"I need to go out and will be gone all day. I have work to do. You will practice with your dagger. Hide it in your clothing and retrieve it quickly. And there is a book about Bel on the shelf. Read it."

Chadas slid Misery from the sheath beneath his shirt. He obeyed for a while as he waited to see if Tomlin would return. When he did not, Chadas was left to creep through the familiar corridors, not wishing to be seen in case Tomlin heard of his slacking. At the door to Rill and Leena's room, he realized he had no reason to be there if Leena had not gone. He tried to think of one, and failing to do so, was about to turn away.

The door opened. Rill smiled. A hand came out to grasp his and pull him inside. How did she know he was there? Did he need to care? He had seen the room before. The room was smaller than Tomlin's, and Rill did not have her own. Her bed was tucked against a wall in one corner. What surprised him every time was the abundance of little decorations. Tomlin's room had none. There were candles and pictures, small vases and trinkets. Everywhere was a splash of color.

Chadas sat beside Rill on the bed and they both smiled. Words were unimportant as long as they were together. Then, as if the forces of the Majick drew them closer, they were wrapped in each other's arms. The kisses grew hot and tender but at the same time, incredibly intense. Each needed the other. Chadas lay back, drawing Rill down onto the bed with him. Rill whispered in his ear, things he could not recall later, but things he knew he loved to hear.

Their bodies pressed closer, their hands exploring. Trapped in the fever of their passion, what they lacked in experience, they completed with enthusiasm.

As he returned to his room, Chadas wondered if what he had done was right, but he smiled inwardly. It felt right.

#

Next morning, as they were breaking their fast, Tomlin grew serious. It was unusual for him to be anything but sleepy at this time of day. "It is time to begin the next phase of your studies," he announced.

Putting down his milk, Chadas asked, "Another weapon?"

"No. It is something with which you are already somewhat familiar. The time has come for you to study it seriously. I will not have you playing at it any longer."

Chadas' brow dropped as he thought. *What could he be talking about? I have never played at any of my tasks.* "What would that be?"

"Stealth."

Now he was more confused. "When have I been playing at stealth?"

Tomlin laughed. "Do you think we do not know how you creep through the corridors trying to remain unnoticed?"

Chadas flushed. "What? How?"

Old Tom laughed again at Chadas' reaction. "Did you think we would not know? We wondered which of you would act first and then how often you would try to be together. We wished to see how well you could hide it. It has been amusing." Seeing Chadas' embarrassment, he settled his mirth.

"We?" Chadas asked in a soft voice.

"Leena and I. But we also wonder about your intentions. Are you just having a little fun, or does Rill mean more to you?"

"I enjoy being with her."

Tomlin was quiet for a moment. He changed the subject when he could see Chadas was becoming overwhelmed by the conversation. "Then tell me, why do we have a need of stealth?"

"In order to not be seen."

Tomlin waited, and when Chadas added nothing, he said, "Partly correct but stealth is more than not being seen. There are times when you cannot hide. Stealth is required most when you expect to be seen but do not wish to be noticed. But how would you not be seen?"

"Hide behind something."

"Yes, if there is something to hide behind. A tree or building, even a barrel in an alley may be useful, but what if nothing exists?" Chadas thought until Tomlin added, "Camouflage. You can use whatever is there to hide your shape, bushes, houses, the night."

"How would I do that?"

"At night, wear a dark cloak, stay in the darkest shadows, crouch to hide your shape, and move slowly. People see movement. If there are animals, slide quietly among them. Steal some clothing from a house and all but the owner will see the person they expect to. If you remain low and still, it will appear as if something has fallen on the ground. With all forms of stealth, be ready to leave. If people become suspicious, that is the time of greatest danger, for you and them."

Chadas could understand the reasons for this, and it seemed obvious. *I should have thought of that.*

"But if done properly, the best method of stealth is to be seen."

"How is it stealth if I am seen?"

"That is the best camouflage. If there are people about, what difference would one more make? The trick is to not be noticed in the crowd. Do not look people in the eye. People will see your intent. And dress to suit the crowd. If you are in an alley full of beggars, dress like a beggar. But if you are in the Lord's tower, look like you are meant to be there. Speak to no one unless you must. Wear a hat or other item to hide your face, and hide any marks that may be recalled. You can put pebbles in your boots to change the way you walk."

"That is a lot to think about."

"Not really. Stealth is having the confidence not to attract attention. It is how you think about it. Now, tell me about your adventures in the corridors and how you should have undertaken them." Chadas began but stumbled over his answer till Tomlin stopped him. "As we expected, Rill's training made her slightly better at this skill. That is why, for the next twenty days, you will go to Leena each morning. She will guide you in the art of stealth while I show Rill how she can use a knife without cutting herself."

# 10 GRADUATION

"There is not much more I can teach you."

"What do you mean? I still have much to learn."

"You are almost sixteen. It is time for me to step aside and allow you to grow from your experiences."

Chadas sat quietly, thinking. It would be sad to leave Old Tom but at the same time he was excited to be accepted into the Guild as a full assassin. He placed his spoon back on the plate. "You have taught me well. I hope that I will live up to your expectations."

Tomlin laughed. "Sixteen in two weeks. The time has gone so fast. It is hard to believe that seven years have passed since I accepted a grubby little urchin as my apprentice."

"I was never an urchin." Then Chadas smiled too. "Well, maybe a little grubby."

I am proud to have been involved in your training. You are smart, a quick learner. There is a great future awaiting you, maybe even becoming Ama one day."

"Ama?"

"You have the intelligence and one day you will develop the wisdom. I hope to see that before I am done."

Chadas laughed. "That would be something special. Imagine, me, Ama."

"Very special, but first you must graduate. Today, you will see the Ama." He grinned. "The current one. Because you have shown such promise, he has decided to set your final test himself. He will not leave it to the leaders of House Eeva."

"Then I must expect him to make it difficult."

"You will not know until you hear his test."

Chadas was ready to say more but was interrupted when the door swung open. His jaw dropped. The Ama came into their rooms. People went to meet the Ama. The Ama did not call on others. Tomlin greeted him and ushered him to a chair while Chadas rose. He knew he should not sit again unless invited.

"So, young Chadas," the Ama began. "You have reached the time of your graduation." Chadas nodded. "Has Tomlin told you that I will choose your final task as an apprentice? Ah, I see by your faces that he has. Good. Sit." When they did, the Ama continued. "Do not be worried. It should be an easy test for someone of your demonstrated skills."

Chadas released a breath he did not realize he had been holding.

"You have one week, time enough to prepare and carry out your test." A week? It must be a massive task. "You must enter the tower and leave without notice or suspicion." Chadas' fears receded. This should not be too difficult. "You will complete the test while you are there. Edur, the son of Lord Rodnel, has a dog, a large and vicious dog. He trains it to attack people on command. You will find and kill this dog."

Chadas' jaw dropped. He sat, unmoving, as Tomlin thanked the Ama and helped him from the room. *Kill the dog? Why could he not kill Edur? He would kill any man the Ama wished, but why kill a dog?*

#

There was no question that he could kill a dog, simply anger that he must. The question was, how? For two days he searched among his notes and those of his mentor, until he found the answers he needed and collected the ingredients he required. They were common items and should not arouse suspicion.

Chadas began by chopping three tulip bulbs and four daffodil bulbs until they were no more than mush. He added a few herbs, some toxic and some for flavor. Taking a juicy slab of goat's meat. He stabbed it a number of times, filling each hole with his concoction.

He waited until night filled the sky before slipping into the darkened streets. The clothes he chose were dark, but not black. Black could betray him like a spider on a gray wall. He carried a bag over his shoulder, the prepared meat inside.

Guards patrolled the wall around the tower, but at most they would be a minor inconvenience. Their role was to protect their Lord from attack. They expected a large group, not a lone youth. And any attack was unlikely under Rodnel's rule. Their real task was staying awake.

Chadas approached the market stalls that by day would be filled with scurrying people. By night they were the home of lost shadows. Slipping between the stalls, he reached the wall unchallenged and began to climb. It offered little to slow him, there were ample places for feet and hands, and soon his eyes peeked above the parapet. He looked to his left and saw no one. To his right were two guards squatting huddled over a small fire while they chatted.

Moving slowly, he eased himself onto the wall and flowed through the darkness to the far side. A glance was all he needed. To his left were the stables with an exercise yard attached. Below, a mound of hay was stacked against the wall for easy access. Chadas took four steps before dropping over the edge. The hay puffed and closed over him as it cushioned his fall. Then all was quiet.

After a few minutes, Chadas was satisfied he had not been seen. He dragged his way out of the hay and, after a quick check, sprinted to the stables. A few snorts and snuffles came from within, but nothing to cause an alarm. The tower was about forty paces of open ground away, with the kitchens off to the right. A few candles burned but the tower was in darkness. The entrance, on the other side, would be well guarded, providing too many opportunities for discovery.

He moved to the wall of the square tower. This face was unguarded, with only the occasional patrol passing, the entry being on the far side. An apse stood at each corner. The one he wanted was on his left, where the lady of the tower did her needlework. The openings were slightly larger there. Where the wall met the apse, he began to climb. The stone here fitted more tightly but still offered no impediment. He climbed until his hand found the stone he had seen from the ground, then he began to circle the structure until the opening appeared. Nothing moved inside. No alarm rose outside.

Chadas squeezed through and dropped to the floor. Six chairs circled the small space within. He had entered the tower unseen, but this would be where the greatest danger lurked. The Lord and his family slept on this level, and there were often guards and servants moving about.

Slipping back into the apse, Chadas removed his outer clothes and stuffed them beneath one of the chairs. Now he was dressed in the livery of a tower servant. Taking a breath, he lowered his head and walked out to begin his search for the dog. He guessed where he would find it. Two guards stood beside one door, the Lord's sleeping quarters as indicated by the glyph of the boar's head on the door. The guards watched him pass but paid him no further attention. Another door, unmarked, he thought to be that of Edur.

The door swung quietly and he slipped into the shadowed interior, confirming his thoughts. He could see no sign of the dog in the blackness. A soft chirp left his lips, like a young bird wishing to be fed. The darkness moved. A large head rose and two piercing eyes looked in his direction.

Chadas held out the slab of meat and the massive dog unfolded itself from the floor. The black beast padded closer and when Chadas threw the meat, it trapped it in two huge front paws before tearing off chunks.

Satisfied that the dog would finish its meal, Chadas backed from the room and closed the door. He had barely taken two steps when the guard appeared.

"You there!" the guard challenged. Chadas froze. "Go to the kitchens and fetch me some cheese and bread. Bring me some milk too." He took his position beside Edur's door without another glance in Chadas' direction. Nodding, Chadas hurried away, realizing how lucky he had been. The guard must have stepped away for a minute.

He hurried back to collect his clothing. He could leave by the main entrance, the guards would not suspect anyone leaving, but they may be curious as to why he did not return. The guard on Edur's room was no problem. Even if he suspected something, he would not admit to abandoning his post, not for a dead dog.

Chadas retrieved his clothing and left the way he came as distant alarm could be heard from Edur.

#

Everyone was waiting in the chamber where Chadas first laid eyes on the Ama. Three other apprentices stood beside Chadas awaiting their graduation. The leaders of the three Houses were present, each with two of their senior members, along with the Ama. Each of the others had their mentors standing behind them, only Tomlin was missing. He had gone out before dawn with a promise that he would be back. He would not miss the ceremony. Chadas stood watching everyone, but keeping his thoughts apart. Everyone was waiting on Tomlin. The Ama met his eyes a number of times but did not disturb his thoughts.

The Ama honored each of the other apprentices in turn, highlighting their work and achievements.

The door opened and the woman in blue entered. Who is she to have free access to this chamber? That is one secret I have never learned or even asked. He decided it was something he would discover. She moved to the Ama and whispered in his ear. Her actions did not go unnoticed. All conversation between the House leaders stopped as they waited.

The woman in blue left without even acknowledging the others in the room. Chadas' eyes followed her out.

"You three may leave. Your mentors will see you out. I have decided this final presentation will be private." They filed out, curiosity turning their eyes to Chadas. When they had gone, the Ama approached him.

In a quiet voice filled with sadness, he said, "I have just been told that Tomlin was discovered while completing his contract." He paused but then continued. "He was arrested by the Tower Guards. While they were taking him to the tower for questioning, he tried to escape. They killed him."

Chadas' jaw hung slack. What had he been doing? Was it bad luck, or too dangerous?

"We will continue with your graduation. You deserve that. But we will be brief. You will need time, but you have earned this day."

He then surprised Chadas by putting his arm around his shoulders and holding him tightly. A gush of grief suddenly clouded Chadas' eyes, and then the Ama stepped back. Chadas was forced to brush away the tears he shed for the only true father he had known.

The three House leaders stood side-by-side as the Ama began.

"Chadas Annear, natapos mo na ang iyong pag-aaral bilang isang aapprentice at ngayon ay nakatayo ka rito bilang isang buyong miyembro ng House Eeva." He seemed to sag. "There is more, but the important words have been spoken. We welcome you to the House of Eeva and the Guild of Masima."

# 11 THE AMA

The brief moment of intimacy was extended when, after the ceremony, the Ama asked Chadas to join him in a meal. The House leaders and their entourages had left and only the two remained.

"Marget," called the Ama. The woman in blue stepped into the chamber. "Chadas will be joining us for a meal. She glanced to Chadas and back before giving a nod and leaving.

"Now, how are you? The news of Tomlin must have shocked you."

Chadas knew he should not lie. "I hated my father. He often hurt my mother during his drunken rages, and he used his fists on us. He was evil and deserved what he got. I hated him. Tomlin was not like him. He was the first man to treat me with kindness. Tomlin was the father I would have wanted."

"It is a story I understand, and too often told in the city. You will feel his loss for a long time, but trust me when I tell you it will become easier. The loss will always be there, but acceptance and understanding will temper the pain."

Marget's head appeared as the door partly opened. "The meal is ready." She stepped back.

The Ama's arm went around Chadas' shoulder again. "We had better hurry. Marget's scowl will tear the skin from my bones if we delay.

*There is much more to their relationship than they allow others to know.*

He was led to a nearby room, the Ama's room, and it was obvious he was not the only one who lived here. Flowers beautifully arranged in a blue and white vase added color. Curtains hung on one wall though there was no window to block out, and the place smelled of lavender, a scent he had learned Rill preferred.

*How did he keep Marget a secret? Or was it a secret? The House leaders must know if he trusts this knowledge with me.*

A knock distracted him and, "Come," called the Ama. A guard entered, leading Rill. He left just as discreetly.

"I thought we should have a real celebration. No more talk of Tomlin for now. Come in Rill. Sit with us." Marget smiled. Rill approached hesitantly but soon all were talking and laughing. After she had become comfortable, the Ama told Rill, "I was once of House Meeya, but now I must be of all Houses. Life was much simpler then."

As the meal drew towards its end, the Ama became serious. "I have avoided speaking of Tomlin and spoiling our food, but he trained you well. Your skills are far beyond those of other graduates. Now, without your mentor, you find yourself with no one to call upon if you require help. I may not have trained in House Eeva but I offer you my support. If you need it, I will be available to talk or help in any way. You need someone to be there, other than Rill," he finished with a grin.

Chadas was surprised by the offer but managed a stuttering, "Thank you."

"I would also hope that I could ask for help if ever I should need it."

"Of course," Chadas promised quickly, eyes wide. "But you are the Ama, the most powerful of the Guild. I cannot imagine you needing my help, but it will always be there."

"Enough of this," scolded Marget, and changing the subject asked, "When is your graduation, Rill?"

#

The following eight years passed slowly and were gone in a moment. Seven times he had been called on to perform secret missions for the Ama, missions that ended in death for someone who threatened to betray the Guild. He had also grown much closer to Marget and the Ama. And there was always Rill. They still met regularly and were the best of friends, but the spark had not grown into a flame. Chadas admitted to himself that he was at fault there. He had been trained not to trust anyone too closely.

Chadas entered the outer chamber. Marget was fussing on the far side with something he could not see. Her eyebrows rose. She was not expecting him. "I must see the Ama. It is important." Sensing something was amiss, Marget's eyes scanned the room. Only the guards were present. They were the most trusted of the Ama's men. "What is wrong?" she asked.

"I cannot say here," he whispered. Her eyes widened and her face grayed. She knew him well and his demeanor warned her.

She nodded and led him into the inner chamber. Chadas turned slowly, searching. It was empty. Again Marget asked, "What is it?"

Chadas did not answer, but instead asked, "Where is the Ama?"

"Not here."

"I must speak with him. He must hear what I have to tell him, and it must be from my lips only. Then he will he know what I say is true. He will know what to do."

Marget studied him. "He is in our rooms, resting. Come with me."

When they entered the rooms the Ama was laying on the bed. "Marg…" he began before spying Chadas. Sitting up, he asked sharply, "What has happened? Why are you here?"

"Chadas has news he will pass only to you."

The Ama looked at Marget, then Chadas. "Go on."

"I was walking in Dragonfang today and overheard a conversation. I heard only a few words and moved closer to listen as they finished."

"What did you hear?" The Ama's impatience showed he sensed the importance of what was coming.

"A man and a woman were talking. There may have been others, but only two spoke. They were discussing a plot against the Ama."

Chadas heard Marget's sharp intake of breath but the Ama ignored her and demanded, "Tell me everything."

"I did not see who they were or recognize their voices. They intend your death. They wish to see one who favors their House in your place. They did not mention where or when they intend to strike, or how they would do it, not while I listened. And they did not say which House."

"You will need guards to stay with you wherever you go," Marget advised.

"Nonsense. If I did that, I would be telling these people I know of their plot. It may force them to act. This may still be nothing more than ambitions. No, the best solution is to find them and show others the futility of betraying the Ama. We will have a better chance if they do not suspect that we know." He turned to Chadas. "When you graduated, I said there may come a time when I would need your help. That time is now. I trust you to do what must be done."

"I will do whatever you ask."

"Find these people. I would know their names. More, I want to know their House. But they must die. You have my contract."

"No contract will be necessary. I do as you ask to protect the Ama and the Guild.".

"Thank you."

"May I offer a suggestion?"

The Ama nodded.

"Finding information that does not wish to be found is not a task for House Eeva. Would not a trusted member of House Bela be more suited?"

The Ama stood in thought. They both knew of who Chadas spoke.

"If there are none you trust, I will do as you ask. It is only that I intend to stay close and keep you safe."

"No, you are right. Marget, find Rill and bring her here."

#

Five days crawled by before the note came for Marget. The messenger did not know where it had come from. It had been left at a drop point and read, 'The sea is turning silver beneath the new moon and soon the boarfish will be patrolling the shores. Knowing your love of boarfish, great lady, it will be my honor to send you my first catch as a gift. Your trusted friend.' It was signed simply with a 'Z'.

This was the message Marget had been expecting. It was from Rill and indicated she had completed her search. Marget dismissed the messenger, thanking him for delivering it. "Boarfish, how lovely," she muttered as he turned to leave, just loud enough for him to hear. She had no doubts that many people, including the messenger, knew what has been written.

Although she wanted to run to Rill, she forced herself to wait. If the ones behind the plot were watching, they would know the Ama knew of their treachery. She waited until her mind could hold her back no longer. Brushing her hands down her dress and taking a few deep breaths, she calmed and walked as casually as she could to Chadas' room. Everyone knew of their friendship and would not expect this visit to be different to any other.

When Chadas opened the door, his expression was of surprise at seeing her. Should anyone be watching, they would not know she was expected. He recovered and invited her inside. Rill was sitting at the table.

"I do not think anyone is suspicious," Marget told them, her face a mask of serenity. Moving to the table, she sat opposite Rill while Chadas perched on the edge of the bed. Without wasting words, she asked, "What have you discovered?"

"Nothing," came Rill's unexpected reply. Marget's brow rose. "I have scoured all the Houses and found no evidence of a plot against the Ama."

Marget sat, thinking, looking between the two. "How do you explain what Chadas heard?"

Rill shrugged and asked, "Chadas, are you certain of what was said?" He nodded. "And are you as sure that the plot came from inside the Guild?"

"Who outside the Guild would know of the Ama? And if they were not of the Guild, how could they gain from his death?" Both Rill and Marget stared for a moment. Chadas' brow dropped and he added more quietly, "Unless it was the Lord, or his staff."

Rill turned to Marget. "Chadas is too good at his work to have misheard, but I can find nothing in the Houses, not even a rumor. If the Lord is behind the words, why? He would know a new Ama would follow. What would it gain him?" He paused. "Unless his goal is to turn the Houses against each other."

Each sat, lost in their own silent thoughts. When Marget rose to leave, she said, "Keep looking." At the door she warned, "Do not leave here until you know it is safe."

"I am sure Chadas and I can find something to occupy us," Rill grinned.

#

The Ama was taking all the precautions he felt were needed. He still could not believe one of the Houses would turn against him but he trusted Chadas more than anyone, except Marget. Six guards of House Alard trailed him wherever he went. These were men and women who had proved their loyalty and he doubted that their minor House would be behind any plot. If he were killed, the other leaders would block any attempt at a grab for power by the guards of House Alard.

Marget had reported that no evidence could be found implicating any House, or that a plot existed. Maybe Chadas was wrong. He needed to speak with the assassin again. If he questioned him once more on what he heard, there could be clues in his story that had been missed.

Two guards stepped into the corridor and confirmed all was clear before the Ama and his other guards left the room. They had gone no more than twenty paces when the clang of a knife hitting the wall sent the guards into pandemonium. Two grabbed him and pulled him into a crouch before scrambling back to the room with the Ama held low between them. Two stood their ground to protect his retreat. The final pair sprinted to where they believed the attack had been launched. He wondered if they could catch the culprit and put the plot to rest. He doubted it.

When they stepped back into the rooms, the Ama was shaking and Marget rushed to him. Until now, he had not really accepted the plot as real.

After waiting in the room for the return of the guards, he was not surprised to learn they had found nothing but the knife.

Thinking quickly, he ordered, "Find Chadas. Bring him here."

The guards returned shortly. The assassin almost beat them through the door. The Ama wasted no words on explanations, he ordered his friend to examine the scene.

Later, Chadas returned. "I have found little more than the guards." He held up a tiny scrap of green cloth. "Whoever did this is good at hiding their tracks. Where is the knife?"

The Ama pointed to the desk. Chadas looked and his eyes widened. He lifted it and turned it over in his fingers before replacing it.

"So, it could be any of the Houses?" Marget asked.

"It could, but I think we can narrow the search."

"How?"

Chadas raised his hand to his chin and thought aloud. "I will not rule out House Eeva. It may be my House, but I have heard nothing. That could be because of our friendship. I think one of the other Houses is more likely."

The Ama was trying to follow Chadas' thoughts and failing. "Why should I rule Eeva out?"

"If the attack had come from any member of my House, they would not have missed, and they would not have used a knife like this. It has no balance."

The Ama shuddered but studied Chadas' face as he considered the words. It lacked any sign of emotion. "I agree about the skills of your House, but I will not rule them out."

Everyone waited as the Ama paced the room, staring at the floor. Suddenly his head came up.

"Send word to each of the House leaders. We will meet in the inner chamber in one hour. They must not be late." And looking to Chadas, he added, "You will attend."

Chadas' head bowed slightly. "I am at your command."

"Is that wise?" Marget asked.

"Marget, by now one of them knows their plot has failed. If I tell them all, they will know the eyes of the other Houses will be on them. Even if they try again and succeed in killing me, the others will never allow them to take control."

Before the designated time, the three House leaders sat at the table brought in for the occasion. What had caused the Ama to demand their presence? Each brought guards, but only the leaders were permitted to enter. The Ama allowed their tension to grow. Finally, he judged the time was right. Six guards entered the room. Two moved behind each leader. Then the Ama entered with Chadas trailing.

Questions came fast, but when he ignored them a silence settled over the group. It lingered, waiting for the Ama to break it.

"Someone tried to kill me today."

"Who?

"When?"

The Ama held up a hand to quell the flow of questions. "Only a short while ago. I was walking in the corridor when a knife was thrown. It missed and hit the wall beside me. The guards could not find the thrower."

The three leaders exchanged glances. "Who would want you dead? And why?"

"Chadas is here to answer those questions." He signaled Chadas to speak.

"When I was in Dragonfang some days back, I overheard a conversation, and no, I do not know who spoke. They were plotting to kill the Ama."

Stunned expressions greeted the news. "Why did you not tell us? We could have searched for these people."

"Because of what they said," Chadas answered. "They intended killing the Ama and have one of their own House take control of the Guild."

The leaders appeared confused. "You cannot believe it was one of us?" Arienh blurted, but the three looked to those beside them and edged their chairs back.

"I took precautions but did not believe it could be true," the Ama answered. "Not until today. Now I believe one of you is a traitor." Looks of amazement and suspicion crossed the faces of the leaders. "I brought you together so that each of you know I have discovered this plot. You will each be watched until I learn which House is responsible. Go."

The three leaders rose and left the chamber. There was considerably more distance between each of them than when they arrived.

#

Marget stood staring at the items on the stall. She had searched many without finding a gift for the Ama. He had been feeling low since the attempt on his life and she wanted to see him happy again, if only for a short time. Now, the gift she sought stared back at her. The small, delicately carved dog had been made from a dark wood she did not recognize, but it was beautiful. It was not long before she negotiated a price and was on her way back to the tunnels.

The object felt comfortable in her hand. As tiny as it was, someone had spent a great deal of time making it an accurate representation. She held it up to admire it as she walked. The eyes seemed to watch her and the mouth appeared ready to bark. I hope he enjoys it as much as I do, she thought. Smiling, she reminded herself that he would. He loved dogs and he would love that she bought it for him.

Back in the tunnels, she hurried to their rooms. Guards stood on each side of the door. She nodded her greeting as she approached. "Has anyone been here?"

"No, milady."

She smiled,

Opened the door,

Stepped through,

And screamed.

The guards quickly pushed past. The Ama sat slumped over his desk, blood staining the back of his shirt. They rushed to his side but were too late. All stood frozen in the moment. The Ama was dead!

Marget was the first to react. "Close the door," she ordered. "We do not want news of this to spread until we have found the murderer." One of the guards rushed to obey. She began to question them on when they began their duty, anyone they had seen, and who guarded the door before them. They answered her questions. One was sent to bring back the guards they had relieved. "Do not say anything," she warned. He nodded his understanding.

The earlier guards were questioned and they gave the same replies. No one had been seen near the rooms. "Help me," she requested and they carefully laid the body of the Ama on his bed. "Now, fetch that screen and set it so he cannot be seen by anyone entering." With their precautions in place, she sent the guards to find the leaders of the Houses and have them brought to the rooms. "And do not forget House Alard," she told them. She held one guard back to help her with her preparations, a woman named Engl.

As they left, she noticed the carved dog on the floor, one of its legs broken in its fall. "Take it away," she demanded. "I do not wish to see it again." There was an anger in her voice she could not control. Engl helped her arrange chairs for the promised visitors, and ensured none would see the body until Marget was ready.

They arrived quickly, hurried along by the guards, Keelia, Arienh and Dyfed as well as Kerwin, the leader of the lesser House Alard. Marget ushered them to chairs, ignoring their questions, "Why are we here?" and "Where is the Ama?"

"I called you here," she told them. "I have news that you need to hear." At her nod, Engl pulled the screen aside. For a moment, no one moved or spoke.

Finally, "What happened?" asked Arienh.

"The Ama is dead, stabbed in the back. We do not know who, or how. He was guarded the entire time."

The leaders immediately moved back from each other. Eyes flicked back and forth and hands moved subtly toward secreted knives. The sword tips of guards were against their backs before any could be drawn. "We need to find the one who did this," Marget declared and they all agreed. "I know of two people who can aid our search, and who can be trusted. Chadas was a close friend of the Ama, and a loyal companion, and Rill, who has been searching for the plotters at the Ama's request."

The leaders agreed that Chadas and Rill should be found, and guards were sent out again. Chadas came quickly wearing his favorite green cape over everyday clothes, but some time passed before the guards reported that Rill could not be found. "We entered her room, thinking she may also have been attacked. She was not there but we found this on the floor beneath her bed." He showed them a green blouse. The sleeve had been torn as if it had been caught on something sharp.

"Find her!" demanded Marget.

Kerwin spoke to the departing guards. "Tell everyone in House Alard that they must find Rill. Do not say why, only that it is my command."

The day passed slowly. The leaders were not permitted to leave. All reports brought the same news. Rill could not be found in the tunnels or in Dragonfang.

#

"She is of House Bela," Marget accused. "Where is she?" It was the fifth time the question had been asked but Dyfed's response remained unchanged.

"We do not know," he admitted, "but Rill could not be at fault. Someone is manufacturing her guilt, and that of our House."

Chadas complained. "I cannot believe Rill is responsible for the death of the Ama. I know she considered him a friend."

"The blouse from the first attempt was found in her room," Keelia reminded.

Chadas protested. "Someone wishes us to believe it was her. I am sure of it. This is not something she would do. I would accuse myself before I accept her guilt."

"I know your feelings for her," Marget replied. "But if she is not guilty, where is she?"

"She has run because she knew she would be caught," accused Arienh.

"Or she is dead," added Keelia.

Everyone stopped to stare at him.

"Why would she be dead?" There was fear on Chadas' face.

The looks he received in reply were a mixture of sympathy and suspicion of House Bela. Dyfed's face, however, reflected Chadas belief that Rill and her House were caught in a trap.

"Perhaps she did this for her House, and they did not wish their plot traced back to the leaders," Marget explained. A pained look crossed Chadas' eyes as Dyfed denied the accusation.

"We will find Rill, or her body, and we will know the truth. But we have more urgent business," Marget told them. "We must announce a new Ama before word spreads of our troubles."

"How?" asked Arienh. "None of us will accept the leader of another House."

"It does not need to be a leader. We need someone who is above suspicion, or the Houses will destroy themselves in bickering and plots as they try to raise their own to become the new Ama. The future of the Guild rests on this decision."

There followed much arguing, many suggestions and even more accusations. In the end, they could think of only one they would all accept, only one they knew could not have killed the Ama. There was only one they would trust.

Chadas protested but his pleas fell on deaf ears. He was proclaimed by all the new Ama.

Privately, each of the leaders believed they may still be of influence in the new order.

# 12 THE CONTRACT

A cold wind swept out of the deep mountain valleys and breathed the chill of snow and ice over Dragonfang before rushing out to the sea beyond. As it passed over the city's marketplace, it grasped Chadas' cape, causing it to shiver in the afternoon light. He worried it might be an omen of evil but his mind dispelled these concerns. It seemed preoccupied with the promise of gold.

The season of the Dragon Skies had passed, and this was the Breath of the Gods, the cold winds that cleansed the dark skies above Dragonfang. The happy chatter of people in the marketplace and the odors of herbs and vegetables relaxed him. It was a perfect day for a kill.

Chadas had been Ama for a little over four years and though he had no need to practice his training, he took on contracts from time to time in honor of Tomlin. This was one such occasion. It would not harm him to be prepared if his skills were ever needed.

He wandered past the crowded stalls occasionally glancing at the various goods on offer. He stopped to admire the skill of one seller who displayed an assortment of shells shaped into necklaces and brooches. His hand brushed the smoothly polished surface of one piece, but he did not notice the gentle interplay of browns and grays that drifted over its snow-white disc. His keen eyes peeked from beneath a broad-rimmed black hat watching across the stall to where his target sat.

The man, a stall holder, did not appear to be seeking buyers for his goods and his wares were sparse and ill-made. He just sat and watched the movements of the markets. Chadas noticed things about him. It had been part of his training. This man did the same. That simple fact should have warned him. He did not even know the name of this man. His client had said something about eliminating competition. He had not paid attention after being offered ten gold coins. Now, all that concerned Chadas was how he should approach his target without being noticed. His client's reasons for wanting the man dead did not matter. His only request was that the target be killed at the market. Chadas was an assassin and his client was going to pay. That was all that mattered.

Chadas' loyalty to House Eeva could not be questioned. As part of the Guild of Masima, it was his home. Some members lived in the tunnels, but most lived among the people of Dragonfang. Even if they took no part in the activities of the Guild, they were a tightly bonded family, and he was the Ama, their leader, and as such, his loyalties must extend equally to include the thieves and beggars, the guards and the inactive members in Dragonfang. A thought passed briefly. How many of them also wandered the market?

He turned away from the stall, disappointing the young woman when he did not buy anything. Walking past his target, he searched the crowd for anything amiss. Then, spinning back toward the stall, he moved quickly enough to catch sight of anyone following, but slow enough to not arouse suspicion.

He saw nothing to alarm him.

The day was still too warm for the dark green cape, but it was a favorite. The intertwined dragons that were embroidered in pale green along its edges held secret pockets for the tools of his trade. All he would need was Misery, his beautiful stiletto blade with black grip and green stone. He smiled. Green had always been his favorite color. It brought him good luck.

Chadas stopped at a stall on the other side of his target. The wooden table was covered with jars of herbs and bowls of spices. The mixed odors stung his nose. He waited. When the herb-woman was distracted, he acted. He was not concerned by his target who only had eyes for the crowds across the square. He was behind the man before anyone noticed. Like a striking snake, his arm wrapped around the man's head, the bend in his elbow quieting any sounds that may escape his mouth or nose. His other hand had already drawn the knife and he felt its tip bite into the stall holder's back.

The stall-holder was more prepared and able than Chadas expected. He rolled in Chadas' grasp as his elbow swung back to strike Chadas in the side of his face. The spin and impact tore the knife from his grip. At the same time, the man's teeth bit into his arm. Instinctively, Chadas pulled his arm away. The man screamed. Sense crashed into Chadas' mind. The man was not screaming, it was a call for help, a demand that could only come from a trained fighter with authority.

Chadas darted away. His mind told him to run, to hide in the crowd. As he blended into the growing throng of onlookers, he looked back. The man was slumped on his chair with Misery still protruding from his back. A guard was already beside him. "Who did this?" demanded the guard, and everyone turned to check their neighbor, all except Chadas. In that moment, the guard gripped of the knife and plunged it deeper into the stall holder.

#

Chadas tried to blend into the crowd. He had earned his gold and planned to disappear quietly. Now he had lost Misery.

And his troubles began. A few moments passed before anyone noticed him. Shouts shook the air. He ran with the tower guards in pursuit. Years of training came to his aid. The wind grasped Chadas' cape, causing it to flare. His feet sought freedom even while his mind chastised him. He darted back and forth between the people as he sought the safety of the nearby streets. It should have been a simple kill. Why had it gone wrong? Chadas shook his head to clear his thoughts. Long tails of thick black hair whipped across his face, slapping his dark eyes and pointed nose. Behind him, the bellowing of stallholders, shoppers, and worse, the guards pierced the air.

Surging waves of humanity ebbed and flowed across the cobbles. The commotion grew as a sea of people tried to flee. Few tried to stop him, and mostly their efforts were only for the benefit of the guards. Above the background of confused sounds was the clank of armor and the bellows of the tower guards. Commands echoed over his head. Someone grabbed at his shoulder. Without thinking, he gave a shove, and the man fell. People stared. His feet drove him on, seeking safety. A narrow road winding between overhanging houses of stone and wood was his immediate goal. Few enough people filled the square so he could move quickly, and yet the crowd was thick enough to hinder those who gave chase. The shadows promised escape. The cobbled surface made running difficult. It would slow his followers. The entrance to the street drew closer. He would soon be free. He should have been clear of the square well before anyone noticed.

Safety beckoned, to suddenly disappear when a tower guard stepped in his path. He was a giant in the Lord's livery, the boar's head of his position embroidered on its breast. Beneath this, he wore leather armor. His boots clad his legs to just below his knees. But the man's most memorable features were his size and the thick slab of red beard that rested on his chest. One arm wore a circular shield, also bearing the boar's head. His other hand held his sword. A grumble like a wild animal grew from deep in the man's chest. The guard's size would make him slow, and on any other occasion Chadas would go around, leaving him to lumber along behind. Not today. The street was not wide enough and the man's arms made longer by the sword. The blade glinted as light danced along its edge.

He had no choice. There was no time to change direction. Desperation required action, and he had no qualms about what he must do, though Tomlin would think differently. He reached for the nearest person, a woman with a basket of vegetables on her arm. Chadas grabbed her shoulders and threw her onto the tip of the blade. The guard tried to avoid the impact, which Chadas hoped. He was too slow, which Chadas regretted. The sword entered the woman's belly and appeared again from her side. She screamed. The guard released his grip on the weapon. Chadas took advantage of this moment. He ducked and ran. *I am sorry, but if the guard had been faster, you would not have died.*

A leather-clad arm reached out to grab him but he was too agile. He raced along the street with the clamor of his pursuers not far behind. He could not breathe easy, not yet.

He ran on.

Dodging left into another street then turning again, this time to the right, he ran past a beggar, a woman hoping for a coin from a passing merchant. As he ran, Chadas raised a hand and extended three fingers across his chest in the sign of the Guild. He was surprised to see her eyes widen and her head follow his dash. It did not slow him. He ran on. Behind him, he trusted the beggar could distract the guards. Maybe she would direct them another way. Had he seen her before? Those dark, brooding eyes and the slightly crooked nose beneath her long black hair seemed overly familiar. He had no time to think further.

If that was what she tried, it did not work. They had not fallen for her misdirection, or there were so many they could check all streets as they chased. Turning another corner, Chadas dived behind a horse trough and listened. His breath came hard to his chest. The thud of heavy footsteps stopped at the corner. The seconds of waiting passed with agonizing sluggishness as his breathing eased. After he had heard no sounds for some time, he dared a glimpse, thinking they may have moved on.

He was wrong.

A cry of discovery, and they were after him again. Their loud calls and the answers from the nearby streets told him they were herding him to where he could not escape. He could hear others moving around to cut him off. One more turn, and he saw his chance. A sign hung from the wall above. He glimpsed the vague image indicating a tavern, though he did not notice which one. A wide door led to darkness within. Chadas ducked into its shadows and allowed his eyes to adjust, being careful not to draw too much attention from the patrons.

A man who appeared to enjoy his work far too much stood by the barrels, a row of tankards waiting. His ponderous belly sagged over blue britches that threatened to part at every seam. Chadas approached and placed a trill in the man's puffy hand. It was the Lord's coin, marked with the image of his face. A trill was rich currency with each coin worth thirty coppers. "Mead," he muttered. Three coppers could have bought food and a goblet but the innkeeper seemed unsurprised.

While he was busy filling a tankard, Chadas slipped quietly into a passage leading to the rear of the inn. At the back door, he listened to the sounds of the tower guards searching. As he returned, he noticed the stairs. He needed no further invitation and hoped the coin was enough to ensure the inn-keeper's silence. The second level had a corridor with rooms on both sides. These rooms would be for the family, and maybe to earn extra coins from those who needed a place to sleep. More likely, the innkeeper had girls that would collect the price of a night many times before the sun returned. Chadas crept along, listening at each door. No sounds came from within. He tried the nearest. It opened with ease, and he slipped through. He was alone. The room contained a bed and a wooden chair with no fancy bed linen, no tapestries, not even a candle to give it life.

A woman's laugh came from the corridor. He moved to where he could listen and be ready. "In 'ere love. Let Nainie make you feel better." A nearby door opened and shut, a slap and more laughing. The purpose of the rooms was no longer in doubt. Should he leave? He moved to the small window. His luck was holding. Just below the sill was the roof of the adjoining building. Chadas climbed through and inched along, leaving the window slightly ajar in case he needed to return. If he moved across the rooftops, he might avoid the guards.

Another building was close, a narrow lane all that separated them. His confidence was returning. The next building was newly thatched and with luck, it would be strong enough. He slid on his seat until his feet neared the eave, leaped, and landed on his stomach with hands searching for a grip. He listened carefully. He heard no sounds of alarm.

Slowly he pulled himself higher. The seagrass ridge was no impediment. He dragged himself over. No one glancing out the window of the inn would see him, and there were no other windows within view. He could rest.

#

Chadas huddled below the thick grass ridge waiting for the sounds of pursuit to Fade. It was during these moments of idleness that he noticed the blood. The smell of it first drew his attention. A dirty smear stained the front of his cape. It had been no wonder he had been picked out in the marketplace. He was grateful for the darkness of the tavern but dared not leave here with that showing or the chase would soon begin again.

With great reluctance, Chadas removed the cape that had served him well. It was of excellent quality but the time had come when he must discard it. The action reminded him of Old Tom's words, you must be prepared to discard that which is no longer useful. But losing Misery and his cape on one job was a heavy price to pay. Immediately he began wondering if he could recover Misery. The thieves may be able to help. He would check. But his cape was different. If he could not return, he may be able to send someone for it. Beneath the cape he wore a yellow doublet trimmed with fur and stitched in silver thread, dark green hose and leather boots. All demonstrated the skill of a craftsman but the clothes were worn, mismatched, and patched. His boots were scratched and mud-covered. They were a perfect disguise for the streets. If anyone was curious, he was a man of wealth who had fallen on hard times, intelligent but not worth robbing. They would not look a second time. Pulling at the grasses, he raised a part of the ridge and slid the cape beneath. If it could not be retrieved, someone would discover it in the years to come and wonder.

Waiting for the dark comfort of night to settle over Dragonfang allowed him time to think. He did not like what came to his mind. It should have been a simple kill. He had done it many times. His client had offered ten gold coins, a small fortune. It had blinded his judgment. That was why he had taken the job and not passed it to another. It was not that he or the Guild needed the coin. It was over-confidence. A kill like that should only cost three golds, maybe four, but the trader who employed him had insisted. He wanted his competitor dead before he could sell his goods. What had the man traded to make ten gold coins worth the cost? He had seen nothing. And why had his target shown skills far beyond any normal trader?

Chadas had requested three coins in advance, and the client had paid without argument or barter. That should have raised more questions, but he had taken the coins without asking them. Those coins now lay hidden in his room. He was to collect the other seven before the night was gone. He had never doubted his client would pay. Anyone who did not complete a bargain with an assassin had his head filled with..., he did not finish the thought, but it raised more questions. In the moneybag tied at his waist were his eight trills, seven now that the innkeeper had one, and he had his silver. He stopped. His silver was in a secret pocket of his cape. He shook his head to clear his mind. He had already made too many mistakes on this job.

Reaching beneath the seagrass, he dragged the cloth free, removed the coin, and returned the cape to its hiding place. Night had crawled into the city when he was ready to leave.

Crabbing down to the eave and checking that no one was looking, he dropped quietly and crouched in an alley. At that moment he was disorientated. He did not know exactly where he was. The city of Dragonfang was a sprawling place. It had grown many times over the years with the wall moving ever outward, but it was not so large that he would remain lost for too long. In the south was always the sea, and he guessed that the water was close judging by the smells and sounds that assailed him. He strolled as casually as his mind would allow. Around another corner he saw the dark door. Above it hung a sign, a blue sea with a maiden's head above it. He knew this inn, the Sha's Maiden. He had been correct. The shore was close. Somewhere out there in the dark stood the tall, black rock that had given Dragonfang its name, Now he could gather his bearings.

Chadas stood at the tavern entrance and surveyed the scene within. In its deep shadows where only a few candles offering their flickering light, the tables were clean and the girls pleasant to watch. He entered and moved to a table at the back. A tall serving girl in a stained green smock approached. The low neckline of her dress displayed the other pleasures she offered. "Mead and food," he ordered.

Her brow dropped. "You got coin?"

"How much?"

"Two coppers."

He pulled a trill from his purse and set it on the table. Her face moved from scowl to smile. She turned and was gone before he could reply. So was the coin. Moments later, a full mug and a plate of stew landed on the table in front of him. Sliding his change forward, she grinned. Her eyes raised to indicate the rooms upstairs. There should be twenty-eight coppers. He counted only twenty resting on the table. She had taken the coin for her night of promised pleasure.

"Not now."

He would not touch the mead. He had only ordered it to avoid the eyes of the patrons and the curiosity of the serving girl. The smell of it made him cringe, the stench of his father. It was one of the two things he remembered about the man, the mead and his fists. Whenever he was awake, his father was either drunk or embracing his anger, or both.

The stew, however, was good. It was hot with a balance of meat and vegetables. His nose tingled at the generous sprinkling of spices. He shoveled spoonfuls into his mouth. When he finished, he leaned back to wait, and thoughts flooded in. Thoughts that angered him.

#

Night clutched at the darkness like a dying man grasping at air. Chadas slid quietly along the street. Night could be a comforting cloak for any who wished to remain unseen. Chadas was one of those, but sometimes it could be a betrayer. The clothing that had served him well earlier would now announce his movement. It may only be a flowing of shapes, a shifting of color, but it would mean much to anyone watching. And why would anyone be about if not to watch?

Back at the Sha's Maiden, when his suspicions had grown too strong, he had gone out the back door hoping to find a Guild member. The beggar woman had been waiting. He told her what he needed. Now he hoped she had been able to find what he needed. Thoughts of the moment she drifted into the shadows returned. He had asked, "Do I know you?" She had smiled and disappeared.

The meeting with his client would be in the yard behind the blacksmith's workshop. He had objected at first, but once again, the promise of coin had won over his concerns. That was before. Now he questioned everything. Why would his client pick a place like that? It was open. It was dangerous. The more he pondered the day's events, the more he convinced himself that his client meant him harm.

Silently, his eyes searched the gloom. A candle still burned in the back of a store. He could not see the sign that would indicate what the owner traded. A clink of stifled movement and he froze, a dagger suddenly in his hand. Though he waited, no other sounds came. Barely ten paces further, and the beggar woman stepped from the shadows to hand him a black cloak. He draped it over his shoulders and smiled. He was a ghost of the darkness again. His eyes studied the woman's shadowed face. He did know her, but from where?

She leaned close and whispered, "Beware, this night holds many secrets," while passing him a sword, sheathed and with a fine belt. "And dangers," she added. Then she was gone. He buckled the sword around his waist, pulled the hood over his head, and wrapped himself in the cloak's comforting darkness before setting out again to meet his client.

When seen at night, the blacksmith's workshop was a shrine dedicated to a lack of light. He still had time before the Tower Crier called middelniht. A slow circuit of the yard and surrounding streets revealed little. In the quiet, he was no more than a dimness sliding from one dark refuge to another. Someone was here. He anticipated the Guild members, they were part of his preparation, but he felt danger on the air. The feeling had come to him many times before. He always trusted it. An old hag once told him he was sensing the Majick. He did not believe in children's stories and had dismissed her. Still, he could sense danger.

He circled the yard twice and was standing in the shadows of the workshop well before the appointed hour. He had learned long ago that patience was an essential ingredient of an assassin. Above him, the tower loomed over the city. Rodnel, the current Lord of Dragonfang, had recently completed the work begun by his father. Now the spires climbed high above the four levels of stone dominance, one massive spire and its four siblings at each corner. The tower was a pillar of black against the stars, but Chadas could almost sense the eyes watching from the small windows and atop the tower wall. It was a poor place to do business if that business was death.

The hour arrived. A lone figure strode into the yard. Chadas broke from the protecting shadows and moved toward him, two cloaked shapes drawn together by darkness. He saw the things that coin had previously blocked from his eyes. The man was broad-shouldered and walked with the confidence that came with understanding his abilities. They stood face to face, though he could see only the man's penetrating eyes. His hooded face, wrapped in cloth, muffled his voice when he spoke. "You have done well." A hand reached out from beneath the cloak. It held a small leather pouch that clinked with the promised coins.

Chadas reached for his payment. He was ready, but the man was fast. The purse dropped, and the man grasped Chadas' wrist in a tight grip. "I have him," the man called, and seven guards stepped out of the shadows. All wore the livery of the Captain's Guard, the elite fighters of the tower.

"What goes there," came the call of a voice from the tower wall.

"All is well. We have captured the man who killed Captain Oswy." *So that explains the man in the market. A captain of the Guard would have the skills to react as he did. But why would he pretend to be a trader?* The man who held him had pulled the cloth down, and Chadas saw a face scarred by battles. It grinned with evil intent.

"Bring him in. I will have the gate opened."

"For Masima," came a call from the shadows, and "For Masima," echoed replies from around the yard. His captor's head snapped up as the ring of guards spun to face the new threat. Chadas had been expecting the calls, and he reacted. Taking advantage of his client's distraction, he dropped. Allowing all his weight to slump to the ground, he caught his client unaware.

Chadas weapon came quickly to his hand. Once again, a dagger would save him. He buried the blade in the man's leg to hear the cry of pain. His wrist came free. Training overcame thought. Speed was essential. He could not allow the man to draw his weapon. He rolled. As he did, his other hand found the hilt, and his sword gave a soft swish of anticipation as it slid from its sheath.

His opponent's sword was halfway out. His was free. In one movement, it spun and cut into the man's other leg. The big man staggered. The cut had cost the man time, but it was not a killing blow. Chadas believed he would be wearing leather armor beneath the cape. He did not waste time proving his thoughts. As the guard's sword finally left its sheath, Chadas shifted his balance. His hand rose, the hand with the dagger. Drawing on years of training, he put all the effort he could find into the stroke. He thrust. Chadas aimed for the spot he knew to be least protected. He suspected the man also wore an aventail beneath his cape. He would, but Chadas was close enough for such a stroke to be possible. The tip of his dagger slid up. It found the guard's chin and continued. The blade traveled up through his head to his brain. The man's eyes glazed, though his body had yet to accept its death. It still convulsed. Chadas drove his shoulder into his client's chest to push him back and clear his blade. He turned to face the others as the body thudded into the packed ground. His sword and dagger both dripped blood.

"Have you killed him?" came a question from the wall.

"He is dead," Chadas assured the guards on the wall.

Of the seven guards, only three still stood. Four had fallen as quickly as his client. Shadows moved in the gloom. Nearby, a shape became too obvious. A guard raised his sword as another shadow rose behind him. An arm reached over the guard's shoulder, and a second gaping mouth opened in his neck. The last two chose attack as their best defense. They charged into the darkened streets. A clash of iron, a scream, then all was silent.

"And so are the seven guards that came with him," Chadas called to the top of the wall.

By the time more guards arrived, the members of the Guild would be long gone.

# 13 REVELATIONS

Sleep eluded him. Something was afoot in Dragonfang, and anything the Guild did not know worried Chadas. He sat alone. No candles burned in the quiet room of his headquarters. Much occurred yesterday that he did not understand. He forced his mind in a different direction by asking aloud, "What do we know?"

"Are you asking me?" His aide had entered the room.

"No, Tulong. I was only thinking."

His client had revealed himself to be a tower guard with enough authority to command others, one important fact. He also had reason to have another guard killed. Why? He did not wish to have it traced back to any of his people, something he found understandable. Then, attempting to kill an assassin? How could anyone in Dragonfang think they could get away with it? Whatever their plot, they did not want it discovered. But what were those plans? Why did they want a guard killed? And why was the guard posing as a trader? Did his client stumble across a plot, or was he part of one? Were the guards hoping to overthrow their Lord? Was his client the leader of this plot? He had suspicions, but he wanted answers. He needed answers.

"Tulong," he called, and his aide hurried to see what was required. "I need to speak with one of the beggars. Find the woman who helped me last night." He sat back to wait while Tulong rushed to obey.

#

Chadas prepared once more to ponder recent events, but Tulong returned quickly. "The beggar woman is here," his aide tried to announce as she pushed past. He stared. Who was this woman? Her confident stride and sure manner were too familiar.

"What do the Ama want wif a poor beggar woman?" Her head hung to face the floor, and her fingers fidgeted.

"Do not take that tone. You may have trained to be meek, but I see an intelligent and confident woman."

Her eyes looked up as she teased, "Is the Ama embarrassed, then, to have a beggar come to his rescue? You are a great assassin."

Her voice carried the sting of someone who did not care for the Guild, or was it assassins she did not like? Maybe it was him. He suspected there was a story behind her words which only added to his suspicions. He was sure he had seen the woman. His mind rushed through his past for clues.

"Is the Ama not pleased with our help?"

"Sit!" Chadas demanded too strongly while Tulong fetched a chair and placed it opposite the Lord. When she settled, he continued. "I made a mistake. The promise of too much coin clouded my thoughts, and I thank the people who came to my aid."

"You could have just sent a message, or coins," she laughed. "Why bring me here?"

"I could. Maybe I wished you to hear my gratitude from my lips. Maybe I wished to see you again." Her eyebrows rose. "I have seen you before but cannot recall where." A smile touched the edges of her lips, but she gave away no more. He changed the direction of the conversation. "Put aside your beggar training. I sense a woman of clear thinking, someone on whom I can rely. There is something inside me that warns of danger. It also tells me when to trust." This time the smile stretched across her face. "I need someone I can trust."

"Can you trust me?" she smirked. Chadas believed he could.

"My client was a guard of influence. The man he wanted dead was also a respected guard. I do not think this to be a case of one man seeking to take the position of the other. I feel there is much more to this tale. The inconsistencies are too many."

"What does your instinct tell you?"

"That I have not met my client." She leaned forward to listen. "The man I met had no reason for employing the Guild, or if he did, I fail to see it. He is trained and commands other fighters. Why kill a Guard? Where did he get the coin? He would know he would not need to spend so much. Someone and something else is behind yesterday. That is where I need your help."

"What can I do?"

"Whoever wished to betray the Guild has forfeited his life. He will die, but not yet. His plot has earned him a few days." Chadas' voice dropped. "I want his secret."

"It may be a woman."

Chadas nodded slowly. "It could be, but I sense the hand of a man. It does not matter. I need the skills of a beggar. Learn all you can. We must discover what our mysterious friend is plotting. As well as giving his life, he may give us an opportunity for much more, a greater prize. I feel there is intrigue in his actions."

The woman thought, and Chadas allowed her a few moments. "I will need others to be involved."

"As long as they are of the Guild. Choose your people carefully. It is not yet time for too many people to know of our investigation." As the woman prepared to leave, he stopped her. "Wait. I do know you. My memory fails me. Have we met before last night?"

"You were always such a bobolyne."

A dim light flickered in Chadas' mind, her words shook free a memory, and he stared. "Alodia?"

A carefree laugh rushed from her mouth. "Of course it's me, you dalcop." Now they were both laughing as he hurried to wrap her in his arms.

It seemed ages before they separated. Chadas held her shoulders. "You know we are the only ones of our family left alive?

"Until I saw you on the street, I believed I was the only one. I assumed you died with the others. I was stunned to see your face. We all heard of the Ama's death and that a new Ama stood for the Guild. I had no idea it was you."

"They died not long after I joined the Guild."

They embraced and stood in silence as memories came flooding back. Finally Chadas whispered, "They executed our father for killing our family."

Alodia stepped back, a deep sadness in her eyes. "Yes, I know."

Chadas' face reddened. "I hate him. He was always violent. I am surprised we got out alive. In my heart, I blamed him for killing you though my mind told me you had joined the Guild. I suppose that is why I did not recognize you."

"Do not hate him. He was a drunkard, and the mead scrambled his mind, but do not hate him."

"Why? After everything he did, he deserved a slow and painful death. Our mother was the only good thing in our lives."

He could see the turmoil behind the tranquil face of his sister. "You know something."

"He did not kill them, not directly."

"What?" When Alodia remained silent, he demanded, "Tell me."

"Our father made a deal. He always made deals. It is the way of a drunkard. He would offer anything for another mug. Anyway, he could not remember making this deal, and once he was sober," Chadas screwed his face. "Well, sober enough to think, he tried to back out of the agreement."

"What agreement?"

"Unimportant, I do not know, but I learned the man came to kill our father. He found him passed out and decided it would be more punishment to kill our family and have him face the guards for their deaths. He wanted our father to sober up and see what he had caused. His plan worked."

Chadas' brow dropped until it almost shielded his eyes. His voice was low and hard when he asked, "What man?"

"We were both in our training, and when I learned of what he had done, I borrowed coin from my trainer and employed an assassin. Their killer could not be found in the city."

Chadas nodded. They sat and spoke, sharing their lives and memories before Alodia left.

#

To begin her task, Alodia set out in search of Sulis. She knew that finding her would not be difficult. Her friend would still be in bed. She did not wonder why she walked in the opposite direction. Without meaning to, Alodia found herself wandering the streets of Dragonfang, her heart avoiding her return to the room they shared, her mind a boiling pot of confusion. Surprisingly, Chadas' request was not in the mixture of her self-doubts. It distracted her, no more. There would be plenty of time to discover the secret Dragonfang was hiding. She walked on, adrift on a sea of emotion and uncertainty.

Sulis had been her closest friend for almost as long as she could remember. She was one of the first people Alodia met when they began their training together. They had only been nine. The years passed as if they were only days. She was happy as they worked closely to develop their bond of trust. At first, the tests were simple, what did their master have for her dinner? Edina, her teacher, expected a detailed list. The tests grew more demanding. How much coin did a particular trader have in his purse? It was not long before their missions became more covert. At age twelve, they entered the tower using the protection of darkness. Their mission was to learn what they could of the Lord's family. They were a good team, and the Guild knew it.

As they grew older, they had both bedded men and an occasional woman to discover their secrets. She had no feelings of pleasure or guilt. It was simply a method of obtaining information.

Then she met Rygan.

She had been begging in the marketplace while watching for anything the Guild might find of use. He had a small stall selling swords and knives. She had not seen him before and moved closer. Rygan was at least twenty years her senior, but this was not what she saw.

His eyes held a smile that flowed either side of his proud nose and flooded his face with charm. His body showed the strength and fitness of a man half his age, but what held her attention were the things he wore. The rings that adorned his fingers were gold set with colored stones. The chain around his neck was also gold, and the pendant it held was a large ruby surrounded by emeralds. Precious stones also shone from his front teeth. This man had coin, a great deal of it. He would be hers.

Alodia hurried to her room, where she dressed in her finest clothes, brushed her face with powder, and removed the bedraggled wig that was her trade. Quickly returning to the markets, she slowed to a casual pace as she strolled past his stall. She smiled and allowed her eyes to flicker in his direction. That was all it took to draw his attention. Over the following weeks, she dressed more to suit him. Soon she allowed him to coax her into his bed. Every time he looked up, it was to catch a glimpse of her. All that remained was to make him believe he wished to marry her. She would be rich beyond her dreams.

The day she heard the news that a stampeding horse had knocked Rygan down, she rushed to his side, but she was too late. Her future was dead.

She had told Sulis of her heartbreak. She told her everything. Sulis had listened and offered comforting words, and when sobs wracked her chest, Sulis wrapped her in arms that held her tight. She could not remember what happened then, but they were kissing and seeking distraction, tearing at each other's clothing. Now they were more than friends. She had found excitement and caring in their new intimacy, but still her mind asked if this was what she needed. Her mind always asked awkward questions.

But what could she do? Staying with Sulis was a comfortable situation, for now. They worked well together. But Alodia had seen behind the mask of her sweet and innocent face. In that hidden space smoldered a cauldron of raging anger. She doubted even Sulis knew why it was there, but Alodia had seen it on occasion. She had even felt its barb. She knew the depth of Sulis' feelings. If she put the relationship aside, it would devastate her friend. There would be no knowing how she would react. Loving her would lead to trouble in the end but leaving her was also fraught with danger. Her mind wrestled with the knowledge that she would probably never meet another as wealthy as Rygan. Sulis could be her only chance of true happiness, if only for a short time. There was no easy answer.

Sulis was still asleep when she finally returned. She stood beside the bed, gazing down at the sleeping figure, wondering what she was feeling.

"Like what you see?" Sulis' husky voice rose from the bed, but still, she had not moved, not even her lips. How did she do that?

"I always like what I see, but we have work to do. The Ama requires our help."

"It cannot be that important." Sulis smiled as she patted the bed. As had happened many times, Alodia slipped obediently in beside her.

#

The gentle snore alerted her to Sulis' slumber. Alodia slipped quietly from the bed and quickly dressed in her street rags, not wishing to be distracted by Sulis again. Would it always be like this? Would her friend take control of her life? She could not understand her feelings. In any other circumstances she was strong and assertive, trusting in her knowledge and abilities. But with Sulis, she was weak, always dominated by her friend's wishes. Was that the answer? Was Sulis dominating her? She tried to think, but thoughts lay hidden in the fog of confusion that was her mind. Was this what it meant to be in love? She loved Sulis. She knew that much, but her mind told her it was the love of a life-long friend, no more. Her heart did not offer any opinion when it came to Sulis. Alodia slapped her hand against her forehead to clear her mind, but the confused thoughts just became more tangled.

She nudged Sulis. "We have work to do. Are you coming?" Sulis grunted. Alodia stormed from the room. Her rising anger was only the frustration of her thoughts. Slamming the door behind her made her feel a little better. Sulis would be awake now.

The blacksmith's yard was where her search would begin. As part of their training, all beggars learned to read the ground for signs of secrets, and she could read marks in the soil as easily as she could read a man. She was one of the best. How often did a patch of bare dirt offer up its cryptic message of past visitors? Even the guards would be surprised. She did not enter the yard. That would have drawn the attention of the smith, and she did not wish him to notice. Instead, she leaned against the fence and stared as if lost in thought. She was. The ground where Chadas had met with his client showed the scuff marks of the fight in the dust and a dark stain marked the place where the man had fallen. The ones who carried him away also left their marks. What had occurred was clear, but there were no clues as to why the guards acted as they did.

A walk around the surrounding area was much more rewarding. Alodia soon discovered the place where some of the guards had waited. The boot marks showed their presence, but more. They stood together and shuffled, leaving evidence of their impatience. Gouges showed where swords had rested, their points stabbing the hard surface. She ran a hand over the marks, wiping them away.

"Looks like they waited for some time." Alodia spun around to find Sulis looking over her shoulder. "What happened here?"

"This is why I came to find you this morning. Someone tried to kill the Ama last night."

Sulis looked at the marks. "Tower Guards." It was not a question.

"Yes, they all died. The Ama suspected a trap, and he prepared, but he believes the guards were only acting on orders."

"Whose?" Sulis asked.

"That is what the Ama wishes us to discover."

They continued their search of the area and found two other places where the guards waited. That accounted for the men who died, but Alodia was sure there was something more. Her eyes searched. If the guards acted on orders, then whoever was behind this attack would have been nearby. She understood the type of man, or woman, who would try this. They would take pleasure in watching their assassin blamed and killed. "We need to keep looking. There is something here we have missed."

Sulis had also been scanning the area. "Where would they hide?"

"We have seen no sign of him, but I know he would wish to watch. It was dark, so he must have been close." Her eyes came to rest on the only place that made sense.

"The blacksmith's," they said together.

Making their way to the street, they strolled to the door of the workshop. They got no further. "Get out of here," came the rough command. "The likes of you are not welcome. Who do you think you are? There be no begging at my door and driving customers away." The blacksmith was big, a man of muscle and sinew rather than a fat belly. His arms were as round as Alodia's waist while a beard hid most of his face. His arms, chest, and beard carried the scars of flying shards of hot metal. Alodia ignored his scowl, walked in, and looked up into his face. Sulis squatted by the door.

"What customers?" she asked sweetly while looking deep into his green eyes. Sweat poured from the man. He was bare-chested beneath his leather apron. Alodia stared into his face despite the stench of old sweat and the heat that hit her like the smith's hammer.

"Get out!" he snarled.

Alodia reached into her rags and withdrew three trills, and held them up to his face. It was a small fortune to a man who relied on coppers. He snatched at them but Alodia was too fast. The blacksmith looked about. "What do you want?" His voice had lost its growl to be replaced by suspicion. "Where did you steal that?"

"It is not stolen." After a pause that allowed him to think, she continued. "I want to know about your customers," she purred. She rested her other hand gently on his chest. "Anyone important, or wealthy, been in here in the last few days?" The words drifted quietly from her lips. She would sense the tension of his muscles if he lied.

The smith looked at the coins, then at her. "No, only a few folks, just some that were wanting knives sharpened and such. No one important."

Alodia pushed one of the coins into his hand. He glanced at it, slipped it into the pocket of the apron, and waited quietly for the next question. Alodia stepped closer to rest her head against his chest. "How about guards?" she whispered.

The blacksmith spat on the ground at her feet, causing her to jump. "Them lot never comes in here. Anything they want, they send a stable boy," he snarled. A second coin found its way into his palm. It, too, disappeared. The blacksmith licked his lips, his eyes fixed on the third coin, and the girl pressed against him.

"Give him the other coin," Sulis called from the door. "He knows nothing more.' Her voice took on a teasing tone, one Alodia knew well. 'We do not want him to beg."

The smith's face wrinkled as he felt Sulis' barb. Alodia looked to her friend, and without another word, stepped back and passed the third coin to the smith. For only a moment, she wondered at the blacksmith's thoughts as he watched her leave.

"Why did you do that?" Alodia asked when they were clear. Sulis kept walking with her eyes turned to the ground. She had to ask a second time, "Sulis, why did you drag me away?"

"Look," she whispered.

Alodia glanced and understood immediately. "These prints came from the workshop?"

Sulis nodded.

Alodia reached again into her rags to withdraw a copper, fumbled and dropped it at her feet. On the pretext of picking it up, she crouched. The marks were not those of a poor man or woman. Only someone of money would leave these marks. The prints were solid, not like the soft leather of working boots, and they had two ridges across them, the mark of a patten. Only someone of wealth would wear them to avoid stepping in the swill of lesser folk. At the front of each footprint was a mark where long pointed toes touched the ground, impractical shoes, only for show. She guessed that these would only lead them to the tower.

Standing and holding her coin as if admiring it she whispered, "You keep going. I will watch to see if anyone follows." Then she turned and walked into the shadows. Glancing over her shoulder, she saw Sulis walking casually away, eyes lowered. Watching for trouble, she followed, but they did not go far. As she suspected, the tracks led them straight to the gate of the tower wall.

#

Alodia waited while the Ama stroked his hairless chin. "So there is trouble inside the tower. Now I must go inside to collect the death he has earned, or her," he added after Alodia's look. "What is their plan?" Another silence followed. "It worries me that we would not have learned of it had they not tried to kill me."

"Is it important? We only need to know who is behind this attempt on your life. Why is of little importance."

"It may be very important. Is someone bold enough to attack the Guild? It is a threat we cannot treat lightly. Is their aim to destroy the Guild, kill me, or is this just another struggle behind the walls?"

"We need to discover the truth then," Alodia agreed.

"First, I must find who is behind this. I have my suspicions, but that is not enough. I need to get inside their lives and learn their secrets."

Alodia laughed. "Is that all?"

"It will be difficult, but we are the Guild. No one can hide from us. I will find someone who can confirm this."

Alodia smiled, and Chadas laughed. "The way your face twists when you smile reminds me of when you were little. If our mother caught you doing something you should not, you would put on that smile."

Alodia smiled again at the memory. "I remember, and more often than not, it worked. No one would believe that a sweet young girl could do anything wrong. They would usually look for you."

Chadas' smile had become a scowl but quickly returned. "I remember that too."

"Back to your problem. Could an assassin get into the tower?" Alodia asked.

"Of course. In the past I often wandered the tower." *And I will do it again when I know who I am hunting.*

"And what about a thief?"

"There are many items that once adorned the tower and now decorate the tunnels."

Alodia stared, her face growing redder, as she demanded, "Then why do you think it is beyond the skill of a beggar?"

Chadas sat quietly.

"A beggar could easily slip past the wall and learn the secrets of the tower."
Chadas' stare made her squirm.
"No one would know I was ever there."
Chadas continued to wait.
"I will find your answers," Alodia promised and Chadas grinned.

# 14 DISCOVERY

The minds of Lima gathered once more. They were concerned. Tremors in the Majick were growing stronger. They had prepared, as they must, but would they be in time?

For a united mind, in this they were not one. Some believed they were, others not. There were even those who thought their efforts unnecessary, that the Majick would heal itself.

The voice of the One joined them. "All the paths of the future have been studied," it said. "Some things are clear. The danger to the Majick rushes closer. The one who could bring about its demise now lives."

"Is there more we must do?"

"All that can be done is ready. We can only hope the Majick gives us time to succeed."

#

It had been Alodia's intention to enter the tower alone. Then she made the mistake of telling Sulis. Once again, she had surrendered to her friend's wishes. Sulis's arguments made sense. That was not what irked her. This was her task.

They did not know where the plotters would be, and they needed to cover different areas. "That is our plan," Sulis decided. "You will enter the kitchens, and I will go to the house servants. Between the two groups, we should know most of what is going on."

"Not yet." It felt good to disagree with Sulis. It felt empowering, if only for a moment.

"What have I missed?"

Alodia could almost see the hackles rising on her friend. She was on the verge of cowering and accepting the plan. But at that moment, a surge of courage welled up inside her. "We need someone inside the stables. If this is a plot of the guards, that is where we will hear of it."

Sulis was dismissive in her reply. "I will entice a stable boy. He will tell me what he knows."

"No. We need a boy of our own in there." Alodia's head spun with the power of her newfound strength. "I know a boy. Isen is sixteen but has a young face." Sulis' eyes could have spit flames at the easy dismissal of her idea, but she said nothing, this time.

"It is dangerous. Do you believe the boy can manage it?"

"Isen may be young, but his courage matches his ability. He will do what we ask of him and not speak of it."

#

Three beggars huddled in the late afternoon shadows. The nearby section of the wall had proved climbable in the past. Hidden in the dark spaces between buildings, they would likely escape notice. The corner of the nearest building also gave them a view of the guards walking on top of the wall. They waited. The sun pulled in the darkness of night and settled it over the city. The noise of a brawl in a tavern was their signal. It would distract the guards for a few moments. Without hesitation, they ran, one behind the other. Hands and feet scrambling, Alodia hauled herself to the top of the wall, glanced to see if anyone was watching, and threw herself over the lip. A quick check showed the others were not far behind. She dashed across the width of the wall and dropped over the edge, hoping the stable boys still stored their hay supply below. They did, and the stack was high.

Rolling aside, she avoided Sulis landing on her. Then Isen thumped into the hay nearby. Soon they crouched, hidden again in shadows. Alodia glanced out from behind the stables.

"You know what we must do. Find out all you can over the next day. We will meet after dark tomorrow," Sulis whispered.

Quieter than specks of dust on the air, they drifted apart.

Sounds of cooks and servants cleaning after the day's close came from the kitchen. Even if she had not been familiar with it, she could have found it easily. Alodia slipped in and scooped up a tray of dirty goblets and plates and carried them to the tubs for washing.

"Who're you?" Alodia turned, every sense on alert. Behind her stood a ponderous woman. She was panting from her effort of speaking, or from hurrying to ask her question. Alodia could not imagine anything that would make the woman rush.

"Maisee, me lady," Alodia whimpered.

"Don't call me lady. The Lord'll have us both if he thinks I'm takin' airs. This is my kitchen and you'll call me Mistress Ezma. Now, what's a Maisee?" The last was a sneer.

"The Lord sent me here."

Understanding passed across Ezma's face. Her eyes took in Alodia's figure. "I suppose you're pretty enough. What'd you do?"

"Me man stole a pig. We was hungry. The Lord ordered him to pay for it, but we got no coin. I was scared the Lord'd do terrible things to him and begged for mercy. The Lord said I should work 'ere to pay his debt." She looked around with arms held wide. "'ere I am." The big woman muttered beneath her breath and turned to see to her other duties.

"You'd be workin' it off." The woman who spoke was the opposite of the big woman. She was short and tiny of waist with her hands submerged in the tub of greasy water. "Yep. You'd be working it off every night for a long time." Did everyone in the kitchens speak like the big woman? Or did they follow her lead? She guessed the second, just as she had.

The kitchen grew quieter as the evening wore itself out. One by one, the women disappeared to find their beds, or someone else's. Alodia found herself alone with the big woman. "Sit a while. The Lord'll give you one night to yourself. He usually does." She examined Alodia again. "Maybe not with someone as pretty as you." Alodia joined her at a table, and Ezma poured two large mugs of mulled wine. "We'll start again. Name's Ezma."

"Maisee," Alodia lied.

"Sit with Ezma a while. The Lord knows where you are. He'll find you when he wants you. Do what 'e he wants, and your debt'll be gone soon enough. You're a pretty thing." She leaned close and whispered, "Much prettier than that wife of 'is. But then, so's his 'orse." A chuckle escaped her causing rolls of fat and ponderous breasts to jiggle, seeking escape from her clothes. "No surprise he takes you for payment." Alodia snickered at the big woman's bold words. Ezma did not know her. She either did not think about what she said or did not care. Her free words were probably brought about by the wine she was drinking. It was not her first of the night.

Ezma warned, "The Lord, he'll not wait when he decides he wants you. Go straight away, but remember, the tower is closed and barred after dark. Only way in is the kitchen tunnel, and there's always two guards who will remove your head if you cannot give 'em the word."

"The word?"

Ezma laughed. "It's a joke of the Lord. Gropewhore. 'e thinks it's funny, but that's the word."

"I'll remember."

Alodia took a large swallow of her wine. "Careful. If you turn up nasty, 'e might make you pay more."

"What would he do?"

"Better you never learn deary." Ezma shook her head slowly. "Much better."

#

Tulong stood over Chadas' bed and regarded the Ama with trepidation. He learned very early his master did not like being woken, but he must. He leaned, intending to nudge Chadas' shoulder. Experience taught him it was wise to be alert when waking an assassin, especially his employer. The dagger was at his belly faster than his mind could comprehend the danger. He froze.

"I am awake, Tulong."

His aide carefully stepped back. "Why do you do that?"

"Because I can, and to test you." The dagger disappeared as Chadas swung his legs from the bed. "If you are to be my man, I want you prepared. You must be aware of the danger you face if you ever betray me."

Bowing low he replied, "I would never betray you, Ama."

"Good. Now, what is the problem?"

"Problem? I did not say there was a problem."

Chadas' eyes fixed on his aide. "You would not wake me if there were no problem."

Tulong scratched his armpit distractedly. "I do not think it is a problem, not that I am aware of. The beggar woman has returned and wishes to see you. She told me to inform you she has brought news of great interest." Chadas' brow rose as he listened.

Throwing himself out of bed, he asked, "Where is she?"

"Your outer rooms, Ama." Tulong's remaining words never found their way to his lips. Before he had a chance to explain further, Chadas disappeared through the door wearing nothing more than his braies.

#

When Chadas entered the room, he was surprised to find three people waiting. Alodia quickly came to his rescue.

"Ama, this is Sulis and Isen. We have each spent the last day inside the tower, and we come to report." Alodia was giving nothing away to her companions that he was her brother. Chadas followed her lead.

"Have you discussed your findings?"

"No, we met at our arranged location and came here. We have not spoken." She smiled. "We barely delayed long enough to hurry a goblet."

Chadas had Tulong bring food and wine while he sat the beggars around the small table. Only after they had eaten did he ask about their experiences.

Isen began. "The talk in the stables is vague. We could not rely on anything they say. It is all rumor, simple things everyone in the tower knows."

"What do they say?"

"It is mostly about the man who died in the market. Everyone he worked with liked him. His name was Wurt of Lord Rodnel's personal Guard, a favorite of his trusted few. They say they could hear the Lord's anger all across the tower grounds when news came."

"The others? Do you know who attacked me?"

"They were only guards. Tattling has it they acted on orders of one assigned to protect Lord Rodnel's eldest son, Edur. Other than that, the stables know little of what is happening."

Chadas turned to Sulis. She began. "What I can tell you also concerns Edur. He has taken pleasure in one of his mother's lady's maids, a pretty little girl named Lynet. She has become his favorite and warms his bed most nights. She fears what the Lord may do, but Edur assures her his father will not cause trouble. He promises to ensure she will be unhurt. He has told her that soon everyone throughout Dragonfang will know her name."

Alodia continued the story. "There have been fights between father and son.

Rodnel keeps his son under tight control, but Edur is trying to prove himself a man. Rodnel has told his son he should enjoy the maid, but she must put her aside soon. If Edur does not send her away, she will disappear."

Chadas sat back, thinking. "So Edur sent the guards. I would guess the Lord was using Wurt to spy on his son, but Edur discovered him."

"So you will kill Edur?"

Chadas smiled. "I must, but not yet. His promise to the maid, what was her name?"

"Lynet."

Chadas nodded. "His promise tells me this story is not over. It appears Edur intends the death of his father and taking the tower for himself. Lynet may even be helping him. We could warn the Lord, but it appears he is aware of his son's ambitions. No, we will wait. Let their little struggle unfold. We will see where we stand then. Now we know his plans, we can prepare. We may obtain much more than his life."

#

It was a strange dream. Chadas floated among the clouds. They drifted past, away from him, or was he moving away from them? It did not matter. The silver road beneath his feet seemed to urge him on, but to what? There was nothing to see except the swirling white that wafted on either side, above and below. He stared at the silver road. Behind, the road grew out of the clouds, and ahead it stretched into the distance. He was having the dream again, the one that continued to plague his sleep. A voice called to him, "Trust yourself. Trust me." He had not heard voices in the dream before. Something in the distance offered a promise of knowledge and power. Around him the clouds drifted past.

"Come to me," the voice called. Chadas did not walk, but the road moved beneath his feet. It was a very strange dream. The silver road had no holes, no ruts, or marks to show he moved, and the clouds swirled on either side, but he sensed his movement, just as he knew without understanding that his body was not here. It was an illusion.

Had he died? Was this the spirit world, or the way to it? Had Edur won? Had he been murdered? His mind spun with possibilities and fretted that it would not like the answers.

Looking up, he was surprised to find he was approaching the end of the road. In front of him were two enormous gates. Each stood taller than ten men. They were so wide he could walk fifty paces from one side and not reach the other. He studied the gates. Enormous slabs of what appeared to be solid cloud flowed with images that were constantly moving. There was a familiarity with the scenes. He recalled them as being similar to the world he had left. But there was also something oddly different though he could not determine what.

Holding the gates in place were two golden dragons. Each stood on what appeared to be a disc of solid air while their forepaws gripped the gateposts. Long, barbed tails waved behind them. Chadas waited. From each side, the dragons' heads lowered to stare into him with deep green eyes. He was not frightened though he thought he should be. Their curiosity amused him. The two great golden dragons sniffed, lifted, and the gates swung open to reveal a world beyond, a world of white.

It made no sense. White animals wandered peacefully among white trees and grasses, yet none were afraid of the others. Chadas could see each as if they were all alone in the world. They were all without color. Again the voice spoke to him. It was a voice that offered comfort and understanding, a woman's voice both soft and powerful.

"The time has come," it greeted. What did it mean? What time? Nearby some of the clouds drifted together. A woman dressed in gossamer appeared. She seemed solid, and yet she was not. Her spectral body was all white, yet he could see the world beyond.

"I am Rata." She waited. "Do you hear me? You must hear me. The time has come."

"I hear you and see you. What time?"

"Good." The woman smiled. "What do you see?"

"I see you and your world. Is this to be my world? All is white."

"That is understandable. Apat will be your world one day, as it is everyone's destiny. It is without color because you have not yet accepted the Majick. It is the Majick that gives the worlds their cloak of brightness."

Now Chadas knew this was a dream. "Majick? Children's stories? Is that where this dream comes from?"

White fire flared around the specter. "The Majick is not a children's story, nor are you asleep. Accept what is inside you. It is time to believe." The woman was insistent. Was this what she meant when she said the time has come? "Some have sensed it, and one tried to tell you. You were not ready to listen. The woman you called the hag spoke the truth. The Majick is strong inside you. Look inward and see for yourself."

This dream was like none he had before. "Who are you? What is this nonsense you speak?"

The woman seemed to grow to tower above him. Her face bore a scowl. "You must listen. I do not wish to repeat myself. My name is Rata, or it was." She paused, lost in a moment of memory. "You claim you carry the blood of Masima. Your mother gave you this news. Believe it. Be ready for me. I will give you time to accept the truth. Remember, if you are to learn, you must trust in the Majick." With those final words, the spirit that was Rata faded and was gone.

Chadas eyes opened and he jumped up, comforted by the room he remembered.

#

"Lord Rodnel is dead." The words burst from Tulong's lips as the door crashed open.

Chadas shot upright in his bed. "When?"

"I only know that rumor speeds through Dragonfang. It says the Lord is dead. The tower crier made an announcement. Edur will speak to the people of Dragonfang from the wall at Sext."

Chadas swung his legs from the bed. "I did not expect him to act so swiftly. Bring me a fresh shirt." While he waited, Chadas wondered what changes Dragonfang would see now, he suspected many. When Tulong passed it, he ignored him. He was lost in thought. "How long before Edur speaks?"

"It is only Terce."

"Good, enough time." He reached for the shirt and paused. "Find the beggar woman. Be quick. I must see her before I go to the wall." There was an urgency in his command, and Tulong ran from the room.

His mind was working again. He examined the shirt. It was the same one he wore on the night the guards failed to kill him. Edur would know the distinctive cut and the pattern embroidered on its breast. He would have people watching for him, knowing the assassin would not miss the news. He threw the garment aside. It was useless for now with Edur's guards searching for him. Even his face and size might give him away.

"What will Edur expect?" he asked the wall.

His mind answered. They will look for people hiding on the edge of the crowd. They will check all who seek to remain in the shadows.

He searched his clothing and selected a blue tunic, something bright and colorful, and tossed it on the bed. He added a red cape and broad-rimmed red hat. Finally, a pair of gilded green boots joined the pile. Now for his face. A smile touched his lips. He would take inspiration from the guard who tried to stop him. He selected a red beard, a wig of long red hair, and red brows from his disguises.

With gum, he began to attach the brows. He added the beard and wig, checking each in the looking glass as he worked. When he was satisfied, he dressed and checked again. He would not even recognize himself. He waited for his sister.

Alodia's arrival was, in itself, insignificant. Tulong merely announced she was waiting for him. With his knives secreted within his clothing, he took time to belt on his sword, the one she had passed him on the street. He was unprepared, however, when he stepped out to greet her. Before he could speak, she fell to her knees amid convulsions of raucous laughter.

"What are you supposed to be?" she finally asked between sobs of amusement. "Do you want to draw the eyes of every guard in the city?"

"Yes." Alodia's laughter stopped. He gave a sweeping bow. "Their eyes will find me, but what will they see?"

He could almost watch his sister's mind as it turned his question over. He waited until, eventually, she looked him up and down and answered. "They will see a man who wants wealth but cannot know how to achieve it or what to do with it if it found him. Your clothes, while well made, appear thrown together by a fool. They are a mash of colors that have no idea how they should look."

"Exactly. When a guard looks, he will see the clothes. He will never look at my face. All he will see is a fool. The guards will expect their assassin to hide among the shadows, not strut about like a mis-formed rooster. Appearing like this, I could stand in front of the Captain of the Guard and ask for directions. He would see nothing but the colors. We should go. I do not wish to keep Edur waiting." He smiled and raised a finger. "Before we go, I have selected some clothes for you. Hurry and dress."

#

He laughed himself when Alodia returned. His sister wore the ugliest dress he could find among the Guild's disguises. It was dark and cut in the fashion of the wife of a wealthy trader, but the similarity ended there. She looked like a flower garden that had escaped the control of the gardener. The patchwork of greens that formed its shape almost hid beneath the abundance of silk flowers that covered it. Every flower was a different type and shade. Lost in the floral wilderness was a profusion of silk butterflies, bees, and other insects. It provided one advantage. The quantity of the embellishment provided excellent places for hiding her various daggers.

"Perfect," he offered. Alodia looked down at the clothes she wore with disgust before they both broke into laughter. "With you beside me, the only danger a guard must be wary of is that he does not die of mirth."

Arm in arm, they walked to the tower wall to mingle with the gathering crowd. The space before the wall was crammed with people, and all faces watched in anticipation. The crier called sext. Everyone quietened, awaiting the arrival of Edur.

A guard walked close by, checking faces. "I wonder if the rumors are true," Alodia pondered, loud enough for all nearby to hear.

"We all know they are true," Chadas replied loudly. "What is the use of a rumor if it were not true? That is its purpose."

"What?"

"To tell the people the news," he said, waving an arm expansively, "and eliminate the shock of hearing it. The speaker can then lead his audience where he wishes, laughter, sorrow, anger." A few people nearby snickered. The guard ignored them and kept walking.

A head appeared to bounce along the wall. An image sprung into Chadas' mind. So many had lost their heads on that wall through the years. Maybe one had returned. He knew the owner stood back where only his head showed, but it amused him. The bouncing head stopped, and the tower crier called, "All hear Edur, first son of Lord Rodnel, Ruler of all Dragonfang."

The crier retreated, and Edur stepped into full view at the edge of the wall and waited. When he spoke, it was in a voice haunted by grief.

"My father, Rodnel, Lord of Dragonfang, is dead." He bowed his head as if inviting everyone to join with his sorrow. When he raised it again, he offered them details. "He was murdered last night while he slept. My mother died at his side. I can only be thankful that my parents did not see the spirits approaching to lead them to their next world."

He paused in apparent thought.

"Lord Rodnel was a great leader, a man who cared for his people and the city of Dragonfang, and my mother was a kind and caring woman. Whoever did this has taken peace and happiness from our lives." He angrily brushed at his eyes with an arm.

"He is good," sneered Chadas.

"Maybe as good as his father," Alodia replied.

"We are all in shock," declared Edur. "We will never see the greatness of Lord Rodnel again. Everyone in Dragonfang must be allowed the chance to grieve for my father. I ask every innkeeper in the city to provide two barrels of your finest ale so that any who wishes may drink a toast to a much-loved leader. Do not worry. After we have all allowed ourselves time to grieve, my people will come through the city to pay you."

"A nice touch," whispered Chadas again. "I wonder if the innkeepers will ever see their coin."

Once quiet had fallen on the crowd again, Edur spoke. "People of Dragonfang, even as we speak, the tower guard searches for the man or woman who did this. When they find them, this person will face your punishment. Now go. Drink to my father and remember the greatest Lord we have known. Tomorrow, search for the killer among you. I want them found. Look to your neighbors and the people you pass in the street. I want proof and I will pay well to find this person."

Chadas and Alodia left amid the departing crowds. A guard looked to them. "Worrying news indeed," offered Chadas. "I hope that you find the person responsible."

Alodia added, "He was a good Lord. It makes me wonder if we are safe."

The Guard replied, "do not concern yourselves. We will find the assassin. Good day to you." He returned to watching the crowd.

#

I looked up from the book to notice Kuwento dozing in his chair. Alerted by my pause, Cara quickly rose to see that nothing was wrong.

"He is sleeping. Your story can wait for him," she decided.

As we sat, I began to tell her and Eath of my travels over recent years. They were both fascinated by my descriptions of far-off places and the people I had met. I know my role is to tell stories, but rarely had my tales brought so much enjoyment and wonder to an audience. Slowly our talk turned to Kuwento, his home and his maal.

"I have never known Kuwento to be a man of such stories. I have only known him these last three years. When my husband died, we moved here to be close to my brother."

"Your brother? Where is he?"

"His house is nearby, but we rarely see him. He is a powerful merchant and travels from place to place to secure his deals."

"That is sad. I am sure he misses you and Eath while he is away."

"He," blurted Eath. "He does not even miss his wife and children."

"That is true," Cara agreed. I think he travels just to be away from them."

"And he always has young Mali to keep him company." The way he said her name, it was clear what Eath thought of Mali.

"His partner," Cara explained."

"His mistress," Eath corrected. Arien looked at her son a moment before nodding. It was a familiar story.

I watched the MaalKeeper slumped in his chair, mouth open and jaw hanging slack. It made me wonder if I would have time to complete his stories before he moved on to the spirit world. I felt suddenly glad that I had chosen to write the story of Chadas. Kuwento's mind held many maal between Awyn and Chadas, but while they were interesting, exciting even, they did not have the appeal of the assassin. The saga if his life captured me when I first heard it. But I hoped Kuwento would hear many more.

Cara's voice intruded on my musings. "He is aging fast."

"I know."

"And his mind is beginning to fail him. Although he pretends, sometimes I do not believe he even remembers us, and we are here each day."

"It is a cruel thing the spirits do. To treat a man who loves them so much this badly is beyond my understanding."

"I try, but some days it is difficult to get him to eat. At times he does not even know if it is warm or cold."

I shook my head. "We can only do what we can."

Kuwento interrupted our conversation. "I am an old man. When you get old, you do not need to eat so much."

"But you must try. The flesh is falling from your body."

"Arrh. Why are you not reading? You came here to read. Do you think that I have a lifetime to listen to your gabber?"

Kuwento would not listen, I knew that. He would hear only what he wanted to hear, and what he wanted was his story. I continued reading.

# 15 DREAMS

Edur's news was a heavy blanket over the city. Chadas could think of nothing other than recent events, Lord Rodnel dead, Edur the new Lord, the attack on his life, the discovery that Edur wanted him and the Guild gone. He needed to sort himself out if he was to be of use to others. He gave up, for now. Thinking that the morning may bring clarity, he blew out the last candle and slipped into bed. It was a waste of time. He could not sleep, even though his eyes were heavy.

"Chadas."

He must have dozed and was dreaming again. His eyelids burned. It was not the dream he knew. When he opened his eyes, he was still in his bed. The ceiling was above him, and light flooded the room. "You are growing to accept the Majick. That is good. Have you accepted your mother's stories?"

Chadas sat up. A gossamer-like figure stood at the end of his bed.

"Not you again," he groaned. "I know the stories of my Guild. I tell them to others. They speak of the great Lord Masima. I know the stories but do not know the truth of them. I have heard nothing of Rata."

"So I have been forgotten in history. That does not matter but what I tell you now is true. Long ago, before the city of Dragonfang, our people walked the land in search of food and peace. We were sleeping when the attack came. Most of my people died, and only eight of my children survived. They were given refuge with another tribe. Of these, the eldest was my daughter, Mayee. She had one child, Masima, who grew to become the leader of his new tribe and built the city you know as Dragonfang."

"But that would…" he trailed off in thought.

"I am now of the world known as Apat. You know it as the spirit world. Long ago, I was of Tatlo, your world. Many of your ancestors have come here and moved on. They have found the next world. I have chosen to wait and be sure that my line lives on."

Chadas tried to blink, but nothing changed. He asked, "The next world?"

"You are not asleep. Listen to me. There are six worlds of Majick."

His mind was catching up. He coughed and then laughed nervously. A spirit? Was his mind becoming feeble? He pulled himself erect.

"Feel the Majick!" she demanded.

Chadas decided he must play her game if he was to rid himself of this dream. "How?"

Rata smiled. "You think to fool me, but it is you who is the fool. The Majick is as real as your bed. You would know this if you chose to accept it."

Chadas was becoming tired of this nonsense. "Majick is not real." The image flared, and he felt the heat of her anger. Then she stood calmly again before him and began to explain. "You sense danger before it appears. You know where to find what you seek. You see what is yet to happen. These are all parts of the Majick. They are small things, but they are only the edge of the Majick. There is so much more you can learn. Many women have known the Majick over the years. You are the first man chosen to experience it since the days I walked among the trees of Tatlo. You knew it was too early to act on the events of the last days without knowing why. But there is much more if you are ready to learn."

Chadas was not afraid. For that, he would need to believe what he saw. Slowly he reached to the pocket in his bedding, found the knife, and in one motion threw it. The knife sailed through the air, passed through the apparition, and came to rest in the wooden door, quivering. Rata stood and waited.

Chadas blinked as he stared at the knife. "Teach me," he conceded.

"I will not teach you. My time in this world tires me beyond your understanding. You must learn from your world, but there are those who can assist."

"Who?"

"I will tell you when you are ready to listen." The image faded. The room that only moments ago glowed with the light of a thousand candles returned to black.

Chadas doubted he could ever find sleep again.

#

Night cast its solemn shadow over Dragonfang when Alodia slipped quietly back into the tower kitchen as if she had never left. She moved to the tubs and immersed her hands in the grimy liquid. For a reason she could not explain, she had not told Sulis of her plan. Maybe she did know. If they had discussed it, Sulis would have decided on a course of action, probably a different one. She would have persuaded Alodia to follow again. That was not what she wanted.

Ezma stepped up behind her. "Lord Rodnel will not be summoning you now." Her voice was almost cheerful. "But listen to old Ezma, my child. Beware of Edur. He has the desires of his father but the viciousness of a mountain cat."

"I will be careful," Alodia promised.

"Have a mead with me when we finish, Maisee?" Alodia nodded. Inwardly she smiled. Already Ezma trusted her enough to release her secrets. It often seemed to happen that way, but she was after bigger secrets tonight. She would need to escape the big woman quickly.

Work in the kitchen continued late as the tower staff took advantage of the dead Lord's mead and food. Eventually, the kitchens grew quiet. Alodia hung about as the others left. When only she and Ezma remained, the big woman sat at a bench and had already poured two mugs. She too had been accepting the Lord's generosity. "Does Edur know you are here?" Alodia shook her head. "Stay out of sight tonight, then. Tomorrow I will send you outside the tower for supplies. Do not come back. If he does not know of you, he will not miss you. Go back to your man." Ezma was a good woman. She felt the gentle touch of guilt as she secretly added the sleeping herbs to Ezma's drink.

Alodia made a show of thanking her, only to be hushed so that others did not hear. It made her task more difficult. She only had the remainder of the night to discover what she could. If she did not take advantage of Ezma's offer, the big woman would become suspicious.

"Tell me, girl, did you send the Lord to the spirit world? I would understand if you did."

Alodia quickly denied any role in the death of the Lord. "Why would I kill him? You know it would leave me worse off. Lord Rodnel would have his way until he tired of me. When the next girl came to his attention, he would forget me. I could then leave without trouble. My man's debt would be paid."

"I knowed you would not kill anyone," Ezma offered as she patted Alodia's arm. "Old Ezma can sense these things but I had to ask. Many strange things are happening in the tower at the moment. Edur is acting very odd, secret meetings and such, but he will be named the next Lord of Dragonfang. It would be wise to stay out of his way." Ezma was mumbling as the herbs took control of her mouth. Alodia left her slumped and snoring as soon as she could get away. She had learned one fact, and she would pursue it.

Her knives were ready in case Edur had changed the password. It was not necessary; the guards allowed her to pass without question.

Alodia crept through the darkened hallways. Nothing moved. All seemed quiet, but she felt the silence hid a great secret. Her skin prickled with it. She could see little of what was about her, but she heard the slow, steady breathing of spent and sleeping bodies. An occasional snore shattered the gentle rhythm and the odd grunt of some still awake but too occupied to notice.

Stone stairs spiraled up to the next level. Alodia climbed, one cautious step at a time, every sense on edge. From somewhere above, she felt the quiet rumble of conversation. Reaching the next level unnoticed, she paused, but the whispered voices drew her on. A soft flicker of candlelight bounced off the wall ahead. It added color to the darkness as a tapestry caught the dancing light.

Pausing a moment to control her breathing, she watched as the tapestry appeared to come alive. The dragon it displayed glistened in shades of green and silver. Was it an omen or merely her imagination? Was the dragon about to turn its fiery breath on the world? Or was its wrath for the people of the tower alone?

A stifled laugh brought her back to the current situation. The dragon would have to wait. Alodia's fingers gently felt their way along the wall. She approached the dragon and the room from which the light flowed. Whispered voices crept out to warn her.

"He is only a man, but he is dangerous. He will come for us all if we do not stop him."

"He is like a spirit. We know he is near, but we cannot find him."

Alodia dared slide her head around the corner to peek into the room. All those inside were too occupied to notice. Edur sat at a table with six of his Captains of the Guard. "He is not a spirit. He is a dangerous man, I admit, but he will bleed like everyone else." Edur was talking. "The assassin killed Captain Wurt. I believe he also killed my father and mother. No man should be able to kill a Lord and remain free to laugh about it. You will find him."

"It is not an easy task."

"If it were easy I would command a laundrywoman to find him. That is why you are Captains. That is why I pay you," Edur fumed.

"I mean, every time we hear a rumor, we raid the place to find he has left only moments before. Either he knows we are coming, or the people play with us, and he was never there."

Edur allowed his eyes to meet each man in turn. "You are here because I trust each of you. If this assassin knows we are coming, it can only be that my trust is misplaced, and one of you is warning him." There was quiet as the men pondered this. "You will put together a squad of six men that you trust. They will not speak with others. When you next hear a rumor, send them. If the people tell you he has fled, you know they play with you. Make an example of the one who passed the rumor. Bind him to a post in the square and open his belly."

No one objected.

"Our assassin is not the only one. We all know there are assassins throughout the city. I want a plan to eliminate them. Have your ideas ready when we meet here tomorrow night."

Alodia slipped quietly back into the darkened passageways. The dragon watched her leave.

#

Chadas and Alodia mingled with the crowd at the base of the tower wall. Once again, they wore their garish disguises of color, and again they had come to hear Edur.

This morning Alodia had returned with news of the secret meeting. Now they waited. Edur had promised to speak to the people, and rumor said he had important information on his father's death. Chadas had been furious when he first heard of Edur's plans. That Edur wanted him dead was one thing, but to plot against the Guild was something far more sinister. Anger twisted his face and churned his belly, but Alodia's hand on his arm and her gentle voice kept him in control.

It was almost time for Edur to speak.

The tower crier called for silence. The new Lord stepped forward. "It seems strange that only days ago I stood here to inform you of the death of Lord Rodnel, my father. On that day, I promised I would find the killer for you." He paused to shake his head. "My mother also died at the hands of this assassin. I do not know which grieves me most, but I promised to find the one responsible. I have summoned you here to tell you that I have, though it gives me no satisfaction."

Chadas' eyes snapped up. If any guards had been watching at that moment, they would have seen the man behind the disguise. Alodia squeezed his arm. Two strong guards stepped into view. Between them, they held a timber. A girl, her arms stretched and tied along the beam, sagged. Her head hung limp. Blood trickled from her nose and mouth. The smock she had once worn now hung in threads exposing red lines of a whip. Shredded flesh hung from her her half-naked body.

"This is Lynet," Edur called. Chadas glanced to his sister, who only nodded. "She was a maid to my mother. I have learned she is a member of a secret group of assassins that roam our city." A low murmur from the crowd followed. Chadas could not determine if it were anger or disbelief. "I promised you justice. We are here to see that justice served."

The guards held the timber with the girl slumped forward. Edur drew his sword and raised it high. "This is the vengeance of Lord Rodnel," he cried as the blade fell. The girl's head dropped, bounced on the edge of the wall, and tumbled to the crowd below. One woman, faster than those around her, caught the head by the hair and held it high as the people cheered.

"My father can now move to the spirit world knowing his blood has been avenged," Edur declared, "and I promise you I will seek out all the city's assassins. Their kind have no place in Dragonfang." The crowd shouted their support as anger tightened the mouth behind Chadas' disguise.

Chadas wanted to do something, to show Edur for the monster he was, but Alodia gently turned him away. "Not yet," she whispered.

# 16 VISITATION

Light seemed to fill his room.

"Wake up!"

Chadas rolled over. His hand sought the knife hidden in a fold of the mattress.

"Weapons are of no use. You should know that. I have little time. Sit up and listen."

The familiar voice caused Chadas to obey. He sat and faced the ghostly figure at the end of his bed. "What do you want now?"

"Only that you listen."

"I heard you. Must you repeat yourself?" This was becoming tiresome. "You have forced me to accept that you speak from the spirit world, but are they all as annoying as you?"

Chadas was surprised when the apparition smiled. "Be nice," she said. "Remember that you are of my blood. Is this how you treat your family?" She laughed before growing stern. "Put the games aside. I am here to help you."

Chadas groaned. "What do you want of me?"

"All that I wish is that you listen and understand."

"Understand what?"

"Your destiny."

Chadas could not help himself. He laughed. "I am the Ama. To many, that is more important than a Lord."

"I speak of the Majick."

Not this again, he thought. He was awake now, and to prove it, he dragged himself from the bed, strode to the door, stopped, and returned to sit in his chair. The desk beside him was laden with notes and messages from all across Dragonfang and even other cities. Chadas scanned them without actually seeing them before raising his eyes. "Where is my place if not here?"

"Your place is for you to find. I only offer to help you look."

"Are you going to teach me how to use the Majick?"

Rata shook her head. Chadas thought she almost looked saddened by his question. "I cannot. I can use the Majick to appear in your world and, on occasion, even influence it. But I cannot show you or teach you its use. I am not yet that strong. You must learn that in your world."

"Then you have nothing to offer."

"I offer you knowledge." Chadas sat wondering. The spirit drifted closer, causing him to flinch. "I can tell you what I have learned of the Majick. There are six worlds traveling side by side through time, though time is different on each. Yours is the third world, and mine is the fourth." As Chadas tried to grapple with this, Rata continued. "The Majick created the worlds and is a product of them. It decides how any being must live in each one." Chadas shook his head to try and put this concept into something of meaning.

"Let me explain. You have seen Apat. The body you are using now will be of no use here."

"But you have a body like mine," Chadas argued.

"What you see of me is only the image I put in your mind. I have no physical body as you understand it."

Again Chadas struggled to understand.

" The body you identify as Chadas will eventually fail. At that time, you may move to take another and be reborn into the world. Only when you have earned your place in the next world, my world, will you move on."

Chadas found that he could accept this. It explained the feeling he had lived before this life began. "What has this to do with the Majick?"

"All the worlds exist for the Majick, and while it is still strong in Tatlo, those who can sense it grow weaker. It has been this way since Agort, the Great Dragon, chose not to become a God, and instead left the world of man to Raiki, the God of the Lands, and to Foehn, the God of the air, and their son, Sha, the God of the Seas."

Finally, something Chadas could understand. If he did not practice his skills, he would soon lose the ability of a clean kill. "Why six worlds?" he asked.

"I do not understand the number, but the Majick created them, so it is as it should be. Isa, the black world, is the lowest of the worlds. All life begins there, spawned from the Majick. When a spirit is born to Isa, it takes the form of a slug or worm, or one of many other lowly creatures."

Chadas cringed at the thought that he could have been one of these.

"When a life begins there, they know nothing better," Rata explained. "As these beings move on, their next world is that of Dalawa, a place of fire and heat. Everything is red. The body a spirit occupies there is one of a larger and more dangerous creature. Imagine a rock lizard as tall as three men or animals with two heads and six legs. These are the creatures of Dalawa."

Again memories returned to Chadas. He dreamed of such creatures when he was a young child. His mother had explained them as nightmares.

"Eventually, a spirit will reach Tatlo, and if it is lucky, become Chadas." He smiled at her words. "My world, Apat, will be next for you. Here is the first of the worlds where a body is no longer required, though each spirit retains its individuality. The remaining worlds are Lima and Anin. I have not been to either, but I believe they are both similar to Apat. On Lima, the spirit may be individual or join with others as they chose, but on Anin, there is only one entity. All the spirits join it when they arrive. They are the Majick."

Rata waited while Chadas sorted the pieces of information into place. "The time has come for your work to begin. There are nine women in Dragonfang you need to find. They are all who remain in the city who can feel the Majick. They are the ones who will teach you. You will need to gain their trust, for they hide their ability. They fear it. Most are not of the Guild, but it is not the time for minor concerns." Chadas' face betrayed his desire for including those not of the blood of Masima. "Put aside your desire for secrecy. Find these women."

"Why women?" Chadas asked.

"Over time, men have forgotten the Majick. Their minds are on battles and other pursuits. Women have the time to feel it."

"Who are they?" Chadas conceded.

The first you have met briefly, the serving girl from the Fat Fisherman Tavern. Her name is Nelda." Rata named the other eight, the last being the hag who saw the Majick in him. Her name, he discovered, was Lorea. "Find them. You will discover more than you think possible."

Chadas leaned back against his chair. It was a strange story.

"I will return if I am needed but one thing before I go. I see grander things in your future than Ama. It is up to you to make it so."

As he watched, the mist and voice that was Rata faded from view, disappeared from the world. At the moment he could no longer see her, Rata spoke her final message. "My blood runs in you. Let it guide you."

# 17 THE TOWER

A small crowd of seven jammed into the darkened room beneath the city. Chadas called for quiet; there was insufficient space for multiple conversations. Six faces turned toward him.

"This is a matter for the assassins." The speaker was an older-looking man dressed in rags, but Chadas knew he washed his long hair and beard in a solution of herbs to take the color away. Behind that false exterior was a man of only thirty-two years and one of the sharpest minds in Dragonfang. Sitting with him was Edyth. Though much older, she was also a person of great intellect.

Chadas smiled as he nodded. "I agree Dyfed, and I welcome the leaders of the House of Meeya. The beggars know as well as any what has occurred recently." His reply caught the room by surprise. "It was my life that my client threatened, and it is my responsibility to see the man pay for his crimes. But I would not gather the council here if it were not important. Allow me a moment. I know you will find what I say difficult to believe. I still find it so, and it happened to me. I do not ask you to avenge the attack on my life. That is insignificant. I wish you to consider a great opportunity for the Guild."

"You have not punished the man responsible. Is this part of your opportunity? Or is this an excuse for not doing what you must?"

"I know that as an assassin you fail to understand, Moire. That is why you are here. I, too, have trained in the House of Eeva, but I need to explain. A visitor entered my rooms while I slept." This news brought their heads up and their ears ready.

"How did someone get past the guards and your aide without notice?"

"Was it one of us?"

"I do not believe a member of the Guild would dare attack the Ama in his rooms."

"But if not one of us, who has the skills?"

Chadas needed to control the speculation. "No, I was visited by the spirits, or rather one spirit. Her name was Rata." He waited a moment for the cries of disbelief and confusion to settle. "I know. I did not believe it either. She took me to the spirit world then brought me back again. She claims to be the grandmother of Lord Masima." The noise that followed was deafening and would not ease until Chadas slammed his hand on the table several times. "I tell you, it is true. The spirit told me it is time for the children of Masima to take their rightful place in the city."

"You require the revenge our Guild demands. Are you afraid of attaining it? Is this the reason for your stories? Have you learned who was behind your attack?"

"I know who commanded the guards, Luden. With the help of the beggars," Dyfed and Edyth both stared at him, "I am sorry. I asked them to hold their silence until I could speak with you. The attack was an attempt by Edur to take control of the tower. He killed his parents or had them killed. The ladies-maid was merely someone who could cause him inconvenience. That is why she died."

"And you want us to believe the spirits spoke with you?"

"Yes. I wish I could make you understand."

"You can." The voice he recognized echoed in the small space. A familiar glow filled the room before the spectral figure stood beside the table. Her radiance shone from the walls. "I am Rata. Chadas speaks the truth. It is time for the children of Masima." Rata spoke to each in turn. "Dyfed the knowledgeable, Edyth the wise, a great burden will fall to you both, but you will handle it well. Luden the strong, your role will be remembered by your children's children. Preada the merciful. Kendric, the leader of men, you will grow the Guild beyond your dreams. And Moire will prove her loyalty to the Guild beyond all others."

Only Moire spoke. "What of Chadas?"

"Chadas must pursue the path of his choosing."

Rata began to fade from the room that now sat in silence. After several minutes Moire asked, "What are we to do?"

"The spirit did not tell me what we must do, only that it is time to do it. The only thing I can tell you is the prediction of the spirit. The time has come for the children of Masima to rise and be recognized." No one argued. They had all seen Rata and heard her speak. Even now, Chadas could see the doubts many still held.

"The spirit says this is a path you must make. What do you suggest?"

"Edur has his guards searching the city for us. Do you think he will be satisfied with the assassins? He intends to destroy the Guild. There is one place he will not expect to find us, in his tower."

"So you are going to kill him?" Dyfed sounded more curious than satisfied.

"Of course, Edur has forfeited his life. Think. There is an opportunity here. We can take the tower, and the Guild will once again rise to become the power Lord Masima intended. It is what the spirits wish."

"We have one advantage," Luden added. "To find us, the guards must search the city while we can move about as we please. The enemies of the Guild have trapped themselves behind the wall."

The council began preparing their plans.

#

Chadas had chosen this night with care. There would be no moon to light the sky or the world beneath. He had not anticipated the cold rain that blew out of the mountains and wondered if Rata had intervened. She had assured him she could not, but he still did not trust her. The wet wall would make the first part of their plan more treacherous. But once they began, the weather would be to their advantage. The protectors of the tower would be reluctant to venture beyond the warmth of their walls and fireplaces.

The first three black-cloaked Guild members dashed to the wall, the same place Alodia had used to enter. All were assassins, and they moved quickly across the narrow open space. Even before they began their climb, Chadas could no longer make them out in the darkness. He imagined them like black spiders skittering up the stones. He concentrated all his effort on listening. If his attention were not so finely tuned, he would not have heard the soft thud. Moments later, the yellow cloth fluttered from the wall's top. Three more assassins were running before it reached the ground. Chadas ran with them.

Two beggars ran at his side carrying a ladder. Soon, all six joined the others at the top of the wall. A guard lay on the stone, a trickle of blood oozing from his scalp. His hands and feet were bound, and his mouth gagged. Chadas gave the signal, and three assassins moved off in each direction. The remainder of their party already waited below. More ladders rose, and the Guild of Masima began its invasion. All was going to plan.

When one of the assassins returned to give the all-clear, Chadas sent the twenty beggars to take their positions on the wall. Their training taught them to observe. They were the best people for the job. Having given orders to take the guards alive where possible, Chadas hoped not too many had died. He had plans for them.

While they waited, they had secured several ropes, and now they dropped them over the inside of the wall.

The first group slid quietly to the ground, and the second was not far behind. The Guild had entered the tower grounds.

#

Isen ran close behind Dyfed to the stables. Six people followed, all members of the House of Meeya. In the way of the Guild, the beggars also trained in some of the arts of the other Houses. Isen ran with his hand on the sword that hung at his side to prevent undue noise. They rested at the main doors and waited. Inside, a lone horse whinnied. From the odors that wafted out, Isen guessed Edur was not as strict as his father when it came to the care of horses.

Unless things had changed in the last days, there should only be five people inside, the stable master and four stable boys. Dyfed signaled them forward. They crept into the center of the space. Individual gated stalls lined the walls, while leaving only the space needed for the back door that led to the exercise area. The staff slept behind a small door on the left.

Isen carefully drew his sword, as did those with him. Dyfed signaled again. As they had arranged, Isen was to be the first through the door. He glided closer. The horses were unaware of the danger, or if they knew, they chose to say nothing. His left hand rested on the latch. Sword ready, he pressed and pushed. The well-greased hinges did not protest.

Livery crammed the small room. Saddles, harnesses, and other items used for the care of horses were everywhere. Isen pointed. In the corner lay a small bed., the stable master sprawled upon it, his snoring slow and regular. Wedged into the tiny spaces between the equipment were the four boys, all sound asleep after a hard day's work. He glanced about for others though he did not expect to find any.

Dyfed nodded. All five woke to find a hand over their mouth and a knife at their throat while quiet voices urged them to remain silent. As sleep left them each was gagged and had his hands bound. They would not be raising any alarm. Isen left as quietly as he came, running back to where he had dropped over the wall minutes before. As he did, he glanced up, knowing that others would also bring the captured guards to the garden at the same time. He continued to the now unguarded gate.

Only then did he realize that someone should have come with him. His small size was against him. How could he open the heavy gates alone? His only hope would be if they were well-balanced. He hoped they did not require great strength. It was the first time he had seen the gates up close. He had not entered this way before, but the large lever on one side gave him hope. He pulled on the mechanism, and the gates moved a fraction and stopped. He tried again, and again, without success. Should he run and get help? Frustrated and with sweat beading on his brow from the effort, he stepped back to gather his breath. His world swam as he gulped at the air.

When his vision cleared and his breath became more steady, Isen approached the mechanism again. He must not fail. They depended on him. The Guild should have chosen someone else; they should have sent someone stronger. He would not let them down, he vowed. He reached up to grasp the lever again. He would open the gates.

His eyes became wide, and a stupid grin filled his face. Fortunately, no one was watching. Releasing the lever, he walked to the gates. At the bottom, where the two timber panels came together, a thick beam spanned the joint. Isen pulled at the handle, and the beam slid easily away. He rushed back to try again. The gates swung wide, as gentle as opening a flower bud and a tide of Guild members flowed in. Isen joined them. The largest of the groups had the most dangerous of all the tasks, the guards in the barracks.

To sneak into the barracks and place a knife in each man's chest would be easy. Chadas did not want that. He wanted as many guards taken alive as possible. They had decided this would be a task for the thieves, with the support of a few assassins.

The barracks door was open. It always was. If there were to be trouble, no one wanted to wait for the keys. Isen was here only to report back to Chadas after the operation was complete. The door opened quietly, and the guards remained unaware. They were all asleep as the thieves flowed in and went to work. He joined them but stepped aside to crouch out of the way and watch.

Both sides of the long, narrow room held rows of bunks, all full. At the far end, the remains of a fire struggled to survive in the stone hearth, adding its dull red flicker to the scene. That was where the officers of the guard would be sleeping, closer to the warmth. Isen watched the thieves move from bunk to bunk, carefully stealing all the weapons they could find. Even with all the activity, the room remained silent except for the crackling of the fire. They had only reached halfway when a guard at the far end of the room rolled over, propped himself on his elbow, and tried to understand what he saw. He intended his bellow to wake people. It did.

Assassins rushed down the room. They ignored the unarmed men, they would offer no threat. The thieves pointed their swords toward them. But half the guards still had weapons. Officers screamed their encouragement for their men to attack. Few did. Some were too slow to wake, and others saw their comrades already defeated and refused to draw their swords. Those that obeyed the commands quickly died. Assassins stepped close, and with a swift slash, left a dead or dying guard on the floor. Thieves came behind and quickly disarmed them.

To Isen, it seemed only moments had passed before three officers were all that remained to stand against them. They charged and on the right, an assassin fell, the blood welling across his chest, but not before his attacker lost a hand when he tried to fend off a swinging blade. Another fell in the middle of the melee, his head landing well clear of his body. Three more guards also lost their lives in the frenzied fighting. Just as quickly, the two groups were so close their swords became ineffective. The guards still tried while assassins lowered their swords to reach for their knives. This close fighting was an assassin's trade. Once it began, the battle was over.

When the guards submitted, three of their number and eight of their officers lay dead while two more would not survive until morning. With them lay three assassins and one thief. Four more of the Guild would carry the scars of tonight. The surviving guards sat on the floor until the Guild was ready for them. Isen risked a glance outside. Had an alarm been raised?

#

Alodia crouched and ran in the shadows at the edge of the courtyard. Sulis ran at her hip with ten of the beggars following. Their destination was the servants' quarters. This had been the second group to drop over the wall and they began their run as soon as Dyfed and Isen had disappeared into the night. There would be little danger unless the alarm was raised.

On her signal Sulis slipped away, followed by five men and women. Their task would be to enter the maids' quarters and capture everyone there. Some would not be present. They would be warming the beds of the noble-born, but most should be taken quietly. The others would take their chances when the tower was raided, as would any that were missing from the kitchen staff. That was Alodia's mission.

Her group slid quietly into the kitchen. The only person present, Ezma, was slumped in her chair with her head and arms sprawled across the table. A steady snore escaped her mouth. One hand still clutched a goblet that lay on its side having spilled its contents across the timber boards. Alodia smiled. She knew their noise would not wake the big woman until morning. She signaled two men into the next room, the laundry. It was empty as expected. A quick check in the larder also yielded no lurking staff.

Leaving Ezma to her slumber, they moved into the smaller area where the staff slept. Bunks were jammed together with barely enough room to walk between them. The smells of exhausted and sweaty bodies filled the room. There were no windows and only a few carefully tended sconces to light the room. No fire burned to warm the staff. Alodia guessed these women would have enough of heat after working over the stoves all day.

At a nod her people went to work. Two moved from bunk to bunk gently waking those sleeping there. Each was roused to find a hand over their mouth and a knife before their eyes. They were taken to join the slowly growing group near the door where they were guarded by Alodia and the others.

No one caused any trouble as Alodia ushered them back to the kitchen. There, she told two of the strongest women to wake Ezma and bring her with them. They pulled Ezma to a sitting position and Alodia stifled a laugh when the big woman mumbled, "One more. Have another goblet with me before we go to bed." Ezma's eyes squinted as she tried to see what was happening. She saw Alodia. "Maisee, me darlin'. Sit and have a drink with old Ezma."

The big woman had been useful. Alodia moved close and placed a hand on Ezma's shoulder. "Come with me, my friend. I have a surprise for you."

Ezma's face contorted as she tried to think. "Whyse you 'ere? Shoulda gone to you man."

"Because I missed talking with my friend, Ezma. Come along. I want you to see my surprise. I know how tired you must be. These women will help you."

"Help me? Yes, tired. All right, Maisee. A nice surprise?"

"Bigger and better than you have seen in your life."

The two women dragged her to her feet and staggered under the weight as they joined the others. Ezma's breath was enough to make Alodia remember her father.

A runner came. This was the role of trusted apprentices from each House. The small girl could be no more than nine years old with long black hair. Alodia had not seen her before. She would be from one of the other Houses. "The cat has caught the mice," she told her and the girl raced away to deliver the coded message. Moire would know that all the staff were captured and no one had died. Edyth waited in the gardens. It was her task to be the central contact.

Soon the runner returned. "The crow has killed the viper," she announced. It told her much. The Guild had taken all those outside the tower itself. Only those inside remained. If the message had said injured instead of killed, then at least one area would be holding out, fighting for their Lord. It was also her cue to move the captives.

"Out," she commanded. "Everyone to the gardens. Be quick and quiet." Alodia was hopeful but being quick was not possible while carrying Ezma. The sensible thing would be to cut her throat and leave her but Alodia had a fondness for the big woman. She may prove helpful in the future.

At the gardens, the first thing Alodia noticed were the ranks of guards sitting with their backs to the tower. With them sat the stable staff. She indicated that her captives were to join them and glanced over her shoulder to see Sulis approaching with the last group. Nervous women hurried to sit where they were told, wide eyes searching.

All had gone to plan and only the last of the tower people remained. This would be the most dangerous, but well worth the risk.

At the edge of the garden, Chadas waited with his small squad. He gave her a smile and nodded as he turned toward the tower.

#

Chadas and the selected few jogged silently across the courtyard and waited moments before Alodia arrived. She led them into the kitchen. When the staff were secured, she loaded a tray with sweetmeats and other treats before showing them into the serving tunnel. The group of assassins pressed against the walls and while they hid in the shadows, Alodia continued alone.

"Who goes there?" came the expected challenge.

"Gropewhore," she replied hoping Edur had neglected to change the password. "I have brought a gift."

The guards stood with their hands resting on their swords, but did not draw them. Alodia smiled. Inwardly she wondered if they were curious as to who had summoned her. Stepping close, she held the tray out. They looked from her to the tray and back.

"Not many think of us," one remarked as they both leaned in to take a treat. At that moment Alodia struck. She dropped the tray. The two knives, one in each hand, that had been secreted beneath the tray flashed up. Both were perfectly aimed. Two throats were slashed before either man had time to react. The assassins came running in case they were needed but the guards staggered back. Alodia had buried a knife in each man's chest. The Guild had embarked on the final stage of their quest to control the tower.

They knew two more guards would be standing by the main door. Others would probably be positioned nearby. There was no way of telling how many and the sounds of the scuffle may have alerted them.

They were standing in the main Dining Hall. This was where most functions would be held and where the Lord and his family would dine. Adjacent to this was the Great Hall, a place of stately events and formal meetings. The large doors between the rooms were closed. The tower's main doors led into a vestibule that served both rooms. Two assassins ghosted across the hall, paused, and slipped into the vestibule. They returned moments later. Two more guards were dead.

The tower had stairs at each corner. The invaders split into two groups and climbed to the next level. This floor housed the lesser officials. As with the ground floor, ornately carved timbers supported both floor and ceiling. The timber floor would not hide much noise but the assassins moved on silent feet.

One after another the officials were woken, gagged, and taken to the ground floor. Other Guild members had followed and now took the captives back to the kitchen. Any that tried to raise an alarm were quietly silenced. The floor was efficiently cleared.

They climbed more stairs.

The next was the Lord's level. Under normal circumstances, only the Lord and his family lived here. Now the entire level was Edur's domain. As Chadas stepped out of the stair he ducked to avoid the sword that attempted to separate his head from his shoulders. As others closed in on him, the guard yelled. Edur was either very cautious or afraid. He hoped it was fear after his failed attempt to take the assassin's life. Three more guards stepped into view and judging by the shouts, others were coming.

The clang of clashing blades told him the other stairs were also well protected. Chadas dived in close to the first guard. His sword blocked the second strike and the knife that had found its way into his other hand buried itself in the guard's arm. The man's sword fell from numb fingers. Chadas brought his sword down to cleave his skull. It gave the others time to take positions where they could fight on more equal terms.

The struggle was quick, but not easy. These guards had been chosen for their skills. They rushed at Chadas' group. Only the well-trained abilities of the assassins protected them from defeat. The guards worked together in attack and defense. When it was over all the guards had died and two assassins lay with them while another carried a severe slash down his leg.

Chadas moved on. He easily found Edur. The new Lord was in the room previously occupied by his father. He was crouched against the far wall brandishing a knife in one hand while his other arm was wrapped around a young girl's neck. He was holding her in front as cover. Both were naked.

"Put the knife down," Chadas commanded.

Edur waved the blade wildly in front of them both serving only to show he had not trained seriously with the weapon. He had instead trusted in the obedience of his guards. Chadas swiped the knife from his hand. Edur's reaction was to throw the girl at Chadas who barely had time to move his sword aside.

Edur took advantage of the distraction to dash between the other assassins. He was almost to the door when a sword hilt struck the back of his head, sending him sprawling. He screamed for his guards, only to be told they were all dead or taken.

The girl begged for mercy. "I am only a maid, forced to obey," she cried.

Chadas lowered his weapon. "What is your name?"

"Immy," she stuttered.

"Do you have any clothes?"

"Yes," she replied pointing to the corner of the room.

"Put them on and come with me."

#

Nothing could have stopped their useless desperation. Lord Edur's personal guard fought until the last man and woman had fallen. Their only purpose was to save the life of the man who had murdered his parents in his bid to rule the tower. Edur had succeeded in his quest, if only for a few days.

Now the Lord was marched down the stairs and out into the gardens. The night air was chill and Edur was still naked. Those of the Guild who were not needed to guard the captives had built a circle of fires around them. These were now lit. Chadas waited until the dancing flames grew tall, casting their eerie red glow over the scene. Finally he was satisfied that all could see. Discarding his cape, Chadas stepped forward and stood resplendent in a doublet of blood-red, generously decorated in gold and silver. The colors danced in the firelight.

"People of the tower," he began as he drew his sword and touched its tip to Edur's chest. The defeated Lord winced. "Look around you." He waited while the captives did so. The guards sat impassive, expecting their lives to be over, while the staff from various places cowered in fear. "The ones who have brought you out here have no reason to harm you. They are all members of the Guild of Masima. We do not desire to have you woken from your rest or to have you sit in these gardens." He turned as he spoke to emphasize his words. "It is a beautiful garden. Who are the people responsible for this work?" Chadas waited but no one moved. "Come, come. Are you not proud of your work? If I created this I would gladly rise to take credit for it."

One man slowly rose. Chadas smiled but still he waited. A woman rose, then a second man. "Is that all? Only three to do all this work?" Chadas turned again to take in the gardens hidden in the shadows. When he faced the captives again, two more were standing. Chadas bowed deeply to them. "My congratulations. You have done a magnificent job. You," he said pointing to the first man to stand. "Come here. Let me shake your hand. Are you the head gardener?"

"No, my Lord."

Chadas, eyebrows rose. "Yet you were the first to claim ownership." He looked to the crowd. "Who is in charge?"

The woman who had been next to stand answered. "That would be me, my Lord."

"Before we go any further, I am not your lord. That honor belongs to Edur, for the moment." He beckoned the two before him. "Your name?" he asked the woman.

"Rheda, my .... I am sorry. How should I address you?"

Chadas scratched his chin. "Ama will suffice. It is my formal title as head of the Guild." He smiled widely. "But you can call me Chadas. Tell me Rheda, why were you not the first to stand and take credit for your work?"

Rheda swallowed. "We are all afraid. We do not know what you intend. I did not think any would stand. But Gareth is my man. I suspect he stood to protect me."

Chadas turned to Gareth. "Brave and honorable as well. You impress me Gareth."

"Thank you, Ama."

"I will speak with both of you tomorrow. Bring all your staff with you, all of them. I wish to hear more of your service to this man." Again the sword tip touched Edur. Again he flinched. "Sit here, near me. I want you to hear what I say."

Chadas ignored them as he turned again to the crowd. "From what my people tell me, you all work hard at your tasks, even Ezma runs a fine kitchen though I may need to lock up the wine." A few chuckled. Chadas slapped his hand against his thigh. "Back to business," he called. "Why are we here?"

When no one moved, Chadas sighed. "For justice," he shouted. It was obvious no one knew what he spoke about. "Lord Edur is correct, his mother and father died at the hands of an assassin. He would have you believe that the Guild provided that assassin. He lied. The Guild of Masima does have members who will kill for a price. When Lord Rodnel lived, the Guild was offered ten golds to eliminate a trader. The trader was a member of Lord Rodnel's trusted few. He was watching this man." His sword pointed at Edur. "Edur was planning his coup."

"A maid, Lynet, was found guilty and executed. Her only crime was to trust Edur. This man," the sword touched Edur's chest and this time blood trickled down the Lord's naked body, "killed his parents to satisfy his lust for the tower."

This brought muttering from the crowd.

Chadas' voice took on a deep and powerful tone. "For this crime, and for attempting to avoid payment to the Guild, Lord Edur has been found guilty. Punishment is death."

Having delivered his verdict, Chadas spun. His sword neatly separated Edur's head from his body. In the stunned silence, all could hear the thump as it hit the ground. Chadas knelt and lifted it by the hair, holding it high.

"Who stands with their Lord?" he called.

#

I heard a faint sound, something like a coughing giggle, and looked up. I saw Kuwento laughing and clapping his hands. "I do not like Edur," he said. "He is a terrible man. Why did you put him in your story?"

I studied him for a few moments, concern biting at my thoughts. "It is your story."

"Is it? Yes, it must be." I waited, watching him. "It is. Read some more."

"Wait. I will be back soon." Rising, I walked to the secret door and went to the room below. The stale, musty smell of unused space filled my nose. I knew what I wanted and the Majick drew me to it. The little clam shell with the tower carved into its shining inner surface was exactly where I remembered it. It tingled with memory as I picked it up.

Upstairs, I took Kuwento's hand and placed the token on it. A look of understanding or memory crossed his features. Nodding, he pointed to the book. I settled myself, picked it up, and read.

# 18 A COUNCIL FORMS

The Guild and the invited people of Dragonfang met in the tower for the first time in known history. Chadas chose the Great Hall for the occasion and a large table had been brought from the Dining Hall. It had been laden with an array of foods, now mostly eaten. He wished to involve many people both from the tower and from within the city. The House leaders stood on an improvised stage facing the guests. Chadas was about to speak when Luden rose and cut him off.

"Citizens of Dragonfang," he called. Chadas was surprised but did not stop him. "Before we begin, I must introduce ourselves. We are the Leaders of the Guild. Lord Edur is dead and he left no legitimate heir. Lord Rodnel had no other legitimate heirs. This leaves our city in a crisis. Can anyone provide proof of an heir to the city?" When no one spoke, he continued. "Then we must find a new Lord. I put forward Chadas, Ama of the Guild of Masima. In his short years he has proved loyal to the city and the Guild. He is a fair and just man, a perfect Lord. Does anyone offer another." Silence followed and Luden asked, "Does anyone think they would be a better Lord?"

Dyfed spoke. "I do not think Chadas is the best choice for our new Lord."

"Why?" asked Luden.

"Chadas is the Ama, the leader of the Guild. He is good at what he does, but I feel that naming him Lord will give him too much power."

"Have you a better person?"

"Yes," then after a moment, "Me."

This was followed by angry mutters from the other Houses. Chadas stepped forward and raised his hands. "No, if Dyfed believes he would be a better Lord, he has the right to believe so." He looked out over the people of Dragonfang. "I leave the decision to the people. Who do you want as your new Lord?"

Chadas, Ama of the Guild, became the new Lord of Dragonfang. Dyfed turned to Chadas. "My apologies, my Lord." Then he offered a muted smile.

The new Lord stepped to the edge of the stage. "I thank you for your trust," he acknowledged. "Being a Lord is not honor in itself. Rodnel was a good Lord but I cannot offer the same words for his son. It is a huge responsibility. I hope I am shown worthy." He waited while calls of support followed. "Now, where are my gardeners?"

The small group approached and bowed.

"Rise, all of you," he ordered. "I feel it necessary to apologize to each of you and everyone else we detained last night, but it was necessary." Turning back to the gardeners, he continued. "My words to you were real. You have made beautiful gardens, which makes what I must ask more difficult." The gardeners were listening carefully, not knowing what to expect.

"I want you to build me a grander garden, only much smaller. There should be paths that lead a person on to find new and wonderful places to rest and relax. Put in some alcoves with benches where a person may ponder your work. Add other things, arches, ponds, and anything else that you think that will enhance the beauty. Make it a garden worthy of Dragonfang."

"Yes, my Lord," they answered in unison.

"And tear up the rest."

Shock filled the faces of the gardeners. Chadas smiled.

"The remainder of the gardens are to be devoted to vegetables and other useful plants, only things that can be eaten or used for medicines will be grown."

The shock had turned to confusion.

"I want my words carried throughout Dragonfang. Once the gardeners complete their work, any person, be they man, woman, or child, who finds themselves in desperate times will receive a gift of the tower. Someone will hear their plight and some of the vegetables these good people grow will be delivered." What followed could only be described as a stunned silence. "Do you understand?" he asked Rheda.

"Yes, my Lord. It will be as you wish, but what of the tower?"

"A portion of what is produced will be used by the tower, but only what is needed. My childhood was not a pleasant one. If my becoming Lord can assist anyone in need, then it will be done." In a louder voice he added, " If anyone has an idea that will assist the less fortunate of Dragonfang, they must bring it to me."

He waved them away and called for the kitchen staff. "Ah, good Ezma, Alodia has kind words for you." The big woman looked confused. "You know her as Maisee." Understanding flowed slowly into the creases of her face. He commanded the kitchens bake extra loaves when they were cooking. These too he ordered to be distributed among the poor. With each group from the tower, he found a way they could help the city's less fortunate.

"We must all do our part to make this city strong. You may wonder how I will pay for this. Dragonfang is a large and most fortunate place. It has many wealthy businesses. My people will come among you and ask how you can contribute to the growth of our home and people. If you have food while your neighbor goes hungry, share your bounty with him. I ask only that you provide what you can. I do not wish to see you harshly treated, you work hard for your wealth. All who provide their fair share will have their names announced with honor in the city square. The Guild and the people will be proud of you. Those who refuse their duty to Dragonfang will also be mentioned. As I say, you will not be forced into payment. But you will be known for your miserly ways. The people of Dragonfang will respond and your business may suffer. That is your choice."

There was a low rumble in the hall as people began to discuss his words. Chadas allowed them to continue for a short time before sending them to their tasks. "The Guild has other business to discuss," he told them.

#

He waited patiently while most people filed from the room leaving each of the House leaders and their chosen seconds. Alodia and Isen attended as guests. The Houses, now the Council of Dragonfang, would spend most of their time overseeing the city.

"That went far easier than I expected, but I spoke the truth. We have things to discuss. Why has the Guild endured for so long? Because we are able to organize and adapt. The first question is how we took the tower. No one must be able to take it from us as easily. I have devoted much thought to this."

"And what have you to suggest?"

"There must be only one entry to the tower, one we can defend. We need the kitchens, so these must be included in the tower defenses. We should have a trench dug around all these and a tunnel to connect it to the sea. When it is filled, no one will be able to approach unless it is across the bridge we build."

This was met with nods of approval.

"And the wall is too easy to scale unseen."

Kendric spoke. "Should we make it taller?"

"No, it could still be climbed. We will begin a second wall ten paces outside and fill the joints with clay. When it dries, it will be difficult to climb. If anyone succeeds, they would then have a second wall barring their way. Guards on the inner wall will be armed with bows. The space between would become a killing field."

Moire sat with brow furrowed.

"Is my thinking flawed?" he asked.

"No, my Lord. What you say is correct and can be improved, but these are decisions that should include all of us. You speak as if they are decided."

"Of course it can be improved. I have decided nothing, but I have put much thought into this and I present my thoughts. I am just excited to see the future of Dragonfang. The decisions are why you are here. What else should we do?"

Moire stared a minute before shaking her head and answering. "I assume you would have gates in both walls?"

Chadas nodded.

"If these were connected with a tunnel, anyone who gets past the outer gate would be trapped until they breach the second one."

Isen seemed overcome with excitement. "We could add platforms on each side with arrow loops so that guards could fire into the tunnel. No one would ever pass."

"Very good. If no one can offer a reason for us not to begin, we will find our workers." Chadas sat back and smiled. "This makes me feel better." After a moment of imagining the future shape of Dragonfang, he slapped his hands on the table. "Other matters. You announced yourselves as the Council. We all know you meant the Council of Masima. After today, the people will know you as the Council of Dragonfang. As such, you must have tasks, a reason for the people to respect you. I told the people of our plans to collect their support for the less fortunate. Of course one in six coins collected should go to our coffers for the construction works and other Guild matters. I believe collecting should be the work of the House of Thieves. They are aware of what people earn and the things they own. This will keep people honest with their charity. They will also manage the coffers of the tower, and all other matters of coin."

Luden and Peadra beamed with pride at their new responsibilities.

"Lord Edur's tower guards," he continued, "will be divided into squads. Each squad will come under the command of an assassin. You will select one man to become the Captain of the Guard. Each squad will answer to him." Kendric and Moire waited, knowing there would be more. "I will select a squad of the best to become the personal Guard of the Lord. House Alard will have the task of building and training an army. The remaining assassins will form a special squad to perform tasks outside the prevue of the army. They will be specialists in what they do best, killing. But they will not work for contracts, they will work for the city. The Guard will be responsible for discipline within Dragonfang, the army will protect the city. Each will come to the aid of the other if needed."

"And what of the beggars?" Edyth asked.

"Officially, they will be responsible for the general operations of the city including justice for all those who feel they have been wronged. Secretly they will be the spies of the Guild. Their business will be knowledge. They must know everything that happens or will happen in Dragonfang."

Discussions continued and suggestions considered, but n the end it was all as Chadas wished. The Council did not even realize they had been led.

# 19 WOMEN OF MAJICK

Chadas rested his arms on the table, deep in thought. Pushing the chair back he came quickly to his feet, causing the guard in the corner to stiffen.

"Find the Captain of the Guard," he ordered. The man hesitated, his eyes bouncing between the door and his Lord. Chadas softened his voice. "Go, I will be all right. Tell him I wish to speak with him now." The guard scurried from the room. As the door was closing, Chadas called, "Then find a kitchen hand. Tell her I wish to see her too, but she is to wait outside until I call for her." The guard nodded as the door clicked shut. Chadas had thought long on Rata's words and decided now was the time to act. Maybe it was Rata that convinced him or maybe it was instinct, but he accepted it might also be the pull of the Majick.

"Come," he called after the knock at his door. The Captain of the Guard entered rubbing his face and straightening his clothes. "Were you sleeping?" Chadas asked, "Or is there a maid in need of rest?"

"Sleeping, my Lord. I am sorry."

Chadas passed him a list he had prepared. "These women are somewhere in Dragonfang. I want them found."

"We will find and arrest them, my Lord? Who are they?"

"People of little consequence to you. I want them all in this room come Sext."

"Yes, my Lord."

The Captain of the Guard turned to leave.

"And Strang," Chadas called. Strang looked back over his shoulder. "These women are important to me. They have done nothing wrong. Treat them well." Strang's brow rose. He said nothing as he left. Chadas noticed the girl outside and beckoned her in.

The girl did as he bid and all was ready in time. A table was prepared along one wall with platters of meats, fruits, and vegetables. At one end was a basket of black bread. She waited at the other end with rows of goblets and two hogsheads. One held wine, the other ale.

Chadas opened the door to see Strang approaching, leading two women who seemed ready to jump and run given any opportunity. He ushered them in. Strang's brow climbed but he offered no objections.

"The others have been found and are coming," Strang advised.

"Good. Take the guards with you when you leave, all of them." He smiled. "These women will do me no harm."

"Welcome," he beamed. "Welcome to the tower of the Lord," he gushed as the women entered his rooms. "I have had food prepared, and drink. I hope my people treated you well." The women were hesitant but slowly they entered while Chadas moved back.

It was only then that he remembered the young maid still standing at the end of the table. He moved close to her. "I would ask you to leave but something tells me you can be trusted." The girl made the sign of the Guild.

His eyes widened briefly. "It is part of my training, my Lord. I am to learn and report back."

Chadas studied her. "To whom?"

"My master, one of the best in the House of Beggars."

"Can you learn and not report?"

"I know when to tell, and when to keep my mouth closed, my Lord."

"I need someone to serve. You will stay, but nothing of what you see or hear goes beyond these walls. If you cannot keep secrets from your masters, then go."

"As you command, my Lord." She stood quietly.

"Your name?"

"Ashee, my Lord."

The two women were huddled close to the door. A knock made them jump.

Three more women arrived.

"Let us introduce ourselves. I am Chadas, now Lord of Dragonfang, but when I was young, I was a pauper. Life has been good to me."

Chadas smiled and looking at one woman, spoke. "I assume you are Nelda? I recognize you."

"It is not often that a man pours his drink on the floor and then orders another."

"Tell everyone about yourself, we will all soon be friends." Nelda looked about. "Do not fear," Chadas encouraged.

"I am Nelda," she said, "I am a serving girl at the Raven's Heart."

She did not continue. Chadas added, "and you still owe me my change." Her eyes suddenly became orbs in her face and Chadas laughed. "Do not worry. I have not called you here to collect it." He looked to the next woman.

Next was a girl of around seventeen with large arms and shoulders. "My name is Wilona. My father is the blacksmith."

Chadas nodded. "And you help your father?" She nodded.

The following woman spoke quickly, sharply. "Bernie, fisherman's wife."

He nodded again. "An honest and hard life."

Chadas turned to the young girl. She lowered her head and mumbled. "What was that?" he asked.

She answered more clearly, "Elrida."

A gentle smile flowed onto Chadas' features. "What do you do, Elrida?"

"I work for Ari."

Chadas had heard of Ari. "And what do you do for him?" he encouraged.

Her face grew red. "He sells me to men."

Chadas voice took on a tone of comfort. "Do not be afraid." Then he moved to open the door. "Guard!" he called. When the man arrived he commanded, "I want you to find a man named Ari." He called Elrida close. "This girl will tell you where he can be found."

With that completed, he turned to a tall woman with long delicate fingers and waited.

"Annis, my Lord. I am known for helping with the birthing of babies and I make clothes to sell."

Wilda, an older woman with graying hair, introduced herself as a widow who did laundry and sewing for her coin.

Chadas was shocked when the next woman spoke. I am Korra. My husband was Captain Wurt.

"I am sorry," Chadas offered.

Her chest filled as she straightened her shoulders. "Did your Guild kill him?"

"No, he died at the hands of a guard under orders from Edur. There is more to the story, but I will tell you when we are alone." Korra brushed a tear from her plump cheek.

"The last then is Lorea who tried to make me aware of certain things before I was ready to listen. The women studied each other. He knew their thoughts. All wondered why were they here?"

The meeting was progressing better than Chadas had hoped. The women began to relax, though Lorea kept casting him suspicious glances.

Chadas sat to one side and chatted idly about his becoming the Lord and life in the tower. The women slowly began to relax. "Ashee, bring fresh drinks for everyone." He waited while she obeyed. "Thank you for your service. It is now time for you to leave. These women and I have matters to discuss. Return when they leave. You can clean away. Remember, say nothing."

When she had gone, Chadas said, "Rata, are you watching?"

"I am here," came the voice that shook the air. The women looked about franticly, fear fracturing their cautious calm.

"There is no need for concern. I merely wished you to understand. Our meeting is the will of the spirits."

"There is something you have not told us, any of you."

He told them that he knew they felt the Majick and expressed his hope that they would help him find it too, but before he could explain further, a knock sounded.

"Come!" he snapped.

The guard entered with a small man in tow.

"Is this Ari?" Chadas asked of Elrida who nodded. He looked the man from his broad hat trimmed with pink feathers to his blue boots with their long, pointed toes. All was of the highest quality. Chadas concluded he did not like this fellow.

"I understand Elrida worked for you?"

"She does." Chadas could read this man easily. How much would a Lord pay for this girl? Then the words penetrated. "Worked?"

"Yes. She no longer is in your employ. Now she works for me."

"But…"

"Of course, I will pay you for her. Let us say two coppers?" Ari spluttered. "Is it too much?" Chadas knew Elrida could earn him five times that much every night. "And when you speak to me, you will address me as 'My Lord'. A fine will help improve your memory, two coppers seems fair."

Daggers seemed to shoot from Ari's eyes.

Chadas returned the stare. "Our business is now complete, but I warn you, should any harm befall Elrida, I will hold you responsible. Your punishment will be to hang in a cage in the town square until you are dead. Do you understand?"

"Yes." When Chadas' brow rose, he quickly added, "My Lord."

"Good. Remember my warning." He called for the guard to take Ari away. As he left, Chadas added, "I do not want to see your face again."

To the women he said, "I will not force any of you to assist me. The decision is yours. When you have finished eating, you may go. I only ask that you return tomorrow with your answers."

"I need no time," offered Elrida. "I will do what you want." He nodded and, one by one, each of the women agreed.

When everyone had left, he called for Ashee.

"Come with me."

He led her through corridors to the kitchen. "Where is Ezma?" he called. The big woman puffed close. "This girl has proved her value to me. I want you to care for her. Show her how a kitchen should be managed. Teach her. She will be the next head of this place."

# 20 SECRETS

The stone steps were worn and blackened with age. Behind them, the doors of heavy oak, though aged and gray, still opened easily on iron pins regularly greased with duck fat. Surrounding them, the thick stone blocks of the tower held the secrets of generations.

Chadas strode out of the tower, down the steps and into the struggling sunlight without noticing any of these. Heavy skies were usual in Dragonfang. He did not see these either. Two guards followed closely as he set out to inspect the birth of his new defenses. Alodia was watching the gang that had begun to dig the moat. "Good news," she told him as he approached. "The ground is heavy with clay. As we remove it we can strengthen it with straw and fashion it into blocks. When the sun dries them they will make a better building material for the outer wall. No one will ever be able to climb it. Not even me," she laughed.

Everything was going far better than he had planned. Not for the first time, he wondered at the extent of Rata's involvement. Could a spirit even change the ground to clay?

The garden, too, was well underway. Most of the planting was complete and it only needed time to grow. When they reached it Chadas turned. "Hold back," he ordered. "Alodia and I have business to discuss."

Chadas and Alodia walked side by side through the maze of plants. He knew this would be as alone as he could be now. As he and Alodia spoke, the guards followed ten paces behind, but he could sense their desire to get closer or listen. "I cannot get used to this," he whispered. "Even the Ama should be allowed his own time. It used to be only Tulong who was always close, and he knew when to keep his distance. These," his thumb cocked toward the guard, "are only happy when they squat beside me in the latrine."

Alodia laughed.

"I need Tulong back."

"Where is he?"

"Strang did not trust him. He does not trust anyone. I doubt he trusts his own mother."

"You are the Lord."

Chadas nodded. "The guards are proud of the role they play. They would not allow another to be close to me. I cannot offer him the role he once held. I could not put him in that much danger, but I can offer him a role where we can meet frequently."

"They would not go against your wishes."

They came upon one of the garden's features, a carved wooden dragon whose outstretched wings formed two seats. Chadas guided Alodia to sit with him, though the gardens were the furthest thing from his mind at that moment. "Find him for me," he pleaded and when Alodia nodded, "I need him back." He glanced over his shoulder at the trailing guards. "I need to speak with you. With your help, I will have a reason for my privacy, and it will give us another advantage."

"What do you want?"

"I do not trust any woman the way I trust you. I wish to tell the people I have chosen you to rule Dragonfang at my side. It will give us a reason for privacy and your help with the city would be appreciated."

"How do you mean, at your side?"

"We will announce that we are betrothed. People would surely give us time alone then."

Alodia took his shoulder and turned him to look into his eyes. After a moment she replied, "We will rule Dragonfang together."

They wandered and chatted for hours, lost in thought and memories, and the promise of aa exciting future.

#

An early evening threatened to steal the remaining light. Chadas relaxed in a deep-padded chair enjoying the warmth of the dying fire. The dining hall was empty and his guards, after inspecting the room, had agreed to stand outside each door. A plate holding the remains of his dinner of roasted boar rested on the floor beside him. No candles lit the room. Soon it would be in full darkness. He sprawled, closing his eyes to luxuriate in a feeling of freedom and relaxation.

A soft click roused him. The fire was no more than glowing embers with barely the suggestion of long-lost flame. Darkness had seeped into the hall while he had been dozing. He watched, ready for danger, a knife already in his hand. He only needed to shout and guards would be about him, but he did not feel the need. He could sense no danger.

Another click, more distinct now he was fully awake. He had not moved. Whoever was here had the skills of an assassin but the Guild had no reason to want him dead, not yet. His training heightened his senses and he heard the gentle rub of soft boots on the foot-worn timber. A faint movement, a shadow drifting in the darkness, alerted him to the location of the intruder. He leaned forward to rise when a shadow moved, closer. He saw the shape lean down to the fire and the flicker as a candle took hold of flame. His knife touched the stooped back.

"Who are you?"

An old woman's voice answered simply, "The MaalKeeper."

"Stand slowly. Hold the candle to your face so that I may see it." When she obeyed he saw a much older woman than he expected, face and hands white from lack of sun. Her long hair hung over her shoulders, the gray now almost gone to white, a hag.

She bowed her head and muttered, "My Lord."

"What is your name?"

"I am without name, my Lord." He did not understand. "I am the MaalKeeper, the current one. My name is of no importance." The musty odors of age masked with lavender assaulted his nose.

"What is a MaalKeeper?"

"Your servant, my Lord."

"What does a MaalKeeper do?"

"We keep the maal, my Lord." She spoke as if he should know this.

This woman was fast becoming frustrating but he slipped the knife away. "Put some wood on the fire and bring up a chair" He sat again. This woman offered no danger. When the logs had caught and flickering light surrounded them, he tried again. "What is a maal?"

Her brow rose. "You do not know, do you?" When Chadas shook his head, she explained. "A MaalKeeper is the servant of the Lord. Long ago, we told the maal to all the people, until one Lord decided the maal were for him alone. He declared that the knowledge they held meant little to the people and would aid in his rule. He made us vow to serve only him and his successors. Only Lord Rodnel and Edur knew of the MaalKeepers." She paused. "The maal are the stories of our land and its people, my Lord."

"You remember all these stories?"

She laughed at that. "Yes, my Lord. That is what we are trained to do, though we have aids to help our memories, and the Majick."

Chadas' ears pricked at the mention of Majick, the first he had heard other than from Rata. But all he said was, "My people have been all over this tower. There is no other hall. Where do you hide? And where are these aids?"

"The MaalKeeper's rooms, my Lord." Chadas had never encountered anyone like the woman before him. "Only the MaalKeeper and the Lord know of it, and the MaalKeeper's apprentice."

"I do not know of it."

The woman's face lit with excitement. "Do you wish me to show you, my Lord?"

Chadas felt he could trust her. He glanced to the doors.

"Your guards will not miss you," the MaalKeeper assured him.

The two rose and she led him to the wall beside the hearth. To Chadas' eyes, it was a solid wall of heavy timbers set on end. The carvings were the best he had ever seen. They depicted the mountains, tall and ice-capped. One, in the distance, belched forth smoke and flame. In one corner a sun, like none he had ever seen shone down on the world. He could see every tree and rock. But above them, filling the sky, flew a dragon. It was beautiful. He had admired it often, but only now was he truly appreciating the wonders in the carving.

"Agort," offered the MaalKeeper as she stepped close to the wall.

"I have heard the name."

As he joined her she took his hands, lifting the left to place his thumb against a small round stone at the base of one mountain. The second finger she placed against the trunk of a nearby tree. His right hand she lifted to the top of another mountain and pressed his palm against its ice cap. "Now push," she whispered. "All together." The three pieces of carving retreated the depth of his thumb and he heard the faint click. An irregular opening swung inwards.

He stepped back. "No wonder my people never found this," he said with wonder. "The door is hidden in such exquisite carving."

Inside was a small landing with stairs leading down to the side. The MaalKeeper ushered him in, followed, and shut the door with the gentlest of touches. A faint glow from below allowed him to see as he descended beneath the tower.

The room he entered took his breath away, not for its opulence but for its size. The Guild had found many rooms but none compared with this. The massive beams and posts, each a great tree, were unadorned, purely functional. They were required to support the tower above.

"This room is as big as the dining hall ," he whispered into the space, The MaalKeeper nodded. It held row upon row of shelves. Chadas was silent as he slowly made his way down the room, amazed to see countless beautifully carved statuettes covered with years of dust. There were shells of various colors, carved stones of various shapes and sizes amid many other ornaments. He picked up a stone to study it and immediately felt the tingle in his fingers that ran through his body. He quickly dropped it. Near the entrance, a small table held chisels and other tools.

"Each piece reminds me of a maal. Only the Lords share the knowledge of this, but only the MaalKeepers can use it. It is a clue to the story that earned its carving." She indicated the table. "I am beginning your story. It will be the ChadasMaal." Chadas saw the indistinct shape that seemed to blend into the surrounding air. Only two things were clear to his eye, a dagger at its side and a ring of gold around its head.

"You could not yet have much to tell," Chadas suggested.

"I have a great deal already, my Lord. The story of your childhood, your training with the Guild, becoming an assassin and Ama." Chadas eyes grew wider as she spoke. Now he stared. "It is the task of the MaalKeeper to know everything. All stories must be preserved for the future."

#

Faint sounds filtered into the room. Alodia woke with a start. Was it a nightmare? If so, the cloud of dread still hovered over her. She lay, trying to understand before rolling over. Sulis was not in the bed. Alodia sat up and examined their small room. It was empty. This did not worry her, but somewhere in the back of her mind a voice warned of trouble.

Her thoughts crawled back through time. She could not recall an instance when Sulis woke first, let alone risen and left without disturbing her. Nor could she remember Sulis coming to bed last night. She would have taken the time to wake her even if she were late. Her mind wrestled with this. Finally she accepted that Sulis had slept elsewhere. They were both willing to find other beds if some piece of information could be discovered.

Today she was to meet Chadas to examine the defenses again. It had become a regular occurrence. The cloud of apprehension followed her as she readied herself. Walking to the constructions, she saw that once again Chadas was there before her. After a brief greeting, they began.

As with each inspection their first task was the progress of the moat and the wall. Chadas always enjoyed seeing his vision come to life. Then on to her favorite duty, a review of the garden. With that complete, Chadas decided they should walk through the city. He greeted the people as long-lost friends and she joined him in each of these reunions. It surprised her how much he could learn from the people.

"A good morning to you," offered one man as they passed.

"Good morning Edard, Is your wife feeling better?"

"Yes, my Lord. She should be back at work tomorrow."

"That is good. Tell her I send my best wishes."

"Thank you, my Lord. I will."

Alodia and Chadas moved on. "It is good for the citizens of Dragonfang to see us" Chadas told her. The people, in return, not only accepted their new Lord, he was their friend. It was a pleasant way to pass the day. Still, the cloud of dread followed everywhere she went like a storm ready to crash down on her world.

When she returned to her room that night, Sulis was still absent. The telltale hair she had placed on the door had not been disturbed. The storm moved closer. She knew she would not sleep and sat in the dark, waiting. The small chair was uncomfortable. It would keep her eyes open.

The loud screech of a rooster startled her and the small movement sent a stab of pain up her back. The sudden noise in the quiet of the morning sounded louder than a dragon's howl. Her buttocks ached. Sleep had found her despite her determination. A quick glance proved Sulis was still not in the bed. A storm of worry crashed into the room and left her gasping.

Why did it affect her like this? Her heart and mind then began to argue which only confused her more. The storm raged around her, leaving her drenched in a rain of sweat while the cold winds of logic numbed her.

She began to examine the feelings that fought inside her. She loved Sulis and had done since their childhood. They had grown intimate yet that only served to drive them apart in many ways. She knew this confusion came from a dark place where she felt threatened by the woman she loved.

Her mind screamed to be heard. You are better to be free of her, but her heart still ached. Joy, pain and fear battled for supremacy.

Her head offered her heart its sympathy, but warned that love was a dangerous emotion.

#

Chadas came to the dining room often. He enjoyed talking with the old MaalKeeper. He told his guards this was a place he could be alone to think. They accepted this knowing that, standing at each door, no one would get past. They allowed him his time undisturbed. Today he did not wait. He went straight to the wall, pressed the secret mechanism, and stepped through the hidden doorway. Almost at the bottom, he wondered if he should have brought a candle, but that would have raised suspicions among the guards. He trusted his memory and the feeling of safety he had with each step.

The MaalKeeper looked up from her work. "My Lord?" she asked.

Chadas wanted to ask about the Majick but he was not ready for that yet. Instead, he asked, "The name of the city, Dragonfang. The sea is Dragonbite. There are tapestries of dragons all about the tower yet no one has ever seen one. Are dragons real?"

To his surprise, the MaalKeeper laughed, a cackle that rose from her feet to shake through her sunken frame. Then she disappeared among the shelves and returned with a chair. When Chadas was seated, she took her seat, stretched, and spoke. "Somewhere in there," his arm waved to take in the rows of shelves, " is an ancient relic of the AgortMaal. It is the first story a child learns if they are to train to become the MaalKeeper. I do not need to hold it to remember the tale."

"Wait," interrupted Chadas. "You say you learned this tale as a child. I have heard you speak of an apprentice. When is a child ready to train as a MaalKeeper?"

"The age varies. I was eight years old but my apprentice was only six. When a child begins to understand and remember the maal, and feels the Majick of the relics, they are ready. My apprentice is now a young woman. Soon she will be ready to take my place and I will return to the city to live the last of my days."

"So, you will cease to be a MaalKeeper?"

"I will always be a MaalKeeper, but I will not be the MaalKeeper.

Chadas nodded, not really understanding.

So, becoming a MaalKeeper was similar to becoming Ama of the Guild, but more secret. "And this young woman will live their life hidden from the world?" he asked.

The MaalKeeper smiled. "Until the next is ready to take her place, just as I did, and many before me." Chadas stared. "But you wish to know about dragons?" Chadas nodded.

"The spirits have given us this story to tell. They called it the AgortMaal, the story of Agort, a memory of time long past." She took a deep breath. "In a time before men walked on the world, before all the things we know, the world was flat."

Chadas imagined the mountains beyond the stone walls. He thought they had always been there.

"Far to the north, in the bleakness of the ice, lives the dragon Agort. She is a creature of Majick. When Agort walks, it was on four huge clawed legs, and when she flies it was with wings so massive they blocked out the sky. Agort's scales of gold and silver glisten and ripple as she takes each mighty breath, her red tongue whips through the air, tasting it. Her tail was as long as a mountain is tall. She was big. She was strong. But she was alone."

Chadas sat listening intently, totally captured by the image the MaalKeeper created.

"So long ago as to be lost in time, Agort decided that she needed children to share her world. She flew south to where the world was not frozen, and there she scratched at the ground to build a nest large enough to hold her eggs and when it was ready she carefully laid her eggs, five of them, in the nest and covered it. She built another nest, and another. In each, she placed her eggs, sometimes four or five to a nest while others held as many as twelve eggs or more. Nest after nest she built until the world was covered in her work.

"When she was finished she flew into the air and surveyed her work. She could see more land to the south where large animals wandered. Fearing the animals would come for her eggs and eat them before her children were born, Agort settled on the land south of her nests. With one great bite, she ate the rock and ground and spat it far out into the Golden Ocean. The sea rushed to fill the bite blocking passage from the south and in this way Agort protected her eggs. Only one small strip of land remained. Connecting south and north. This was far to the west on the shores of the Spiritwater, in the darkness where the sun rested at night. Agort returned to her world of ice to await the birth of her children. But one of her teeth broke off and stands as a reminder of her power. It rises out of the new sea to stand tall, not far from the shore. It is for this that our city found its name.

"Agort waited while men came to the world to scratch their lives around the edges of her nests. She saw them but was not worried as they did not attempt to harm her nests, structures that towered so far above the men that they appeared to reach the sky. The men called her nests mountains and the scratches she had made in the ground valleys.

"Occasionally an egg would hatch and the young dragon would blow away part of the nest with its newfound breath of fire. The flames would push the rock aside, much of it running molten down the side of the nest while more was flung into the air as rock and dust and smoke. The young dragon would emerge from the nest hidden in the cloud and race north in answer to Agort's call. Eventually, the trembling of its escape would settle until once again the nest was quiet.

"This is how the mountains were born and if a man would see these moments and if his eyes were fast enough he could glimpse the birth of a dragon. If his ears were good enough he could listen and he would hear the dragons breathing within. This is the maal of Agort, given to us by the spirits."

Chadas remained silent, his mind lost in the hidden mountains.

#

Work on the gardens had been completed and all that remained was for the gardeners to maintain them. They had risen to his challenge and while small, a person could easily become lost in its maze of pathways. The MaalKeeper's secret room was where he went to learn. The gardens were where he came to think. He sat on the bench in one of the many alcoves the gardeners had created. He needed answers to questions that chased each other through his mind. Did he possess the Majick? Could he learn to use it? What could it do? Other questions tried to push them aside. Why was Rata taking such interest in him? What should he do? That last question ruled all others.

The swish of drawn swords and the harsh words of his guards dragged him from his reverie. "It is Alodia," he heard his sister call. "I need to speak with the Lord." The guards were always close but pockets of shrubs and small trees hid them while the scents of assorted flowers masked their odor.

"Let her come," he called.

Soon, Alodia appeared from around a corner. He slid along and invited her to sit. Behind them, a young maple stretched its infant limbs, protecting them beneath a natural pergola. A star magnolia was beginning its crawl up the new trunk, enhancing the surrounding hues of daphne, witch hazel, and pussy willow. It was a place Chadas could enjoy. He closed his eyes again and allowed the heady scents to take him to a faraway private sanctuary.

Alodia's voice intruded on this peace.

"What?" he asked.

"I was trying to tell you, Sulis is missing." Chadas tried again to return to his peace. "She has not returned in three days."

He tried to ignore her but his sister's voice was growing more desperate, and with it, more high pitched. He would not find his peace again until she was gone. "So?" he asked.

"I am worried for her."

Chadas opened his eyes and twisted to look into her face. Their noses were almost touching. "The last time you spoke to me of Sulis, you were concerned that she was controlling you. You were unhappy."

"I know. She is controlling but she is my friend and I miss her. We are also an excellent team for the Guild," she added hopefully.

"She may have tired of the friendship and gone away."

"She would not have me worry. She is strong and determined, but she is also caring. If she wished to leave, she would tell me."

"Maybe she found someone else."

"Again, I would be told."

Carefully, Chadas raised another possibility. "She could have been discovered stealing information. She may have died at the hands of someone she was spying on."

"She was too careful for that."

"But why do you concern yourself? If she made you unhappy, you are better off without her."

"In these last three days, I have come to learn how much I care. Will you help me find her?"

Chadas nodded. "If she can be found, I will find her for you."

"Thank you." Alodia rose and left the garden. Chadas closed his eyes and sat back to try and recapture the sweet comfort of the garden. He knew he would not, just as he knew he would send no one in search of Sulis.

# 21 A TALE OF TRUTH

The following morning, Chadas wandered silently, with Alodia trailing. Eventually, he sat on the ornate dragon bench beneath an arch of iron his gardeners had commissioned from the blacksmith. He patted the seat, but he did not speak. His stare took in the beautifully pruned bushes, the young trees, and the carpet of color. Beside him, a vine crawled up the arch, its scented yellow flowers brilliant in the evening light. He stared, but he did not see any of these things. His mind ignored his vision to concentrate on what he should say.

"What do you know of Sulis?" he asked.

"I have known her since she was seven. I doubt there is anything I could learn of her that would surprise me."

"What do you know of the time before she joined us?" Chadas pressed. Alodia concentrated, finally realizing Sulis had told her nothing of her life before her training began. She turned to her brother and waited. "Do you know she is one of only two people in the Guild who cannot claim to be descended from Lord Masima?"

Alodia's eyes widened. "But the Guild is only for Masima's people."

A tired smile twitched at Chadas' lips. "Not true." His sister had the sense not to speak. "Sulis was secretly sponsored to join us. Her heritage may not be pure, but we have never told her this. Only if she had children to another outside the Guild would she find out because her children would not carry the blood of Masima."

"But..."

"Allow me to tell you the story of Sulis, the Sulis you do not know. Her mother was a prostitute in the fishing quarter. She died years ago. There is no way of knowing who fathered her." Alodia listened quietly.

"Sulis suffered many beatings from her mother's clients who disliked a young girl interrupting their pleasure. Others thought it might be enjoyable if she joined them, and her mother obliged them."

"That would explain some of her moods," Alodia suggested. Chadas only nodded.

"After one brutal beating, Sulis was left almost dead. An important member of the Guild knew her and had realized her intelligence. He spirited Sulis away. When she was well, we told her she was one of us, and her training began. That is how she came to meet you."

Alodia shook her head. "Poor Sulis."

"Her life before the guild left her with many scars that time could not heal."

A quiet followed as each became lost in their thoughts. "Our father was not shy in giving beatings. I can understand why she said nothing," Alodia pointed out. "Can we find her?"

Chadas ignored her question and instead asked, "Did you tell her of our family?"

"I told her our father was a drunk."

Chadas nodded. "Did you tell her about me?" After some thought, Alodia shook her head. "And mother?" Chadas asked.

"Yes, I spoke about her often. I missed her." When Chadas did not speak, she asked, "Why?"

"Sulis was jealous of your family life."

"But our father…"

"She did not know her father, and the men she knew mistreated her. Her mother did not want her, and hearing about our mother and family, things she never knew or understood, made her wish for more."

While Alodia absorbed this information, Chadas asked, "Who told you of our father's wager?"

Alodia only needed to think for a moment before answering, "Sulis."

"She lied."

Alodia's hand went to her mouth. "Why?"

"Because you were the closest thing she had to a family, and she did not wish to share you."

Alodia was afraid of the answer before she asked, "Who killed our family?"

"Sulis." Despite anticipating his reply, Alodia was stunned into silence. "It was almost a year after I joined the Guild. You and Sulis would have begun your training with weapons. She saw her actions as a way of keeping you to herself."

A long, tense silence followed, only to be broken by Alodia's voice. "I will pay for the Guild to find her, and I will pay for the assassin."

"You will not pay," her brother told her. "There is no need." Alodia's brow creased, and her eyes squinted as she waited for her brother's brutal words. "Sulis will not be found. Her spirit has moved on, and her body is no more. She will not be missed."

Alodia sat silent but emotions boiled within her, emotions that would take time to unravel. Sulis, her friend, her lover, the murderer of her family. Eventually she decided Sulis would be missed, if only by her.

# 22 MAAL AND MAJICK

Weeks passed.

Chadas worked with the women of Majick but nothing seemed able to unlock the powers he had been told hid within him.

Chadas slept uneasily. Since he had last seen her, Rata's words followed him like a lost dog. If what she told him was true, the problem was with him and he would need to face the fact that he could not blame someone else. He had always thought of the Majick as a children's story, something told at bedtime but never believed. That was what his mind held to. He had never truly believed in the spirits either but Rata convinced him otherwise. If she told the truth, how was he to convince himself?

That night, he sought out the MaalKeeper again. "I need your help," he began.

The MaalKeeper listened in silence. When he had finished, Chadas asked, "Can you tell me any stories of the Majick? Can you tell me anything to help me accept it?"

The old woman considered his request. "Come back tomorrow night. I am sure there are some, there are many maal from early times. My apprentice and I will look."

The next evening Chadas climbed down the stairs once more. The MaalKeeper was expecting him and waited with a smile creasing her ancient face. "We have found two maal that speak of the Majick," she gushed. "No one has heard them in my memory." A young woman stood at her side. This was the first time he had seen the apprentice, but he had been distracted by the news they had found what he wanted. The apprentice held a tray with two objects on it, one a yellow gem cut in the shape of a sunburst and the other a gray stone vial with a woman's face carved on it.

"Bring them to the Dining Hall, both of you. We will sit, and you can tell me the memories they hold." Excitement made his words gallop, but then he remembered and thought he should warn them. "There are others waiting in the hall that I wish you to meet."

#

After overcoming their reluctance or surprise, they followed him back up to the Dining Hall. As Chadas expected, no candles burned but he could hear their breathing of the group of women. One of the women moved about the room with a taper bringing flickering candle light to the room. The women of Majick were about to meet the MaalKeeper and her apprentice, who she introduced as Matilda.

They sat at the large table usually kept for the Lord and his family. Matilda gently sat the tray before them. "These objects contain the past. Within them are images placed there by the Majick. Those who are sensitive to the Majick are able to see them."

"May I?" Korra asked as she delicately reached forward to touch the nearest, the gem. Images flashed through her mind until she pulled her hand away.

The MaalKeeper's brow rose. "You see them. How long have you had the gift?"

Chadas was impatient for the story but held himself. "All these women have the gift," he told her." The MaalKeeper looked slowly to each of them.

"This is an ancient token. Reaching out, she took the golden gem and wrapped it in her palms." When everyone was ready, the MaalKeeper began to recite.

"Listen to the words of the GodsMaal, passed from the spirits to Awyn, the first MaalKeeper. Awyn passed it through the generations until it was committed to this gem by Eldric.

Matilda sat wide-eyed with jaws gaping. The MaalKeeper raised her head and stared.

"What is wrong?" Chadas asked when the silence had grown. The MaalKeeper opened her clasped hands.

"In all my life, I never expected to hold a maal made by Eldric."

"Who was he?"

"Eldric was the seventh Maalkeeper of Dragonfang. It was he who learned how the Majick could be called on to put the images into a token. More than that, this is a story told by Awyn." When she said the word Awyn, her voice took on a tone of pure trembling awe.

"Awyn was the first MaalKeeper, from the days before Lord Masima," Matilda explained. "Awyn was here even before the first stone of Dragonfang."

The MaalKeeper composed herself, closed her hands on the gem, and continued to recite.

"In the days before time, and long forgotten, there lived only the Majick. The Majick gave birth to the six worlds that are one world. They gave these worlds for the Great Ones to enjoy. Though the Great Ones could move with ease between the worlds, three chose Tatlo, our world, for their home. These were Raiki, Foehn, and Agort. They filled the world with trees and grasses. They created the animals to wander the land and fish to swim in the sea. They scattered the skies with clouds. But their grandest achievement was to fill the night with stars to celebrate their new home."

"Agort?" asked Chadas. "The dragon?"

The MaalKeeper looked up. "Maybe, remember this is the first time I have heard this Maal, but I know of no other Agort." She returned to the story.

"Raiki wished for a world of his own. He convinced Foehn they should divide this new place among them. 'The rocks and trees are strongest,' he told them. 'Since I am the strongest, I should be God of the land and all things on it.' Foehn added that because she loved the skies, she would be God of the air. Agort can be God of the seas, Raiki decided, but Agort told them she did not desire the sea, and she did not wish to be a God.

"Raiki stamped a foot and shook the ground with such force that in places, the ground cracked. Foehn brought the winds down upon Agort, who stood quietly and accepted their anger. Without her reaction, the Great Gods settled and asked why she would not be one of them.

"Agort explained. 'I am not a God. I do not wish to rule a world.'

"Foehn understood, but Raiki raged. 'If you do not wish to be one with us,' he declared, 'then you are not welcome in my world.'

"Agort reminded, 'I can fly. I will live in the clouds.'

"'No,' corrected Foehn. 'That is my world.'

"'There is a land to the north where no trees grow and no animals walk. Ice covers the rock. There I will live as a being of both the land and the air.' It was agreed. And so, Agort the dragon came to the Northice Bleak. The Majick was happy, and the Great Gods were satisfied.

"Raiki and Foehn had a problem, neither was interested in the sea. 'If there are no Gods to be found, then we have no choice but to make one,' boomed Raiki. And so Foehn found herself with child. Many years later, for the life of a Great God cannot be measured by the lives of man, Sha was born.

"Sha loved the sea. He would swim and frolic all day in the waves. He loved to watch the fishes and delighted in the colors of the corals and sands. As he grew older, he was spending more time in the sea than on land. He was the son of two Great Gods, and the Majick flowed through him like water in a river. He began changing his shape to better play in his new world until the day came when he would not leave. He was home.

As the MaalKeeper finished, the hush remained over the room. They knew the maal had ended, but they hoped for more.

#

While the maal had been interesting, it gave Chadas no insight into finding the Majick. He sat, lost in thought as the sun gem was returned to the tray.

"Would you like to hear the other one?" the MaalKeeper asked, interrupting his pondering. Chadas wanted to hear it though he believed it would get him no closer to understanding the Majick. He nodded. "This is the EevaMaal. Again, I have not held this token, but I have heard of Eeva in other Maal. She was a woman of Majick."

"Go on," Chadas instructed, hope entering his body.

"This is the maal of Eeva. It is her tale as told to her brother, Awyn. It is how she came to find the Majick."

Chadas came upright. Was this the story he sought? He was sure it was.

"Eeva was a young girl of only nine summers when Ixaka's tribe found her. Warriors hunted her and her brothers and sisters. During the chase, the children escaped, but they had become separated. When Eeva saw three of our siblings taken by a new tribe, she determined to save them, though she was one against hundreds. She was a bold child, but it was not enough. She was captured.

"Though they were not yet all together, Ixaka and his people adopted the children. Even so, Eeva's boldness constantly found her facing Ixaka for punishment. Soon the time came when Eeva must grow up. Her new family tired of her rash behavior. She was taken by Flet, Ixaka's mate, to the place of growing. There she would meet her future.

A large, flat rock projected from the side of the mountain. It was about as high as three men above the ground, the place of growing.

"Flet told Eeva to gather two handfuls of red bark from the spirit tree and scrapings of yellowrock. With this and a flint, she was to climb to the rock. There she would build a small fire. The smoke would take her to discover her future."

Chadas was listening intently.

"When Eeva put the flint to the bark and struck it with her knife, the yellowrock flared and flashed her eyes. For a moment, she could see nothing. As her vision cleared, she was no longer on the rock. Instead, she floated on a cloud. She was impressed by what she saw, though she knew it could only be her imagination. Around her floated more cloud and beyond that even more. She did not know how she came to understand this, but she knew it within her body and mind. Above her, the sky was white, filled with white stars. Beside her, a white sun shone brightly."

Chadas recognized the dream.

The spirits had taken Eeva to the spirit world to teach her the Majick. They gave her the path to her future, though they would not say what that future held. Her growing took many days. But when she returned to her world, barely a morning had passed.

"Eeva offered this as a guide to others, to help them accept their growing. She would never speak of her time in the spirit world. She did, however, say that each person faces a different growing, and each must find their own understanding.

"So says the EevaMaal."

No one spoke.

#

Chadas could not sleep. His mind would not allow it. He expected Rata to appear to tell him again of her disappointment. She did not. But questions circled in his head like birds of death. What had he learned? Could the women of Majick help. Did the maal offer an answer? The women he had gathered told him the Majick would show itself when he was ready, but they did not know how he could summon it. They did not know how they did it themselves. Before he knew it, the sun had brought the new day, and he had nothing to show for his worries.

It was a day that provided few distractions. People left him to dwell on his mood, and those that approached did so with caution. He walked the streets of Dragonfang seeking something without knowing what. His personal guard trailed as far back as they dared. Somehow he stumbled into the marketplace, the stalls where his journey began. Was he meant to be here? Did the Majick lead him here, or was this merely coincidence? Could the answer be here?

He wandered among the many stalls. Some provided fish and other bounties of the sea. Others sold fruits and vegetables, while a few offered clothing, boots, dyes, and similar items. In one of these, he saw a cloak. It was well made and dark green in color, with paler green stitching on its edges. It had aged, worn from rain and partly eaten by rats but he remembered it. Looking closer, he found the secret pocket where he had once kept his coins. A smile touched his lips and grew. Soon he was laughing loudly while the stall holder watched on nervously. His guards rushed closer.

"How much?" he eventually asked.

"My Lord, it is yours. I will take nothing from you."

"No, no," laughed Chadas. He looked again. "There is blood on it."

"I will have it washed for you, my Lord."

"No, I do not wish that. I prefer it as it is."

"What price do you have on it?" The man seemed confused.

"Three coppers, my Lord," the stall keeper stammered, "but I will take two."

Chadas opened his money bag. and withdrew a coin. "It is worth a silver to me as it is." He passed over the shiny new coin and handed the cape to one of his guards to carry. Everyone stared as he moved to the next stall.

Further along, he spied a stall filled with herbs. On the table, he saw a strange powder in a small bowl. "What is this?" he asked.

"It is ground yellowroot, my Lord. Some say it will help a man in bed."

Chadas laughed again. "Why would a man need that? All he needs is a pretty girl. She will do the rest for him." He was about to walk on when he stopped. Was this the clue he needed? He felt it was. "Is it also known as yellowrock?" he asked.

"No, my Lord. I have no use for yellowrock. But I know it is in the mountains. It looks like veins of color through the dark rock."

"Do you know where to find it?"

"No, my Lord, but I have spoken with those who have seen it. They say it is a long way into the valley behind the city. Would you have me look for it?."

"No, it is all right. I heard of it and was curious."

Chadas had found his answer. He called his guard close. "Prepare the horses in the morning. We will be going riding in the mountains at sunrise."

Suddenly the lack of sleep caught up, but he felt he could now rest. They returned to the tower, knowing tomorrow would be a full day.

#

The following morning, Chadas was dressed and ready before Tulong arrived to wake him. He had been wondering how Alodia was handling the loss of another person from her life. Now she informed him that she was with child. Did she make the child to hide her loss? He had said nothing when she told him, and that angered her. He had left her sitting in the garden.

"I am going riding today." Tulong's impassive face and stony mask offered no comment to his words. "I do not know when I will return. It may be today, or it may be days. Find Alodia. She will take care of anything in my absence, and you will take care of her."

"Yes, my Lord."

Dressed in dark green riding clothes, his sword bouncing at his hip and his new stiletto in the pocket in his boot, Chadas left his rooms to join his guards in the courtyard. His favorite horse, a tall black stallion, stood saddled and ready, a stable boy holding its reins. As he approached, the horse raised its head and stared, unafraid.

Chadas approached and rubbed its neck. "In the morning light you appear much more than a horse," he whispered. You hold secrets and watch the world. You are more like a raven, a careful and wise creature. That should be your name. Good morning Raven," he laughed as he rubbed the big horse's neck. "Are you ready for a ride?" He mounted and waited as his guards settled themselves into their saddles. They rode out of the tower, and through the city. Outside the wall, Chadas felt a freedom come over him and grinned at the thought of Alodia with child and caring for his city. "We will go up the valley." It was the first they knew of his destination, but with their help he would find the mountain with the protruding rock.

They rode all day.

With night approaching, Chadas ordered his guards to prepare a camp. There was water in the small river that ran down the valley and they still carried enough food. Tomorrow, if he was still searching, they would take time to hunt in the afternoon.

After three days of riding and searching the valleys, he decided it was time to return to Dragonfang. The place of growing did not wish to be found.

As the third night grew closer and his guards were again preparing their camp, Chadas decided he needed solitude. He needed time to think, and a place beneath the mountains should provide that. He began to explore. This part of the valley was quite flat, a surprising feature. But not far away, a mountain grew up into the clouds. It almost hurt his neck trying to glimpse its peak. The power of it drew him closer, though he was wandering further from the camp than he planned.

Other peaks cast their shadows into the valleys, but this magnificent mountain spread its shade over them. To Chadas, this was beauty. His tower and the delights of the city held no appeal. They were the things of man. In his mind, even the sea was a lifeless expanse of emptiness. This mountain, however, possessed dominance and power over its world. It was all the things he wanted for himself.

It was then he noticed the scar. Even such a perfect thing can be damaged, it seemed to say. A large slab of rock lay on the ground. Chadas walked closer to investigate. It was as he suspected. It had fallen, leaving the mountain broken. Imagining the slab attached above, he realized what he had found, the place of growing. But would the spirits still come now it was broken?

Chadas searched, and to his surprise, he found a seam of yellowrock and a stand of trees he thought matched those of the Maal. He did not need to climb the mountain. Instead he made his way onto the rock slab and prepared his fire. He had no flint, and did not want to return to camp to retrieve one, but drew his dagger and soon discovered that striking it on the rock could produce a spark. After several attempts, the yellowrock flared and the bark began to burn. Smoke engulfed him.

As the smoke drifted away on the wind, Chadas was startled to see a face looking back into his own. "He is ready," the woman said, to be echoed by others around him. He turned slowly and counted five people sitting on the rock with him.

"Why do you come to this place?" one woman asked.

"To learn."

"What do you wish to learn?" asked a man and Chadas twisted to face him.

"The Majick."

"Why?" asked another man on his other side. Again Chadas twisted.

Chadas was confused by the question. "Because I was told I must," he answered.

The spirits looked to each other until a young woman behind him suggested, "Look around you."

Chadas did as instructed. The near-by trees were not the ones where he had collected the bark, yet he could see that in some way they were. But he had never seen trees of gold and blue, and he could see the yellow air that danced around them.

"Come and see," suggested a third woman, and as Chadas watched she changed to become a blue dragon, scales glistening with the unseen reflection of a thousand candles. "I am Ugu," she introduced.

"How can I come with you? I am not a dragon."

"You are what you wish yourself to be," the first woman told him.

Chadas imagined himself as a dragon, and suddenly he was rising on massive purple wings. Ugu flew into the sky and Chadas followed. Flying seemed as natural as walking in his imagination, and he was enjoying the experience.

Below, he saw the land he knew, but in colors he did not recognize, red grasses studded with blue rocks, and he could even see the yellow wind. The massive peak that had drawn his attention stretched skyward in brilliant hues of pink splendor and capped in thick green ice. The two dragons flew side by side toward the orange sea. On its shores sat the gray smudge of Dragonfang, but the city was not so much gray as colorless. Not everything about it was drab. He sensed, rather than saw, the glowing white orb within the tower.

"That is the Majick of the ones who teach," Ugu told him.

They flew out over the sea and above the land beyond. Ugu led him in a circle out over a world of water and back to the mountains. High over the peaks and down through the valleys they soared, and north to a place where the world was buried beneath a blanket of ice. In all these places, the colors amazed him.

Eventually, Ugu settled back on the rock where their journey began. He came to rest beside her. The other spirits had gone. He took his old form again and Ugu became the woman once more. "It is time for me to go," she told him.

"But I thought you were going to show me the Majick."

"All that you have seen is Majick, and there is Majick in all that you see."

"But how do I use it?" he pleaded.

"You must accept the Majick and appreciate it before you can use it."

Chadas felt disappointment engulf him. "Can you show me nothing?"

Ugu thought for a moment, or was she asking the other spirits. Finally, she nodded. "The fire you started on the rock still burns. Find it." Chadas looked down. "Not with your eyes. Use your mind." Chadas tried again, Stretching his mind, he found the small flame still flickering. "Good," Ugu complimented. "Now feel the warmth it offers. Draw some of that warmth into your body." Chadas reached around until he felt the comforting heat of the little fire. He drank it in and he felt his skin begin to burn. "Stop," Ugu yelled in his mind, and Chadas released his hold on the flames.

"If you draw in too much, the body you wear cannot hold it. It will perish." She pointed. "See that tuft of grass, remember it. Now try again. Find the fire and absorb its warmth, and as you do, direct that heat to the tuft of grass." Chadas tried again, doing as Ugu instructed, and suddenly the grass burst into flame.

"Now you have used the Majick," Ugu stated. "I must go."

Chadas was still staring at the burning grass when Ugu vanished. Around him the world had returned to the colors he recognized.

It was time to return to the camp, and tomorrow, Dragonfang.

# 23 FARTOWN

Far to the south, beyond even the imagination of Dragonfang, slumbering on the western edges of Langit, rests the little fishing village of Fartown. The simple cottages are all brightly colored with large, inviting windows and shingled roofs, the streets wide and clean. The town has little structure and mostly, Fartown resembles houses scattered over the rise and fall of the land as if tossed out by one of the Gods.

Pigfish Bay lies on the northern flank of the town though it is more of a large, salty lake connected by a narrow channel to the unending expanse of Spiritwater. The unfortunate name for such a beautiful calm body of water surrounded by trees and the town derives from the fish that can be caught there. Smoked pigfish is a prized delicacy throughout Langit and the small fishing village profited from their catch. Traders buy the fish and carry the catch to larger markets but they bring exotic goods to Fartown on their return. One of the most sought-after is salt. Salted pigfish is something everyone must experience at least once before the spirits call them.

Eight miles south of the village is the Bellin farm, run by Torne Bellin whose father had died two years before. He lived here with his family, his wife Shayla, his mother and his sister. Still only twenty, he has much to learn about farm management, but it had always been a good farm.

Torne was not working today, his first day off in two years. Instead, he paced back and forth in front of the house, his black dog trailing his every step. He stopped and turned to the house when he heard the piercing scream inside. He wanted to race in but his mother would have none of his meddling.

The screams had been tearing at his heart for the last hour, though it felt longer, and they would continue. He began to pace once more.

The door opened and his sister came out to join him. "It is over," she said.

The One of Anim was pleased.

The collective of Lima was pleased.

Torne tried to read her face but could not. "Shayla?" he asked.

"Your wife is in need of rest, but she is fine." Mavie smiled. "And you have two new baby girls."

"Two?"

Mavie nodded. "Twins, and both are healthy and hungry. Shayla wishes to name them Hope and Faith, if you agree."

"Hope and Faith? I have twin daughters?" His face split in a grin that would not go away. He ran to hug his sister then yelled at the top of his voice, "I have twin daughters."

# 24 CHADAS' VISION

Chadas checked his preparations.

The tables were laid out and waiting. There was plenty of mead and ale. The Great hall had been cleaned and he had been to the kitchens where Ezma had prepared a fine feast. All that was missing were his guests. The first to arrive were Dyfed and Edyth. Five other members of the House of Meeya trailed behind. Chadas was glad to see that Isen was one of them.

"I bid welcome to the House of the Beggars," Chadas began. "Tulong will provide you with anything you wish to drink while we await the others." Tulong brought a tray of goblets as he spoke. "As you see, Alodia will be joining us, but she is here as my guest, and will not represent your House today." Eyes turned to Alodia but no one objected.

They did not wait long before Kendric and Moire led in four unassuming men and women, but Chadas knew every one of them was a successful assassin. Luden and Preada followed them, leading their guests.

"Good, we are all here." Then in a louder voice, he called, "Bring out the food. There will be plenty of time to talk when our bellies are full."

Servants entered with trays laden with vegetables, and for each there was a tray of meat. Venison, rabbit, chicken, along with bread, cheese and other delicacies. The Great Hall was far to large for this gathering, but this did not concern Chadas. Fires burned in the hearths and the posts that held the floor above seemed to dance with the carvings of squirrels and dragons, trees and birds. Most ate carefully and drank little, for they still did not know what Chadas would ask of them. But they knew he could do nothing without them.

Finally, Chadas called for their attention and silence settled over the Hall. "You all know why we are here," he began, but looking about at the blank stares, he was surprised. "I am sorry. I did not explain because I thought you would understand." He waited, but no one replied.

"The Lords have always ruled Dragonfang as they saw fit," he explained. "Lord Rodnel was a good Lord, the best we have seen in many years. He cared for this city. Edur was nothing like his father and Dragonfang would have suffered for long after his rule." This time, nods of agreement met his words.

"Dragonfang has seen many good Lords, and there are many who were worse than Edur could have been. I hope to be remembered as a good Lord, but I cannot speak for those that follow me, unless we make changes to protect this city from those who would destroy it."

"How can we do that?" Preada asked.

"Through the times of all the good and bad Lords, what is it that remained constant?" Blank stares waited for his answer. "The Guild," he laughed. "Through all the years the Guild has remained strong. Why?"

"We were not one person," Kendric answered. "We worked together and each did what they were best at."

"Exactly," exclaimed a jubilant Chadas. "We only did what we did best. A Lord will run this city much better if he has the best people for each task." The blank expressions were replaced by curious faces. "Why does the Guild operate so well?" Before anyone could answer, he continued, "Because an Ama is not a Lord, and he does not try to be."

Chadas took a moment to smile. "The Guild has the structure that is ready to run this city. We should have seen this before. Together we will make Dragonfang great. You made me Ama, then the new Lord, but you are my power. Each of the Houses has skills that are needed. The Guild should be running Dragonfang."

Everyone appeared surprised though they secretly agreed. They had given him the Lordship, and he seemed to be passing it back to them. Behind Chadas, Alodia smiled.

"I proposed that the Houses use their trained abilities to run Dragonfang. That is working well, but we must be organized. The people must see and respect their Council. Each House will nominate two of their members to sit on the Council of Dragonfang and meet with the other Houses and make decisions for the city. That is right, you cannot be seen as only being of the Guild, we must be of the city. As Lord, I will also be there. My task will be to settle any disputes and see that the people follow you."

A babble followed as each House wished to be heard.

"I know you currently have two leaders for each House, and I do not wish to change that. I am only suggesting that they meet regularly with the other Houses to decide what needs to be done. When any of you are unable to fulfil your duties, your House will elect a new member. I, or the future Ama, will sit on the Council and we will manage this city together."

Everyone quickly agreed, knowing they would wield as much power as they had before, and more.

"I would like to make one change," Chadas added. "I would add another to the Council." All eyes turned to Alodia. He could read their thoughts. They believed he was giving the balance of power to the Beggars and were ready to object. "No, not Alodia," he laughed. "I think it is time for the House of Alard to be represented, only with one seat, but two when they grow strong enough." No one objected. He did not wish to alter anything for they all knew that House Alard would never grow as strong as them. "Good. The Council of Dragonfang is formed."

He then gave them his final surprise. "As second to the Lord, I name Alodia."

His sister smiled.

#

After the meeting, the leaders of the Houses left, chatting among themselves, to determine how they would achieve what was asked of them. Alodia began to speak, but Chadas signaled her for silence. Instead, he invited her for a stroll in the garden.

They wandered aimlessly between blooms of white, yellow and red, ending when they reached the place Chadas felt was the most secure from prying ears, his little grotto bench.

Alodia lowered her head so that no one could read her lips. "What are you doing?" she asked.

"I am trying to be a good Lord."

"But you have given away much of your power to the Houses."

"I have given away nothing," Chadas replied. "All the tasks I handed out need to be done. I would much rather the Guild perform those duties than leave them to Lord Rodnel's people. If any of his staff are good enough, I would expect the Houses to make use of them."

"If they know you are not needed, they could take your position away."

Chadas smiled. "They will not. Think about it. Until today, they may have thought of it. Now, they believe the power is with the Guild. They see me as no more than a figure head."

"But that is the truth."

Chadas laughed. "It may seem so, but no one has considered the truth."

"And what is that?"

"Today, the Guild died."

Alodia's eyes widened to become great orbs in her face. "How? What have you done? Have you betrayed the Guild?"

"I have done nothing, other than see the future," he assured her. If his sister could not understand, he doubted anyone else would. He decided to explain. "The Guild has always been strong, not because of Lord Masima or any other person. It was strong because it remained secret. Now Dragonfang is ruled by a Guild Lord and the Guild takes up key positions in the city. The people will soon learn to live with us and see what we do. Very quickly, all the positions the Houses took on today will be staffed by ordinary citizens as well as Guild members. The Guild will grow weaker and die. Meanwhile, the Lord will be seen by everyone as the man who brought change and the rightful ruler of Dragonfang."

"I am loyal to the Guild," Alodia warned.

"And the Guild will be around for years to come, but it is inevitable that its power will weaken by mixing with the people of the city. I am not causing it harm, I only see what will occur."

Alodia studied him for a few moments before nodding. "So, the people of Dragonfang will achieve what no Lord has ever dared."

"With our members blending into the city, all will become part of the Guild in time. Dragonfang will be one people, and all will be of Masima's blood. It will happen but the Guild will be forgotten. There will only be Dragonfang," Chadas stated.

# 25 EXPANSION

Chadas rode through the streets of Dragonfang. His large black stallion bumped walls and pushed people aside as it tried to navigate the narrow streets. Behind him, Alodia and the grey mare he had given her suffered the same troubles. In his mind, Chadas knew this was not good, if anyone wished him harm, this was their chance to achieve their goals.

"Dragonfang is becoming too crowded," he called back over his shoulder. He knew the whole city was not like this. Some areas were not too over-packed, but this close to the gates, it was congested.

"It would be fine if we did not have so many people," Alodia laughed.

"And I need these people if this is to become the strongest city in Lilim."

They rode on quietly, eventually passing through the gate and out of the crowded city. Together they stopped to admire the scene beyond. Tall mountains climbed into the sky, and even now with the warmer days showing off their hard black rock, there was still touches of white at their peaks. Large tracts of open ground surrounded the wall, protecting it from the trees ahead.

Chadas swung from his mount and Alodia followed suit. Side by side they led them as they walked to the trees. Chadas' personal guard followed, at a discreet distance. At the tree line, they both turned. The city wall with its closely packed rocks and clay mortar formed an imposing barrier. Occasionally he saw movement as a guard walked along its top, checking all was well. Beyond the city, the gray sea glistened like stars in the daytime.

"What are you thinking?" Alodia asked after a drawn-out silence. Chadas did not reply. He was too deep in thought. Eventually, he mounted the horse and suggested, "We should get back."

His sister joined him and they rode in silence. She did not wish to interrupt his thoughts, or his mood, if that is what it was. With the gates close, Chadas finally spoke. "I want you to find me a good map-maker, someone you trust. Bring him to my rooms, and then pass the word that I am calling the Council to a special meeting. We will meet in three days. You chose the time."

When Alodia arrived with the map-maker, Chadas was waiting. "This is Archerd," she introduced. The Lord did not check his skill or discretion. His sister would have chosen well.

"What I ask is needed tomorrow. When I see it, I will ask for any changes needed. I do not wish anyone to know of this until after I speak with the Council." Archerd said nothing, only waiting for his instructions.

#

Chadas took his seat at the table with Alodia at his left side. His knife would come easily to his right hand and he could trust no one more to protect his left should anyone feel the desire to become Lord. The other seven filed in and soon the Council was convened.

"Why have you called us together?" demanded Dyfed. Chadas knew he was not annoyed, merely curious, and he was determined to assert his authority.

"I will come to that, but first, are your people encountering any problems with their new roles?" None were reported. The city did not care who ruled, only that they could live in peace. A few of Lord Rodnel's people complained about the Guild taking their senior positions, but no one objected too strenuously.

"So, why are we here?" Dyfed repeated.

"I have been thinking." Chadas signaled his sister to admit the mapmaker. Both stood back while he spoke. "No one can deny that Dragonfang is overcrowded, and will become more so."

"What do you propose? That we kill off the excess people?"

"No. It is the people that make Dragonfang strong." The Council waited. "I went riding a few days ago and at times my horse had trouble getting through the streets."

"We all know the difficulties, unless we use the tunnels. Is that what you suggest?" asked Arienh.

"You have thought of a plan, or we would not be here," added Keelia.

"The city must expand."

"Do you want us to build a new wall?" The thought of such an undertaking was daunting.

Chadas allowed his eyes to slowly wander over the group, assessing their response to what he was about to say. "No," he finally answered. "Why do we face this problem? Not because the wall is too small or that we have too many people. The problem is that we have too many people inside the wall." He waited.

Gradually, what he was saying began to come clear. "You want to put the people outside the wall?"

"They will not go."

"Who will protect them."

"You cannot make them go."

Chadas waited for quiet to settle again before answering, "When was the last time anyone attempted an attack on Dragonfang?"

"There have been no attacks for many generations," Arienh answered. "They would not dare. The walls of Dragonfang are too strong."

Chadas stared directly into her eyes. "It is not the wall that makes the city strong, it is its size. We have more people than any other city could bring against us, and our guards are trained too well. What I propose is that we make use of the land around the city to grow stronger." He called the mapmaker to lay out his drawings.

" Here is the city," The mapmaker began. "We have so much space outside the wall that is not used. This is a grid of ordered roads with houses either side. There is space behind the houses for gardens or animals, kilns whatever the people wish to do. A blacksmith or tavern keeper can build a larger place with less land for other uses." His enthusiasm grew as the words rushed from his lips.

"But what if we are attacked?"

"You admitted there have been no attacks in generations, but if someone should try, they would face a wall of people ready to protect their homes, and the Guard could rush to their aid. If things go badly, they could fall back inside the wall," Chadas explained.

His hands slapped the table as he sat back, grinning. A ring of faces leaned forward to study the drawings.

#

Returning to the tower with Alodia riding at his side gave him pleasure. Then his sister spoke. "You seem happy," she observed.

"Why should I not be? What we saw today warms my heart. He people are accepting the decision to move beyond the wall, though with reluctance. Dragonfang is starting to grow. They accept the rule of the Guild and the Council is satisfied."

"And the people seem happy that they have land to grow their farms and their families."

Chadas nodded, smiling. "They will overcome their concerns and then everything will be better."

They rode on, each deep in thoughts of a new Dragonfang. As they approached the tower, Chadas reined his horse to a stop and called one of the guards forward. "Take our horses to the stables. Alodia and I are going walking in the garden." He swung his leg across the saddle and dropped to the ground while Alodia hid her surprise and dismounted. The two walked toward his private sanctuary. Glancing over his shoulder he saw the other guards following at a discreet distance while one man led the horses back to the stables. This was as private as he could expect.

Alone on the winding paths, or as alone as they could be, Chadas broached the subject that nagged at his mind with a question. "Do you know where Isen is?"

Alodia paused to cup the purple flowers of a lavender bush and held it to her face to sniff. Her eyes turned to see how far away the guards were, checking they could not be heard. Whatever Chadas was thinking, it would be better if it stayed between them. "I can find out," she whispered."

"Good. I have a task for him, one that must remain private for the moment."

Alodia rose from her crouch, slipped an arm around his, and led him deeper into the garden. "What are you planning now?" she whispered.

"Nothing of importance, not yet." She squeezed him in encouragement for him to continue. "The people move outside the wall. I told them there would be no danger, but if it did come, it would probably be from the nearest cities. Bel is the most probable. I want him to go to Bel and learn how strong the Guild is there. I know we have a presence but do they have any power to control the city? I wish to know what influence we can exert there. I will feel safer then."

Alodia nodded and whispered in his ear. "That sounds a sensible thing to do, but I know you too well. You have more on your mind than safety, but you can keep your secrets. What will you do if they are weak, and they probably are? Can you do anything to make them stronger?"

"When Isen brings me news I can assess the next questions."

They reached the little grove that Chadas loved and he led her to the bench where they sat side by side, enjoying the scents and colors of the plants, the heady flavors of roses and the sweetness of jasmine drifting on the air. Brilliant red amaryllis jostled for space amid the stunning white of daisies and the subtle yellows of primrose.

Chadas broke their quiet contemplation when he asked, "Who can I trust?"

Confused by his question, Alodia answered, "You are the Ama and Lord of Dragonfang. The city grows stronger. Why should you mistrust anyone?"

"There have been many good Lords found with a knife in his chest because someone craved his power. Lord Rodnel is only the most recent."

"Do you fear anyone in particular?"

"No, just everyone." At her glance he added, "Except you." She smiled.

"And what makes you believe you can trust me?" Her evil grin caused him to sit erect and stare. "You are my brother, my family. Of course I would not harm you."

"Rodnel was Edur's father."

"But Edur was a selfish goat." Chadas laughed at the description.

"It is because of who you are and what you understand that I trust you completely."

Alodia placed a hand on his shoulder. "You are the only family I have. I will protect you, little brother."

In a sudden torrent of words, Chadas said, "I want you at my side. Together we can make Dragonfang the power of the land. It will be a better place to live."

Alodia wrapped his shoulders in her arms. "I will be here."

"I know, but I wish the Council to know."

"How?"

"When we are married, it would put certainty in their minds, at least long enough to give them warning."

His sister stared into his eyes, then nodded. "It would make us a more powerful team in their eyes."

"So, do we announce the day of our wedding?"

Alodia smiled and nodded. "Yes."

#

Many weeks passed before Chadas found the time to ride outside the city wall again. He did so today, with Alodia at his side and an escort of six. Reining the big stallion to a stop, he turned to look behind.

"Is anything wrong?" asked Alodia.

"No, and yes," he replied. Alodia's face twisted in confusion and she looked to him for clarification. "At ease," he instructed. "I am not sensing any danger."

Chadas searched ahead and found a guard by the side of the new road. He nudged his horse forward to stop beside him. "Who is in charge here?" he asked.

The man searched frantically about before admitting, "That would be me at the moment, I think, my Lord." Chadas waited. "The others have all gone inside." He pointed a thumb toward the gate.

"Your name?"

"Jaykse, my Lord. Guardsman Jaykse."

"And why would they go and leave you in charge?"

The man shrugged. "Nothin' much to watch, so they make me do it. Only a few houses being built."

"I see that. Why do you think that is?"

Guardsman Jankse scratched his head. "Dunno."

"Then run and find someone from the houses and bring them here." The man ran off clumsily, the leather armor and sword at his hip hindering him. But he was back quickly with a woman in tow. Chadas asked her the same question.

She answered immediately. "They do not like coming outside to live. They are afraid of living without the wall's protection." Chadas thought about her reply, but the woman must have believed he was waiting for more because she added, "my Lord."

After learning her name, Chadas thanked her. They rode on and at each house he spoke with whoever he could find. They finished visiting very quickly. Chadas dismounted and passed his reins to one of the guards. "There is no need to follow," he told them. "I want some time to think."

"Should I wait too?" asked Alodia.

Chadas waved a hand. "Come if you wish." She slid from her horse and passed her reins to a guard. They walked down the empty road, and turned to move out to one side, among the field of plot markers. Chadas strode, head down and hands clasped behind his back. Alodia trailed at his shoulder knowing he was lost in thought and would not notice the world around him until they were organized.

Finally, he stopped.

Alodia looked back.

The horses were more than two miles distant, under the protection of a solitary guard. The other five trailed at a discrete distance.

"If Dragonfang is to become a great city, the people must come outside the walls. And if the promise of more space does not encourage them, I must make them. It is for the good of the city and their families."

"What do you have in mind?"

"Two things. First is to make them move. The guards will announce in all quarters of Dragonfang that any who have not begun their new homes in forty days from today will pay a tax for remaining. I will call it a wall tax. Each day they will state the number of days before the tax is imposed."

"They will not like that."

"I know, and the second idea will go to removing their concerns. They will have an army to protect them."

"An army?"

Chadas laughed. "Yes. They will have their army, but some may not like it. The Lord's Guard will remain and half the House of Alard will become the City Guard. The remainder will join House Eeva as leaders of the army."

"It will be no more than they have now."

"It will grow. Every man and woman over the age of sixteen will be required to join them for one day in every ten to learn the skills of fighting. They will soon become their own army."

"What about the Council?"

"They will see the sense in what I propose and Dragonfang will grow stronger when every man and woman is ready to fight."

Alodia considered his proposal. "It might work. No, it will work if you can win over the Council."

"It will work. I will rely on the leaders of the Houses to make it work."

"They may think it better to see their taxes in the hands of the Guild."

"With extra land to use for vegetables and animals, kilns and forges, and other trades, the people will become more wealthy, and we will have more taxes and other benefits."

With a grin splitting his face, Chadas started back to the horses.

# 26 NEW BEGINNINGS

Chadas and Alodia sat astride their horses watching the spectacle. His army was in training and he was closer to his dream, one that he dared tell no one, not even Alodia.

Nearest were the archers. These men and women had been chosen as the best for their skills of the weapon. He expected them to be good. A city that relied strongly on hunting should produce excellent marksmen. Still he fidgeted in his seat.

"Come," he said at last. "We should go and see what the others are doing."

When they stopped near those practicing with maces, he winced. "What are they trying to do?" he groaned. 'They are in more danger of opening their own heads than stopping an attacker." Many swung the tall timber pole as if it were a sword while others poked at the air as if attempting to put holes in it. No one had any understanding of what was required or the conviction to do it.

They moved on to the swords to find they were no better. After watching for only a few minutes, he kicked his horse forward, into the army. "Stop!" he yelled. "I can tolerate this no more. Stop."

One of the trainers came closer. "My Lord, what is wrong?"

What he watched was only as he expected of his newly formed army. They would improve their fighting skills, but now was the moment to direct them to what he wanted. "Send runners. Have the army stand down and wait. I wish to speak with all the trainers, all of them." He looked about and pointed. "I will wait there and tell them to hurry." With his orders given, he and Alodia nudged their horses into a walk, but not before Alodia had glanced his way and raised a brow. Without looking back, he could imagine the scene behind him, with men running about to fulfill his orders.

Soon, they sat their horses as the trainers gathered around. One bold individual called, "You have not given us time. We have been given farmers and no time to teach them."

Chadas called the young man forward. "What will you teach them?" he asked.

"We will show them how to use the weapons you have provided, my Lord." His demeanor had changed the moment he was singled out.

"Is that all?"

The trainers stood waiting but what Chadas saw was a glimmer of understanding in the young man's eyes. "What is your name?"

"Allyn, my Lord." No flicking signal came to show he was of the Guild. This was one of the men chosen for his skill rather than his breeding.

"Well Allyn, of what do I speak?"

"The man hesitated before answering. "When they know how to use their weapons, they must also know discipline."

"Exactly." Chadas lifted his head to ensure all could hear his next words. "At my command, Allyn is now commander of the army." This was followed by a few gasps but no objections. "You may return to your training while I speak with him."

When they were only three, Chadas slid from his saddle and passed the reins to Alodia who had also dismounted. With hands clasped behind his back he began to stroll through the short grass. "With untrained troops, it will not matter what you do, if your enemy has more they will defeat you. That is why we train. As you suggested, an army requires discipline, but this has no meaning without organization. Work has started on this with the division of skills. You may have other thoughts but I would divide skill into groups of around twenty. Groups this size could easily be managed by a group captain who would be responsible for the training and discipline of their group." Allyn nodded. "They must ensure their group works as one, each man supporting the others. Some competitions of skill between the groups would help. They must also work alongside these other groups. A squadron Leader could be in charge of around ten groups, with one person to lead each discipline, say a division commander of archers and so forth. You would take charge of the entire army."

"I understand what you desire, my Lord, and I am honored to serve in this way."

"We will make any changes that we see as being necessary as our army grows, but that brings me to another problem."

"What would that be, my Lord?"

"Communication. Each leader from yourself to the group captains must be able to communicate with each other whether they are twenty paces apart or in the next valley." Allyn's face creased in thought. "I am sure you will find an answer, but while you think on it, consider whether the army is stationary or moving." The young man's eyes widened. "We cannot expect to sit and wait while our enemy prepares and attacks when he is ready. There will be times when we must become the pursuer." He turned to take the reins from Alodia as she trailed behind and climbed back on his horse. She did the same. "I have faith in you Allyn." Then as he turned to leave, he added, "And you will need one of these." He patted the horses neck. "I will see that a suitable mount is provided." He left Allyn staring as they rode away, only then realizing the man had probably never been on the back of a horse. Chadas reined and turned. "I will teach you to ride." Then he kicked his heels and galloped away.

#

Three carts covered in heavy cloth waited just outside the gates. Two traders had left for Bel over the last nine days but Isen had deemed them unsuitable. Their horses were not cared for and the carts were in need of repair. They would not be carrying any goods of value and so have no need of an extra hand. This trader was different. Everything about the caravan showed he knew the value of his equipment and his clothes announced his ability to make good coin.

With a broad-rimmed hat drawn down over his face and his body hidden in loose clothing, Isen approached the trader, glancing continually over his shoulder as he did so. The man looked up from his loading. His cape and clothing were colorful without being garish and he wore no hat over his long black curls. "Get away, you little ragamuffin."

"Sir, could you use another guard on your journey?" Isen asked.

This brought a guffaw from the trader and laughter from the two large men who would protect the cargo. "I have no need to guard myself against mice."

"I have a sword," Isen pressed as he fumbled beneath his clothing to prove the truth of his words.

Again the men laughed. "On your way lad. You have a few years before you can play with men."

"I can drive a cart," Isen continued while looking behind.

The trader placed a large hand on his shoulder. "Tell me lad, why are you so keen to go to Bel?"

"You travel to Bel? That should be far enough."

The hand tightened. "If you are not going to Bel, what do you run from? Are the guards looking for you?"

Isen squirmed under the pressure, though it was not great. "To tell you the truth, there is a young girl and a father I would not wish to meet for a while."

The hand came free of his shoulder to slap him on the back. Trying to speak around his laughter, the trader agreed to take him to Bel. "You can share our food and water, but I will not pay you unless you prove your boast as a driver."

A grin split Isen's face. "Thank you."

"You can call me Mott. What shall we call you?" Isen stumbled around a few meaningless words. "It need not be your real name. What would you prefer?" Isen shrugged. "You talk big for such a puny lad. We will call you Giant. How would you like that?"

"Fine."

"Well come along Giant. The carts are loaded and we will leave soon. You will ride in the second cart with Nobbs. It is not his real name either."

They were soon rattling over the ground with Dragonfang a distant mark on the land.

"Nobbs?" The thin man grunted. There was not much of him, but it was all sinew and muscle. The reins draped over his hand allowing the two horses to have their heads and follow the cart in front. "How do we get to Bel?"

Nobbs looked across the seat to where Isen sat. "Only one way. How ya think?" He spat over the side of the cart. "Long the coast."

Isen took his cue from the man and spat over the other side. "Dunno. Never been outa Dragonfang afore."

Nobbs frowned and a hard look came to his eyes. "Wacha doin'?"

"What?"

"Ya make fun o' me. Don' preciate that. I sees ya got learnin'."

"I am sorry. I had no intention of upsetting you. I only want to fit in."

"Then no bally nonsense. Just be you self."

"That is why I am here."

"Wha'?"

"I was being myself with a lovely young girl when her father caught us. I ran for my life until I saw this caravan about to leave."

Nobbs grinned. "E'll ferget soon 'nough."

"I hope so. I would love to see his daughter again and finish what we started."

Nobbs loud laugh had all the drivers and guards looking. Word would spread. He had become part of the team."

On the first night, the three drivers and Isen sat apart. Nobbs whispered that it was not considered good practice by the guards if they associated themselves with such lowly folk. He did not mind. Nobbs had shown a good sense of humor and kept everyone entertained.

He had been truthful with Mott. He had never been beyond the outer walls of Dragonfang. As they traveled the next day, he stared, fascinated, at the sea and the mountains. He could see these things from the city, but here they were different. They were free. Waves tumbled along a far-stretching shore. He spied a turtle scurry into the sea as they approached. To his left, the mountains climbed to the sky, their hard black rock dotted with patches of green, while the peaks were dressed in white.

"Is it always this beautiful?" he asked.

Nobbs replied with a shake of his head. "D'pends on the Gods. When Foehn's breath is cold, She blows snow off the mountains an' turns the skies gray. But if Raiki angers, He turns the mountains red an' they melt. If that happens, get outa here." Isen looked again at the mountains. He would love to see them turn red.

Late in the day, as they crossed a small river deep enough to wet the axles, Nobbs asked, "Ever play Raffle?"

Isen looked at him quizzically. "Raffle?"

"We gonna play af'er we eat if ya wanna try." Isen nodded. Although he had never played, he understood the concept. Played with three dice, each player had one throw. The one who threw the highest three-of-a-kind was the winner, and if one was not thrown, the highest pair. "A quarter copper a throw. Don' worry. If ya lose, we'll wait till we gets to Bel fer ya to pay."

A journey of four uneventful weeks brought the first glimpse of Bel. Isen was driving at the time with Nobbs beside him. Bel appeared almost as large as Dragonfang, which surprised him, but its walls were not as tall. He would need to examine them in more detail.

"What ya think?" Nobbs asked.

"This is the first time I have seen any place other than Dragonfang. I do not know what to think yet."

"Ya be right. They be pretty young girls here too." He grinned.

Isen walked into Bel. Somewhere nearby, someone was baking biscuits.

#

Chadas and Alodia sat in the private garden relaxing and chatting. The sweet odors of tranquil peace allowed him to think. Occasionally the trill of a small bird interrupted the silence.

"I cannot understand it. I feel the Majick. I know I do, but it will not reveal its secrets to me."

Maybe you try too hard," suggested Alodia.

"I have tried everything. The spirit said the Majickers would teach me. They have not. Do I accept that the Majick is beyond my ability?"

Alodia watched him a moment before replying. "I believe it is within your grasp. The spirit would not have contacted you or given you this task if it were not."

"I will not give up, if only to prevent the spirit annoying me again. But the skills the Majickers have discovered could be very useful. The army would benefit from their learning."

"What is it?"

Chadas did not reply. Instead he rose and wandered out of the garden to the open area beyond. Alodia followed. As they walked, Alodia asked again.

"Let me show you." Chadas had a guard run and ask the Majickers meet him in the Great Hall.

When they were gathered, he spoke quietly with Elrida and sent her to run to the city wall. Then he sent Wilda to climb the tower stairs. They waited to give time for the two to reach their alloted location before Chadas asked Alodia to select one of the remaining women. She chose Wilona.

"Ask her a question."

"What should I ask?"

"I cannot tell you. It must be your question."

At that moment she heard the tower cryer.

"What is the time? Alodia asked. Wilona smiled.

A few moments later Nelda came back down the stairs. "The cryer has just announced Prime, my Lady," she said.

Alodia's head snapped toward Chadas. He had kept his dealings with the Majickers secret. This was the first hint at what they could do.

"Elrida is at the gate, my Lady," Bernie announced. "Do you have a question for her?"

"Do not make it too easy for her," Chadas advised.

Alodia turned slowly back to face Bernie. "Is the gate open?" she asked.

Bernie replied almost immediately. "Yes."

"Could you think of nothing better?" Chadas asked.

Still staring at Bernie, Alodia asked, "How many guard the gate?"

Again the response came quickly. "Six, my Lady."

Chadas was about to speak but Alodia responded before he could. "Who commands?"

Moments seemed to pass before the reply came. "Podge, my Lady."

"Have her return," Chadas ordered. Soon they were all together again. "Do you see what this means, Alodia?"

His sister was quick to comprehend. "You can send messages to the army without runners."

"More than that. I can pass and receive information in moments. I will know the state of a battle as it occurs and my orders will be acted on instantly. If there is a stronger army in Lilim, this will give us the advantage."

Alodia smiled, understanding the implications. Chadas discussed some of his plans.

"They have yet to discover the limits of their skill, if there is any, and the learning has just begun. Unfortunately they do not know how to show me what they do."

#

"The Spiriteer has told me he has called the banns on the last two Spiritdays and has received no objections. If none come after tomorrow, we can be wed on the following Spiritday."

Chadas shook his head.

"What?" asked Alodia.

"The spiriteer will officiate at our wedding. For more generations than anyone can remember they have controlled the thoughts and ceremonies of Dragonfang because they claim to be able to speak with the spirits. I know this is not true."

"Does that matter? He will perform the ceremony and all will accept it."

"No, it does not matter. But if we are going to rule Dragonfang, how do we reduce their influence?"

"Then why the concerns?" Alodia used her thumb to wipe away his scowl, trying to calm his thoughts. "No one knows us to be anything but members of the Guild."

He brushed the hair from her face. "I fret because the Council would not wish to see us together. It would make me too strong in their eyes to have you at my back."

"They cannot stop us. They have no reason to offer the Spiriteer."

They sat quietly on the bench in their little grove, the sweet scent of lavender filling the air around them. Finally he said, "The living may have no reason, but what if the spirits object?"

Alodia's face suddenly showed concern, but she masked it as she answered, "Why should the spirits object?" Before he could reply, she added, "The spirits do not concern themselves with such matters."

Chadas knew she was trying to convince herself more than him, but he allowed the topic to drop. Instead he said, "Isen should be close to Bel. Soon we will know the strength of the Guild there, but I do not think Lord Masima had the same influence outside of Dragonfang."

The days passed slowly until it was finally the eve of their wedding. He had given his instructions and been told all was in readiness.

Next day, festivities began early across Dragonfang and developed as the day grew older. When the crier announced Nones, Chadas and Alodia were waiting on the steps to the entrance of the Tower. Chadas wore a new red cape without cowl, trimmed in white wolf fur. It covered a red doublet and britches, both trimmed with gold. On his head was a white cloth cap slouched over his left ear. At his side stood Alodia in her new blue dress with white ruffle collar and silver embroidery around the sleeves and hem.

"Are you ready?" he whispered.

Alodia only smiled as her matron of honor fussed over the dress, making everything perfect. Four trumpeters raised buccinas to offer a mighty fanfare. Chadas took Alodia's arm and they stepped out to begin their procession. His best swordsman, chosen for his skill from the Lord's Guard, moved in behind, riding a horse and holding his sword ready to protect his Lord and the new bride. The Council would follow him to represent their new family.

The procession from the Tower to the House of Spirits was short, no more than a hundred paces. About them people played reed flutes, drums, and anything else that would make a noise.

As they arrived at the closed doors of the House of the Spirits, the cacophony died away. The Spiriteer stood waiting. The bride and groom took their places along with the wedding party. When all was ready, the Spiriteer called the mandatory questions.

"How old is the bride and groom?"

"Old enough."

"Are the bride and groom related by blood?"

"No."

"Does the brides family permit the marriage?"

Keelia gave the Council's permission.

Alodia's thought was so strong that she feared others may hear it, I wish my mother was here.

"Were the banns called properly?"

All that could hear called "Yes."

And finally, "Do the bride and groom consent freely into marriage?"

Both agreed.

With all the questions asked and answered appropriately, Chadas offered

Alodia a coin purse containing thirteen coppers. After the ceremony, Alodia could distribute these among the poorest of the city as a sign of her authority to make decisions in her husband's name.

Next, Chadas plighted his troth, vowing to have and to hold his bride in bed and at the table, whether she be fair or ugly, sick or of good health.

The Spiriteer blessed the ring and passed it to Chadas, along with a kiss of peace on his cheek. Chadas then placed the ring on and off Alodia's first finger, then the second and the third. With each finger he recited, "Before the spirits of our ancestors and with this ring, I thee wed." He then passed on the kiss of peace to his wife.

The Spiriteer then opened the doors and invited everyone to enter and praise the spirits for the marriage. Chadas and Alodia faced the people, accepting their enormous cheer.

Now we are officially family again. Dragonfang will thrive through our bond, Chadas thought. His mind flashed briefly back to Rill, and he wondered.

#

The Majickers had learned a new skill, they could make the wind obey their command. They could make it come or stop it. They could make it whisper or roar. Still Chadas could not feel the Majick. The one thing that made him accept this was that Rata had not reappeared to harass him. He suspected she would soon.

They were in the field normally used for festivals. Small stacks of timber were scattered around, some now fallen. Nymphs of spinning dust danced between them. One nymph turned, pirouetted, and cavorted a circle around one of the wood stacks.

Annis laughed. *What was that?*

*Just having fun.* Nelda giggled. *I thought the Lord would appreciate the show.*

*I did.*

Suddenly the nymphs disappeared, the dust settling to the ground.

*How did you…*

*Do that again so we can watch.*

Chadas' eyes widened and his jaw dropped. He staggered a little as the shock of realization took him. I heard them, he thought. They did not speak, but I heard them. All the women were staring.

"What did I do?"

*My Lord?* Wilda was speaking to him but her lips did not move, her mouth did not open. Then they were running to him, excited that he had found the Majick.

He stared at them in shock. "This could be a problem," he said aloud.

"How?"

"I do not wish to make my thoughts open to you all. There are things I am not ready to announce."

"We will keep your secrets, my Lord," Annis assured him, "but it will not be necessary. We will give you your first lesson now. We will show you how to control or direct your thoughts." *Like this*, she added. *The others cannot hear these words.*

"Your training can now begin," added Annis. "We can show you in your mind what you must do."

Chadas' face twisted into a huge grin. He was going to achieve his destiny. For some reason, his next thought was, Rata will be pleased.

"What do I do?"

Nelda was in his mind. *The fire. Look at it. No, not with your eyes, but with your mind.* Chadas did as instructed and saw the flames dancing on the logs like nymphs at play. Now look deeper , she encouraged. Chadas tried, and was surprised. The fire was no longer fire, but a ball of pulsating white energy. *You see it. Good. Now, hold out your hand and ask a small amount of the energy to come to your hand.*

Chadas jumped, shaking a hand that was already beginning to blister. Annis was at his side ready with a bucket of water.

*You pulled too much. Never do that again. The Majick can be dangerous. With time you will be able to perform multiple tasks at the same time, like put gloves on that do not burn. This is not like burning grass, this is control.*

# 27 A RIDING LESSON

Hope and Faith ran, squealing, to the horse yard. Their little legs seemed hardly to touch the ground, so filled with excitement were they. "Are you ready yet?" they called in unison.

"There is no rush," Torne laughed. "I must first saddle the horse and make sure all is ready." They groaned. "This is not your first lesson. You know you must be prepared." On seeing their disappointed faces he stopped what he was doing. "I know you have both been on the horse before, but you are eight now and if you wish to ride solo, it must be your responsibility to make sure all is ready. First, check the horse to make sure it is healthy and able to carry you. Make sure your saddle is properly cinched. Most of all, do not rush. If you go too fast, you will scare the horse, and he may react badly to your riding him. Wait to see he is not skittish and will accept you on his back."

"Yes father," they answered, slightly crestfallen.

Farm life was good for Hope and Faith. They enjoyed the animals and birds, the crops and the sheer pleasure of being outdoors. Torne and Shayla had expressed concern that their girls had little interaction with other members of the community. Twice their father had taken them to Pigfish Bay on an outing. Their parents thought the people there may encourage their daughters to meet others. They ignored all the people to watch the expanse of water that held them in awe.

Today, however, was one they both anticipated with joy. Today, their father would not lead them around the yard. He had promised they would ride without his help. They were going to sit the horse and guide it unaided.

Shayla had walked quietly over to watch. "Are they too young?" she asked.

"No, mother. We can do this. Let us show you, please!"

Shayla smiled. "Of course you can. I was only teasing."

The girls squealed and went back to their father's tasks.

The chill morning air heralded the beginning of the cold winds and rain. The scent of ripening maize competed with the usual odor of the chickens.

Bouncing and hopping, they watched their father saddle the brown mare. Their mother caught up, calling for the children to behave and wait for their father. "Are you nearly ready?" she asked Torne. "The girls will jump out of their skins soon." Shayla remained unconcerned. She trusted Torne and her children were smart. All three would take no chances, no matter how excited the girls were. Watching her family, Shayla felt the sorrow she knew so often. It would have been lovely to give Torne more children, maybe another three or four.

"Is the horse ready?" Torne called, and both girls stopped to look.

"I think so," they answered.

"Right, he is." Torne bent to lift Hope into the saddle. He then took Faith's hand and stepped away. "Be careful," he advised, "and remember, go slowly"

Hope flicked the reins and her parents watched with pride as their daughter rode around the yard. Torne laughed. "She is a natural," he called to his wife. They watched as the horse circled the yard five times.

"Is it my turn yet," Faith pleaded.

Torne looked down into his daughter's eyes. "Soon," he promised. Looking up, he called," One more time around Hope, then give your sister a turn."

Hope did as instructed and brought the horse to a stop in front of her father, who reached up and lifted her to the ground. Patting the horse and speaking to it quietly, he and Shayla both wore enormous smiles.

"You look like you have been riding for years," Shayla complimented Hope.

"My turn," squealed Faith, and both her parents laughed. Torne lifted her into the saddle and gave her the same instructions. "I know. Can I ride now?"

"Yes," her father answered as he stepped back. Faith kicked her heels into the horse's flanks as she had seen her father do. She began riding around the yard, a little faster than her sister.

"Slow down," called Shayla. Faith replied by flicking the reins and moving even faster. She giggled with delight as she bounced up and down in the saddle. Then her foot slipped out of the stirrup. The giggles stopped. She gripped the horse with her legs. Her flailing arms whipped the reins to slap against the horse's neck. The horse obeyed the command. It jumped into a fast trot.

Faith screamed.

Torne rushed to catch the horse, but it turned to evade him. Suddenly Shayla was in its path, grabbing at the bridle. With a shake of its head, the horse turned again. It knocked her to the ground. Torne cried out. The horse panicked and bolted. Shayla was on the ground. The horse leaped. A rear hoof caught her in the chest. Faith dragged at the reins, and Torne caught up to hold it still. Hope ran to her mother. Torne grabbed Faith from the saddle and they ran to Shayla. His wife had not moved.

She was still breathing.

Torne lifted her and carried her into the house to lay her on the bed. He sent his sister into Fartown to find help. Blood trickled from his wife's lips. Torne sat or slept in a chair beside her, his farm work forgotten.

Nothing could be done to save her. She was taken by the spirits three days later.

With tears running down their cheeks, Hope and Faith hugged. Faith whispered in her sister's ear, "It is bad, but it is necessary."

# 28 THE TREATY OF BEL

Mott gave him twelve coppers for his work. It was not what the others earned, but he was here, and without suspicion. After paying what he owed the drivers, he left with two in his pocket. Nobbs waved him off with a leering, "Keep ya eyes open fer fathers."

He turned. "I just have to run faster," he joked. Isen waved as he called, "Maybe I can find a willing lass before night."

Laughing, Nobbs returned to his work.

The first thing Isen needed was a place to sleep. In Dragonfang, he would have no difficulty. He knew of places that were safe, whether in a dark alley or a girl's bed. Bel was unknown. He did not know what dangers lurked or where they hid. Chadas had given him some coins to use and he decided a few would be well spent on a room and meal. Mott had suggested a place, cheap and clean enough. As he made his way to the tavern, he kept one eye open for beggars, the most easily found of the Guild if you looked for them. He passed three, and though he passed the three-fingered signal, none responded.

'The Serpent's Tongue' was as he had been told. Almost concealed in the narrow alley, its dark walls hid it from passing trade. Isen stepped through the black door. Once inside, the serving room was well lit with candles. Three patrons played stones in one corner. He called for an ale and took a seat at one of the empty tables, well away from the game. The patrons and the innkeeper stopped to examine the intruder in their domain. He gave the Guild signal again, just in case. Again no one reacted. The innkeeper turned to the barrels behind him and drew a mug. Isen made a show of taking out a coin and putting it on the table.

"Anything to eat?" he asked when the serving girl delivered the mug.

"Got a rabbit. Caught fresh yesterday. And some vegetables." Other than the words tumbling from her mouth, the serving girl's face remained devoid of expression as she wiped her hands down a plain yellow apron.

"That would be nice," Isen smiled. "And would you have a room for a few nights?"

The girl turned to the innkeeper who rubbed his prominent chin between thumb and forefinger. "Got a room upstairs, at the back, not big, but got a bed," he suggested.

Isen thanked the girl and placed two more coins on the table. That was probably the most words the innkeeper had put together in some time, he thought. The girl scooped up the coins and took them back to the innkeeper.

A short time later, an older woman brought him his meal.

#

Later, the serving girl led him up to the room where she passed him a candle and opened the door. He offered one of his best smiles but her face remained impassive as she walked away. With a shrug, he entered. While his eyes adjusted to the darkness, his nose was assaulted with the raw odor of stale air, unwashed linen and urine. Beyond the door, the small windowless space took on the flavor of wet wool. There was no window and barely enough room for the crude bed. Squatting beside the bed like it deserved its place of honor stood a stool that Isen dared not sit on for fear of it collapsing.

It had only been his first day but he thought he would have contacted the Guild by now.

He closed the door and placed the stool against it. If anyone tried to enter, he would hear. With the candle on the floor beside it, he removed his outer clothes and hung them on the peg in the stone wall. Carefully he lay back on the rickety bed. Resting his hands behind his head, he wondered where he should look tomorrow.

The crash woke him.

Before he could retrieve his hidden knife, three men wearing tan leather jerkin over brown doublets rushed in and pinned him where he lay. A woman stood to one side. Their livery was emblazoned with the symbol of a bear. They quickly searched and removed all the other knives he had before dragging him to his feet. "What …" he began before a fist took the air from him. As his eyes focused, he saw the innkeeper and the serving girl watching from outside the door.

He directed his questions to the woman. "Can I help you? I do not see how. I have only just arrived in Bel. You must be looking for someone else."

"We know who we seek. Your words only make us certain we have the right man."

"Why?"

"Save your breath. Lord Beed will question you himself."

He was dragged out into the hallway. The girl darted into the room and returned. "His clothes," she said as she passed a bundle to the guards. They left, Isen with his arms pinned between two burly men. They marched him out into the street in his small clothes and did not stop. He was herded through the night like a common criminal.

Bel's tower was not as magnificent or imposing as the Lord's tower at

Dragonfang, but that did not detract from its sense of power. Isen was taken to the center of a long, sprawling structure of two floors and many windows. The Lord of Bel had no intentions of using this as a defensive structure, there were too many entry points. This Lord intended to live and die with his people.

The guards dragged him inside and threw him to the floor. They had still not offered a word he could use. His clothes were thrown a few paces away.

#

A huge man stood over him, his black fur coat hanging from his shoulders to the ground. A hood of the same fur covered his head. Beady blue eyes peeked out. Isen attempted to rise but a guard's booted foot pushed him back to the ground. "No man stands before the bear of Bel unless told to," he snarled.

"This is him?" asked the man in black.

"Yes, my Lord Beed."

The big man crouched and pulled Isen's head up by the hair. "Your name?" he demanded.

Isen felt his only chance of survival was the truth, or at least enough of it to be convincing. "Isen, my Lord."

"Why are you here?"

"I have been sent by Lord Chadas, Lord of Dragonfang."

The man dropped his hair and walked to the window, staring out, hands clasped behind his back. "Let him up," he ordered.

The boot left Isen's back and strong hands grasped his arms to pull him to his feet. Isen waited.

"There are none of your kind in this city. I will not have them, and neither will the good people of Bel."

"My kind?"

The Lord of Bel spun, anger in his eyes. "The Guild of Masima," he spat. "We know your signal and it only warned us of your presence among us." He spun back to the window. From the rise and fall of his shoulders Isen knew he was trying to calm himself. Finally, without turning, he demanded, "Why are you here?"

"Lord Chadas sent me."

In one long step Lord Beed towered over Isen, his hot breath steaming in Isen's face.

When words came, it was a command to the guards. "Take him to the dungeon."

He stood watching as Lord Beed stormed from the room. Isen wondered if he would ever get back to Dragonfang.

#

I glanced up to catch Kuwento smiling.

"Did I say something amusing?" I asked.

"No. On the contrary, I am enjoying the way you tell Chadas' story."

I waited a moment.

"It is just that you are making Isen's role in our past known, and that pleases me."

"I must," I told him. "I can see from your maal that Isen was important to both Chadas and Alodia."

"He was. Without Isen, things would have been different in our world. They may have been better or worse, but they would have been very different. But few people remember him or his role in their lives."

"Then I will accept your smile as a compliment on my writing," I said, and Kuwento's smile broadened.

#

The first day in the dungeon left Isen confused. Why was there such animosity toward Masima or the people of Dragonfang? Three more days did little to answer his questions. He was a prisoner but this was larger and more lavish than the room at 'The Serpent's Tongue'. The bed was sturdier and topped with a feather mattress. A small window without a view cast light on a timber table and chair. He had been given a candle, and when it was discovered he could read, a book on the history of Bel was brought in. It contained much on their hatred of Masima and warnings of the cruelty of the Guild. He did not understand. But now he learned something else. There was one section describing ways to recognize the scum of Masima, as the book described them. The guards even took him out for a walk twice each day to exercise him.

One of the guards, a woman named Keela, brought him good food and was always present on his walks. She was smaller than his other guards, though blessed with broad shoulders and strong arms. The way she walked, Isen had no doubt she was skilled with a sword. They quickly became friends, chatting while they walked.

On the fifth day, Keela brought him his meal of black bread, cheese, and a piece of cold fish. When he began to eat, she sat on the bed to talk.

"Is it true? Are you a member of the Guild of Masima?" She shuddered as she asked.

"Yes," he answered.

After some time she spoke again. "Masima and the Guild are despised in Bel. Is it not the same in Dragonfang?"

"No."

Nothing more was said until Isen finished his meal. Then, "Why?" she asked.

"Why what?"

"Why is the Guild not hated in Dragonfang?"

Isen wondered how he should answer, and chose, "For many years we remained hidden. Only the members knew our secret. But when the Lord of Dragonfang, Lord Rodnel, was murdered by his son, Edur, it soon became apparent the people would suffer at Edur's cruelty. The Guild decided they had no choice. They had to step in."

"What did they do?"

"Lord Chadas, the current Lord of Dragonfang, is also the Ama, the leader of the Guild." He gave a sly grin. "You might say that Dragonfang is the Guild."

Keela looked stunned as she gathered the plate and left. At the door, she turned to shake her head before locking it and leaving.

#

Early in the morning of the following day, Isen woke to the sounds of the guards' taunts.

"Wake up you miserable Masima lover. Get your God-cursed bones out here."

Isen dragged himself from the small bed. As he reached the door, he was roughly grabbed and pulled into the knot of men outside. "Time to face the bear," one snarled.

At first, sleep clouded Isen's thoughts. Then, bear he remembered. They must be taking him to see the Lord. He followed quietly as they led him away, but his mind was like a stirred hornets' nest. Is the Lord going to have me killed? Will I be sent back to Dragonfang? Will I ever see Dragonfang again? Scenarios followed, one chasing the other through his mind.

He soon found himself standing before Lord Beed, and fell to the floor before he was thrown there. He did not speak, waiting for the big man's questions.

"So, Dragonfang is ruled by the scum of Masima," the Lord growled.

Keela must have told him, he thought. Of course she did, She was one of his guards. When he realized the Lord was waiting, he answered, "Yes, my Lord."

"And he sends you to find any of his misguided followers to incite them to rise against me."

"No, my Lord."

A kick in his ribs took the breath from his body. "Do you challenge me?"

"Only when you are wrong, my Lor…"

This time the boot struck him in the face. Isen could taste blood in his mouth.

Isen lay prone on the floor. He will not hurt me too much, not yet. I just have to wait.

"Do not lie to me."

Isen braced himself for another blow, which did not come. "I do not lie," he tried.

The Lord of Bel walked to the window, staring out but seeing nothing. His mind fought to comprehend this little man. "Get him up," he commanded. Rough hands dragged Isen to his feet. "Why did you seek members of your Guild?"

Isen took a deep breath. This was the chance he had hoped for. "I wished to speak with you, my Lord. I thought if any of the Guild lived in Bel, they could best advise me on how to do that."

Lord Beed spun sharply and Isen waited for the next fist.

"Why?"

"I am merely a messenger, my Lord. Lord Chadas asked me to approach you and your city with regards to a treaty."

The bear approached slowly, looking deep into Isen's eyes. "What sort of treaty?"

"One to benefit both cities. Lord Chadas believes Dragonfang and Bel are the two most powerful cities in the world. He seeks a treaty of peace and increased trade. He says it will aid the lives of the people of both cities while adding to the treasuries of its Lords." Lord Beed stared and after a moment Isen added, "my Lord."

The Lord returned to the window. Isen waited. Eventually Lord Beed spoke. How do I know your Lord will not betray me just as Masima did to this city and its people long ago?"

"Lord Chadas is a good man and a fair leader."

Time stretched. "Take him back to the dungeon. I must consider his words."

Two more days passed before he was called back before Lord Beed. This time he was not man-handled. The Lord spoke immediately. "I will not make deals with a messenger. Your Lord can too easily deny all you say. No, you will remain here where I can find you. I will send my messenger to meet with your Lord Chadas."

"That is wise. Must I remain in the dungeon?"

The bear scratched an armpit before answering.

"No, but I will have your word that you will not try to leave Bel, and guards will be with you at all times."

"You have my word."

Lord Beed nodded.

"But, my Lord, may I add my message to tell Lord Chadas that you treat me well and that I believe his treaty is possible?"

Lord Beed agreed. "But I will read it before it is sent."

"Of course."

"Take him away." This time it was Keela who stepped forward to lead him from the room. Later that day, parchment, ink and quill were brought and he sat to compose his message. When he finished he read it back in his mind. *Lord Chadas, all powerful ruler of Dragonfang, I could find no one to introduce me but I did not require them. Some guards presented me to Lord Beed and I must report of the great courtesy he has shown. Your treaty interests him, but he is untrusting of dealing with a messenger. I will remain in Bel to guarantee the safety of his man but Lord Beed will meet only you to discuss terms. I trust your vision of greater trade with Bel comes to pass and hope for peace between the two cities.*

He smiled as he added his name and passed the parchment to Keela.

#

Alodia sat staring out of the small window of the sewing room in the corner of the tower. Her eyes looked but her mind did not comprehend. The city below did not reach her thoughts. She did not notice the mountains or the vast expanse of water. Even the open sky remained unseen. Her mind was turned inward, throwing reason around in a maelstrom of confusion. At one moment she felt the overwhelming joy of life, only to have it dashed aside by sudden terror. Then her tears would flood down her cheeks.

*This is not me. I am trained to be in control. I was taught to observe and think. Why can I not do it now?*

Still her sense was overruled by emotion. She jumped to her feet and fled the room, drawing anger along with her. Reaching the stairs, she rushed down. By the time she stepped into the sunlight, the tears had taken control again.

*No one should see me like this.*

She ran to the garden with guards trailing at a discreet distance. Running along the twisted pathways, she reached the hidden grotto, her grotto, hers and Chadas'. Her face fell into her hands as the tears flowed unchecked. Emotion may control her body, but her mind listened to her ears. She heard Chadas approaching.

Someone saw me and sent for him.

In her heart she was pleased but her mind was disappointed that she should be seen in this state. The heady scents of lavender and rosemary filled her nose and her stomach rebelled. She barely turned her head before her breakfast erupted to splash on the ground. An arm came around her shoulders. Chadas had arrived.

"Get someone. Hurry," he called to the guards.

Feelings of warmth and comfort filled her. "I will be fine. It happens sometimes," Alodia said.

"What happens? Why?"

Alodia took his hand and rested it on her belly. "I am with child," she whispered.

"How?"

"The usual way."

"Why? Who?"

Anger found its way back. Alodia was on her feet. "A baby. My baby. Your baby," she screamed.

Chadas put his arms around her and eased her head to his shoulder. "I am sorry. I know what, and how, and who. You just took me by surprise."

She looked up into his eyes. "You are not disappointed?"

"Disappointed?"

"With me."

Chadas laughed loudly then. "Why would I be disappointed with you. If my memory serves me, I had an equal part in this. It is good news."

"Good news," Alodia whispered and pressed herself closer into his body.

"Yes, very good news," Chadas laughed. "It will be a boy. We will have an heir to rule Dragonfang after we are gone."

"And if it is a girl?"

"It will be a boy. I forbid you to have a girl."

The runner arrived while Chadas was still accustoming himself to the news.

"What?" he snapped. The young girl cowered but passed him the rolled message. Taking it, he asked, "Where did this come from?"

"A messenger brought it … from Bel."

Chadas read, then passed the parchment to Alodia. While she read, he studied the girl. She was new to the tower and did not know her place, but he was certain she could not read. There was no way she could know what the words contained. Even so, he stressed, "No one must know of this or that you brought it to me. Do you Understand?" When she nodded he continued. "Where is he?"

"It is a woman, my Lord. She is in the Hall. She carries another message but will only pass it to you."

There followed a grunt from Alodia. As the girl began to speak again Chadas cut her off. "We heard you. There is no need to repeat yourself." He looked to Alodia, thinking, before adding, "Have food and ale brought to the woman. Tell her I will attend her shortly. Go. Run." The girl hurried off. "Is Isen a prisoner of the Lord of Bel?" he asked.

"That would seem to be the case," Alodia answered.

#

Chadas and Alodia took the time to ready themselves for the meeting. Alodia donned the dress she had been married in while Chadas placed a deep blue cape over a yellow doublet.

"Ready?" he asked. Alodia nodded.

Side by side they entered the Grand Hall. The woman jumped to her feet but Chadas waved her to sit again. "Finish your meal. You have had a long journey."

"Thank you my Lord," the messenger stumbled before pulling a scroll from beneath her tunic. "From Lord Beed," she offered as she held it out.

Chadas unrolled it and his eyes scanned the words. His glance to Alodia was all that was required to have her go along with what he would say. Turning to face the messenger he said, "So, the Lord of Bel is interested in my proposal for a trade agreement? He paused as if considering. "Tell your Lord that I will come after I have completed some business here."

Then to Alodia he added, "If this is a trap and I am betrayed, tell the army that no stone of Bel is to be left standing and no citizen breathing."

"If you fear a trap, then why go?" Alodia asked.

"I want this treaty. The most important aspect of any treaty is trust. I must demonstrate my trust in Lord Beed and he must see that trust. The army is only required if my trust is not returned."

To the messenger he said, "You will leave in the morning. I will be two days behind."

#

"We have discussed this. You will not come to Bel. Dragonfang needs you here. I want you to watch over the city while I am gone. Others must not see this as an opportunity to replace me."

"No one would dare challenge Lord Chadas."

"Maybe not, but with you here I would feel more comfortable."

Accepting her fate, Alodia warned him to be careful before they walked hand in hand out into the courtyard. There, they joined Chadas' traveling companions. Twelve of the Lord's Guard stood waiting by their horses. Twenty foot soldiers were with them. Three more horses were loaded with supplies. It should be only a short journey.

The air was beginning to chill but Alodia stood watching as Chadas left the tower and Dragonfang in the early light, avoiding pomp or ceremony, and began their march along the shore. Then her stomach betrayed her again.

While Chadas wanted to see Isen free, the lad had given him an opportunity, he had plans and it was more important that Lord Beed agree to a treaty. Chadas had no interest in trade with Bel, but there were benefits. Isen would be freed and the risk of attack by Bel would be reduced. It would give him time.

Throughout the morning they walked across firm sand, the sea on their right and the mountains climbing into the sky on their left. A number of small streams flowed from the valleys to the sea, but none caused any impediment. By the time Chadas called a halt for rest and food, they had covered twenty miles. At this rate they would be in Bel in less than two weeks. Chadas understood it would probably be longer, not every day would be this easy.

Maybe because of the recent dry weather, their journey went more quickly than Chadas expected. As the sun climbed to its peak on the twenty-second day, Bel came into sight. Eight guards on horseback greeted them.

"I am Kon of the Bel Guard. Lord Beed bids you welcome to our city."

One of Chadas' guards nudged his horse forward. "This is Lord Chadas of Dragonfang, Ama of the Guild." With the introduction, Kon's brow dropped and his lips tightened. "I am Captain Daric of Lord Chadas' Guard." He searched the group. "Does your Lord feel it is below him to greet my Lord in person?"

Kon squirmed in his saddle. "Lord Beed waits in the manor."

Daric frowned, but Chadas spoke. "It is fine, Captain. Are you a captain?"

"I have no title other than guard, as do all the guards. None is made to stand above others. One is chosen to lead each task the Lord desires."

Chadas smiled but said, "Lord Beed still does not trust me. He wishes to meet where he feels safe. I am here to show he need not fear us. By now, he knows I have not brought an army."

Kon tried to make himself more insignificant as he asked, "Do you wish to enter Bel?"

#

Chadas rode at the head of the guards as the entered Bel, known as the second largest city of the mountains. The houses and shops they passed were similar to those of Dragonfang, though they had a little more room around them. He saw none that resembled the house where he and Alodia had spent their early years. As he was guided to Lord Beed's manor, the name he was told he should use, Chadas studied its inadequate defenses. The outer wall offered the city's only real protection. He wondered how Lord Beed protected himself from his own people. The thought that no protection was needed did not occur to him.

He entered the manor with only Daric, Urk and Jerad as an escort. The others gathered in the courtyard.

Lord Beed sat waiting. His seat was not brightly colored cushions on a throne of worked gold or silver, but a simple wooden chair. Another sat opposite, with a small table between. Chadas signaled his guards to stand where they were and strode to the chair. Lord Beed was about to speak when Chadas said, "Good day to you Lord Beed. I am told you do not trust my messenger. Is this correct?"

Lord Beed's eyes widened, but he recovered quickly. "Welcome Lord Chadas. The city of Bel welcomes you and your guards, but I admit I was surprised by the invitation. It occurred to me that your man may be speaking out of turn."

"So, Isen is your prisoner?"

"No. He has agreed to stay here as proof he tells the truth."

A hardness came to Chadas' eyes but he forced his face to relax. "Where is he?"

Lord Beed raised a hand and beckoned. A door opened and Isen was escorted into the room.

"Are you harmed?"

"No, my Lord. Lord Beed has proved a gracious host."

Chadas waited to see if Isen would provide more details. When he did not, he turned his attention back to the Lord of Bel. "Isen is one of my most trusted advisers. That is why I sent him to speak with you."

"My deepest apologies, Lord Chadas."

"Why was he detained?"

Lord Beed dropped his eyes and mumbled but recovered quickly. "He made it clear when he first arrived that he was a member of your Guild. The Guild is not welcome in Bel. When our people discover a member walking among them, It is soon reported to the guards. They must act on the people's wishes."

Chadas was silent, waiting.

"It is the people of Bel who reject the Guild of Masima. I or my city bear no ill-will toward the Lord of Dragonfang."

"Anyone who rejects the Guild casts aspersions on me. We are not monsters who eat children or murder for fun. We have done great work in Dragonfang which leads me to my offer of treaty. The people of both cities will benefit from an agreement of trust and trade, but if you do not trust me, I do not think a treaty can be reached."

Lord Beed considered this. "What do you propose?"

"First, You and I must agree on a pact of peace between our cities. Without this, any agreement cannot succeed."

Lord Beed nodded. We are a peaceful city. I see no problem, but I will not have members of the Guild living or wandering about in Bel." Chadas' brow dropped. "Then I and my people will leave in the morning."

"What? Why?"

"I had intended leaving Isen here to act as my agent."

Isen's head snapped up.

"Wait." Lord Beed thought in the silence of the room. Then, "What would an agent do?" he asked.

He would speak for me on all but the most important decisions. He would check all loads going to and coming from Dragonfang."

Again there was silence.

"I would pay for his rooms and expenses," Chadas offered.

Lord Beed was quick to respond. "No. I will provide rooms in the manor and he will eat from my kitchens but you must agree that no further members will stay in Bel without my knowledge."

With a smile, Chadas assured him, "If it were my intention to infiltrate your city, I would have done it, and I would not be speaking with you now. But I wish to send two more people to help Isen with his work. To demonstrate my respect for Bel and its people, I will find two who are not of the Guild, though they would be loyal to Dragonfang."

The tightness of Lord Beed's face disappeared. "Agreed. And the trade agreement?" he asked.

Chadas turned to Isen. "Do you agree?"

"Of course my Lord."

"Then, when this agreement is ready, you will become Envoy of Dragonfang. You will be authorized by my seal to sign it." Turning back to Lord Beed he said, "I will leave the details to my Envoy. I have only one stipulation. In order for our cities to grow, the people must benefit. Goods in each direction will be taxed when they enter the city at a rate of one coin in twenty. That must be spent to aid both our cities to grow."

Lord Beed scratched his chin as a broad grin filled his face. "Agreed," he said.

#

Chadas laughed at the story one of his guards was telling of his exploits with the women as they rode into Dragonfang. The morning sun took the chill from the air and this, combined with his success in Bel, had put Chadas in a good mood. His thoughts drifted to his visit. Alodia would be pleased that he had obtained Isen's freedom, though she would probably not be happy that he had left him behind. She was fond of him.

The future of Bel had been on his mind and his plans had improved during the journey and he was anxious to share them with Alodia. Approaching the tower, however, he began to grow concerned. His wife was not waiting for him. His eyes flicked back and forth, searching for danger. The door of the tower opened and Tulong came down the steps. His worry had not left him, but if

Tulong was alive, there had been no attempt to replace him. He would have been the second to die behind Alodia.

He dismounted and passed the reins to Daric.

"Tulong, where is Alodia?"

"She is in your rooms, resting."

"Resting? Why does she need to rest?"

"She is feeling ill, my Lord."

Chadas rushed inside and up the stairs. Pushing past the guards he saw Alodia in her bed.

"What is wrong?"

Alodia smiled and began to speak, but threw herself to the side of the bed where a bucket rested on the floor. She lurched and emptied the contents of her stomach into it. When she lay back, she dabbed at her lips with her handkerchief. "Can you pass me some water?" she asked. Having refreshed her mouth, she explained, "It is the sickness of the baby."

"Is the baby ill?"

Alodia chuckled. "No, many women feel the illness when they are with child. It is worse in the morning but it goes soon enough. I should be feeling much better in three or four weeks." She patted her belly. "I hope he realizes what he is putting me through." But she smiled to reassure him.

Chadas' concern must have shown on his face because she added, "I am all right. Allow me to rest a little and I will join you in the Hall. Before you go, can you send someone in to take the bucket? The smell of it will make me ill again."

Chadas picked up the bucket. If it would help Alodia, he would remove it quickly. He would tell her later of his idea. After speaking with a number of people and satisfying himself that Alodia's sickness would pass, he sent word for Arienh and Dyfed to attend him in the Hall.

#

By the time the two leaders arrived, Alodia had joined him, looking better than earlier.

"Welcome," he greeted as each arrived. They were seated at a table in the Dining Hall. Trays of various foods waited while a fire spluttered in the hearth.

"I trust your trip was successful?" Arienh asked.

Chadas grinned. "You would not hold the position you do if you did not already know."

Arienh returned the grin. "I know you smile a great deal and I know Isen is not with you. Rumor has it that we now have a peace agreement with Bel."

"The rumors are partly true. Isen remains in Bel to negotiate a treaty of peace and trade."

"We have no need of a peace agreement. Our army is far stronger than anything Bel could put against us." Dyfed declared. A few heads nodded. "Why not take the army there and win Bel for the Guild?"

"I agree, but this agreement gives us other advantages. Why should we fight? We did not fight to win Dragonfang, only to remove an troublesome lord. The

Guild works from within. Lord Beed will soon come to accept that I mean peace and his feelings toward the Guild will relax. That is what we are here to discuss."

They waited quietly.

"Bel is not like Dragonfang. It has no army. The guards have no structure. They do not know who will lead each mission until someone is appointed by the Lord."

Dyfed's eyes widened. "So, we could conquer Bel without too much trouble."

Chadas nodded but explained, "The Guild does not exist in Bel. It is despised by the Lord and all his people. That is how Isen was taken. As soon as he was suspected of being a member, the people turned him in. If we try to force our way into Bel, the people will never accept us. It is easier to win their trust. I have convinced Lord Beed that Isen should stay to act as my representative in his city."

"Will he be safe?" Alodia asked.

"I believe so. Lord Beed knows that any act against him will incur the wrath of Dragonfang.

"What do you want us to do?" asked Arienh.

"Isen will act in my name, but he will need staff. He will need a tax man to oversee the shipments in and out of Bel. They will require a scribe to document and authorize each load. All deliveries from Bel must carry the scribes mark. They must also find a method of passing messages back to Dragonfang. House Bela will provide the tax man, and the scribe will be from House Eeva. I want good people, but it must never be discovered they are of the Guild."

Arienh and Dyfed nodded. "What is your plan?" Arienh asked.

"I want to know all they can learn of Bel and earn the trust of Lord Beed. The Guild has not spread throughout the city, but now they will. We lived in the shadows here for many generations while Dragonfang thrived and suffered under many lords. Bel will not be permitted to take that long."

# 29 CHILDREN OF THE TOWER

Chadas was late getting to bed. He had been reading more of the piles of reports that came to him daily. Trade seemed to be growing and many suggested that the people of Bel were more tolerant of the Guild. It would soon be time for some of their members to find their way into Bel's community. Already a few had been selected who would be accepted.

Laying down, his eyes had barely closed when Alodia grunted and moaned. Moments later his eyes flew open as she screamed. His knife was in his hand. Soon she settled, looked at him, and laughed. "What is that for?" she chuckled.

"You screamed. I thought someone was attacking."

"Put it away and get the mid-wife. The baby is coming." Chadas sat, stunned. She had to push him to get him moving, but once the spell was broken, he ran to the door. "Alodia laughed again before suggesting, "Put some clothes on first."

Eventually the mid-wife and two ladies-in-waiting were in the bedroom with Alodia. Chadas was exiled to his outer rooms. Deciding to make use of the time, he sat at his desk and pulled another pile of reports toward him. Taking the first, he sat back to read.

Excited women's voices woke him. The two ladies-in-waiting were coming from the bedroom. "Is Alodia alright?" he asked.

"Yes, my Lord," they answered in unison.

"And the baby?"

One stepped forward to curtsy. "May I be the first to offer my congratulations, my Lord?" You have a beautiful baby."

Chadas grunted. "No son of Lord Chadas should be described as beautiful." She waited, still crouched in her curtsy. "But I thank you." He then had a terrible thought. "It is a boy, is it not?"

"Yes, my Lord, a healthy baby boy."

#

Crowds began to gather even as the sun crept into the sky. Most of Dragonfang was already there, many of them busy at stalls in the food and goods area. Archery targets stood ready to draw attention. The swordplay area had been fenced off while other areas awaited the wrestlers, knife throwers and participants in the other activities.

Chadas watched through the narrow slit opening in the tower. Behind him, five women fussed with dressing Alodia and the baby. Alodia would be wearing green, she had told him, and the baby would be resplendent in yellow silk and much lace. He could not understand why a woman needed to spend so much on a child's clothes that would only be worn once, but he did not argue or even voice his thoughts. This was to be the baby's day, he did not mind too much. *But his clothes cost more than my sword.*

Finally, the attendants announced both were ready. Chadas turned from his view of the festival grounds to see what his people would see. Alodia's long gown, split for riding, was also new. *Another sword, maybe two.* He nodded. "The city will be impressed. It is time for us to go." He strode to the door with Alodia following. The five attendants trailed, one holding a basket with the baby.

In the courtyard their horses had been saddled and stood ready. His and Alodia's wore blue caparisons while the guards' horses had red. All were trimmed with gold tassels. When everyone was mounted, the baby was carefully passed up to Alodia. At his signal, they moved out. Five guards abreast rode in front with another five abreast behind. Three rode in single file on each side with Alodia and Chadas in the middle of this impressive box.

As they moved through the city, cheers surrounded them and people began to follow. Their numbers swelled moment by moment. They reached the festival grounds ahead of a long procession, all cheering and singing.

Slowly making their way through the crowds, their guard protecting them, they inched closer and closer to the stage that had been erected for them. Chadas climbed the wide steps with Alodia at his side. The crowds hushed.

"Welcome to today's festivities," he called. "This day of fun is to honor a new arrival to Dragonfang." The crowd grew even quieter with anticipation. Alodia held the baby high. "Meet my son, Lukin." A roar of approval greeted the announcement and spread as word of the baby's name spread to those out of hearing. Chadas allowed it to continue. When they settled, he thanked them on Lukin's behalf. "The book of names says that Lukin means light. He has certainly brought light into my life, and to Lady Alodia's." The crowd cheered again. Then he bade all those competing his best wishes.

Alodia gave Lukin a soft tickle under his chin as she passed him to her attendants who, under escort, returned him to the tower.

Chadas sprawled on his chair. From his position on the stage, he had an overview of the events going on in the various arenas. Color and noise were everywhere.

"I am going for a walk," he told Alodia. "I would like to see some of the events from a closer distance."

"I will come with you."

Chadas took her hand and helped her to her feet. Together they descended the stairs. With guards around them and clearing a path, it was not long before they were watching the wrestling. This was the only event where men and women competed separately. At the moment a women's match was taking place.

The aim of the match was to prepare the army for fighting in close quarters. Each contestant was to put their opponent on the ground where they could be easily dispatched if it were a battle. In the match that was about to start, Aivi, the wife of the blacksmith, a big woman with arms like a man's thighs was to face a girl Chadas did not recognize. She was a small, nimble lass. Aivi was expected to win but Chadas knew from his training size was not always an advantage. He was going to enjoy this match.

The girl was cautious, dancing around her larger opponent without closing. Aivi made three lunges, trying to catch the girl, only to grasp at air. After the third attempt, Chadas knew who would win. On the next lunge, the girl darted left and ducked beneath the outstretched wrist as it passed. With a pull she caught Aivi off-guard, increasing her momentum as she passed. Aivi stumbled forward, but she was not beaten yet. Her heavy legs pushed beneath her falling body until she was able to stand again. Aivi began to turn. The girl had followed and swung a kick into the back of Aivi's knees. Maintaining her balance, Aivi gave a roar and lumbered after her miniature attacker as the girl skipped away.

And so the match went on, the girl darting in as if to attack, before falling back making the blacksmith's wife chase her. Once, she even slapped the big woman on the rump. This made Chadas laugh aloud, to which the girl nodded her thanks.

Aivi was tiring. In a desperate bid to end the match, she stopped chasing and beckoned the girl to come closer. In reply, the girl began to run circles around the big woman, around and around, always just out of reach. Chadas watched with interest. This was a dangerous game. Aivi turned to watch as she ran, but when the spinning became too much, she stopped and followed her with her head. The girl continued and when she was behind Aivi, who was forced to turn her head to the other side, she attacked. Another kick to the back of the knees and a solid shove in the back had Aivi desperately seeking her balance again. As she moved her feet, the girl threw one leg in front of them. Aivi crashed to the ground, raising a cloud of dust.

The girl looked back. Chadas applauded and called, "Your name?".

"Aiolos, my Lord."

"Well done, Aiolos," and Chadas nodded his head.

*My Lord, the archery is moving into the next round.*

*Thank you Nelda.*

At the archery, one group had just finished and the next competitors were preparing. Someone called, "My Lord, would you care to demonstrate your skills?"

"No," he answered shaking his head. "Let those competing entertain us."

"Can I try?" Chadas looked to his sister.

"Of course, my Lady. Let me find a bow for you." One was quickly brought and Alodia took her stance. She fired three times in quick succession. All three arrows hit the target, one slightly to the left and two well high. She thanked the owner of the bow and returned to Chadas' side.

As they continued their walk, their guards clearing a path through the people. Chadas whispered, "What were you doing?"

"Shooting arrows."

He scowled. "You know what I mean. You are better than that."

"I have shown your people what they needed to see. Those that watched know I can shoot, and word will spread. Any that have ideas do not know how well I shoot."

"You are the Lady of Dragonfang. It is expected that you are the best," Chadas growled.

She smiled. "As long as you know it."

They continued in silence.

When they reached the knife-throwing, Chadas watched with undeniable interest. Each contestant was asked to hit seven targets from seven throws. Four of the targets were stationary, but spaced and at different heights. The other three were moving, the final one resembling a small bird in flight.

They lingered there. Most throwers hit the four stationary targets, but few were successful with the moving ones. While they watched, everyone failed at the final challenge. The most successful competitors had all been trained by the Guild.

When he heard the call to try his skills, Chadas stepped forward without hesitation. Someone approached with the knives, but Chadas waved them away. He spun, raised his hand, and a knife appeared in it. As he threw, another knife was suddenly in his other hand. It, too flew, before the first had reached the targets. The knives followed as he threw with each hand, the knives appearing and launching as if possessed.

The crowd was stunned to silence and the only sound was the thud, thud, thud of knives hitting the targets. When he stopped, all seven targets were pierced by knives, all dead center. Chadas retrieved his weapons. They disappeared into his clothing as fast as he pulled them from their resting place. He returned to Alodia and was halfway there before the silence was broken. Cheers erupted from the people.

"And what were you doing?" his sister asked.

"Throwing knives."

They turned and walked away. They had gone twenty paces before Alodia whispered, "Showoff."

#

Lukin was two when his brother was born and almost four when his sister arrived. Tomm was named in remembrance of Chadas' old mentor while they called the girl Wynne in honor of their mother. As the children turned five, Chadas introduced them to the duties of being a Lord. He began by having them listen whenever he was required to offer judgment on a dispute among his people. "You must watch and learn," he told them. "There will come a time when you will be asked to decide."

Before passing on his decision, he would often ask how they would handle the situation. Later he would explain where their answers were right or wrong. "It is not a decision our people are requesting," he would explain. "It is our understanding. It is the role of the Lord when hearing their complaints to show we can appreciate their problem and offer a solution they can accept, even if it is not the correct one."

When they turned eight, younger than when he began his training, Chadas explained they would learn from the masters of the Guild. They were to train for two years in each of the four Houses. They would begin in the House of Bela, followed by the Houses of Meeya and Alard. Finally they would study in House Eeva. When they were finished, they may choose a House to continue their training if they wished it. Lukin had obeyed but when Tomm learned of his father's wishes, he complained, "That will make me sixteen before I finish my studies."

Chadas had replied, "Yes."

As the children progressed with their studies, not all the reports were favorable. Lukin was an excellent student , gaining praise from all his mentors. One report said, 'He is a son worthy of his father's ambitions."

When she was nine, Alodia took Wynne to the private garden. At a secluded seat, and with the guards at a suitable distance, she spoke quietly. "You have been training with your brothers, and we are both proud of what you have achieved, but it is time for you to become more."

Wynne looked up from her round face surrounded by curls, waiting.

"The people want to see Lukin and Tomm as great warriors. But they want something else from you."

"What mama?"

"The people want to see a lady. They want to see a gentile and well presented young woman. You do not need to give up your training, in fact it is more important for you than your brothers. An enemy will stand up to them and expect a good fight, and your brothers can give them that. But when they look at you, they will not see what you will be able to do. This will put you at the advantage."

"I can trick them."

"No, not trick them, surprise them. Your skills must be kept secret."

#

Wynne followed in her elder brother's footsteps.

The same could not be said for Tomm. At first, his reports were less than good, claiming he was easily distracted or disinterested. One said, 'Tomm shows he does not share the interest in learning that his brother displayed.' At age ten, Chadas read, 'Tomm shows more interest in girls than in his studies.'

Chadas had always blamed these on the unachievable expectations of the mentors following Lukin's efforts. Now he decided the time had come to speak with his son.

"I have no problems," Tomm assured him, "and if I am not as good as Lukin, why should I be. He studies all day and has no interest in other pursuits. I like girls. Lukin will one day be Lord of Dragonfang. That is what he trains for. I will only ever be his brother, but it has advantages. The girls know that Lukin is distracted with his role and see me as a good alternative. I am happy to allow them their dreams."

Chadas considered Tomm's reply. Putting an arm around the boy's shoulder he said, "Let us walk." They went out to his private garden and strolled between the shrubs. "Do you believe I would not have plans for you?" Chadas asked. Tomm turned to his father but said nothing. "I have had plans for your future since you were born, since Lukin was born."

"You have told me nothing of them."

You were not ready to hear them. You are not ready to hear them now."

"Why?"

"Because if anyone discovered them, it could cause trouble. It would not be trouble that would cause us disaster, but it may raise tensions in the city and beyond. I only ask that you trust me and put effort into your studies."

Tomm continued walking beside his father, his head turned and face squinting on one side. "I will think about it," he promised. If he considered the words, it did not stop the inadequate reports.

#

On the occasion of Lukin's sixteenth birthday, Chadas declared another festival. The people of Dragonfang were becoming familiar with their Lord's ways. Whenever Chadas wished to make a happy announcement, he did it at a festival. There were no doubts this was to be a celebration of his son becoming a man.

The usual events were being competed but today was something different. This festival was for the common folk. Guards who had trained with the sword were not permitted to enter. The archery was for the farmers and storekeepers. Those who usually challenged or won watched from the sidelines.

The day was becoming a huge success with lots of laughing and surprisingly few injuries, and they were minor.

With the heats completed and everyone resting before an afternoon of finals, Chadas turned to Tomm. "Have you been watching?"

"Of course. It has been fun. I particularly enjoyed the women wrestling."

"That is not what I meant."

Tomm squinted as he tried to think of what his father wanted of him.

"Have you been watching?" Chadas asked again, heavily emphasizing the last word. "When the finals begin, I want you to watch all the events you can. You will later tell me all the skills that each competitor exhibits. In the swords, watch how quickly a man moves from defense to attack. Which archers release their arrows without pause. Anything that makes them stand out, no matter if they win or not."

"Yes father," he replied.

Chadas then rose. He waved Tomm away and moved to the front of the stage. All ears turned to hear what the Lord was about to say. They were surprised by the formality he chose to use.

"People of Dragonfang," he called. "Honored members of the council." He paused and bowed in the direction of the House leaders. "Competitors, ladies and gentlemen." An expectant silence greeted this introduction. "That means you, the Store holders and blacksmith, the farmers and mothers, and everyone in the city." They cheered then. "We are here today to celebrate my son, Lukin. On this day he becomes a man." A roar of applause shook the air. When it quietened, Chadas continued. "He has become a man that Lady Alodia and I can look on with pride. I think the city of Dragonfang can also be proud." Further cheering and calls of congratulations followed.

It took some time before they noticed Chadas still standing and a respectful silence fell over the crowd.

"I have been Lord of this city for a long time," he told them. The councilors exchanged glances. He had not told them what he was about to say. "I grow tired." Again, he waited. Everyone was now listening intently. "I have trained Lukin well, and he has been a good student. It is time for me to relax and enjoy my life with my wife. From today, Lukin will be known as Regent of Dragonfang. I will remain Lord but he will take over the daily operation of the city."

The loudest roar followed. Chadas glanced across to where the councilors stood in silence. Each knew his time as Lord would not last forever and each hoped that when he grew tired, the next Lord would come from their House. Now the city expected and wanted Lukin. Chadas hoped his son would be safe from their political maneuvering. Each House had been involved in the training of Lukin. Would that satisfy them?

Chadas turned back to the crowd. "Of course, Lady Alodia and I will be available should Regent Lukin wish our advice."

The new Regent stepped up beside his father to tumultuous appreciation.

Moire stepped up beside them. She called, "On behalf of the council, I welcome our new Regent and remind him that he has great boots to follow. I hope he proves worthy of his role."

More cheers followed.

Lukin thanked her. "My father is the best that Dragonfang has seen. I will try to live up to his high standards. Now, let the games continue," he called.

#

The festival to celebrate Tomm's coming of age was a less exciting but more memorable affair. Chadas chose not to have tournaments of skill. Instead, a large number of cooks prepared meats and delicacies of all types. Ale and mead was abundant and a great party began. There were no speeches until the end of the day when good humor was in vast supply.

Regent Lukin called Tomm to stand beside him while Chadas approached to hang his arms around the shoulders of his sons. Alodia and Wynne sat on their chairs behind.

"People of Dragonfang," Lukin called. "I know it is hard to believe, but my brother has become a man." He glanced to Tomm with a grin. "I think many young girls of Dragonfang have thought this happened long ago." Tomm's beaming face bowed to his brother.

Lukin continued. When I became a man, I was named Regent of Dragonfang." Cheers rose from the crowd. "It has been a difficult task. My father was difficult to follow. But Dragonfang cannot have two Regents." Laughter followed while Lukin stood scratching his head. "Can you imagine two Regents?" he asked. "One is more than enough."

More laughter was punctuated with calls of "Long live Lukin."

"But my brother deserves his place in the city, something to keep him out of mischief. And give our girls time to hide," he laughed.

Tomm scowled at his brother.

"That is why I have decided Tomm will begin his training tomorrow, as commander of our army. The party is almost ended but Tomm's training is about to begin." Expectant silence followed. "In order that he may learn his duties, he will lead our army on a march at sunrise tomorrow. I want all members of the army here and waiting, but some will remain behind to protect Dragonfang if needed. Be prepared to stay away until my brother learns." He gave Tomm a grin. "I have never seen my brother out of his bed at sunrise. It will be a new experience for both of us."

"Why does the army need to go before the day has begun?" Tomm called.

The laughter that followed was free and loud, partly from Lukin's speech but more from the ale and mead. But all would be ready at sunrise just to see Tomm's discomfort.

Lukin held his arms high and waited for the noise to subside. When it did, he spoke to them again. "I know we celebrate Tomm today, but I have another duty to perform, a very pleasant one." From somewhere, a man appeared. He had not been noticed before that moment, which was surprising because he led a massive gray dog.

Wynne rose to stand beside her brothers.

"Before I became Regent, my father was very busy caring for the city. Now he has more time, we have decided to present him with this gift." Lukin turned to his father. "Now you have a companion to go hunting."

Chadas thanked him and crouched to nuzzle the big dog's face.

"Her name is Nola," Wynne offered.

"Hello Nola," Chadas whispered. Her fur, if it could be called that, was a tangle of gray and white, stiff and wiry beneath his hands. "Do you like to hunt?" Nola licked his face.

Chadas looked up to his children and smiled.

"Now you have something to do," Lukin called, "we might be able to live our lives in peace."

"That is very unlikely," Chadas laughed. The crowd laughed with him.

#

Lukin and Tomm teased each other on the ride back at the tower.

When all had returned to quiet, Alodia led Wynne to the private garden. At a bench, Alodia sat and patted the seat beside her. "We need to chat," she began. Wynne's curiosity showed in the way she twisted her body to face her mother while pulling at her blonde tresses. Her head tilted in question. The scent of flowers hung in the still air as if awaiting gossip.

"What do you think of Lukin's announcement?"

Wynne stared a moment before answering. "Which one?" she asked and when Alodia did not reply added, "I was surprised."

"Your reason?"

"I will not speak ill of my brothers."

Alodia smiled. "No one will know what is said here. I will not think less of you for answering my question with honesty."

Again Wynne waited before answering. "Tomm may learn, but I do not think he has the ability to lead the army. He can barely look after himself."

"And why would that be?"

"He ignores his studies and is more interested in what lies beneath a girl's skirts than fighting, Dragonfang or anything else."

Alodia patted her knee. "You are exactly right."

"So why did Lukin name him commander?"

"That was your father's and my suggestion." Wynne's brow rose but she did not speak. "What I am about to tell you was also our decision." Wynne leaned forward and the garden scents seemed to come closer, awaiting Alodia's words. "We want you to ride with your father and Tomm tomorrow."

"Why? I am not trained in war. I can use a knife or sword, but I have not been instructed in the strategies."

"You will not need to be, but you will be gone more than a day or two, as will Tomm and the army. You must not mention this to anyone until the time is right."

"When will that be?"

"You will know when those with you know. Your brother is to be no more than a figurehead of your mission. His destiny is not with the army, and neither is yours. Your father will be there to give him his true role, and you will be at his side to ensure he succeeds. You may be younger, but you have been trained for what is required."

"What must I do?"

You must guide and support your brother, just as I do for your father."

Wynne's eyes widened as the words assembled in her mind. "Are you telling me I must marry him?"

"Do not look shocked. We have told no one, but Chadas is my brother, one year younger than me. It was easier for us. The people did not know."

Wynne's jaw dropped. "Does father know?"

Alodia laughed. "Of course. It was his idea." They sat in silence. The scents withdrew to think. "When the time comes, you will understand. Let Tomm have his girls. It will keep him occupied. You will act in his name.

# 30 CHOSEN

Far to the south, the twins, Hope and Faith, had moved on from their mother's passing and grown into the young women they now were. Torne, however, could not understand. It had taken him years to accept Shayla's death. He put this down to the innocence and acceptance of childhood.

His girls, now fourteen, rushed home. Their father watched their approach with amusement as he rested on his chair on the porch. It had been a long, hard day on the farm. When they were close enough, the girls began to shout. Both tried to outdo the other in the babble of their excitement.

"Guess what we found Papa."

"You must come and see Papa."

"It is blue."

"A sword. We found a blue sword."

"Not like any sword I have seen."

"Me either Papa."

"Have you seen a blue sword Papa?"

"We were going to bring it to you."

"It got angry Papa. Do you think a sword can get angry?"

"Come and see."

"Yes, you must come and see."

With their tirade concluded, they turned and ran back the way they had come. Hope stopped long enough to call, "Come with us Papa."

Torne could feel every one of his thirty-four years. He was tired and only wanted his rest, but he loved his daughters and their enthusiasm dragged him to his feet and he followed.

"Hurry Papa."

#

Torne caught up with his daughters near a tuft of rushes beside the small stream that ran through the farm. They were both pointing. There, among the green stalks, a blue sword stood with its point in the soft ground. He stared. He worked his fields most days and had done so for years. Why had he not seen it? He turned slowly to see if anyone was watching.

Hope spoke. "It does not like us Papa. I will show you." Her words delivered, she approached to sword. With each step, the sword changed from blue to an angry red. When it began to pulse with dark power, she stopped.

"It does the same with me," Faith told him.

Hope withdrew and the calm blue returned.

"You try," Faith prompted. "It might like you."

Torne was doubtful. Why would the sword like him? But it would only grow angry again. It had not harmed anyone. He took a step forward, and another. It was not growing red which confused him. Why should it not do the same, he wondered. He stepped closer. The sword had been like polished stone, solid. Now it was different, the blue was fading, becoming something he could almost see through, like a thin blue curtain at a window.

He was close and the color was almost gone. When he hesitated and ripples of blue ran along the blade. The sword seemed to be calling to him. He stepped up beside it, sensing his daughters holding their breath behind him. A soft glow now surrounded the blade.

I must be tired, he thought. I can hear it purring to me like a kitten. Reaching out, he wrapped his fingers around the hilt. Energy filled him. The exhaustion left him. With one swift movement, he pulled the sword from the ground and held it high, and almost dropped it. Golden flames burst from the blade flooding the darkening air with light.

The flames only lasted a moment before the sword grew calm, but he felt its exultation as if it were his own. He studied their find. The hilt was patterned in scales, like a fish, and protected by a guard shaped to resemble a dragon, its head on one side and wings on the other. The dragon's body wrapped around his knuckles with its tail returning to the bottom of the hilt.

The fingers of his free hand traced up the blade. It felt cold, like any bronze sword, but it was not bronze and it was smoother, slipperier, like water. At the hilt, the double edged blade was quite narrow, widening as it went up until, close to the tip, it turned in and came to a point. At its broadest place, an image marked the blade. It was not painted on, nor was it carved into the surface. It was part of the blade varying only in that it was a slightly lighter shade. In the middle was what appeared to be the sword, above it three wavy lines and below, a dragon with a long body, four legs and two massive wings. Six circles surrounded the image; each linked to the next with a thin line. He did not understand any of the images, but felt it was important.

Torne turned to stare at his daughters.

"What is the trouble?" Faith asked.

"I do not know. I have never seen anything like this sword." Torne tried to put it back where he had found it but the blade turned deep green like a storm about to break. In his mind he heard the sword speak with one word, No!

"It has chosen you Papa," Hope gushed.

Faith added, "Where did it come from?"

Torne studied the sword that seemed to have bonded with him, but what was the bond, good or evil? Was it the bond of an eagle and its prey or that of a dog and his master?

# 31 BEL

The army gathered. As the sun peeked over the horizon, Chadas, Tomm and Wynne mounted and rode from the tower. Nola loped along beside them. Their personal guard followed.

It had been decided that a quarter of the army would remain behind to protect Dragonfang. The rest would join the march. When they arrived at the field, officers were assembling the mass of men and women into divisions. Drawing close. Tomm shielded his face with a hand and groaned, "Where is the sun?" This brought a few chuckles and word of his discomfort would spread.

Everything was working out as Chadas planned. The wagons carried enough food and water to last the journey. Ample arrows and weapons were hidden beneath covers. And hiding in plain sight, dressed as waggoners' wives and cooks were the Majickers. Korra would stay in Dragonfang to send reports of events in the city.

A short time later, Tomm kicked his dappled horse into motion. Dressed in a red cape, a broad-rimmed red hat with black plume and shining black boots trimmed in red, he was every part the spoiled upstart prince in command of the greatest army in Lilim. Chadas and Wynne rode side-by-side behind him. A block of guards flanked them on each side while a third trailed close behind.

The archers and swords followed in groups of twenty-five, alternating to give the best protection to the trailing wagons. Axmen and pike brought up the rear. The five-wide column snaked along the beach for over a mile. The first day and the second went smoothly, but on the second night, Tomm called, "I am covered in dust. Where is my bath, and put some water on to heat. I cannot go on like this."

A soldier he could not see called back, "This is the sarding army. We have no bath or water to spare for spoiled brats. Be dusty like the rest of us."

"Well, at least bring me my spare clothes."

"Did you pack any more? If not, you're wearing all you are going to until you learn."

Tomm held back his grin.

As they set out on the third day, mutters of discontent began to trickle through the ranks. Chadas had expected this and had prepared for it. As each complaint flowed by, a second comment followed. "How can we teach Tomm his duties if we do not allow him to be tested? After all, the poor lad has to go without his bath."

A reply came. "Maybe his sister should lead the army. She rides without complaint." This brought a wave of laughs from those nearby.

The army marched on, over sand and through small rivers. Days passed.

Then Tomm turned them inland. The unexpected turn brought comment and rumor. They marched into the valley chilled by the shadows of the mountains, beside a freshwater stream, they stopped.

"We will set our camp here," Tomm announced. "You have all earned a day or two of rest."

#

The wagon laden with exotic goods rumbled into Bel. Inside the gate it was stopped by Isen's inspectors. The old man at the reins glanced over his shoulder and shook his head. The city was not protected by an iron gate but a simple wooden structure and two guards. The low stone wall that surrounded the city offered little more protection. In all the years Bel had traded with Dragonfang, had they learned nothing?

While the inspection was taking place, the assessor wandered around making a mental tally of the duty. He would add it to the records later in his room. But the wagon's most important cargo was not on the manifest. The old man driving the horses was not as he seemed. The clothes, beard and coloring disguised one of House Meeya's most skilled spies. The young woman at his side was clad in heavy work clothes and could have been his daughter or niece if not for her obvious servitude. She may have been a grand daughter straight from the farm.

As the assessor passed, the driver passed his hand across his chest with three fingers extended as his hand rose to scratch his beard vigorously.

The assessor did not flinch at the signal. "That will be three silvers," he calculated.

"Three silvers? The duty should be no more than two silvers, not even that."

"I said three silvers."

"Thief," the driver yelled. "I will not pay that.

"Guard," the assessor called in a steady voice. One man left the gate to approach menacingly. The assessor turned back to the wagon and demanded, "The duty is three silvers. Pay."

"I will give you two silvers and not a copper more. I will not pay to make you rich."

"Take these two and their wagon and lock them in the holding house. Post two men to watch the door and then return to the gate. They must speak with no one until I question them again."

"Very happy to," the guard grinned. "Right you two, move along, straight down the road. I will show you where to go. If you try anything, you will have the might of Bel to face." Not far down the road they were turned into an old stone and timber barn. When the doors closed behind them, dark shadows filled the windowless space. The two sat on the wagon and waited. Isen would not keep them waiting long. By touching his face after giving the signal informed the assessor their message was urgent.

The voice of the assessor broke the stillness. "Get down. Follow me." They dropped to the ground and the voice said, "Over here." A hatch opened and pale light rose to offer its comfort. "Down the ladder," the assessor instructed.

They descended quickly into a narrow tunnel that reminded them of the early tunnels beneath Dragonfang, built before the Guild grew their strength. The assessor led holding the dimmed lantern while they followed, running fingers along the rough-cut stone walls. No side tunnels offered alternative paths. No chambers offered a place to rest. They walked until they reached the far end where another ladder led up. They climbed to the open hatch.

Isen sat at a table that held goblets of fine wine. The assessor turned back to the tunnel saying, "Come back when you have finished."

The girl stopped him. "You should wait. What I tell Isen, you should hear." The assessor turned to Isen who nodded. "My name is Elrida. What is your name?"

"They call me Yol."

Elrida smiled. "It is good to meet you both. I am one of a group of women loyal to Lord Chadas." She indicated the old man with her. "This is Roh, a senior member of House Meeya."

Isen's eyes grew large as he glanced back and forward between his guests. Who is this girl that someone this important defers to her?

Elrida motioned the assessor to a chair while she took the other. Roh stood against the wall, hands clasped behind his back.

"Lord Chadas sends his greetings," she began, "and his instructions to you both."

Isen held out his hand awaiting the coded message. When none was passed, he lowered his hand. "Do you have a message?"

"Not yet. Lord Chadas has not given anyone the message yet."

Isen glanced to Roh who shrugged, then back to the girl. "Then how can I act if the only one who knows the message is in Dragonfang?"

"I am speaking with the Lord now."

"What! How?"

"I told you. I am one of a group of women loyal to Lord Chadas. We have special abilities." Isen's eyes widened as the thought came to him. "A witch?"

"If that is what you wish to call me."

A gasp left Yol's lips.

"How do I know you speak with him now?"

"Lord Chadas says I should demonstrate my skills." He paused for a moment, and a gush of air spun around the room upsetting papers on the desk. When it stopped, Isen spoke again."

"Tell me when the Lord decided I should stay in Bel," he demanded.

"You were held by Lord Beed. The Lord came to Bel to demand your release. When he heard your story, he supported it and left you here to demonstrate your importance to Dragonfang." Isen sat quietly for a moment. "When he left, he told you that the time would come when you must obey. I do not know what it means, but he says the time has come for the yellow dragon to bare its teeth. "Isen sat up. This was the code he was told to expect. "What does Lord Chadas desire of me?"

"You each have a task to perform." She turned to Yol. "You must gather all that is valuable, coins, artworks or papers, and hide them for safety but where they can be collected later. Do not allow anyone to know what you do, then return here."

To Isen, she passed on his instructions. Lord Chadas says you both must act quickly. He wants everything complete and both of you ready to leave this afternoon. We will wait at the wagon until you are ready."

#

Isen strode to the manor house and told the guard he must speak with Lord Beed on a matter of urgency. He was soon ushered before the leader of Bel.

Lord Beed began. "I have heard that a wagon driver refuses to pay the duty. This is not something that requires my attention."

"No, my Lord, but the driver carried a letter for me." He pulled from his pocket the letter and hoped the Lord did not look too closely for the ink was barely dry. He passed it to the leader who read it.

The Lord looked up and passed the letter back. "I am sorry. I know how frail mothers can be. What can I do?"

"With your permission, my Lord, I would like to return to Dragonfang to be with her in her final days."

"Of course. When?"

"As soon as possible my Lord. The wagon that arrived today can be sent back for not paying the duty. We can put it out today and I can ride on it."

Lord Beed looked concerned. "Will you be safe? The driver may have a grudge for the profits he did not receive."

Isen scratched his head. "With your permission again, I could allow him to pay only what he wishes to. We could have him unloaded and leaving this afternoon. He will think he has fooled us, but when I return, I can add a copper to each load he delivers. It will take time, but his debt will be paid with a little extra for our troubles."

"I agree. Go back to Dragonfang and help your mother. I will see you when you return."

#

When the wagon left Bel, the hunched old driver looked slightly different. No one noticed. The wagon rumbled along, and when it was clear , Isen slapped the driver on the back. "You did a good job."

Yol pulled away the fake beard and hair and stretched to remove the kinks from his back. "He did," Elrida agreed. "Now turn into the valley up ahead."

They had not gone far when the army came into view. Isen and the assessor stared. The army sprawled through the valley like an undulating mat of bodies. They had not seen this many campfires and people in one place outside Dragonfang. As the wagon approached, a familiar figure rode out to greet them.

"My Lord Chadas," Isen offered as he arrived.

Chadas greeted them then apologized. "I am sorry the hurried summons, but I did not want either of you in the city in the morning. It is a danger that was avoidable." They joined Chadas in his tent while the confusion of activity filled the valley. The sky had darkened as the Great Dragon ate the sun before they emerged. "Walk with me," Chadas requested. They walked down the valley, Chadas leading his horse. Elrida dropped back to join the women following.

Having completed its preparations, the army followed. No one rode, and other than Chadas' stallion, all the horses were at the tail of the column. Swords were wrapped in cloth to prevent noise while spears and other weapons were carefully packed for the same reason.

The line marched down the valley and turned towards Bel. Each group knew where they needed to be. Travel was swift. As they neared the wall, Chadas spoke with his Majickers. "Are you ready?" They replied that they were. "Begin then."

Nothing seemed to happen for a while but soon a cold wind blew in from the sea. It carried with it the smell of unease, a promise of danger yet to happen. Dark clouds lit by internal lights crawled toward the shore. Chadas' army closed and the defenses of Bel loomed large in the flashes of light. He signaled and the army spread into the darkness. A Majicker marched with each group and only Elrida remained with him.

Night was dying when it was reported that all were in position. Sunlight tried to break through the storm. "Now!" Chadas sent to his Majickers.

A bolt of lightning like nothing he had seen lit the clouds, emphasizing the boiling blue, black and green of the sky. The light coalesced and drove toward the ground. In a moment of anger, it struck. The section of wall did not explode; it disappeared in a cloud of dust that was washed away in the rain.

With its anger sated, the storm subsided. Clouds dissipated. Rain and lightning dispelled.

A shout of alarm from the city wall, followed by others. It was not long before half-clad guards joined the defenses.

#

Daylight showed the full extent of Chadas' betrayal. The city was surrounded and armed soldiers were sitting just beyond the range of arrows. Many in the ranks wondered why they had not attacked while they held the advantage of surprise, but their orders were to hold.

Chadas had other ideas. His army was beyond anything the guards of Bel could muster. He trusted Alodia back in Dragonfang but others may have ambitions. This was his opportunity. Whether it was what Rata spoke of he could not know, but it felt right.

He passed his command to the Majickers. Almost as one, the army rose and called, "Lord Beed, Lord Beed. Come out, come out. Dragonfang is here." Having delivered their message, they sat again.

The Lord of Bel came striding along the wall, looking resplendent in yellow. Chadas stepped in front of his troops and, using he Majick, propelled his voice above the city and his army. "We are here to witness your surrender of the city of Bel to the army of Dragonfang and the New World of Masima."

"Bel will never surrender!" came the reply.

Chadas laughed. "You will, it is only to be determined how." In a voice that reverberated over the land, he called, "Wind." The Majickers were ready. A tunnel of air swept across Bel. Along the wall, guards hunched against the icy blast. Lord Beed stood his ground, but his flapping cape looked like a small dragon ready to take flight.

"Stop!" Chadas called and the wind was gone as fast as it had arrived. Guards rose, appearing confused as they stared out to where Chadas waited.

Again, words echoed over the city. "Is Bel ready to accept defeat?"

"Never!" came Lord Beed's reply.

"Water!" Chadas called. The first wave hit the shores of Bel smashing canoes and flooding nearby houses. A second followed, and a third. The waves continued until all along the shore was destroyed. A small price to pay.

"Stop!" Chadas called, and no more waves came. His voice boomed above the city once more. "Lord Beed, do you accept the rule of Masima?"

His reply came quickly. "Masima is a demon of our past. His Guild will never be welcome. Your attack only shows my people that the stories of our past were correct. Bel will not accept Masima or his followers."

Chadas knew it would come to this. Lord Beed would stand against him till his death. Only what happened after was in doubt.

Chadas had never asked his Majickers to kill. He would not ask it now. He reached for the Majick as he had never done before. He felt it enter his body, burning through his veins, energizing his mind. He spread his arms, accepting it completely, bathing in its glory. The strength of Agort flowed through him. As two forces watched, he grew. Wings sprouted from his back. His neck reached for the sky. A blue tongue flickered from his horned snout. The Majick tingled in him. He commanded it, and the air obeyed. Breath rushed from Lord Beed's lungs and would not return.

The Lord of Bel grasped his throat, thumped his chest, and desperately sought life. His agony seemed to last an age. Finally, his staggering body fell from the wall, his spirit long since departed.

The dragon that was Chadas roared. "Who is next to speak for ?" No reply came. Everyone was staring at the dead Lord. "Then lower your weapons and stand down from the wall." They were slow to obey, sluggish. Chadas was not concerned. A stunned city was far easier to subdue than an angry one. Shrinking back to his normal form, he commanded, "Open the gates." One life to save a city, but now the Guild can grow.

Bel accepted, if not welcomed, the army of Masima.

#

Rows of soldiers marched through the gates while the defending guards stepped back, awaiting commands. As Chadas anticipated, it was an almost bloodless coup. The defeated guards were ordered to wait in the town square while the army took charge of the city. The Guild now controlled two cities, though Bel was yet to be tamed.

That evening, Chadas approached the square and stood beneath a large oak tree. He could not be missed in his red and gold cape. When quiet had settled, he addressed the prisoners.

"My people will now walk among you. If you are selected, rise and come to me." He waited while ten people were selected at random, six men and four women. When they stood in a line facing their people, soldiers approached from behind and placed nooses around their necks. The ropes were pulled up over a branch until each balanced on their toes, their eyes wide as they stared at everyone watching.

"You must all remember this moment. The Guild knows all that occurs in Dragonfang. It will be the same in Bel. These people have done nothing, yet, but what you see is the fate that befalls anyone who plots against the Guild, or if you fail me." He raised his arm and the soldiers reached to be ready to pull.

Someone screamed.

Chadas walked across to where the ten prisoners could see before dropping his arm. The soldiers dropped the ropes. Ten guards collapsed onto the ground.

"You are all free to leave, but do not forget," Chadas called as he walked away.

#

Nola trotted along at Chadas' side as he walked through Bel. It had been two weeks since his army had entered the city and only now he began to feel at ease. There had been no trouble other than the usual disquiet when so many people were crammed into a small area. His spies had told him that no one wished to see the dragon again. Now he had time to see the beauty of Bel. The carefully cut stonework of the houses was beyond anything the masons of Dragonfang could produce and the carved wood panels that decorated the city were to be admired.

He stopped in the town square and turned around. Bel was a city to be appreciated. Lord Beed and his predecessors had made it lovely but at the sacrifice of its protection. He could see what was needed, but he must return to Dragonfang, and Alodia.

A woman approached hesitantly and prostrated herself at his feet. "My Lord," she mumbled.

"Rise woman."

She came slowly to her knees and waited with head bowed. There was something about this woman, in her attitude and her presence.

"What is your name?"

"Pavane, my Lord."

"Stand up Pavane and tell me what you want."

She rose, head still bowed and hands clasped before her. "I wish to go to Dragonfang."

Chadas smiled. "Tell me about yourself."

"I am the daughter of a potter. I am married to Mika, a storekeeper."

"How old are you Pavane?"

"Eighteen, my Lord."

"Why do you want to go to Dragonfang? Does Mika beat you?"

Her eyes widened suddenly. "Oh, no, my Lord. Mika is a good man."

"Yet you would leave him to come to Dragonfang, or would you want him to come too?"

"Please, no, my Lord. He must not find out. He would not understand."

"Understand what?"

His voice dropped to a whisper. "The women who travel with you, my Lord, they are … special?"

"Yes, they are."

Her voice dropped further and he had to strain to hear. "Witches?"

Chadas studied her closely. She wore a pale yellow blouse over a long black skirt. Both were marked with soot, as was her face. Her feet were bare. Beneath the grime he sensed something more. Her appearance was a subterfuge, the grime a disguise, and her feet were not used to walking without shoes. But more, he could sense the essence that was in each of his Majickers.

"Those women work for me. They are loyal and I trust them."

"I can be like them, my Lord."

This woman was almost admitting she was a witch. "If I say no?"

"My mother had the gift. When the people of Bel discovered her secret, she was stoned to death. If they learn of me, I will die. I do not fear death, but I am with child. My baby must live."

Chadas hesitated only a moment before answering. "I am returning to Dragonfang in the morning. Meet me outside the city at dawn. Bring only what you must, I will provide what you need."

"Thank you, my Lord. I will be there."

#

That afternoon Chadas called the most important people of Bel to a meeting. These were the ones who could influence opinion and help him rule the city. Members of the Guild would rule Bel in his name, but these people's support would make things go smoothly during the transition. They could also be the ones to lead a revolt.

He awaited their arrival in the Great Hall, a cavern of a room decorated with banners and tapestries. Nola sprawled at his feet, only her ears betraying her level of alertness. In all other respects she appeared to be dozing. Tomm and Wynne waited by one wall with the Majickers.

His guests began arriving to be ushered to the seats that had been prepared for them. There were a few mutters, but they ignored him until the last was seated. Chadas raised a finger, his signal to the Majickers, and the doors closed as if of their own accord. No one moved to check them, but if they had, they would have found them sealed. He rose and paced while they waited. Eventually he stopped and spoke.

"Gentlemen, and ladies, you are here because I wish to ask for your help, for which I can be most appreciative."

A sudden display of interest spread through the room.

"I see great changes in Bel's future, and you will be part of that. I need people who understand this city and have the ability to make it grand. I intend to implement some of the changes our Guild has introduced at Dragonfang that have shown to be successful. The people of my city have grown stronger, and the traders grow their wealth."

At this, his audience grew more attentive.

"I will be leaving Bel in the morning to return home. My son, Tomm, will remain to implement my vision, for which he will be accorded the title of Regent of Bel. Wynne will remain with him. She is the most capable at offering the support he will need and with your help, Bel will grow as powerful and wealthy as Dragonfang

#

As the sun cast its first glimpses of color across the clouds, Chadas was preparing to leave Bel. Tomm and Wynne were there to see him off, which surprised him. Maybe it was a sign that he would take his position seriously. More likely, his sister had a stronger hold over him than he knew.

The army was also ready to leave, those who were going back to Dragonfang. One in six would stay. They would protect his new city and train the army it produced. They saw it as an opportunity for rapid advancement as Chadas' power grew, a belief he encouraged.

He hugged his son and daughter before swinging into the saddle. By the time he saw them again, they should be major figures in the growth of Bel. The black stallion waited patiently while the army, those with horses, did the same. He looked around to plant the image of Bel in his mind.

"Take care of my city," he said to Tomm before nudging his horse into a walk. Reaching for the Majick, he drew enough to allow his voice to boom in the air. "Goodbye Bel. I will return soon."

As he passed through the gate and out of the city he noted that his new defenses had begun and next time he came, he would bring a few stonemasons back to Dragonfang to teach the masons there.

Nola loped along at his side, occasionally darting off when she spied something in the grass and brush along the side of the road. She always came back with empty jaws, having failed to catch the wary prey this close to the city.

He was passing a small grove of stunted trees when Pavane stepped out. A bag carrying her few possessions was slung over her shoulder. "My Majickers are following in a wagon. I have just informed them to watch for you. Join them and we will speak when we get to Dragonfang."

Two days out of Bel, Chadas was growing restless. What drove him on was the thought of seeing Alodia again, but the journey was slow and tiresome. Waking on the third morning, he had made a decision. He passed word that the army would rest for the day. After all, why own a hunting dog if you did not hunt. He would take only two soldiers for protection and two extra horses to carry back any prize. Hunting must be done without distractions. Their journey would resume tomorrow.

They rode up the nearest valley putting about two miles behind them before they heard snorting. He signaled a stop before going on alone, with only Nola at his side. A boar dashed from a patch of brush to race across his path and into shelter among some rocks. A moment later, four followed. Chadas was ready and his arrow struck the third in line in its neck. The stunned boar staggered on a few steps before dropping to the ground, legs thrashing while blood stained the rocks and dirt. Before he could draw another arrow, the rest were gone. Nola ran to the fallen boar, sniffing at the blood. He called the soldiers up and instructed them to prepare and load his kill. Nola seemed disappointed but she would receive some of the offal.

#

A mile further into the valley a husk of fat hares dashed across their path. There must be more than fifty. As Chadas reached for his bow, the two soldiers were also drawing arrows. Three shafts flew straight and true and they had time for one more flight before the hares scattered.

All three dropped to the ground to gather their catch. The meat they now had would make a welcome addition to the food they carried.

Chadas lifted his first hare and extracted the arrow. When he reached the second, Nola was already munching on the creature's head with one large paw pinning the body to the ground. He reached for it, but when he tried to take it, Nola snapped, sinking her teeth into his hand. A stiletto was suddenly in his other hand, but he held back the strike. Nola backed off but a deep growl rumbled from her throat.

The soldiers were at his side. A stunned Chadas stared at his hand where dark blood covered it and dripped from his fingers. One man tore a strip from his shirt to bind the wound while the other drew his sword and approached Nola.

Chadas stopped him. "No. It is not her fault. I should not have tried to take her meal. Let her keep it."

At the first soldier's insistence, they returned to camp where his wound could be properly treated.

#

As Chadas and the two soldiers prepared to ride back and rejoin the army, a cool breeze drifted down the valley. It grew quickly and soon an eerie whistling filled the air as the wind wound its way past the many bumps and hollows. Chadas shivered. He could feel the Majick at work here. It took little encouragement from the soldiers for him to push his horse to a canter.

Many were surprised at his early return but as news of his injury spread, Pavane, his new Majicker, came hurrying. She carried the bag of her possessions. Nola still waited at his side, her head hung low, rubbing against his leg as if in apology. He reached down a hand to stroke her head.

"Show me your hand." Pavane's voice was curt, brooking no nonsense.

"Leave me alone. There is nothing wrong. Nola bit me for trying to take away her food." At the mention of her name, Nola's head came up.

"Hand!" Pavane demanded.

Chadas extended his arm, the hand still wrapped in the bloodied strip of linen. Carefully she unwound it to expose the wound, or rather two wounds, punctures from Nola's teeth. Looking closely at the hand she agreed, "I can see nothing." She was not finished. She placed a hand over Chadas' wound and concentrated.

"Something is wrong," she stated. "I feel a fever in your hand, and the presence of evil." She reached into her bag and rummaged toward the bottom. As she did so, she called to a nearby soldier. "Bring me a bowl. Fill it with hot clean water."

From her belongings she withdrew an unmarked wooden box. Inside were various compartments, each filled with a different herb. When the water was brought she ordered, "Find me some honey, I do not require much. The soldier jumped to obey.

While he was gone, Pavane placed Linum, Ulmos Rubra and Lavender into the bowl of hot water. With a small rock, she ground the herbs to a pulp. Tearing a strip from her petticoat to replace the soiled bandage, she also tore a square for the concoction. The honey arrived and she wrapped the herbs and honey into a parcel. The poultice was then placed on Chadas' hand and bound with the fresh bandage.

"This is the best I can do. It should remove the evil."

Every morning of their return to Dragonfang she repeated the process before she allowed anyone to ride, and each day she said less, which Cadas took to mean his hand was getting better.

# 32 SWORD OF MAJICK

Torne carried the now almost colorless sword back to the house, his excited daughters chattering at his side. For the entire walk the weapon flickered through various shades of blue and green as if it muttered to itself in strange and indecipherable phrases. He looked to Hope and Faith, but they did not seem to notice, or they ignored it. The tickling of small bells played in his ears. It felt like the sounds of happiness, a joy that it had found what it sought. It was a feeling of completeness.

But as he neared the house, another desire pushed those feelings aside. He sent the girls in to help with supper while he waited outside. The last vestiges of exhaustion were now gone to be replaced with the overwhelming desire to practice. He needed to wield the sword, to feel its balance. He took a stance he imagined right and held the blade high in readiness. In that frozen moment he understood. These were not his thoughts but the desire of the sword to test him, or maybe train him.

He swung the sword down and left, then back up and right. Lifting the sword above his head, he fended off an imaginary blow and felt the impact in his hands and radiating up his arms. Spin, twist, parry, strike, the exercise continued until he lowered the weapon. The sword spoke clearly. "You are the one."

Muscles were again aching but pleasure that the sword had accepted him overcame the tiredness. Then he wondered if he should be pleased but the sword glowed with a happy pink. As he turned to go inside, he saw Mavie standing at the door.

"What are you doing?" his sister asked.

"Practicing."

"Practicing what?"

"With the sword."

Mavie looked around. The sword spoke again, more clearly than it had before. "Others cannot see me. I am for your eyes only, yours and your daughters." He stared at the sword.

"Are you ill?" Mavie asked into the silence.

"Yes. I mean no. I was just imagining a sword in my hands." His sister looked confused. "I am finished now." The sword turned a joyous yellow, as if it were laughing.

"You have a very good imagination," complimented Hope.

"Very good," added Faith.

Then they both giggled, spoiling his praise.

As they went inside Mavie commented, "I have never seen you move so fast, or anyone else. At times you were no more than a blur."

Torne gave no answer, he could not, but he wondered more about the strange object they had found. He corrected himself, the sword that had found him. Maybe it had fallen from the spirit world. He heard the voice of the sword. I am only what I need to be.

Torne practiced each of the following evenings, becoming confident of his movements and control. Then on the fifth day did not go to the fields. Instead, he prepared a leather strap to carry the sword at his side. It was something the weapon seemed to desire. There was no need for a scabbard to hide a weapon that could not be seen, and an empty one would raise more questions.

When he tied it to his waist, the blade shone bright green. He felt its satisfaction.

# 33 CHADAS, RATA AND DRAGONS

An evil redness surrounded the wound on Chadas' hand. Alodia wanted to call a physician, but he refused.

"Nola meant no harm. I should not have tried to take away her meal. It was just a bite, and there is nothing wrong with her. The poultice will heal it quickly."

On hearing her name, Nola, who had been dozing in front of the hearth, raised her head to look in their direction. Having satisfied herself that she was not required, she rested her head once more on her forepaws and closed her eyes.

Alodia tried again, only to receive an angry, "Go away woman. Leave me in peace. I said there is nothing wrong."

But there was. He had refused to show it, telling his Majickers and the physician they were not required. They continued to pester him, but this only fueled his growing anger. His hand began to ache and quickly became pain, and to increase his annoyance, it began to itch. This, he decided was worse than pain. He understood pain.

He grew more short with Alodia, though he knew she was concerned, He was too.

Four days later, Alodia approached him as he climbed the stairs of the tower. "Where are you going?" she asked.

Chadas stopped, looked at her, then up and down. He shook his head, trying to clear the fog that engulfed it. "This is my tower," he exploded. "These are my stairs. I will go where I wish."

Alodia started at his sudden response but casually changed the subject. "There is something wrong with Nola."

"What?"

"She sleeps all day in front of the heart and has not moved or eaten in days."

"She is ashamed, and she should be. She must learn not to bite me."

"Show mw your hand. You have not allowed anyone to see it in days either."

"Leave me alone woman. Does everyone think they know more than me? I am Lord of Dragonfang. All knowledge is mine."

"Chadas!" Alodia chided. "We have known each other all our lives. I know when something is not right with you."

Chadas raised his hand threateningly and took a step toward her, but then he sagged against the wall. It was impossible to stop his slump to the floor.

"Guard!" she yelled. "Get help and carry the Lord to his bed." Help arrived quickly. As they struggled with his weight, Alodia began to give instructions. "I want two guards at his bedside, another at his door. No one is to see him like this." They lowered him onto his bed. "Send someone for the physician. I will get him some broth."

On her rush to the kitchen, she spied the sleeping Nola. "Nola," she called. Having the dog at his side might comfort him. She called again. "Nola!" The big gray dog did not move. Changing directions, she approached and reached down to wake her. Nola was cold. Startled, she looked closer and saw the bubbles of white froth around her mouth. Calling a guard, she ordered him to take the dog outside and burn it, pointing to the symptoms of mad animal disease. As the guard obeyed, she ordered, "Do not allow anyone to see you or discover what you are doing, and say nothing."

Ignoring the broth, Alodia rushed to sit beside Chadas, He was not sleeping but mumbled incoherently. With the door closed, she carefully unwrapped his hand. As she did so, the stench of rot filled the air. She put a finger to her lips to warn the guards that they too were to say nothing. She then ordered one to go and inform the council that Chadas had ordered a meeting that afternoon. They were all to attend. As he left Chadas began to moan.

She finished unwrapping the bandage. For the first time she was truly shocked. Chadas' hand was black and swollen. Pustules had broken out all over. Most alarming were the three red lines that traced up his arm beneath his shirt. She tore the shirt open to see them spreading across his chest.

"Get Lukin," she ordered the other guard.

#

Chadas was dreaming again, a familiar dream. Where had he seen it? When? A memory returned. It had not been a dream. It was a place Rata had shown him. She said it was the way to the spirit world. Why was she showing it to him again?

He was floating along the road to the spirit world. What had Rata called it? Apat?

Something felt different. He searched about and it only helped confirm his misgivings. A horrible image penetrated his mind. With it, the silver road stopped, or he did. He looked to either side, then back the way he had come. Swirling white clouds surrounded him, seeming to press closer. Reaching for the Majick, he changed. He was the dragon again. He felt none of the sensations he felt when he had changed before. This time he just thought it and it happened. He thought of a mighty stag, and he was. The dragon returned, he was comfortable with that image.

He was becoming distracted. Refocusing, he imagined the clouds behind moving back. They moved apart and an image appeared. He saw himself on his bed. Two guards stood either side of him. Alodia waited with them while the physician moved away from the group. Alodia said something he could not hear, and everyone left the room. Alone now, Alodia fell to her knees sobbing. He looked closer and understood. He was dead.

It shocked him, not his death, but that he could not complete his vision of Dragonfang ruling all Lilim.

A nearby cloud coalesced into the shape of a woman. "Keep going," she said.

He looked once more at his body lying in peace. His final memory was Alodia sobbing into the bed. My work will go on, he thought. Alodia will see to it, and Lukin and Tomm will grow my empire.

Without thinking, he allowed the clouds to return and hide the scene. He was moving again towards the gates of Apat. Soon the great cloud gates appeared, and the two golden dragons that supported them. He heard the voices of the clouds welcoming him, telling him they had been awaiting his arrival.

The two dragons leaned forward and sniffed. Only then did he remember he still held their shape.

#

The dragons pulled back and the gates began to open. Behind them, Chadas saw Apat, but not the Apat Rata had shown him. The world beyond the gates was awash with color, all the colors of the rainbow and many more. A spirit appeared in the clouds beside him to explain.

*If someone looks into Apat from outside, they only see white. Only when entry is granted do you see the splendor of the spirit world.*

*So, I am dead?*

*You are not dead. The body you wore on Tatlo no longer holds you. Even in the void between worlds you are not dead, only lost forever.*

*Then I can enter?*

*You must. Your place is now here.*

Chadas drifted forward but stopped again when a booming voice screamed.

*No!*

A swirling, oversized image of Rata appeared to bar his way. Other spirits began to coalesce from the clouds.

*He has earned his passage*, challenged the first.

*And I say he cannot enter*, countered Rata.

*You must not stop him.*

Anger blazed around Rata causing the air surrounding her image to glow in layers of fiery color. A flare of blinding Majick was cast at the spirit. Chadas acted instinctively. He willed a barrier to the Majick, a thing he was familiar with having held one most of his life. The Majick hit and exploded. Sprays of orange, red and yellow lit the clouds.

The spirits warned him. *Beware the void.*

Chadas was ready, but he was confused. Rata had always guided him well.

*The Majick demands his passage. If you attempt to stop him, it will harm the Majick.*

Rata replied with another blast of Majick and again Chadas' wall deflected it.

*We are unable to stop Rata, but you can. We will stand with you.* He could feel the voices of the spirits.

*Fool. I am the Great Author. I write the Majick and it is mine to command.*

Chadas stood his ground and challenged her. *I am strong in the Majick too. I was Ama and the Lord. I will enter.* Then more quietly, *why would you do this? You showed me the Majick. I was happy without it but you encouraged me to use it.*

*I am the strongest in Apat. The Majick is mine. I will not allow you to take it from me.*

With her last words, Rata shot a bolt of Majick toward Chadas, a spear so powerful it glowed whiter than even the surrounding clouds. The shield he threw up slowed it but the power cast at him caused it to bulge. Lines of cracks zig-zagged out from the impact. Almost off-handedly Chadas wondered what would happen when it shattered.

The bulge grew. Cracks radiated from cracks. Chadas knew Rata was about to win. At that moment he felt the Majick rush to his aid. The bulge retreated and the cracks solidified. He did not know how or what he had done. Voices filled his mind.

*We will help but you must fight.*

They were right. Chadas called on the Majick, drank of its power. He felt the wings of the dragon grow large. He strengthened them with fibers of Majick and when they were ready. He knitted the strands together. Free to think, he wove more between and around the scales that covered him. Should his wings fail, his scales wound give him time to react.

*That is good,* came the spirit voices.

*We can win, but I will need your help.*

*What should we do?*

*Be ready to call on the Majick, all you can hold. I will tell you when to strike.*

Sparks sprayed from his wings. He had an idea but no belief that it would work. Behind the shield of his wings he began to work. A tiny spot of darkness appeared. As it grew, even the spirits behind him gasped. It was black, not the darkness of night where even an assassin could be noticed, nor any other black of Tatlo. This was pure swirling black, the essence of nothing.

*Prepare your bolt of energy, the largest you can control.*

The spirits began their task. Chadas hid the darkness with his wings, not knowing what he had produced, only that it would destroy Rata. He tensed. His wings parted briefly, only long enough to hurl the ever-expanding nothing at his enemy.

The spirits behind him gasped.

Rata was caught by surprise. She had not anticipated that even Chadas was foolish enough to do this. The hole of nothing shot toward Rata absorbing all the Majick she cast at it. It reached closer and the image of Rata turned the putrid green of fear. She knew what Chadas had done and it terrified her. It fed on Majick. She could not allow it to touch her. But she could not allow it to grow either. She stopped casting Majick, killed her weapons, shut down her defenses.

*Now!* Chadas called.

A lance of white-hot Majick shot toward Rata. Chadas added to it with a ball of flaming energy. It should have been the end of her. It was not. The attack did not reach its intended target. Instead, it was absorbed into the growing darkness. Rata wrapped it in a ball of silver. But the blackness continued to grow, eating at its confines from within. She kept adding layers of silver as those inside were eaten away.

*What have you done?* Rata roared.

Chadas radiated confusion. *I only tried to think of something that would stop you.*

*Fool,* broadcast the spirits behind him. *You have killed us all. You have destroyed Apat. You have slain the Majick.*

*How?* He asked.

*You invited the void into our world,* Rata accused. *It will grow now until it devours all. The Majick is lost. The void has won.*

Rata continued to build the silver barrier, but as fast as she worked, the blackness ate away at it from inside. The other spirits came to her aid, adding their strength to hers in the losing battle. The swirling darkness would not be stopped. The barrier was constructed of Majick and it ate Majick.

*You must help*, Rata called.

Chadas began to add his strength to the silver ball.

*No! You make it stronger.*

Chadas withdrew. *What must I do?*

*Make a portal to the void.*

*That is what I tried to do.*

*No, you asked it to come to you.*

*Tell me how.*

*Just look. Find the barrier that stands between Apat and the void. It is all about us.*

*Then what?*

*Open a window, a portal, to look beyond. Look out, do not ask it in.*

The silver-clad darkness had grown as large as a house. It had been no larger than a fist when he threw it. Soon Rata and her supporters would not be able to contain it. He sensed other spirits converging from all across Apat, hundreds of them, thousands. Chadas searched for the edge of the world, found it and opened a portal as instructed. Beyond was an enormous nothing, swirling, powerful and angry. He could sense tiny specks of lost entities in there, desperately holding to the last vestiges of themselves in a tumultuous place, not living yet unable to die.

Rata and the spirits pushed the blackness toward the portal, rather they pushed their silver barrier hoping it would survive long enough. Chadas watched for a moment as the silver ball was attacked from both inside and out.

It shattered into a myriad of pieces. That was his mistake. Rata attacked. She took control of the portal from him and turned it in his direction. Before Chadas could think, the portal was charging toward him.

He tried to grasp back control, but in the moment she took it from him, she had protected it. Closer it came, rushing at him like a charging bear. He searched for help. The portal was almost upon him. He cast bolts of Majick that only disappeared into the void. He constructed a barrier that was eaten just as quickly.

Rata was too strong. She had used the Majick far longer. His only chance was escape, He created a portal to the one place he knew, Tatlo. There he could regroup and try again. He dived through. Rata did not follow.

He had seen what Rata had done and protected his portal so he could return whenever he was ready. But Rata constructed a barrier so intricate as to confuse the senses. When it was complete, she wove the strands into the fabric of the portal. No one would use this again unless she released it.

#

Chadas raged at the barrier. He smashed Majickal fists into it. He created lances of fire, balls of flame and much more to cast at it. Nothing worked. The people of Tatlo watched his efforts, heard the crashes of his attempts, and they hid in fear. He even tried to understand the knitted threads, but the weave was too tight. Again, he attacked with everything he could think of until finally his temper eased and logic showed its face. There is an easier way, it said.

He looked to the edge of Tatlo and tried to open a portal back to Apat. There was only the faintest of splutters that faded quickly to nothing. He tried to think. A deep, tired voice spoke within him.

*No one can create a portal up through the worlds. It is against the laws of Majick.*

Chadas stopped. If he could not create a path to Apat, there was one he could use, the silver road. He began to search. For years he hunted in every corner of Tatlo but could find no sign of it. Frustrated, he screamed at the sky.

Where is the silver road?

The deep voice answered.

*You have used it once. It no longer exists for you.*

*I have used it more than once. Rata took me along it to show me Apat.*

*Rata only showed you an image. Each entity may only travel to the next world once.*

*Why?*

*It is the law of Majick.*

*Who are you?*

*I am the Majick. I am the Great Author.*

*Rata says she is the Great Author.*

*All can say who they wish to be. Only by our actions can we be who we say we are.*

Chadas thought about this.

*If you are truly the Great Author, you could allow me back into Apat.*

*I cannot.*

*Why?*

*The laws were the first words I wrote in the book of Majick. The first law says there are six worlds. The second was that we begin on the lowest world, Isa, and that there exists but one path to the next world and when used, it no longer exists for us.*

*What about portals?*

*I had not anticipated portals, but when they were created, I wrote that they could be used to leave the worlds, or go back to a world you have been, never to a world above.*

*Then write that I can return to Apat.*

*The words of the book of Majick have been written. Once written, they cannot be changed. They have become the laws of Majick.*

The voice was gone. Chadas was trapped. He could never move on.

He stopped. The voice did not say he could not travel up through a portal, only that he could not create one up to Apat. If someone in Apat opened a portal to Tatlo, he could go through. Could the spirits open a portal for him? Did they see that he had escaped to Tatlo? Or had Rata cast them into the void?

#

It quickly became apparent that a portal would not be opened for him. A thought struck him, maybe Rata had cast his supporters into the void. An anger filled him, an anger so powerful he must release it before it overwhelmed him. He called on the Majick that was Tatlo. It rushed to him, wrapping him in power he had never felt before. With this, he would defeat Rata but first he had to get back to Apat.

He would make her open a portal to stop him. Majick flowed through him. Winds howled and screeched across the land. They screamed through the valleys and tore ice from mountain tops. The winds blew for days that became weeks. Chadas discovered Langit, and the winds blew there too.

The people of Tatlo suffered. Those that lived on the shores watched helpless as the ocean became violent mountains of confusion. Where people lived on farms, the winds blew away the topsoil leaving bare rock and clay. Everyone asked the spirits how they had offended them and what they should do to be forgiven.

The winds brought clouds that grew heavy across the world. Chadas' anger was only in its infancy. The clouds ate the sun and the people of Tatlo found themselves in a night that lasted more than a year.

Chadas opened the clouds and the rains came, rain that would not cease. On the shores the rain came so heavy, it flattened the sea and damaged the boats. On the farms, where the people still tried to survive, land that had been dried by the winds became creeks that soon turned into rivers, washing away hope. The rains continued until the clouds could supply them no more. Tatlo had been devastated.

For the people of Tatlo, the spirits had been appeased. The weather began returning to what some still remembered.

#

Chadas had been distracted, his fury forgotten for a moment. In his tantrum he had discovered something far to the north, something only remembered as legend. In the place known by the people as the Northice Bleak, he had found dragons. They were a group of more than fifty, and he watched them with awe. He could feel the Majick in them, a great Majick, as if they were made of it.

He found them laying on the ice, sleeping, but something disturbed them. Their long necks came up and heads searched about before looking directly at him. They leaped into the air, screeching loudly. He did not wait long before he found cause for their alarm. As they circled overhead, a great shadow fell over the ice. With a roar and a flapping of mighty wings, another dragon approached. Ripples of color rolled down its body and across its enormous wings. Stretching out her legs, she settled to the ground, coiling her tail around her and waited. In his mind he heard her speak. Return, he is of no threat.

The dragons settled before her, the ice reflecting the many hues of their scales into the sky. He could hear their voices as they greeted, Mother Agort.

Chadas tried to understand. When he lived on Tatlo, the MaalKeeper had told him of a dragon named Agort. Could this be the same one? The others called he Mother Agort. Were they all her children, born of the dragon nests? If so, it meant the legend he had heard must be true. That would mean, incredulity filled him, she was here before people came to the land.

The younger dragons began to speak. Tell us again, Mother Agort. Tell us about the six worlds.

Agort began her story. Before time, there was nothing. The worlds and everything on them had not been born. The Majick hid in tiny pockets in the void. It was weak. When one of these pieces of Majick discovered it could shield itself from the darkness, it approached others and united until, together, they became strong.

The Great Author was born.

The void was not concerned. It was vast and the Majick, though stronger, was of little consequence. It was no more than an irritation.

The Great Author saw this and gathered more Majick until there was enough to build Isa, the first world. Others followed, Dalawa and Tatlo, then Apat, Lima and Anim. The six worlds of Majick were born. Onto these worlds, the Great Author placed beings of Majick.

Chadas was captured by the tale and listened as she told the story of life until she came to present time.

Eventually, you were born and dragons flourished.

But why must we remain in the Northice Bleak?

The time of dragons has come and gone. Now is the time of man.

The young dragons spread their wings and flung themselves into the air to circle a few times before landing again. Chadas tried to imagine being a dragon, a heady thought. An idea began to germinate and before it left him, he acted. If he could enter a dragon's body he could feel the sensations of flight and power. He could feel life with a body again. He selected a dragon, a beautiful red creature with yellow flashes on either side of its head. It lay at the back of the group, and when none were watching, he dived in.

He soon discovered its eyes and could see what it saw. No alarm had been raised. He felt around. More sensations, taste, smell, and he could hear. Then he found the dragon's mind. He reached for it, wrapping it in himself. He WAS the dragon.

Fly, he commanded, and the beast leaped into the sky. He tried control, left, right, swoop, soar, and relished the feelings that came to him. But then he heard Agort's bark. Tygrane, behave. What is wrong with you. Startled, Chadas fled from the dragon and watched as it settled before its mother.

#

Chadas knew instinctively what he must do. Rata could not ignore an army of Majick. He withdrew and waited, watching, until Agort dozed.

With a stealth far greater than he had ever used, he approached, wrapped in a blanket of Majick, woven in the guise of a young dragon. He slipped quietly into the body of Agort and searched, finding first her senses, eyes, ears and such. He masked each with his own fabric. Then he turned his attention to Agort's mind. She awoke.

Startled, the great dragon roared, but with one last rush, Chadas won. Agort was alive and well, trapped in the shielded chamber of Chadas' Majick.

Chadas commanded and the body of Agort rose to stand on the ice. And the Chadas flew. Mighty wings beat at the sky and Chadas exalted at the experience.

When he was ready, he called, and a great cloud of color filled the air as Agort's children flocked to their mother.

#

Over the mountains Chadas flew, leading his army of winged warriors. They fell on farms, tearing down homes, chased away livestock ripped up the ground with massive claws. They attacked villages, destroying buildings and terrifying the inhabitants. And they descended on cities of stone and timber with screeches and bellows. The people tried to defend themselves but all they could bring to the battle were spears and arrows, useless against the might of a dragon and less so against a horde of them.

Chadas kept an eye to the skies but still Rata ignored him. He needed to do more. He must make her pay attention. He had to alter the Book of Majick.

He looked further south, across the great sea Dragonbite. The dragons spread their terror across Tatlo. They raged across the mountains of Lilim. They caused havoc from Wellow to Wyrmwatch. Everywhere between Fartown and Dawnreach came under attack. On the shores of Pigfish Bay, everything was set alight and burned for days. Chadas looked beyond to the Wylds, but nothing lived there. He ignored it. Other than the Wylds, nothing and no one was exempt.

It was a difficult time for the people of Tatlo. Dragons ruled the skies and the lands beneath. People hid in their houses, in forests, anywhere they thought they might escape. No one traveled unless they were desperate. They never knew when a roar would break the air and a colored monster would fall on them from the clouds, and they did, often. A piercing scream would see grown men fall to the ground shaking in fear. Women would freeze where they stood before instinct took hold and they ran with their children in search of cover.

Dragons would drop on a large building for no reason other than to grab stone and fly up to drop them from a great height. Livestock was easy prey. Being Majickal, a dragon had no need to eat but Chadas saw the fear when they took a cow, opening its belly with a single slash of a claw, or biting off its head.

A thunderclap broke the air and Rata spoke to him. *Stop this or I will turn the Majick against you.*

*You are powerless to stop me, Chadas replied. These are my dragons and I will rule here.*

*I am the Great Author. I will write you out of the Book.*

*I see the truth now. You are not the Great Author. You are not even good at what you try to do. I have discovered the Majick that lives within these dragons. I rule them, and with their power, I will rule all Tatlo.*

*Why?*

*You would not allow me to enter Apat. You confined me here. So I intend to rule Tatlo as you try to rule Apat.*

*I must protect myself. I am the Great Author.*

*Chadas laughed. You are a deluded spirit who refuses her future. I control the dragons and I will control Tatlo for all eternity. When I am finished my destruction, there will be none left to enter Apat. Your world will be no more.*

Rata roared. Chadas knew he had enraged her and he must be ready. She would come for him soon.

# 34 TORNE'S DESTINY

The people of Fartown suffered the weather no more and no less than others. On his farm, Torne hid in his house to avoid the winds when they began. He thought they would soon ease, he discovered they would not.

On one occasion during the night, Torne woke to hear the screech of wild wind tearing at his house. The air whistled as it rushed past every perturbance. Then a gust hit and for a moment, the wind became violent. He heard cracking as timber tore away from timber. The entire roof lifted. Torne screamed for the girls to wake. But as fast as the gust came, it moved on and the roof fell back into place. He rushed to their beds, but Hope and Faith slept soundly. Leaving them there, he found rope to secure the roof. He could repair it tomorrow, but he prayed it would hold until then.

When he could, he ventured out, rescuing the remains of his plants and relocating them to the lee of the house. He collected rocks and built small walls against the winds to protect his animals. He did these things, but water was scarce. Behind one wall, he dug a well in the hope of finding a clean supply. He did not need to dig deep for the sea was close and water was plentiful under the ground if it was not tainted. His luck was with him. Rather than use a rope and bucket, he widened a path down to the water. Animals, his as well as wild ones, used this. With his small garden and the animals he killed, Torne's farm became a haven in a confused land.

When the clouds brought the rains, it became almost too much for his little garden. The plants had more water than they needed and lay flattened to the ground under its onslaught, but the roots survived.

Throughout this run of disasters, the sword lay against the wall becoming more and more excited. It flashed to him in many colors, it called to him, it pleaded. When he touched it or listened, it repeated the same message. It is nearly time!

"Time for what?" he would scream.

The sword would only repeat, *It is nearly time*!

#

Kuwento was sitting up in his chair, eyes wide and clapping his hands. A dribble ran from his mouth to dangle from his chin. He must be enjoying the story, I thought. I was pleased I could bring him so much pleasure in his dying years.

#

When the rains finally ceased, Torne began rebuilding his farm, but each night, when he returned to the house, his daughters were waiting.

"It is time, papa,"

"You must listen to the sword, papa."

"The sword understands."

"It sees your destiny."

"And mine."

"And mine."

"We all have our destinies, papa."

It did not matter which girl spoke, it was always the same. Torne heard their pleas, heard the sword. But he had work to do. It would take years to rebuild the farm. He needed to find fresh seed, find the best place to plant it. There was work here for the rest of his life.

But the desperation of the farm, the nagging of his daughters and the demands of the sword wore him down. One evening after a long, hard day, he picked up the sword and walked outside to practice. The blade spun easily in his hands, it gave him strength. More, it gave him trust and an optimism for the future. It gave him purpose.

When he finished, the sword spoke. *It is time.*

"Time for what?," he yelled. "Time for sarding what?"

*Time for us both to fulfill our destiny. It is why we were brought together.*

"Brought together? By who?"

*By the spirits, and the Majick.*

"I do not believe in Majick."

*Then where do you find the strength to train as hard as you do after working all day?*

Understanding, then shock, slowly seeped into Torne's mind. He suspected the sword had fallen from the spirit world, but he never truly believed it. Now it told him not only was it born of the spirit world, but the spirits had sent it to him. And the Majick!

"Why?"

*We must save the Majick.*

"Save the Majick?"

*The Majick of the worlds faces extinction. It is for you, with my help, to save it.*

"How? I do not know what to do."

*You were chosen. Your path is clear.*

"And if I do not?"

*The Majick will die, and all the worlds and their peoples will die with them.*

"All the worlds?"

*"There is more to life than just the human world."*

"But my girls, I must care for Hope and Faith."

*They will come with us. They have their destinies to fulfill.*

"But the farm?"

*Give it to your sister. She will be happy here, and soon her new husband will arrive. Your life is elsewhere, yours and your children's.*

#

Torne was working in the garden behind the house when he saw them, six specks of different colors. It was the third time he had seen them and knew what they were, a weyr of dragons. He watched for a few minutes as the shapes became clearer. Soon he could make out their long necks and beating wings. Only then did it occur to him they were coming straight toward the farm. He ran for the house, the only cover nearby, calling for everyone to remain hidden. "Dragons," he explained. When he saw they were led by a big red creature with yellow flashes on its head he knew it was the same dragons coming again. Torne rushed inside and crouched beside the window to watch. They moved with purpose flying low to the ground and coming straight toward the farm. The dragons were hunting, searching.

Suddenly they stopped, hovering on beating wings. Their heads swung back and forth as if seeking a lost scent. They came forward slowly, heads down, hunting. Torne counted the distance in his mind, a thousand paces, eight hundred, five hundred. They came so close he count the scales on their bodies if he wished and see the sinewy veins of their wings. The red dragon swooped. It passed so close he imagined he could hear the scrape of its claws across the roof. He was certain he was about to meet the spirits. Worse, his sister and daughters would go with him.

The dragon roared, a long, wailing cry that sent shivers through his bones. He scanned the room. His sister hid beneath the table, her head covered by her arms. He wondered stupidly if that could save her. But his daughters sat at the table finishing their meal. They did not seem at all fazed by their impending deaths. He had never seen Hope or Faith show fear but there were times when fear was deserved.

His eyes came back to the window. If the dragons attacked he would not turn away from his demise. As he did, he spied the sword. He expected an angry red, or a violent green. Instead, what he saw was no more dangerous than a toy, a sword made by a child from pieces of wood. He ignored it. What was the value in a sword that was afraid to fight.

The dragons had not attacked. Instead, they ignored the farm and continued their search towards Fartown. Then they banked and swooped on the town tearing at buildings, ripping off roofs and peering within. Even at this distance he could hear the damage being inflicted until they climbed to fly east.

When he could see them no more, he sat on the floor and tried to calm his breathing. Air struggled to avoid his lungs. His chest ached. Eventually his body relaxed and he was able to stand, if unsteadily.

"Are you ready to go?" Hope asked.

"Yes," he replied. "You two stay here while I go to Fartown to help repair the damage."

Faith spoke. "No, Papa. It is time to take the sword north. If we do not leave now, it will be too late."

The thought of a sword that hid from a battle returned. Torne studied his daughters; he would never understand them. "Too late for what?" he demanded.

They answered in unison. "The sword must go where it is needed. You were chosen to carry it."

Torne looked to where the sword rested against the wall. It was shimmering in ripples of pale blue. Walking across the room, he picked it up and asked Where must you be?

*I have a task. I must be where and when I am needed to complete it.*

*What can a sword that will not fight do? And why must I go now? Why cannot it wait until I have helped the people of Fartown?*

*There is a time and place to fight. This is neither. The people of Fartown have no need of your help, but only you can save them. You must take me to my destiny or Tatlo will be no more. There is no more time.*

#

Torne finally accepted that the sword must go north to do what it must. He also accepted he was chosen to carry it. He would do it, but once it reached its destination his part would be over. He would return to the farm. He was not sure if he believed this but that was his intention.

They set out the following morning beneath gray skies that promised nothing more. They took the remaining horse, the only one to have survived the troubles, but they would walk leaving its emaciated frame to carry the little food and water they had. Torne carried the sword on his belt.

"How long until we get there, Papa?" Hope asked as they left their home behind.

"I do not know where I am going so we can only walk until we get there."

To the sword he asked, *How long until we are there?*

*We will arrive when we must. To be late will mean the end of the worlds. To be early could endanger my task.*

"The sword says we will arrive when we must."

Hope and Faith exchanged smiles.

The day passed without incident and by nightfall they had traveled twelve miles and found a stand of trees for protection. A meal of dried rabbit washed down with a single gulp of water had to satisfy them before they settled in for a night of rest.

*Beware!*

Torne came awake to find the sword had taken on the shape of a child's toy again.

"What…."

"Quiet," Torne warned. Moments later the dragons passed overhead. They watched as the creatures grew distant, flying north.

It is safe.

The sword had come back to life.

*Why do you hide from them?*

*It is not time to face the dragon and the one I seek is not with them. If I show myself, it will be warned.*

*You are hunting a dragon?*

*Yes.*

*And I am to take you to this dragon?*

*We must stand together before Agort.*

Torne's heart was pounding in his chest. He wanted to throw the sword down and run home. He was a farmer. What did he know about facing a dragon?

Faith put an arm around his shoulder. "What is wrong, Papa?"

He looked at his daughters. How could he tell them what the sword wanted of him? He could not. First thing in the morning, they would start for home.

Hope came to squat before them. "I saw the dragons, Papa. The sword must have an important task if dragons are sent to find it."

"That does not matter. We are going home tomorrow."

The girls swapped glances before speaking together.

"No! The sword must go north. We must go with it. You are chosen to bind us all together. You must take us."

Before he could say more, the girls returned to their places and were quickly asleep.

When Torne awoke next morning, his daughters were ready to travel. "Time to go, Papa," they chimed. And began walking north, leading the horse. Torne caught up with them and continued walking. No one spoke.

They saw the dragons six more times on their journey and each time there was convenient cover nearby, rocks, trees, and once, a cave. Each time the sword hid and they were not noticed.

#

Agort beat her mighty wings as she propelled herself across the lands. From Northice Bleak to the Wylds and back again she struck terror into the minds and hearts of the people of Tatlo. There was only one place she did not go.

Chadas sensed the Majick, something so powerful as to stagger the imagination. He had felt nothing like it and he stayed away. He would not approach until he knew what awaited him. It may be a natural bubble in the fabric of the world. If that was it, he may be able to use it against Rata. But it could also be a trap set by the spirit to draw him in. He would not be caught so easily.

He had ordered Tygrane and five of his brothers and sisters to find it. If it were a trap, he would know. They would probably die, but he would know. They had been close many times but on each occasion it disappeared. He concluded that whatever caused the bubble was afraid of them.

The time was rapidly approaching when he would have to find it himself.

He banked Agort's wings and swooped low over a village, briefly wondering its name or even where it was. He had traveled so far back and forth he no longer noticed where he was. But he felt the exhilaration of the dive, the rush of wind past his face, and when he roared, the power of his voice excited him.

As he climbed back into the sky, he saw Tygrane and his siblings approaching. Finding an empty field, he glided in descending circles until he could extend his massive legs and settle on the ground. Agort relaxed and waited. Tygrane landed while the others circled above.

*We were very close but it hid again.*

Chadas expected this answer.

*Did you do as I commanded?*

*Yes, Mother Agort. Tourak, Ruu and Aeryz continued the search while I watched the air with Deagh and Ahnook.*

*Did you see any holes?*

*There were none. I am sure of it.*

Chadas was not as certain. Rata could do many things but he had not seen her open a portal that he could not see. He did not think Tygrane would have been deceived either. So, whatever this Majick was, it was probably not of Rata's doing. Could he use it? There was only one way to find out. First, he had to find it.

*When did you last sense its presence?*

*Two days ago. It is moving slowly north. It will soon be at the place where the two human lands meet.*

*I will look. Do not return there. Whatever it is, it may know your scent.*

*Yes Mother Agort. We will stay away.*

#

For many days, Torne could not tear his eyes away from what lay ahead. He had never traveled this way before and did not know anyone who had. At first he thought they must be strange hills but no matter how far he walked, they were always over the horizon, yet they climbed impressively higher and higher as they reached for the sky. How much farther must they walk to reach them? And ow high would they be if he stood at their base?

*They are known as the Mondoghats.*

He had not expected the sword to speak.

*That is where I must go.*

Those words brought back the reality of what awaited them there, a dragon.

*We must hurry if we are to arrive in time.*

*I told you I will take you there, but then we are going home.*

*You are charged by the Majick to carry me.*

Torne decided to accept this to be the sword's agreement.

Many days later they stood at the base of a high cliff, the face of the nearest mountain.

*We must climb.*

Torne stared at the mountain, then at the sword.

*I brought you here. My work is done.*

The sword remained silent.

*How do you expect me to climb that?* he said, pointing.

*Your path lies before you.*

Torne approached the cliff and soon a trail became apparent following along the face and climbing quickly. Why had he not seen it before?

"We will wait here, Papa," his daughters chimed.

"That is probably better." He looked up. "I do not know where this track will lead me but I do not want to have to search for you later."

He stood at the start of the track, looking up. His senses were on alert. He could hear his daughters behind him, hear the scuffle of the horse's hooves and the twitter of birds as they laughed at his folly.

*If I am going to climb,* he told the sword, *we had better begin.*

He set off, not thinking that a moment ago he had no intention of climbing. The air closed in around him, cutting him off from the world. He could no longer hear his daughters, the horse or the birds. There was only silence. Looking back over his shoulder he could see nothing. Behind him was silence and shadows.

*Where are my daughters?*

*They walk their own path.*

Confused, he walked on. The sword glowed the soft green of content at his hip.

The trail seemed to follow the cliff face, a broad track with a chasm to the valley on one side and a wall of rock on the other. How had he climbed so high? The trail offered no obstacles, no barriers to his path. Soon his mind began to wander.

A large dog bounded toward him, knocking him to the ground. He laughed and reached up to put his arms around its neck. The dog barked and began licking his face. He felt its breath, reeking of old meat, felt its wet slobbering tongue as the coarse member ran over his face. He pushed. "Get off, Toby. Let me up." The dog dropped on him before rolling to the side, legs in the air, waiting for the inevitable belly-rub. "Do you have to be so rough, Toby?" But then he obliged and pushed his fingers through the thick layer of fur to scratch the beast's belly.

Strange, he thought. Toby died when I was eight. Why did I think of him now?

Another memory began to form. A house appeared in his thoughts, a farmhouse, his home. The door opened and a young girl stepped out. She had flowers in her hair. It was Shayla. It was their wedding day.

With an effort, he pushed that image aside. He had thought of Shayla often, but he could not face meeting her again, not when he knew what was to come. To distract himself, he spoke to the sword.

*How much farther must we walk?*

*We walk until we arrive.*

He swore angrily. *You know what I mean.*

*Some find their destination quickly. Others search all their lives without finding it. Your path is as short or as long as you make it.*

Torne decided he would hear no more of the sword's twisted words. He walked on in silence, not even noticing if the sword spoke. Memories continued to plague him, the birth of the girls, their first steps and words, Shayla's excitement at receiving the horse he had carved for her from a piece of fallen timber.

Then came the moment of her death and he staggered with the pain of it. His hand reached for the rock wall to steady himself. Instead, he was shocked when his arm disappeared into the mountain. He jerked it back.

His other hand came up to check. His arm was intact. Reaching for the wall again he gave a gentle push. Once more his hand disappeared. Withdrawing his hand, he tried the other. It, too, disappeared. Leaning forward, he placed his face against rock and carefully pushed. On the other side of the barrier were many paths intertwined in a tangle of confusion. He pulled back.

We must go on.

The sword was encouraging him. Looking down, he saw the glow of orange. It was afraid, but for itself or for him? He took another step, and another.

*What was that?* he asked.

*You must walk your own path.*

Torne stopped and pulled the sword free, and held it as if he would strangle it. The sword was now brown, but flickering as if shaking.

Tell me!

The sword turned blue. *You must walk your own path.*

*Or?*

*If you turn to the valley, your life will be over before you reach your destination.*

*And the mountain?*

*It is not a mountain, you only see what you expect. You walk in time with the help of the Majick. Beyond are the paths of others who have entered or left your life.*

Torne looked at the mountain. *So, Shayla's path is in there?*

*It is, but if you step off your path to follow another's, you will be lost. You must follow your own path just as they must follow theirs.*

*But I could be with Shayla again?*

*The memories of your wife are with you but your time with her is gone.*

Torne stood for an unknown time while the sword waited, as if afraid to speak. He began to understand that all would be won or lost in this moment. Finally, he placed the blade back at his hip and started to walk.

*How long?*

Your destination is close.

A memory of dragons over his farm came and went quickly. Then the air shimmered and pulled away. All around him was ice, but he was not cold. He knew, somehow, the sword, or the Majick, would keep him warm.

He stood on top of the mountain. It was a circle of rock and ice with a depression in the middle filled with a flat expanse of ice.

*Down there*, the sword instructed.

Without thinking, he began his descent. He was surprised at how easily he could navigate this unforgiving place. Soon, he stood at the center of a large, flat ice-field.

It is time to set me free.

Torne took the sword and held it high, its tip pointing to the sky. The sword flared white, brighter than he had ever known it. A column of white fire reached up above him.

#

Rata watched.

The sword did not worry her. She knew it was of the Majick, and she was the Great Author. The Majick was hers to control. But she also knew that Chadas could not resist. He would come, and he would be distracted.

She was ready.

#

Chadas had called on all of Agort's senses but weeks had passed and he had not found the spike of Majick. Flying back and forth over the land had yielded nothing. Now he was soaring high above the mountains the people called the Mondoghats.

On the verge of giving up and believing the spike to have been only a temporary thing, maybe a trap of Rata, he felt it, or Agort did. A burst of Majick so powerful it sent tingles through the dragon. Even her scales shivered with the strength of the disturbance.

Agort's head swung back and forth, searching. He saw it, on top of a mountain at the south end of the range. A white flame had burst into existence. White fire flared up, and up.

Putting Agort's wings over, he dropped and swooped toward the Majick for a closer look.

#

Torne saw it, a dragon so large it made the ones he had seen previously look like squirrels. It came toward him faster than any horse could run, faster than an arrow loosed from a bow. Even so, he could see its features clearly, its head aimed at him baring large, pointed teeth. Horns swept back over its long neck. Its wings were loose and tatty, like an old woman's arms and four huge legs hung from its body. Each one displaying ferocious curved claws. Its scales, though old, reflected the light in many shades as it moved.

The fire winked out.

Have you used all your Majick? He screamed.

If I had, you would not be here, neither would I. The time must be right.

The dragon came closer. With senses heightened by fear he saw each beat of its wings as if they took an hour, each snarl a day.

*Stand true.*

What did the sword expect? He was a farmer. A dragon the size of a mountain was about to kill him. There was nowhere to run, nowhere to hide. He felt the sword encouraging him, enticing him to practice as they once had. Without thought of his actions, the sword spun in his hands, faster and faster. Colors blurred as the blade spun until all he could see was a bubble of brilliant shades surrounding him.

*Now!* screamed the sword.

Torne swung it in an arc that began beside his right knee, came up and over his head before stopping inches from his left leg. The blur of color faded.

Agort was above him.

#

When Agort saw the fire of Majick, she understood. She hid her knowledge from the one who had invaded her being. He had caught her and taken control but not completely. She still knew herself. But he had made her do things she would never do. Worse, he had made her encourage her children to do the same.

She knew it was the Chadas thing, but it was her body that terrified the people, her claws that tore animals apart, her roar that made the world hide.

She flew straight at the tiny insect that wielded the Majick. The Chadas thing sensed danger and flew high enough to remain clear of the sword, the blade that held the power. Agort gathered all her willpower. She would have one opportunity, one moment. The Chadas thing had her fly low over the mountain. The right time would come and go in a heartbeat.

Almost.

Almost.

Now.

She threw her will against Chadas. He had not anticipated it. She pulled her wings back and dropped The sword came up and cut across her chest. She felt terror rush through Chadas' thoughts and her control over her body returned.

Chadas was not injured, he had fled the body he thought doomed. He did not know what would have become of him if was still in control when Agort died.

She had not been injured either. The sword was made of Majick. It purpose was not to cut flesh, but to sever the ties that constrained the Majick. Chadas did not know what it was to be immortal. Agort turned and with three huge beats of its wings was well on its way back to the Northice Bleak. She called her children to join her there.

#

Rata saw her opportunity. She established the portal and rushed through. Her first instinct was to build a barrier of Majick, protecting both her and her passage back to Apat.

Chadas did not understand the truth of the sword, but she did, and she was cautious. It was a weapon unlike any other. It could cut, but only one thing.

Someone had created it, she did not know who, but she knew its purpose. She may be able to use it. It was made to separate a spirit from the Majick.

Below her, Chadas had fled the body of Agort thinking the dragon doomed. He had been lucky, he had escaped the sword's first cut. She only needed to get him close enough. Holding her barrier in front, she plummeted from the sky. Her intention was to push Chadas close enough that the sword could do its work.

But Rata's attack had been anticipated. Chadas dashed to the side, far enough to evade her barrier, then rather than attack, he raced for the portal. Rata screamed, shaking ice from some of the mountains, and threw bolt after bolt of energy in his path. One almost hit. Chadas was forced to pause and shield himself. It gave Rata enough time to weave the Majick across the entrance. Now, no one could access Apat until she removed the seal.

The battle that followed lit the skies above the Mondoghats. Lightning clashed with lightning, fire with fire. The world shook with the power of their fight. All the colors of the rainbow and more streaked through the sky, to be seen as far away as Bel and Dawnreach Dragonfang and Fartown. The Majickers felt the world shake and tremble. The people of Tatlo must think the spirit world was at war.

It was.

Rata prepared a beam of pure white and aimed it towards Chadas. He countered with one of absolute black. Where they met, the air seemed to catch alight. The explosion of color sprayed over the world before falling to the ground.

They came together, only their two barriers separating them. Fists of Majick punched. Chadas was above Rata pushing with all his strength.

#

Far below in the valley, Hope and Faith watched the battle unfold. They knew what was happening, they had planned it and all was going well. Now, the time had come for them to play their part. This was the critical moment for the world, all worlds, and the Majick.

"Ready?" Faith asked her sister.

Hope nodded.

If anyone had been watching, they would have been stunned by what occurred next. The two girls stood side by side, and began to grow. In moments they were teenagers, then young women. In no time, two women of around thirty years acted.

They started to grow. Soon they were taller than the tallest tree and they grew. In a blink they each stood as high as a hill. As Rata and Chadas came together, their shields flaring, Hope opened a portal to the void on the ground behind Rata. Faith gathered the air until it was almost solid, and pushed from behind Chadas.

The air closed against the void.

At that moment Rata realized what was happening. She fought, trying to escape, throwing up shields and barriers. Who was doing this, Chadas was not strong enough. Screaming as the void engulfed her, her last thought was that Chadas would follow. He would not win.

Chadas had a moment longer, and he had escaped once before when Rata had tried to cast him into the void. He reacted the same way. He did not know who created the portal but he created another just in front of it. This one led to the first safe place he thought of, Dalawa, and since he created it, he thought he could always return.

Hope and Faith had other ideas. After dismissing their portal they began weaving the threads of Majick, a thin curtain at first, that became a heavy blanket, then a plug. They wove it into the portal and through the ground around it. Chadas would not return this way.

# EPILOGUE

Hope's thoughts reached for the top of the mountain where her terrified father still stood clutching the sword. She gently cradled him in soft folds of air, lifted him and lowered him to the ground. They had assumed the size of normal women for his benefit.

Without the air to hold him, he slumped to the ground. Then he saw his daughters. "Hope? Faith? Have I been gone that long?"

"No, Papa. Things are the same, but they are different."

Torne laughed, a stupid half-hysterical cackle. "Now you are sounding like the sword." He sat for a while, and they waited.

"Are you both alright?" he asked.

"We are fine papa."

"We have completed our journey."

"What happened?" he asked after his senses began to return.

Hope answered. The Majick was being misused. Two spirits each wanted to control it. They had to be stopped or the Majick would have died, and the worlds would die with it."

"Two spirits of great power in the Majick fought today. There was only one way they could be stopped," explained Faith.

Hope continued, "Rata has been banished to the void, the space between worlds, from which there is no return, and Chadas fled to Dalawa. That is the world before this world. His powers will be limited there. And having walked the path to the next world, it can never be traveled again.

"But why fight here?"

"They chose the place of their confrontation. We came here to see that it ended."

"Came here? But you are my daughters. I was there when you were born."

"We are from Apat, the place you know as the spirit world."

"We returned as your daughters to await the time when we would be needed."

Torne stared, not understanding what he was hearing. Feeling lost, he answered, "Apat? The spirit world? How? Why?"

"We had to be born of this world again so we could use the Majick without destroying it. We are sorry, Papa."

Torne tried to take in the story, but he had so many questions.

"The sword?"

"We created the sword. We needed a weapon that would separate Chadas from Agort. You were the only one we trusted to wield it."

Those words brought back recent memories. "The dragon, is it dead?"

"Agort is immortal, she cannot die."

"And Shayla? Was her death a part of your plan?"

"No, papa. It was just the time for her to walk the path."

Torne stared at his daughters. "What now?"

"The conflict is over. You could return to your farm, but we see you beginning a new farm further south with your new wife. Your sister will be fine."

"Will you come with me?"

"No. Our journeys have ended."

"And you will return to Apat?"

"No. We have traveled the path once. We can never walk that way again.

Torne stared, confused.

"We returned to save the Majick, and the worlds. It was our sacrifice," Hope told him.

Faith added, "We will never see Apat again, or the worlds beyond."

"Then come south with me. We could be a family again."

"We cannot do that either. If we lived in Tatlo any longer, our presence would cause a greater distortion in the Majick. Our journey is over. And though they will never know it, the people of all the worlds owe you their gratitude."

Torne looked to each of his now-grown daughters. Tears ran unchecked down his cheeks. "So, we will never meet again, here or in the next life?"

"We are sorry, papa, but that is true." A single tear leaked from Faith's eye.

Torne threw his arms around his daughters in a massive hug, pleading for them not to leave, but eventually he stepped back and saw the sorrow on his daughters' faces. In a choking voice, he asked, "Will you take the sword with you?"

"No, that is yours. It will be needed again, but not by you." Hope passed him a box sealed with Majick. It appeared to be of white stone with a rune carved on top. At his raised brow, she explained. "It is the mark of the Majick. When it is needed, the one who will use it will be ready."

Faith added, "You must take the sword and the box. Both must be protected until they are required. This is the task for you and your children."

"My children?"

You will marry again and have a happy family."

"We must go, but there is one last task we must perform."

The ground began to shake beneath Torne's feet. The shaking grew stronger to the accompaniment of loud cracks and rumbles in the air. The mountains on each side of the valley shook violently and rocks began to tumble from them. Dust filled the air. Much later, the noise eased and the air cleared. Where the plug of Majick had been was now covered by rocks that formed a wall from one mountain to the other.

But Torne stood dumb-founded at what stood at each end of the wall. Some of the rock remained untouched and two massive stone figures looked down on the wall, his daughters. Something inside him whispered, "We will always stand watch and protect Tatlo. Now it is time for you to go."

Torne turned and walked away. When he looked back, the rock images seemed to smile.

#

I looked up from my book. All eyes were upon me, staring in silence.

Finally, Kuwento spoke. "That was a wonderful story. Where did you hear it?"

I looked stunned at the old man.

"From you. It is your story, the Chadasmaal."

Kuwento's hand came up to his head. "Of course it is. I remember." He slapped the side of the face with his palm, then smiled. "You just tell it so well."

I stared at my friend.

"I am tired," Kuwento declared. "Cara, could you help me to my bed?"

Cara came to assist.

After seeing to Kuwento's needs, she returned to tell me that the old man's mind was failing. She had seen it before. "He tries to hide it but I can see it more and more."

I left, promising to return as soon as I could. "Here are some coins for your help," I said, pushing a bag of coins into her hand.

"It has been my honor to serve someone who knows so many things." She smiled.

I did not know if she was referring to Kuwento or me.

# OTHER BOOKS BY STEVE REILLY

Tam's Journal

The Saga of the Society trilogy
Hidden Enemies
The Hopes of Kings
Return of Magic

The Telling of the Maal
Dragonfang

www.ingramcontent.com/pod-product-compliance
Lightning Source LLC
LaVergne TN
LVHW091051080826
845145LV00002B/702

* 9 7 8 0 6 4 5 7 5 5 5 8 9 *